DO UNTO OTHERS

MARK JENKINS

ALSO BY MARK JENKINS

With One Stone

The Golden Rule is decisive and omnipresent. It exists pole to pole and can be found in some form or fashion in almost every religious or ethical heritage.

Baha'i Faith

"Lay not on any soul a load which ye would not wish to be laid upon you, and desire not for anyone the things ye would not desire for yourselves."

—*Gleanings from the Writings of Bahá'u'lláh*

Buddhism

"Hurt not others in ways that you yourself would find hurtful."

—*Udanavarga 5:18*

Jainism

In happiness and suffering, in joy and grief, we should regard all creatures as we regard our own self and should therefore refrain from inflicting upon others such injury as would appear undesirable to us if inflicted upon ourselves."

—*Yogasastra*

Confucianism

Zigong asked, "Is there a single saying that one may put into practice all one's life?" The Master said, "That would be 'reciprocity': that which you do not desire, do not do to others."

—*The Analects of Confucius*

Wicca

Ever mind the Rule of Three
Three times your acts return to thee
This lesson well, thou must learn
Thou only gets what thee dost earn

—*The Rule of Three*

Christianity

"In everything, do unto others as you would have them do unto you."

—*New Testament, Matthew 7:12*

PROLOGUE

"Let me tell you how you're going to kill them."

For the next five days, Bradley sat across the oak table, listening to every word from his mentor, absorbing everything. Every detail was permanently forged onto his memory like a brand to cattle. The information was substantial, but he had no problem becoming well-versed in the plan. He was told not to take notes, for anything written was fodder for discovery.

But truth be told, he didn't have a choice.

They did not allow him bathroom breaks but provided him with a bucket. He was only allowed water and a few crackers for provisions, but he knew if he drank the water, he'd have to use the bucket, and that was something he did not want to do. The last time he urinated in front of them, it was from humiliation and embarrassment. He did not want to revisit that period in his life, so the bucket was out of the picture. But occasionally, his thirst forced him to drink during these five arduous days. And inevitably, urination would follow. He would wait until they left, of course. He dared not move from his spot for fear they returned, and he'd be gone.

Once again, he saw no choice in the matter.

So, not budging from his chair, and only when he was alone, he would urinate into the empty water glass and then, grudgingly, drink the warm, yellow broth. Pee and repeat.

It wouldn't be the first time.

But by not moving from his chair, it proved his discipline. It demonstrated his fealty. And there was nothing more sacred than his loyalty.

Bradley was deathly allegiant to his tablemate. He knew it, and they knew it. The deaths he had already caused had already proven his deference to them. He was a soldier. A zealot. A protector.

He was told to pay attention. Always pay attention. And so, he listened, heeded every step of the plan, understood every possible outcome, and agreed to whatever consequences might befall him.

On day one, he learned he would need a dog. A big one. It was a crucial part of the plan. The dog would be a pawn, and Bradley would use him to ensure checkmate. He would need to train the dog, as he himself was being trained. A parallel world that would ultimately mirror more than Bradley bargained for.

On the second day, Bradley learned the "who": who his targets were and how he would love, laugh, and engage with them. Or at least he learned how to fake it, to go with "motions without emotions". He was given their home addresses and phone numbers. He was schooled on their favorite movies, flowers, hobbies of the parents, and, of course, fears. The phobias that would come to life like a reanimated corpse. Every puzzle piece fit cohesively with the next, interlocking perfectly until the victim had no game left to play because by then, sadly, it would be too late.

Day three comprised of the "what": the heavy machinery, the succinylcholine, the ladder, the map of Yosemite, the poppies, the fence around the lake, the Adirondack boat, and most importantly, the rescues, the very things that would make his targets dependent on him. In addition, he would need a wilderness permit and a library card. Simple tasks in theory, but it was an enormous risk, having his name out there when so much was riding on the concealment of his identity. And to lighten the tasks, even Dr. Seuss would play a role, believe it or not.

On the fourth day, he learned "how" he would do what he needed to do. It was the most complex day of them all. His brain clicked, and he accepted the heavy material with as much ease as a child learning to stack blocks. He never left the room, but he studied the books and manuals presented to him, and he learned the basics of scuba diving, hiking, and cave exploration. Essential acts with necessary results. But when his lessons took sharp turns he was unsure about, he could feel sweat beading down his back. But he trudged on, determined to make this his proudest moment of display of his devotion yet. He sat up straighter, his back groaning in protest. He had been sitting in the hard chair for four unending days, and his body was beginning to revolt. But despite that, he listened. And learned.

Sitting and listening was excruciating, but whenever he looked across the table, he could see the pain they suffered, and it was minuscule in comparison; no one should go through what they went through. It was monstrous and inhumane. How close they came to dying, to leaving him. It was all something he refused to remember. However, sitting face to face at this moment was a brutal jolt to his memory. His mind relented. So, he would do this and not complain. He felt a sense of pride for being chosen to execute the agenda. Bradley listened to the now familiar, stern voice. Onerous and stringent in its delivery. He feared it.

He revered it.

The last day, the fifth day, was one of no questions, no recaps, no issues. They did not afford him those luxuries. It consisted of only two pieces of instruction: the photographs and the phone calls. They were the most essential part of the plan because they were the last parts, the final acknowledgments of trust. *I will not fail them.* They gave him three burner phones: one for each component.

Bradley sat with his thoughts. He had figured out how to compartmentalize his lies from the truths and how to pull from each compartment as needed. He learned how to take emotions off the table. He would be the best imitator. A chameleon. And he would accomplish the goals they had entrusted him with.

His duties were immense. But at the end of this project, three women would meet their quietus. And since he was going to be carrying all this out while seeing all three women at the same time, he couldn't afford to fuck up. He took in a sharp intake of air.

"Are you ready?" was the question.

"Consider it done." He trembled at the thought of displeasing them.

Bradley saw the slight nod before they rose from the table, leaving him to his own devices. He grabbed his phone and looked up the number of the San Francisco Pet Humane Adoption Center.

"Hello? Yes. I'm interested in getting a dog. A big one."

It had begun.

PART ONE
BROOKE

CHAPTER 1

Brooke Carson's eyes snapped open.

She was lying in her bed, and something was wrong. She looked at the clock on her wall: 4:48 p.m. *Shit!* Hank would be here in twelve minutes. And he had zero patience. She looked down beside her and realized she had a huge problem: Oscar was still in her bed, and she needed him not to be. Oscar had plenty of patience and was never hurrying to go anywhere. Proving her point, he was on his side, a soft snoring sound emitted from his nostrils.

To be honest, Brooke liked both men: Oscar was sweet and attentive, like a cute puppy, eager to please and always jubilant, and could never hurt a fly. On the flip side, Hank was like a grown-ass Pitbull, a mountain of a man, full of energy and always up to play roughhouse. With Oscar, she got adoration, rest, and lovemaking; with Hank, she got raucousness, ferocity, and, occasionally, some bruising.

Oscar acted like he was a choirboy, and Hank acted like he just got out of prison.

It was the best of both worlds.

Brooke jumped out of bed and threw on her robe. She quickly tied it around her waist as she walked to the other side of the bed.

"Oscar," she said, sort of softly. She needed to wake him up but still found it rude to wake someone up.

"Oscar," she repeated a little more loudly, nudging his feet. He was 5′6″ and was snug in any bed like a baby in a crib. The nudge didn't faze him one bit. She stopped in front of his face, which was crunched inside a fluffy pillow. He wasn't the cutest thing in the world, but he was sweet and loving and definitely knew how to please her in bed. She smiled and looked up. The clock showed 4:50 p.m. *Ten minutes.* Her eyes widened.

"Oscar!!" she yelled.

He bolted upright like he'd been electrocuted.

"Wha? What's wrong?" He rubbed his eyes.

"Time to go, baby. I have someplace I need to be, and I'm already late. So -" She began to pull the covers off him. He didn't budge. To her horror, he laid back down.

"Come back to bed. I'll just stay over -" he yawned "- and leave in the morning." He pulled the covers back up to his chin.

This isn't happening.

Brooke had always been conscientious when balancing her love life. There'd never been any crossover, and her secret was safe with her. But it had been a busy month for her at the real estate firm where she worked, but when Oscar called her for a bit of afternoon delight, she couldn't resist, and they had spent the afternoon together. Only, she had forgotten she had scheduled an early time with Hank on the same day. For 5:00! She smacked her head. *Stupid.* Brooke knew she was cutting it close. Now she'd overslept and – *8 minutes!* She was wasting time. She had to act fast.

"On your feet, soldier," she bellowed, yanking the covers off the naked man in her bed. She admired his lean body for only a second. Not very muscular, but lean and *very* long in the best way possible. She caught her breath.

She grabbed his legs and swung them around where his feet barely touched the floor. She grabbed his jeans and tee shirt off the floor and tossed them onto his lap.

"Hey!" he said, startled.

"Sorry," Brooke said. "But I really need you to go. I have an appointment I need to get to -"

"Now?" he asked. "But it's almost 5:00."

She looked at the clock. *Seven minutes.* Brooke threw off her robe and started to get dressed. She slipped on slim-fit jeans and pulled a thin sweater over her head. She slipped her feet into some pink tennis shoes, then pulled her long blonde hair back into a ponytail.

"Yes, I know, but it's the only time my client was free for me to show him a house." She hated lying, but, hey, desperate times.

Oscar stood up and pulled his jeans on over his short legs. He grabbed his shirt, put it on, and pulled it down over his taut stomach. He moved up behind her and wrapped his arms around her, pulling her back to him. They were the same height, and she felt his head touch hers.

Any other time, Brooke would've been ready to go again with Oscar, but not tonight. She couldn't risk him and Hank running into each other. Hank wouldn't be too appreciative, and that made her nervous. She gently pulled away from Oscar, and he swung her around to face him. He kissed her deep and slow, and she felt her legs wobble. He was good; she'd give him that, but he wasn't her type- at least not for the long haul.

She backed away. "Save that for another night, tiger," she said, and she gave his crotch a squeeze. He groaned. She ran around behind him and started pushing him out the bedroom door.

"I'm going, I'm going," he protested, his arms going up in surrender. His legs weren't long, and Brooke felt he was moving at a molasses pace. They were in the den, close to the front door. "Oh, I forgot something," he said and ran back into the bedroom.

Oh my god, she thought. *Hurry up!* She felt a bead of sweat on her hairline.

Two minutes later, he came bounding out of the bedroom, putting his watch on his wrist. "Didn't want to leave this behind," he said, smiling.

Nope. Can't leave any evidence.

"Come here, you," he said and pulled her close. "I'm glad you could squeeze me in tonight. I know you've been busy…"

Yeah, yeah…

"…but I like you. And I think you like me…"

I do, I do, but not right now. You need to go!

He could see something in her gritted facial expression. "Fine," he smiled. "I'll go. But I'm calling you tomorrow." He stood on his tiptoes and kissed her on the top of her head.

He always could take a hint. She reached for the door handle.

"Good luck with the showing," he said.

"The...oh yeah. Thanks. Talk tomorrow?"

His sweet, frustrated smile curved up to the right. He sighed. "Tomorrow," he agreed.

She opened the door for him to leave.

Oscar stepped over the threshold and came face to face with a balled-up fist, ready to knock on her door.

Brooke followed his eyes to the gigantic man on her porch. *Hank.*
Shit!

She had no recollection of the moments that followed.

CHAPTER 2

Brooke woke up, and instantly, her head began to throb. She tried to open her eyes, but everything was so white and bright, she closed them immediately.

"Ahh, you're awake," a deep voice said.

"Barely," she whispered. Her mouth was dry. "Where am I?" She could tell she was sitting up in a bed.

"You, my dear, are in Saint Francis Memorial Hospital. I'm Doctor Kaufman. Now, can you open your eyes again for me? This time, for a little longer than two seconds?"

She squinted them open slowly, then felt fingers gently pulling her lids open. Another bright light aimed directly into her eyes and swooped back and forth. He moved his fingers to the other eye's lids and wavered the light again.

"The left pupil is a little dilated. Nothing to worry about. Just a very minor concussion." He looked over the glasses at the end of his nose. "How's your head?"

"Haven't had any complaints yet," Brooke said, wincing a bit.

The doctor pulled back and smiled. Then gave a hearty chuckle. "That's funny. I'll get the nurse to draw up your release papers." He sent a text and then started to walk to the door.

"Doctor Kaufman," Brooke said.

He turned.

"What happened? How did I get here?"

The doctor took his glasses off and put them in the pocket of his white coat. He walked back to her bedside.

"It appears you were caught up in the middle of some -" he paused to think of the word – "melee between two young men. There was a fight, some slugging, name-calling, lots of yelling, and you stepped in to break them apart, but you took a left hook to the side of the head. The physicality of the hit sent you slamming into the side of your front porch, and you hit your head on the brick wall. Then you slumped to the ground."

Brooke's mouth was wide open. "You can tell all that just from looking into my eyes?"

"Heaven's no," the doctor said, smiling. "Actually, Ms. Carson, it was the young man that brought you in. He witnessed the whole thing. When he got up to the porch, he found you passed out and saw the two men running off. One, he said, was worse for the wear. Very hurt and bleeding. Limping away. I think your friend said he heard him crying."

Poor little Oscar, Brooke thought. *I'm sure Hank pummeled him raw.*

"Well, he's such a little fellow, I'm sure his injuries -"

"What? Oh, you misunderstand," the doctor said, surprised. "It was the *bigger* fellow that was crying. Like a big ol' baby. Apparently, the little dude just went all angry elf on him." The doctor shrugged. "Not my words. Your friends'."

Brooke found her mouth open wide again. She covered it with her hand and began to laugh. *Hank? Big ol' Hank was crying?* She laughed harder. Then her head started to pound again, and she winced.

"Ahh," he said, noticing. "I'll write you a prescription for some pain medication just until everything subsides."

"Oh, I have some Tylenol in my purse – *my purse!* Where is it?"

"I don't know," Dr. Kaufman said. "You didn't come in with it."

Brooke looked perplexed. "Hmm."

Dr. Kaufman turned.

"Wait," Brooke said, remembering something else. "You said a young man brought me in here. Who was it?"

"He said his name was Gio, but that's all he gave me," the doctor said. "He was a big, strong guy. Carried you in his arms into the E.R."

Brooke paled. *Gio? What the hell? This is impossible.*

"Are you sure he said Gio and not, maybe, Leo, or something?"

Dr. Kaufman referenced his notes. "Nope. Gio. Why? Do you know him?"

She did. Well, she knew *a* Gio, but this couldn't be the same one. "No," she replied.

"He drove you here in your car and left it in the parking garage for you. I'll have the nurse -"

At that moment, a nurse walked in with a file folder and a small manila envelope.

"Perfect timing, Judith. Ms. Carson would like to leave."

"Wouldn't we all?" Judith replied. "Here, honey. Sign this, and you're free to go."

Brooke signed the release papers, and Judith handed her the manila envelope.

"These are the belongings you had on you when you arrived. Wasn't much. Your car keys are in there, too. And your car is parked on the fourth level in the South Garage."

Brooke looked inside and pulled out her keys. She looked back into the envelope and saw something shiny. She pulled it out. It was a necklace with a dangling orange poppy charm. She looked at it and took a deep breath before hooking it behind her neck. She warmed the charm between her fingers.

"That's a pretty necklace," Judith said. "Where did you get it?"

Brooke thought for a moment before responding. "It was a gift. From a friend. A long time ago." *Was it really that long ago? Just over a year...*

"Well, it's mighty pretty."

Brooke's eyes were almost closed, and her mind seemed elsewhere.

"Are you going to be okay to drive, honey?" Judith asked her.

Brooke looked up. "Yes," she nodded. I'll be fine." She got up and left.

Brooke headed to the South parking garage, mad at herself for even being in this position: two men going at each other and knocking her out as a bonus. She cursed at herself for being so stupid. Entering the elevator, she pressed the button for the fifth floor. The elevator shook as it slowly carried her up, and the doors finally opened on the fifth level. She stepped out and instantly felt lost. *Did she say the fifth floor? Or fourth?* She walked around looking for her car, using the key fob to search for her vehicle. Nothing. No beeps. There were several cars still in the garage, even at this time of night, but she couldn't find hers. Her head pounded. She was in a labyrinth of cars and ramps. Then she heard footsteps echoing in the garage.

"I'm alone in a parking garage. At night. With footsteps." Brooke took a deep breath. "Great, I'm a horror movie cliché," she frowned. And now there was this business with Gio. *Literally, what the fuck?*

Brooke hurried back to the elevator, and the footsteps increased in pace and loudness. *Someone is following me!* The doors opened, and she hurried inside, frantically pressing the button for the fourth floor in rapid succession. She peered outside the doors and saw nothing. "Hurry up!" she yelled at the sloth-like elevator. Apparently, the elevator didn't care if she got murdered here or not because nothing was happening.

She heard a loud thumping noise. Her eyes widened, and she turned her head to hear better. Brooke closed her eyes, and her shoulders slumped as she realized it was her own heart making the sound. Finally, the doors started closing at a glacial pace, connecting after what seemed an eternity, and she felt a bit safer in the small, enclosed tin box as it lowered to the fourth floor.

Leaning against the inner wall, Brooke suddenly heard a loud boom as the elevator abruptly stopped one level below. She looked at the floor as the doors slowwwwwly opened with a long creak. She began to step off the elevator.

Out of the darkness, a shadow loomed above her.

CHAPTER 3

Brooke screamed. Her hand slammed to her chest, and she took in a quick breath of air. "Oh, my god!" she said. "You scared the crap out of me!"

It was Dr. Kaufman from her hospital room.

"Sorry, my dear. Are you lost?" he asked. He no longer wore his white lab coat, and he looked like a regular Joe Schmo.

"I…uh…." she was still trying to catch her breath. "I…yes. I mean, no. I mean, I *was* lost, but now I'm found." *Why am I reciting Amazing Grace? Damn concussion.* She pressed her key fob and heard a faint beep to her right.

"Ahh," Dr. Kaufman said, nodding towards her car. "Was blind, but now you see." He gave her a gentle smile.

"Yeah, I guess," Brooke said. "Well, good night." She hurried towards her car. A large SUV was parked close to her BMW, and she had to shimmy past to get to her car door. Once inside, she locked the doors and leaned back against the headrest. She closed her eyes and sighed out a huge breath. Her heart was still thumping out a loud noise, but inside the confines of her car, she felt a little less threatened. *A little.*

She rested her head back and shut her eyes. "Breathe, Brooke. Breathe." Her body was shaking, and she placed her hands on the steering wheel for support. "I need a drink," she said to the car's interior. Her head came up off the headrest. She looked over at the passenger seat. Her purse was sitting on the soft leather. She eyed it warily. She didn't have that going into the hospital, so maybe the stranger that brought her here went into her house and got it and left it here for her?

Brooke shifted her eyes back and forth, wondering if she really was any safer here in the car. Many cars were still in the lot, and a big black SUV was parked very close to her. But there was no movement. She grabbed her purse from the passenger seat and dug inside for her cell phone. Pulling it out, she touched the screen until it lit up. A quick punch of a code, and she was in. She clicked on the phone symbol and called her friend.

"Hey. What's up?"

"Misty!" Brooke said breathlessly. "Alley Bar. Fifteen minutes!"

"Uh, okay. Everything good?" Misty asked suspiciously.

"Yes. I mean, no. Whatever. Just be there, babe." She hung up.

She adjusted her rearview mirror. A tall figure stood between her car and the big black SUV next to her.

"Shit!" she cried, whipping her head around to look out her windows. Her glass had a dark tint, and she couldn't see clearly, but she was pretty sure she had seen someone. Or some*thing*. But now, as she looked, there was nothing there. She cracked her back window down an inch. "Hello?" she called out, but an eerie silence greeted her. Brooke shook the hallucination from her brain.

"Fuck this!" she said, suddenly remembering she was a horror movie cliché. She started her car and slammed it into reverse. The squeal of her tires echoed throughout the garage as she bolted down the ramp.

"Oh my god, *what*?" Misty asked when Brooke tried to regale the evening's events. "Both of them *fought*? Over *you*?"

"Don't act so surprised," Brooke said crabbily.

"I didn't mean it that way. I meant – well, maybe I did mean it that way," Misty replied, smiling. "You've got these two guys fighting over you and then -"

"….and then they knocked me unconscious!" Brooke said rapidly.

"Yeah, yeah. But *two*! That's pretty cool! I wish I had just one knight in shining armor to fight for my honor."

"They weren't fighting for my honor, you titmouse. They were fighting to exhibit their social dominance. That's all."

"Oh, that's right. I forgot you were a psych major," Misty said, rolling her eyes playfully.

"Whatever," Brooke said, taking a sip of her margarita. "So, tell me, how're things at work?"

"Boring as hell," Misty said with a flourish. "I hate being in a cubicle. I can't get anything personal done. Everyone knows everyone's business because there are no walls and people walk by all day long and -" Misty suddenly stopped talking mid-sentence. She just stared off into space over Brooke's shoulders.

"Uh, Misty?" Brooke asked.

"Holy crap!" Misty said, leaning in to whisper to Brooke. "My husband just walked into the bar."

Brooke knew two things: 1) Misty was not married, and 2) if her 'husband' walked in, then it was probably a very handsome man that Misty wanted to be her husband. "Dare I turn around?" Brooke asked.

Misty just smiled and nodded in the man's direction. Brooke swiveled on her stool and followed Misty's gaze. Brooke saw the man in question. He sat in a booth across the way and, indeed, looked very handsome. As he sat, his jeans fit him perfectly, tight around the thighs. He wore a simple white tee shirt that barely contained his torso. His biceps flexed with every gentle move of his arms, which caused a couple of tattoos to come to life. A waitress was by his side lickety-split, sidling up to him to take his order. Brooke noticed how she reached behind her and pulled her top tighter into her skirt so the front would be like a second skin against her $8,000 boob job. He ran his fingers through his thick hair and looked into her eyes. They both knew what they were doing.

He leaned forward around the waitress and caught Brooke's eye.

Then he smiled, teeth white as snow. She felt her legs shimmy a little. *Yes, he knew what he was doing.* She spun away, her cheeks flushed.

The waitress did her best to flirt and get a number, but the man showed no interest, only politeness. In surrender, the waitress stormed off without a phone number nor a chance in hell.

Misty nudged Brooke. "Go."

"Go where?"

"To him! Go talk to him. He's obviously smiling at you, dammit," Misty said.

"No, I'm not the dating kind," Brooke replied.

Misty knocked Brooke on the top of her head.

"Ouch!"

"Well, maybe you *should* be the dating kind. The one-man dating kind. Like me. With Tyler."

After Tyler and Misty had had one date, Misty was already planning their future. He was literally from the other side of the tracks, but they were perfect together, and Brooke always felt a pang of jealousy every time she saw them together. Deep down, she wanted a relationship with someone, but for now, she enjoyed what she did. She was a modern-day woman and felt like settling down was just that: settling. She just never found the right one that did for her what Tyler obviously did for Misty. One day…

Brooke looked up and saw Misty gathering three margaritas.

"Three?" Brooke asked.

"Yep. Two for us and one for -" she whipped her head in the direction of the muscle man.

Brooke's face showed no amusement as she smirked at Misty's brazenness. *What the hell,* she thought. Gamely, Brooke pulled back her shoulders and grabbed two drinks before heading over to the hot man. As she walked, her nerves started to drain, and she hesitated. He looked at her and smiled. She picked up her pace and continued her campaign, reaching his table and then sitting down opposite him in the booth.

Brooke shifted her eyes towards Misty, who had a Cheshire Cat grin on her face. "Bye," Brooke mouthed. She saw Misty feigning being hurt. Brooke just smiled, rolled her eyes, and gave her a thumbs-up. It was clear to Brooke that Misty was pleased with her matchmaking skills. Brooke turned her thumbs up into a thumb sideways, indicating Misty to leave them alone.

I'm going, I'm going, Misty mouthed back in surrender. She chugged her margarita before gathering her purse from the bar and heading out the door.

"I'm sorry for just barging in on you over here," Brooke said, turning her attention to the man across from her. "Are you meeting someone? I mean, you don't look like you'd be here alone, and well, what I mean is you're too good-looking to be alone, and you look like you should be on a date with a hot chick, and I don't know why I just said that. I'll shut up now." *Nice going, Brooke.* She rolled her eyes.

Bradley laughed louder. "You're cute," he said.

Her face flushed.

"Actually, yes, I am on a date. Well, technically, not anymore," he said. He peered around the bar. "Guess I've been stood up."

Stood up? You?! Then there's no hope for the rest of us, she thought.

"So maybe I should just go," he said, sliding out of the booth.

"No!" Brooke said too quickly. "Stay, please. Have a drink." She slid the margarita across the table.

"I guess I could stay for a bit," he replied, settling back into his seat. "I'm Bradley."

Brooke was relieved and smiled. She took a long sip of her drink and felt the tequila beginning to work its magic. They began to talk.

"So, what do you do for work?" she asked him.

"I'm in the landscaping business. I'm working on a large estate in Sonoma. I have to travel there occasionally to do things on the property. In fact, I'll be there later this week. It keeps me busy."

"That's not too far from here. Are you from the area?" she asked. "I mean, I haven't seen you around."

"Not from San Francisco proper. Cupertino."

"Ahh, Silicon Valley," Brooke said. "I know it well."

He took a sip of his drink and shifted in his seat. "You do? How's that?"

"I'm a realtor. I've sold a few properties there." Brooke shrugged. "The area is nice. The houses basically sell themselves." She sipped her margarita. "Where about did you live there?"

"Oh, well, it's been years since I've been there. The house is probably torn down by now. So, your friend. Did she leave?"

Ahh, the old subject change. An air of mystery. I can live with that, she thought.

"Yeah, I guess she did," Brooke said. "Three's a crowd, right?" she laughed. *Oh, my God, why did I say that?* She felt her cheeks burn. She looked into her margarita glass, blaming the alcohol. "Sorry," she muttered. "I don't know why I...I mean, I wasn't insinuating that the three of us.... I'm so embarrassed and I .... shut up, Brooke."

He let out a hearty laugh that went on for a while.

"What?" Brooke asked. "What's so funny?"

He kept laughing and Brooke joined in. Their laughter continued until tears streamed down their faces.

"You!" he said when he finally caught his breath. "You are what's so funny."

"Oh," she chuckled. "Yeah, I'm a barrel of laughs tonight."

"Well, I haven't laughed like that in a long time," he replied.

"Me, too."

"And for what it's worth," he said, reaching across the table and grabbing her hands, "I'm very glad I got stood up tonight."

"Me, too," she repeated quietly.

"So," he said. "I want to hear everything about you. Don't leave anything out."

"What do you want to know?" she asked.

"Well, for starters, your name."

Her eyes flew open. "Oh, my god!" she blurted out.

And the laughter began again.

Three hours and six margaritas later, the bar was closing, and Bradley said he needed to get home. Feeling a little fuddled, Brooke wasn't sure if it was the margaritas, the company, or the concussion, but she found herself enamored. The margaritas eliminated any headache she might have had, and now she just felt she was floating around a handsome,

God-like man. *Get a grip, Brooke,* she told herself. *He's just a man. Just a man in tight jeans and a perfectly fitting tee shirt and arms that could choke a horse and –*

"What?"

Brooke snapped to. "*What* what?" she asked.

"You said something about a horse. Is that how you're getting home? Because I could give you a ride," Bradley said, his smile revealing he was being playful.

"Umm, no. No horse. I'll call an Uber," Brooke said. She shook her head. *Stupid!*

"That's probably best," he said, motioning to the empty glasses on the table. "Besides, I've already called one. And I just got a message they're here."

"But...my car..." she mumbled.

"You can get it tomorrow."

They both slid out of the booth, holding onto the table for a bit of support.

"The floor's moving," Brooke said, then realized to her horror it wasn't.

He took her arm and walked her to the door. The Uber was waiting for them, and he helped her in. The drive was curvy and fast and did nothing to help her tipsiness. Twenty minutes later, they were outside her house. She wanted to kiss him but also wanted to throw up. She hoped she wouldn't combine the two.

Bradley was a complete gentleman and didn't offer to stay the night, although Brooke wanted him to. She had a long day and an even longer night and, in the long run, felt he made the right decision for them. He got her number to call her later, walked her to the front door, and left, saying only a soft "good night".

She closed the door behind her, leaned against the hard oak, and sighed. Her smile was huge. She was definitely smitten, and her pounding heart gave the confirmation. She felt something on her shins and looked down. Her fluffy Himalayan cat was rubbing against her, looked up, and then meowed hungrily. He batted at her leg for ignoring him.

"Hey, Bongo," she said, bending down to scratch the top of his head.

Then it hit her. "I'm a single woman with a cat, yearning for a man I just met." She breathed heavily. "Great. I'm a Hallmark movie cliché." She rolled her eyes.

The night had begun with her and two men she couldn't care less if she saw again; it had ended with one man she *needed* to see again. With Oscar and Hank, she had the best of both worlds. Or so she had thought. But with Bradley, he was something different. The angel on her right shoulder whispered: *what the heck is wrong with you? You've only known him for three hours!*

But the devil sitting opposite overrode the angel. *Go for it! This is unlike anything you've experienced before.* Brooke could almost feel the devil's nudge. She felt warm inside. Tingly. Nervous. Whatever this reaction was, it wasn't familiar to her, but it was a welcomed invasion of her emotions. And for the first time in her hectic life, Brooke knew. She just *knew.* Bradley was the one.

"Oh, my god, this is nuts!" she told herself. "That bump on your head really messed you up." But she was only kidding herself. She was a goner. Bradley would be the man to turn her life into something she never knew was possible. He was the easiest man to talk to she had ever met. He was gentle and sweet, had a good construction job, and just seemed perfect. Something inside told her that if it seemed too good to be true, it probably was. But she was too busy being swept off her feet to trust her instinct. She wanted to trust her heart, which, at the moment, was fluttering like a hummingbird's wings. *Or was that the margaritas?*

"Thank you, devil," she said, brushing the imaginary angel off her right shoulder. This was new to her, and she never wanted this feeling to end. She imagined her and Bradley connecting on a visceral level, an instant, spontaneous, explosive love. They would come together and never separate again. She had never felt such certainty. Or happiness. She picked up Bongo and kissed him on his forehead. "I'm head over heels, buddy," she said. He hissed angrily and sunk his claws into her shoulders before jumping down, meowing angrily. Brooke playfully hissed back.

But she was too happy to be angry. "This is crazy!" she told herself.

Brooke, in a state of euphoria, threw herself onto her bed. She and

Bradley would talk again tomorrow and sort things out. They would talk and discover each other on a fundamental level, without margaritas. She was looking forward to tomorrow like she never had before.

With the broadest grin on her face, she fell asleep, knowing tomorrow would bring nothing but happiness.

CHAPTER 4

U nfortunately, tomorrow came and went four times without a word from Bradley.

Brooke jumped every time the phone rang but was disappointed every time. None of the calls were from Bradley. However, she received plenty of calls from other guys, including Oscar (*"I'm so sorry, Brooke. I panicked! Let me make it up to you! Please?"*) and even Hank, who seemed to be aroused by the events (*"That was a fuckin' awesome night, eh? Think you'd like to be hit like that again, only while you're riding my dick this time?"*). Brooke found herself disgusted by both guys. After what they did and then left her there, on the porch, unconscious, it was unforgivable. In no uncertain terms, she told them both to go to hell. She felt a surge of power course through her and imagined the little shoulder-sitting devil applauding.

Brooke wondered why she wasn't into any of her guy friends anymore. They used to be her comfort zone. They would scratch whenever she itched. But now she had no desire to even think about those boys. She only wanted Bradley. *And there's your answer,* she thought to herself.

And yet, he was M.I.A.

Four days was a long time to wait for anybody. And the more she thought about it, the angrier she became. "How dare he! I can't believe I let myself get bamboozled by some guy in a bar!" *Screw it.* She decided right there she would wait for no man. She called up Mel, her go-to guy, the one who was always there for her no matter what. Mel was neither attractive nor ugly. But he was an excellent partner in bed and never asked for anything. He wasn't into commitments or questions, which suited Brooke just fine. He was precisely the kind of guy Brooke liked to keep around – the "wham, bam, thank-you-ma'am" type. He was a relationship with no heartstrings attached.

She invited him to come over for dinner, and though food wasn't normally on his brain where Brooke was concerned, he had agreed to come over that evening. Brooke headed to the grocery store to buy things she needed.

Up and down the aisles, she felt anxious, but she was not sure why. Her mind was on Bradley's absenteeism and why she hadn't heard from him. It still nagged in the back of her head, even though she had basically given up on him. She couldn't concentrate and realized she had passed the pasta aisle ten minutes ago and had to re-circle.

She grabbed a bottle – fine, two bottles – of Meomi Merlot. It was her favorite comfort wine, and she needed major comforting after the week she'd had. As she rounded the end of the aisle, she heard her name. But it was soft and sinister, almost ghostly. The little hairs on the back of her neck prickled.

Brooooooke. Brooooooooke, the voice called, almost soundlessly. She froze in her tracks.

"Who's…. who's there?" she asked, shaking.

Silence.

She grabbed a bottle of wine from her buggy and held it by the neck, like a flashlight, ready to strike out.

Brooooooooke, she heard again.

She bounded around the corner to surprise whoever was calling her name – but there was no one.

Brooke crinkled her brow, sure she'd heard someone from this direction –

"GOTCHA!" Misty yelled, grabbing Brooke by the shoulders. Startled, Brooke dropped the bottle of wine. It smashed to the floor and wine started to bleed across the floor.

"Misty! What the hell?"

Misty laughed and hugged Brooke. "For someone who loves scary movies, you sure are a scaredy cat!"

Brooke composed herself. "Ha ha," she fake laughed.

"What are you doing here?" Misty asked.

"I'm cooking dinner for Mel tonight. Just picking up a few things."

Misty looked in the buggy and started rummaging. "Don't forget to lock up that mean cat of yours. He hates people."

"He's not so bad."

Misty held up her arm to show a faint pink line on her forearm. "I've got the scar to prove otherwise!" She picked through the tomatoes, lettuce, and mushrooms in Brooke's cart. "Is Mel on a diet or something?"

"No, but then maybe we won't eat at all." Brooke tried to sound upbeat, still unnerved by not hearing from Bradley in four days.

"What happened with the hot guy from the bar? Did that go nowhere? Awww, poor Brooke." Misty's concern was patronizing in a friendly way.

"Who?" Brooke tried to deflect her hurt. "Oh, him. Bradley. Nothing. I haven't heard from him. I think he said he had to go to Sonoma for work or something." She shrugged.

"*Bradley*," Misty said sweetly, trying his name on her tongue. "Well, you will if it's meant to be! I gotta run. I'm meeting Tyler at the movies. Ant-Man and something. Wanna come?"

"You know I hate those superhero movies."

"Oh, yeah. You like horror movies. Ick!" Misty went to hug Brooke goodbye.

"Huh," Misty said.

"What?" Brooke asked, releasing the hug. She noticed Misty's eyebrows were furrowed.

"I'm sorry...what?" Misty said, distracted.

"Earth to Misty. Are you okay?"

Misty recovered quickly. "Oh, yeah. It's nothing," she said, opening her eyes fully. "I just thought I saw someone I knew leaving the store. But I was mistaken."

"Okay, fine. Don't tell me."

"Whatever!" Misty said. "But I'm gonna head out. Have fun with Mel tonight!" She went back in for another hug.

Brooke squeezed back. She liked Misty a lot. There were a lot of memories between the two of them, along with Cathy, Dana, and Alicia. *That seems like a lifetime ago*, she thought. She hugged Misty tighter before releasing her friend.

Misty pulled away, blew her a kiss, and left.

Suddenly, Brooke felt all alone. Her friends were no longer in the picture, and now this incredible man she had just met was M.I.A. He probably hooked up with that girl who stood him up at Alley Bar. *Get a grip, Brooke*, she told herself. *He's a free agent.* Only, she didn't want him to be, really. She sighed, and her heart sank. She was livid at herself for letting herself feel this way over a man she had met just once. *Dammit, Brooke*, she told herself. *Why am I letting this bother me so much? Don't do this to yourself.*

But it was pointless. As ridiculous as it sounded, her heart was breaking. And she felt a hot tear streak down her cheek onto the ground, mixing with the blood-like wine that now encircled her feet.

As Misty got into her car, she sat in her seat and reflected on who she had just seen leaving the grocery store: Bradley.

He had told Brooke he would be out of town working in Sonoma. Misty knew that most men were liars, and apparently, Bradley was no exception. *He has his own life, and the two of them had just met. Technically, he owed her nothing.* "But why lie?" she said.

Her Uncle Mike was a detective, and he used to always say, "If it walks like a duck, acts like a duck, and quacks like a duck, it probably needs more time in the oven." That always made Misty laugh. But she knew what he meant. She just needed a little more information before she decided Bradley was, for sure, a duck.

Misty's gut was telling her something was up. And the more she thought about it, the more suspicious and incensed she became. *I blame you, Uncle Mike, for turning me into a junior detective!*

Misty started her car and then glanced back at the grocery store where she had left her friend. "Don't you worry, honey. I've got your back," she said before leaving the parking lot.

CHAPTER 5

When Brooke got home from the grocery store, she gathered her bags in her arms. She stepped onto her front porch, opened her mailbox on her wall, and pulled out the mail. "Ooof," she said, adjusting the heavy bags in her arms. She put the mail in her mouth and bit down to hold it in place. After a few minutes of fumbling with the key and the ever-shifting bags, she managed to get in her house, make it to the kitchen, and plop the bags down on the countertop. The soggy mail fell from her mouth onto the floor.

"Ugh!" she moaned, catching her breath. She collected the mail from the floor and rifled through the stack.

"Bill. Bill. Voter's registration. Bill." Brooke scoffed. "You're a bad boy, Bill." She kept flipping. "Lawn care. Bill……hmm," she murmured, coming across a postcard. She set everything down on the countertop and flipped the postcard over. It was from Peterinarians, Bongo's vet. *It's time for Bongo's annual checkup!* Dana, her friend from college, owned Peterinarians, and they hadn't spoken to each other since the wedding. *Not since the accident…*

The memories flooded Brooke's head in a torrent, and it seemed the room was spinning. She closed her eyes and let the movements subside. After a long moment, she opened her eyes. They had grown watery from the thoughts. She was proud of Dana accomplishing her dream of opening her own vet clinic. She got a pen and wrote a note on the card: *Call Dana!* Brooke laid the postcard on the counter and took a deep breath. Her eyes saw the bags of groceries and knew she had to get to work for Mel's dinner.

Brooke Carson's mother used to say, "The way to a man's stomach is through food, but if his stomach ever gets too big, the way to the gym is down the street." Her mother believed in reeling them in but also in making sure the sight of him didn't embarrass her. Her mother's way of having her cake and eat it, too.

Because of her mother's philosophy, Brooke was an excellent cook, but unfortunately, she never really had anyone to cook for. She was looking forward to having Mel come over. She would insist they have dinner first before any other indulgences. Mel would be a pleasant distraction. And she needed a distraction after the afternoon she had at the grocery store.

So tonight, she was making toasted Orecchiette with veal meatballs. Her pasta was cooking, and she had already chopped the bacon and added it to the veal. Next, she added garlic, onions, coriander, allspice, paprika, and breadcrumbs, then formed small meatballs, rounding them gently in her palms. In a pan, she cooked the mushrooms, onions, and kale. After mixing the mushrooms, she added the mixture to her pasta and placed the veal meatballs on top. She added a layer of shaved Parmesan cheese on top, then used a small spoon to taste and gave a chef's kiss. She covered her dish and let it simmer. The house smelled of a rich sauce and earthy, vibrant spices. *Mel will love this*, she thought.

She heard her phone *bing* a text message.

> Need to cancel. Stomach upset, sick and nauseous. Can we reschedule our tee time?

It was from Mel. And it was in the code he used sometimes in case someone else saw the text. *'Stomach upset, sick and nauseous'* was a coded acronym, and the first letter of each word spelled out 'Susan', his girl-friend, who must be coming over to his apartment. *'Can we reschedule our tee time'* was code for "Can we pick another time you can play with my balls?". Brooke rolled her eyes. Bongo jumped up on the stool, putting his big, furry paw out to touch her arm. She put the phone down on the island top.

"Men!" Brooke said, rubbing the cat's head. Bongo licked her fingers. He could taste the veal. He started nibbling at her fingertips. Brooke saw the Peterinarians postcard on the countertop and picked it up again. Absentmindedly, she ran her hand over the card as if the feel of it would somehow bring a sweeter memory back to her. The doorbell rang, and Bongo meowed before jumping down off the stool. *Maybe Mel canceled his cancellation*, Brooke thought as she opened the door.

But it wasn't Mel. It was Bradley. And he was holding a bottle of Meomi Merlot in his hand.

Brooke's eyes opened in surprise. "What…what are you doing here?" she stammered.

"Well, I wanted to apologize for not calling," he said sheepishly. "I was out of town for work and got busy installing a humongous hot tub at the estate where I'm working, and you should see this tub! It's huge! Anyway, there were a lot of details to work out and pavers to install, and, well, time just got the better of me, and I forgot to call." He lowered his head. "Sorry…" he left the sentence hanging.

Brooke cringed. She had thought he was with another woman. She shook her head in frustration with herself.

"So…" Bradley continued, waving the wine in front of her. "Am I forgiven?"

"Oh, shit, yes! So sorry! Come in, come in!" She opened the door wider for him to enter her house. She smacked her forehead with her palm. *Idiot.*

"Here. It's my way of apologizing: with drink." He handed her the wine.

"It's…it's my favorite, actually," she said. "I have another bottle – fine, two bottles - in the kitchen. Come on, I'll pour."

"What's that?" he asked, pointing to the card in her hand.

"Oh, this? It's just a postcard from the vet, Peterinarians. Time for Bongo's yearly checkup."

"What's a *Bongo*?" He took the card from her and looked it over.

Brooke laughed. "That's my cat. If you see him, run. He's a bit territorial."

"And who's Dana?"

"Huh?" Brooke said, caught off guard.

"Here," he said, pointing to her note to call Dana.

"Oh," she said quietly, taking the card back from him. "A friend from, like, a lifetime ago. Just someone I need to call."

There was a quiet pause.

"Peterinarians. Cute name," he said, breaking the silence. "Not as cute as Meomi, but…"

"Oh, gosh, yes! Sorry. Let's get these opened."

They went into the kitchen, and Brooke got two glasses from the cabinet. She got the corkscrew, but he took it from her. "Let me," he said.

So, she did.

"Something smells great," he offered, handing her a glass of wine.

"Oh, that's just dinner. Toasted Orecchiette with veal meatballs."

"Wow," he said, impressed. "That sounds…amazing."

"Then stay. I insist. I've got plenty."

He looked down and saw a big, furry cat rubbing between his legs. "This must be Bongo," he said. They could both hear Bongo purring like a freight train. "Beautiful kitty," he said, bending down to pick Bongo up.

"Oh! Be careful," Brooke exclaimed. "He might claw you. He's been known to -" but she stopped when she saw Bongo in Bradley's arms. Curled around Bradley's biceps, Bongo placed his head on Bradley's chest, occasionally rubbing his whiskers against Bradley's cheeks.

Brooke's mouth popped open like a ventriloquist doll's.

"Aww, he's a sweetie," Bradley said. "Aren't you, big fella?" He rubbed the cat's tummy for good measure before setting Bongo back on the floor. Bongo retreated to another part of the kitchen and began licking his paw.

"I love animals," Bradley said. "I have a dog, myself. A big black Russian Terrier named Kong. He looks and sounds ferocious, but he's really a sweetheart."

Brooke's mouth was still open at Bongo's reaction to Bradley. "K… Kong?" she asked absentmindedly. Brooke looked quizzically at Bongo.

"Yeah. He's a rescue. Big ol' sweet boy."

Brooke's face reacted to the word 'rescue'. "That's so kind of you," she said sincerely. She clasped her hands over her heart. She couldn't help but feel Bradley was a big ol' sweet boy, too. "Come on. Let's eat before it gets cold."

As they sat for dinner, she eyed Bongo suspiciously. *Who are you, and what did you do with my killer cat?*

Over dinner, Brooke and Bradley fell into an easy and comfortable conversation about jobs, hobbies, and reading.

"Tell me more about your landscaping business," she said.

"Well, it's not my business. I just work for a couple of guys and help them out wherever they are working. We did all the landscaping for Kaiser Permanente in Monterey two months ago. And now, we're working on that large estate outside of Sonoma. We do all sorts of projects up and down the coast. But so far, Sonoma is my favorite."

"I love wine country," Brooke said. "The smooth hills and coastline, it's just all so beautiful. I did a hot-air balloon ride over Sonoma once. Just breathtaking."

"It is. But I don't get to see the ground from the air. Usually, just from being in enormous holes I've dug with the Bobcat excavator."

"What's a …"

"Just a smaller version of a bulldozer. It gets into smaller spaces and is much more straightforward to operate."

"So, what else do you like to do in your spare time besides digging holes?" Brooke asked.

"Hmmm. I like country music – not the new stuff. I'm more of an old-school country music sort of guy: Waylon, Willie, Alabama. Life was simpler back then, and I like to pretend I was simpler in a previous life."

"I like the old stuff too: Dolly, Emmylou, Tammy. What else?" Brooke asked.

"Vintage cars. I like to look. I can't afford to buy them, but they certainly are pretty to look at. Oh, and I collect stamps. I know. I'm a bit of a nerd."

"Stamps?"

"Yeah. I'm a -" he shrugged, a little embarrassed "– philatelist."

Brooke blinked. "My dad collects stamps, too! That's so cool!" Brooke couldn't believe how much they had in common.

"So, who was your friend with you at Alley Bar?" Bradley asked.

Brooke deflated. "Oh, that was Misty. A longtime friend. Why? Did you...like...her?" Brooke didn't know why she asked the question or why she felt scared to receive the answer.

Bradley laughed. "No!" He laughed some more. "I was just making conversation."

Brooke was relieved. "She's at the movies with her boyfriend." Brooke spoke louder on 'boyfriend' for emphasis. Just in case Bradley needed any clarification.

The left corner of his mouth rose. He got the hint.

"Some Marvel movie," she continued.

He pulled a face. "I hate those superhero movies. Give me a good ol' slasher flick any day!"

"Me, too!" she said. She smiled inside and out, feeling the night was going very well.

"I like to try to figure out who the killer is," he said. "I'm usually pretty good with that. I love a good psychological thriller book, too: Freida McFadden, Natalie Barelli, Nina Travers. They keep me guessing. I can't always guess their endings."

Brooke liked Bradley more than she cared to admit. Their conversation was easy and uncomplicated. And he was very easy on the eyes. A fantastic, tanned build, no doubt from years of working in the landscaping business; a couple of tattoos on his biceps that seemed to have lives of their own every time he moved his arms; deep green eyes. And a tight butt that would rival any rugby players' out there. But besides the physical, he seemed to be a simple man, unlike the needy bores she'd been with in the past. She found herself filled with hope. *This is nuts,* she told herself. She'd never reacted to a man this way before. *Who are you?* she wondered about herself.

After a couple of hours of food, wine, and conversation, Brooke had all but disowned every man in her life except for Bradley. She found herself staring at him, eyes all goo-goo, not unlike a Disney Princess swooning over her Prince. *I need a psychiatrist,* she told herself. She thought of what a psychiatrist would say to her.

Doctor: So, what brings you to see me, Brooke?

Brooke: You're the doctor, you tell me.

Doctor: So, you're a smart-ass.

Brooke: Excuse me?

Doctor: I call 'em like I see 'em.

Brooke: Well, that wasn't very nice.

Doctor: Tell me I'm wrong.

Brooke: I can't.

Doctor: Fine. Then tell me why you're here.

Brooke: (silence)

Doctor: I can wait. I'm paid by the hour.

Brooke: I have man problems.

Doctor: OK.

Brooke: (laughs) I mean, don't we all?

Doctor: I don't.

Brooke: (silence)

Doctor: (looks at his watch)

Brooke: (sighs) I like to sleep around. I mean, I used to. But lately, I've met someone. And…for some reason, I don't want any other man…in my life.

Doctor: Or in your bed.

Brooke: Yes.

Doctor: And why do you think this is a problem?

Brooke: Well, I'm not sure. I think I fell for this guy rather quickly. I admit that. But I'm rather smitten with him. (takes a big breath) You should see him.

Doctor: No, thanks.

Brooke: Umm…

Doctor: Again, why do you think this is a problem?

Brooke: (cocks head) Well, my friend, Misty, lovingly calls me a slut, (laughs), and where there may be some truth to that, I don't feel that way anymore. I feel…respected. Honored. And that's new to me.

Doctor: Interesting.

Brooke: So, what you're saying is, it's not necessarily a problem, but something worth building on.

Doctor: If you say so.

Brooke: I hear you. And I should let Bradley know this so we can stay connected through communication!

Doctor: That sounds good.

Brooke: That what I've really done is manifested all the best parts of my past men into one perfect person for me!

Doctor: Do you feel better?

Brooke: Oh, yes, doc, I do! Thank you so much! I feel like you've done so much for me today. Thank you! I feel cured of my problem and am ready to fly from the nest!

Doctor: So, same time next week?

She felt the sofa shift. Bradley was getting ready to leave, and Brooke was not ready for the night to end. Egged on by the bottles of wine consumed, she moved her hand to the front of his jeans and squeezed. Bradley smiled, but he eased her hand away.

"I'm sorry, Brooke. I like you, I really do. But I don't want to ruin things by moving too fast. I...I...just want to take things a little slower." He looked into her wide eyes. "Wow. That sure didn't sound manly, did it?" he chuckled.

"No, no...it's fine. Really. I understand." *I don't understand.*

He went into the kitchen. When he came out, he handed her a piece of paper.

"Here's my phone number and address. It's a bit scribbled. I don't have the best handwriting, but if you ever want to...talk, or...whatever."

She took the paper from him and laid it on the coffee table. She stared blankly as Bradley cupped her chin in one hand, pulling her face towards his. He kissed her deeply, better than she'd ever been kissed before. It was hot and sweet, erotic and loving, soft and shattering. It was unlike any kiss she'd experienced.

She was a puddle.

After what seemed like an eternity, he pulled back. Her eyes were still closed, and her neck was still leaning forward.

"Good night," he said, then walked out the door.

It was at that very moment Brooke knew her life had changed for good. She had completely forgotten that Bradley was away for four days with no contact. None of that mattered. The only thing that mattered was that he was back, and she would never let him go again. She looked over and saw Bongo on his back, legs splayed out and purring deeply.

"You and me both, buddy," Brooke sighed. "You and me both."

CHAPTER 6

M isty was shaking.

Brooke and Bradley's romance was over a month strong, Brooke was in a complete state of euphoria, and Misty had been all but forgotten. It was as if her best friend had replaced her with Bradley, a man she barely knew.

This man Misty had yet to even meet.

Misty had begged to hang out with Brooke and Bradley to get to know him better, but Bradley had insisted he and Brooke needed their time alone to build their relationship. To get to know one another without interference from anyone else in their lives.

Misty remembered when Brooke told her about Bradley's idea.

"What? That's weird," Misty said. "I mean, it is weird. Right?"

"Um, maybe, but it's what he wants, and I kind of agree," Brooke replied. She saw Misty's head tilt in doubt. "You and me? We already know each other. We're besties." She grabbed Misty's hands in solidarity. She smiled. "But Bradley...Bradley doesn't know many people, and I get the feeling he's not close with his family back in Cupertino. So, I can understand how he would want to have some sort of strong connection to someone in his life, you know, before letting someone else in. Does that make any sense?"

No, Misty thought. But instead, she said, "Yes."

"Look," Brooke said warmly, "I've never had a relationship like this. I've always been the girl who...who -"

"– slept around?" Misty goaded.

"Stop!" Brooke laughed. "Yes, I suppose I did. What can I say? I like men."
She saw Misty nodding in exaggerated agreement. "But now, I like one man. Just one. And that's new to me."

"But you don't even know him. You know nothing about him, and now he doesn't want to share you with anyone? That's just so strange to me. No matter how hot he is," Misty added quickly.

"You're right. I know next to nothing about him, but I'm learning. And it's been fun. I'm intrigued. So, can you give me this? Just a little more time alone with Bradley, and I promise he'll come around and want you to join us in everything."

Misty's eyebrows shot up.

"Not that!" Brooke squealed. They both laughed. Brooke quieted. "Are we okay?"

"Yeah, fine. We're good," Misty said begrudgingly. "So, what are you two lovebirds up to tonight?"

"Going to dinner and a movie. The new "Scream" is out."

"Scream?" Misty exclaimed.

"Yes! He loves scary movies as much as I do! Isn't that amazing?"

"Yeah..." Misty said, almost doubtfully. "Amazing."

And there was the time Misty had seen Bradley at the grocery store when he was supposed to be out of town working. She never told Brooke about it. She didn't want to ruffle any feathers until she had concrete evidence that.... *that what?* Misty asked herself. She didn't have an answer. She only had a gut feeling. *I'm going to find out if that duck is an actual duck.*

Even though she was nervous about what she was about to do, she felt a determination flourish inside. *We're best friends,* she told herself. *This is for her own good.*

She grabbed her cell phone and scrolled through her contact list until she found who she was looking for. Her finger hovered over the 'call' button for four seconds before finally resting on the red circle. She heard ringing.

After the third ring, a male voice greeted her.

"Hello there, Mist! How's my favorite niece?"

"Hi, Uncle Mike. I'm doing good. Work's keeping me busy. How's Aunt Karen?" She made small talk, her heartbeat furiously.

"She's fine. Sitting right here. Misty says hello," he yelled away from the phone.

"Tell her 'Hello' and come for dinner this week," Misty heard a female voice in the background.

"You heard her?" Mike asked.

"I did. I'll call later to confirm…" Misty left the sentence hanging.

"So, what's up, Mist? Why are you calling now? I know it's not to say 'hi'. You could've texted that."

Misty knew this next part was a point of no return, but she also knew it had to happen. Then again, maybe nothing would come of it. Maybe it was all good, and she was worrying about nothing. She took a deep breath.

"Well, I need my favorite detective uncle to do me a favor."

Mike laughed. "I'm your *only* detective uncle." He paused in the silence. "So, what can I do for you?"

"Well, I have this friend -"

"Oh! A *friend*, huh?" Mike laughed.

"I do! Seriously!" Misty said. "And, anyway, she started seeing someone and, well, I'm a little concerned for her because -"

"Concerned? Do I need to contact my police buddies?"

"No, no, nothing like that. I don't think, anyway."

"Okay," Mike said, suddenly serious. "Continue."

"I'd like you to check him out for me. Do your…detective thing."

"A background investigation?"

"Yeah, that," Misty said.

"Hold on. Let me get something to write with." A minute passed. "Okay, go ahead. What's his name, and where's he from?"

"His name is Bradley Harris. And I think he's from the Bay area. Cupertino, maybe?" She had gotten little information about Bradley from Brooke, so she didn't have too much to go on. She'd hoped what she provided Uncle Mike was enough to use. "Uncle Mike?"

"Yeah, I'm here. Just writing everything down." There was a pause. "Harris is a common last name, so it may take a little while to come up with something, but for my favorite niece, I'll do my best."

Misty smiled. "Thank you, Uncle Mike. I really appreciate this."

"Now you know, usually when I look up someone in the database, 84% of the time, it doesn't end well. So, I have to ask: are you still sure you want me to do this?"

Misty hesitated. *Was* this the right thing to do? Brooke would be furious if she found out. But if Uncle Mike came back with nothing, then Brooke wouldn't know the difference. Misty decided on her answer.

"Yes," she said but found herself shaking her head "no." After promising to call to confirm dinner, she said goodbye, hung up, and closed her eyes.

I feel good about this. I did the right thing.

She flung her eyes open.

Crap. What did I just do?

CHAPTER 7

The next couple of weeks were a whirlwind for Brooke. She and Bradley decided the best way to get to know each other was to dive in and spend almost every waking moment together. They both had shared interests in traveling, and so they did.

From their home base in San Francisco, they went north. In Sonoma, they were in the heart and soul of wine country and stayed at Dawn Ranch. They kayaked the cool water of the Russian River, took a hot-air balloon ride over sprawling orchards and vineyards, and then caught a delightful show at Main Stage West.

"Don't you just love seeing the ground from way up here? Everything looks so small and delicate!" Brooke said excitedly while they were floating over the California landscape in the hot-air balloon.

"Uhhh...." Bradley moaned.

Brooke looked at him. He had turned green.

"Oh, god. Are you sick?" Her hand flew to her mouth as she stifled a giggle.

"Why's that so funny?" he groaned, leaning his head over the balloon's basket.

"It's just a big ol' guy like you, afraid of heights and all. You just look like you can handle anything."

"Aren't...aren't you afraid of anything?" he asked, holding his stomach with his hand.

"Enclosed spaces. I'm a bit claustrophobic. But out here -" she spread her arms wide for emphasis. "Out here, I'm wonderful! Everything is so open and free!" She took a deep breath. "Ahhhhh!"

The basket jiggled with her movements. Bradley's eyes grew wide.

"Stop shaking it. Ohhhh...." He looked queasy.

Brooke laughed. She felt very connected to Bradley. She could relate to his phobia and wanted to help.

"Sir," she acknowledged their balloon handler, "we can go down now." She rubbed Bradley's back. "It's okay, big guy. We'll be down soon."

Twenty-five minutes later, they were safe on the ground and continuing their adventure.

They explored the towering beauties in the Redwood National Park, the shade making the day chillier than Brooke had expected. Bradley bought her a sweatshirt with the California Bear logo to warm her up. She snuggled up next to him as they walked the smooth trails that wound in and around the five-hundred-year-old trees.

Bradley still had made no moves toward Brooke, and after the last time she tried and failed to initiate contact, she decided it was best to wait and let Bradley determine when he was ready. As much time as they'd spent together, she still felt they were strangers, never destined to blend as a couple. Two separate people who would eventually go their own way. She could feel her heart begin to sink. *Maybe Misty was right.* Brooke felt a little feather tickling the back of her mind about what would make a man like Bradley – or any man for that matter – put off making love to a beautiful woman. Maybe he was gay. That would certainly explain the stereotypical 'man-with-the-perfect-body-who-didn't-want-to-sleep-with-a-beautiful-woman'. Right? Brooke shook her head. *God, I sound like an arrogant princess. Give it time, Cinderella. It'll be worth the wait.*

The next morning, they headed one hour east to their next destination, Bodega Bay. When they checked into room 411 at The Lodge, there was a bottle of champagne and a note from the owners welcoming them:

Hope your stay with us is magical! Aaron and Scotty. Brooke smiled at the kind gesture. Afterward, they explored the grounds. From their private back patio, granite pavers ran parallel to seven-foot-tall hedges of coffee-berry laden with bright red berries. The fruit bushes stretched the length of the grounds towards the cliff's edge. Brooke and Bradley walked right up to the cliffs overlooking the harbor, whose waves crashed violently along the rugged Sonoma Coast directly below. Instinctively, Brooke wrapped her cardigan tighter around her waist.

The grounds were magnificent, with incredible views from every spot on the habitat. Sunsets as if plucked from a Chagall burned in the panoramic views of the bay just beyond the bucolic fields. Bradley and Brooke filled their days with playful, relaxing activities: they played bocce ball, enjoyed a soothing spa treatment for two, and savored artisanal dishes and several bottles of local wines at Drakes. After detoxifying at the spa, the wine rejuvenated her senses, and she felt sanguine and uninhibited.

They decided to check out the inside of The Lodge. As they walked the travertine floors, they noticed framed antique photographs and memorabilia from the resort's rich history hanging on the walls: male celebrities on the golf course, wearing argyle vests and newsboy hats; before and after shots of the resort before a major expansion; letters from visiting Royalty. Brooke brought Bradley over to one of the letters.

"Look! This one was written by the Queen herself!"

"Pretty cool," he responded.

"And that stamp? It's so unique-looking. What does that mean, 'Half Crown'?"

"How would I know?" Bradley asked.

"Oh. Well, I thought you said you collected stamps, and I just -"

He swung his head to her. "*American* stamps. Not British ones. I'm not an expert at everything."

Brooke's eyes got big.

"Can we just go? I want to check out the gift shop," he said as he walked away, leaving Brooke with a confused look on her face.

"Sure," she responded to his back. *Maybe his job was stressing him out.*

After some shopping, they sat at the Lodge's bar, drank wine, and rested. High on the wine and relaxation that the resort afforded, they walked in the dark along a foot-lit path and retreated to their secluded guest room. Brooke felt the wine rushing to her head, and the warmth made her mellow. She could also sense Bradley was more relaxed than earlier. Bradley started a fire in their room's fireplace. The extra heat made Brooke more flushed. Without thinking, she disrobed until she was nude. Bradley stood and looked at her. She suddenly felt her nakedness.

"Oh, god. I'm sorry..." she stammered. "I was just feeling warmish suddenly."

Bradley moved to her and looked down at her. The fire danced in his green eyes, and she felt hypnotized. He swept her in his arms, but instead of taking her to the bed, he led her to the French doors, where he deftly opened them with one hand. He carried her out onto their private patio, where the warm air from the room mixed with the cool breezes from the outdoors. It was intoxicating, and Brooke melded into Bradley's arms. He gently stood her up next to him. Her skin was covered with goosebumps. Bradley unbuttoned his shirt and put it on her but left it open, her breasts barely hidden beneath the poplin. Her hands drifted down his hard chest, moving downwards to unhook his belt, but she paused and looked into his eyes. He smiled his affirmation, and her hands continued their journey. She unbuttoned his jeans and yanked them down, then stood and stared at him, taking him all in.

In one fell swoop, he grabbed under her legs and the small of her back, lifted her, and carried her to the thick pad on the lounge chair. He lay on top of her, and Brooke trembled, knowing this was the first time they would make love. She had waited so long for this. She wasn't sure if it was the wine or the headiness of the mixing temperatures or the seclusion of the bay, but for the next several minutes, there, under the northern California stars, the only sounds louder than the waves crashing fifty yards away were the muffled, pleasurable eruptions between two strangers finally coming together as one.

"I love you," Brooke panted in his ear.

"I love you, too," Bradley said. "More than anything." He was trembling.

The next morning, she was still wearing his dress shirt, and they were having coffee and Danishes on their room's terrace.

Bradley sat at the computer. "I was just reading up on the Black Chasm Caverns! We can go tomorrow, our last day!" Bradley said with a smile that of a little boy.

"The...*what?*" Brooke said, nearly choking on her fig croissant.

"The Black Chasm Caverns," he repeated. "It's only about three hours east of here. In – get this! – Volcano, California! Isn't that the coolest name for a town? We've got one more day here, and then we'll head there tomorrow. If we left after breakfast, we could be there by noon."

"What exactly is this place?" Brooke's voice quavered.

He referred to the website. "It's a cave system discovered in 1854 before the gold rush. Explorers discovered a bright blue lake and millions of sparkling, twisting crystals now known as helictites." He showed her a picture of the stone formations. "Looks like visitors can go down about 100 feet into the darkness!" His excitement was palpable.

Brooke felt nauseous. She was deathly claustrophobic. When she was six, her brother's friend locked her in the trunk of her parents' car and forgot about her. In the darkness, she could feel icy fingers slowly constricting her throat, her breathing lost in the complete blackness of the trunk. Fear froze her in place, rendering her unable to move despite not having lost consciousness. Ever since then, enclosed spaces had been her worst enemy, and she had avoided them at all costs. Until now, apparently.

She felt close to Bradley, closer than ever before, and she knew he was the one she wanted to spend the rest of her life with. But this! This was not okay. Black Chasm Caverns just *sounded* like a foreboding tightness. She could feel her airways beginning to constrict just from the thought. She felt faint.

"Are you okay?" Bradley asked. "You look pale."

"I...I..." She looked at this man. His eyes were filled with concern and, dare she say, love. He wanted this. And she wanted to do this for him, to prove to him they were meant to be together. If she complained this early in the relationship, surely, he'd resent her pettiness, and that would be the end of them. She was too far gone in their alliance to throw it all away on a silly phobia. She swallowed hard.

"I...I'm fine," she said. "It sounds exciting."

It sounded like death.

After breakfast, when she was getting dressed for the day, she overheard him on the phone while he was out on the patio. His voice was raised slightly, enough for Brooke to hear bits and pieces but not enough to form a complete conversation.

"...I can't...not right...I made...mistake.... scared.... go wrong..."

She saw him hang up the phone and come back inside.

"Hey. Everything okay?" Brooke asked innocently.

"Mind your own business," he barked.

Brooke felt like she'd been slapped. The sting was lasting. And she never asked again.

Today was going to be a good day. Brooke was determined. Bradley acted like the morning conversation had never happened. Brooke didn't want to bring it up, so she left it alone. Bradley and Brooke drove down Highway 1, turned right onto Bay Flat Road, then straight onto Westshore Road. They passed hundreds of fishing and leisure boats lined up at the docks at Spud Point Marina. They pulled into Spud Point Crab Company to grab a quick picnic lunch of chowder and crab sandwiches. Back on the road, their destination loomed in the distance, and Brooke could feel her heart begin to flutter. Bradley reached over and grabbed her hand. They pulled into the bluff-top parking lot at Bodega Head peninsula and parked their car.

Several trails offered spectacular views from the bluffs, but Bradley and Brooke decided to head down to the massive flat granite boulders at the southern end of the parking lot for their picnic. They found a perfect spot on a rock with amazing views of the bay and ocean. Bradley spread out a thick blanket, and they sat facing the calm, azure waters. Though the sky was a brilliant cornflower blue and the sun blazed on the rocks, Brooke felt a chill sweep across the harbor's waves as her blonde hair tousled in the breeze. She loved being out in the open where her claustrophobia could not rear its ugly head. She scootched closer to Bradley, handing him a sandwich thick with Dungeness crabmeat. Together, they sat and looked out into the vastness. The anticipation was discernible.

Finally, the show began. Brooke could hear the whoops of excitement from other neighboring spectators, all of whom focused their eyes on the pageantry in the sea: a pod, at least thirty strong, of massive gray whales heading south to Mexico after their primary migration from Alaska breached the crests of the waves, hissing plumes of sea spray high into the air. The elegant, noble beasts swam effortlessly through the swells, their flukes on full display before propelling their immense bodies beneath the surface. Suddenly, a huge forty-foot gray whale stopped swimming and seemed to stand straight, its body vertical to the water.

"That's called spy hopping," Bradley said. "They're using their pectoral fins to inspect their surroundings. Gray whales are very protective of their calves, so a baby must be nearby. Nature is pretty amazing, isn't it?" He hugged her closer to him.

Brooke felt a tear flow down her cheek. She wasn't sure if it was the awe of nature she was witnessing or the shock of legitimate love her heart was feeling for the first time. Either way, she had inwardly forgiven Bradley for snapping at her about the phone call earlier. She looked out at the fantastic migration and said a silent *thank you*.

When they returned to their room at The Lodge, Brooke saw a large vase filled with red and yellow variegated poppies. She never told Bradley poppies were her favorite flower – at least she didn't think she had – and she wondered how he knew.

"How did you…?" she asked

"You like them?" he asked. His smile looked like that of a five-year-old boy asking his mother if she liked her Mother's Day handmade clay ashtray.

"I…I love them," Brooke said honestly. "They're my favorite!" Instinctively, she reached inside her shirt and felt the necklace with a poppy charm she'd always worn since Alicia and Ryan's wedding. Her shoulders sagged at the memory. *Poor Alicia*, she thought. Lifting her head, she came back to the present.

"How did you do this? We were together all day?"

"Oh, I just asked the concierge to help me out. Threw a little money at the situation and he came through. I should go thank him."

"Later. Right now, I need to thank *you*." She moved slowly towards him and pulled him down into a deep kiss. His tongue found hers, and she fell limp in his arms. Still pressed against his lips, she smiled.

Brooke knew at this moment nothing could ruin their happiness.

CHAPTER 8

The next morning, Brooke felt sick.

Not from food or from drinking too much or anything like that: it was because they were driving towards the Black Chasm Caverns. The *enclosed* Black Chasm Caverns. Just twenty minutes in, Brooke made Bradley pull over so she could throw up. Now, thirty minutes later, she was asking again.

"Are you sure you're okay?" he asked.

"I'm fine," she lied. She took a sip of Pedialyte, her go-to for stomach issues. "Mind if I try to doze for a bit?" she asked.

"Go right ahead," he smiled. "I've got you."

She grinned and laid her head on the upholstered padding around the window. No sooner had she closed her eyes than she was asleep.

She awoke with a jerk. She was being throttled left and right. Something was wrong with the car. It was swerving across the center line and back again, and she heard the squealing of tires. The road looked wet – had it rained while she was asleep? Her left hand gripped the door for stability.

"Oh, my god!" she screamed. "We've lost control!" Her eyes were on the road, the car moving closer and closer to the steep cliff on the left that plunged into a bottomless crevasse. Suddenly, the car swerved back to the right, closer to the jagged rocks protruding from the side of the mountain. She was trapped between being impaled on razor-sharp boulders or plummeting into a dusty abyss.

She screamed! She looked at the driver. *Gio?*

"What...?" she tried, but the car swerved again. She banged her head on the window and heard a crack.

Frantic, she reached for the steering wheel and tried to straighten the vehicle out. Four hands on the wheel, working against each other, the car barreling down the twisty road, racing towards – Brooke looked up. Trees loomed ahead, and she knew this was it. One way or the other, this was the end.

The car zoomed uncontrollably at the trees, faster and faster, barreling towards death. Brooke screamed just before she heard an explosion of crunching, metallic noises. The car came to an instant, grinding stop, jarring and twisting her, slamming her into the dashboard. She was still conscious, her neck stiff and pained as she looked out the splintered windshield.

Like a flash, the engine caught fire, and flames blazed up on the windshield, shutting out her line of vision. The car's cabin filled with smoke, and she could see orange flames flickering behind the air conditioning vents. The inferno started licking her hands and arms, and her skin began to sizzle.

My god, we're on fire! Alicia!

Startled, she popped upright as if struck by an electric shock and gasped.

"Whoa! Are you okay?" Bradley asked.

Brooke tried to catch her breath. She looked around. There was no cliff. No jagged rocks. No trees or fiery car engine. She was breathing fast and shallow.

But she was safe.

"I'm...fine," she lied again. "Just a...a bad dream."

"Must've been. Sounded like you were whimpering."

"I'm sorry. I just…"

"And who's Alicia?" he asked.

"What?" Brooke asked, startled.

"Alicia. You called out her name. Just before waking up."

Did I? Brooke wondered. *What else did I say?*

"I don't know. Did…did I say anything else?"

"Nope. Just 'Alicia'. Maybe it was someone you met at the whale watching or something. New names pop up in dreams all the time."

"Yeah," she said. "Maybe that was it."

But Brooke knew better. She turned her head and looked out the window at the landscape passing by in a blur.

The dream was horrible. So maybe, in comparison, the Caverns wouldn't be so bad.

As it turned out, she was wrong.

The tour guide was speaking. "Now, we stay in our group. There are twenty of you today, and I don't want to come back with only nineteen. Again."

The crowd standing around the guide laughed and murmured light-heartedly.

Brooke's eyes just grew wide.

She looked up at Bradley. He was grinning at the guide's joke. She elbowed him in his ribs. "Not funny," she said.

"He's kidding," Bradley said. "I think."

"Stop it!" She grabbed Bradley's hand. "Just don't let me go."

"Promise," he said. "Love you!"

She gave in. Brooke didn't want to be *that* girlfriend, the one who was all wussy and scared of every little thing. She had always taken care of herself, but ever since she got locked in the trunk of her parents' car, she couldn't deal with dark, enclosed spaces. It never ended well, so she avoided them altogether. But she would do this for Bradley. For them. She took, then released, a deep breath.

"And that's it. That's all the safety talk I have today. Any questions?" the guide was asking.

Shit. I wasn't paying attention, Brooke thought. *I'm gonna die here.*

"Everyone can walk into the cave, which is right below the gift shop. "Oh, and one more thing: touch nothing in the caves. And if anything – and I do mean anything," he said, pointing to a young blonde-haired boy, "drops or falls to the cavern floor 120 feet below us, you will never get it back." The little boy's eyes were wide with frightened excitement. "Ever." He paused for effect. "Cool?" the guide asked, grinning. "Then let's go."

The group walked past tee shirts and magnets before entering a door in the back of the gift shop. The chill from the caverns enveloped everyone. In an instant, the group held onto the stair railings and started heading downward. The cavern was vertical, and the stairs descended deeper into the cave. Brooke held Bradley's hand tightly as if she were squeezing a lemon barehanded.

"Ouch," he toyed.

"Get used to it," she said

Despite not being as enclosed as Brooke initially thought, she could still see the cavern's bumpy, craggy, wet (with something) roof, which reminded her she was definitely in an enclosed space, just not a trunk-size one. She closed her eyes and kept climbing down. She breathed a bit easier.

Finally, the group reached a platform, and the cave surrounded the group. 'Oohs' and 'ahhs' echoed throughout the chambers. The guide pointed out the helictite, the stringy mineral deposits that branched out and spiraled in a direction that, to Brooke, resembled long, root-like fingers, stretching in every direction, seeming to defy gravity. They gave her the creeps.

"There are literally hundreds of thousands of helictites throughout the caverns, some even reminiscent of animals," the guide informed them. "See there? That's a butterfly. And there's a reindeer." The crowd nodded in agreement. "Now, if you look jussssst over there, beyond that big stone, in the Landmark Chamber" - he used a laser pointer to illuminate something – "what do you see?"

"A dragon!" the blonde-haired boy exclaimed.

"Very good! And he's our mascot here at Black Chasm Caverns."

Brooke heard the tour guide blathering on about the damage throughout the cavern because of the miners and their carelessness in the uncharted subterranean areas. *Subterranean. Underground.* Brooke shivered. The tour continued, descending further down until everyone reached the second platform, a long, skinny dock where the twenty guests had to stand side by side.

Brooke's foot slipped a bit, and she remembered the dripping cavern juices lubricated the stairs and platforms. Even with her trusty Nike's, she knew one slip, and she'd be gone forever, snapping her neck in two on her way down.

The guide spoke: "I would like everyone to step up to the railing and grab hold." The tourists all stepped up to the rail and placed their hands on the cold metal.

Holding Brooke's hand, Bradley stepped forward, but he felt resistance. He looked back. She hadn't budged. He moved to her side. "Come on. I've got you. Promise. It'll be okay." Reluctantly, she allowed him to guide her to the railing, where she let go of his hand and grabbed the metal bar with a death grip. *That wasn't so bad,* she thought to herself.

"Now," the guide continued. "If you lean over and look waaaaay over the edge -"

The tourists craned their necks to look down.

"- you will fall to your deaths," the guide announced.

"What?" Brooke asked incredulously. She jerked her hands off the railing and backed up.

"Just a little cavern guide humor," the guide said, chuckling.

"Not funny," Brooke huffed. Bradley was laughing. She poked him in his side.

"Seriously," the guide continued, "it's 100% safe. Now, for real, grab the railing and look down."

Like lemmings, the tourists replaced their hands on the wet railing.

Brooke heard more 'oohs' and 'ahhs' from the tourists as they all leaned over.

"See? It's fine," the guide was saying. "The railing is made of chromium steel and can hold the weight of fifty elephants without bending. It resists warping and melting and is one hundred percent resistant to the conditions here in the cavern. It will hold every single one of you leaning onto it with full force." He smiled, proud of the construction. Then he cocked his head and raised his eyebrows. "Learned *that* the hard way," he said with a chuckle.

Everyone laughed. Except Brooke.

I'm going to faint.

"Kidding again. You're not going anywhere with this baby here," the guide said, hitting the railing with his hand.

Disgusted with his morbid sense of humor but not wanting to draw more attention to herself, Brooke stepped up to the railing. With a deep breath, she slowly leaned her head over the railing. She could see the sheer drop of the cavern, one hundred feet straight down to a pool of water. The water was calm, but her heart was in chaos.

"Back in the early days, the miners would take raft trips in the lake to transport minerals and supplies. We don't do that anymore because some of the helictites have blocked passageways. Shall we continue to our final platform?"

Almost every area in the cave could be seen from the third platform. The room was massive, filled with stalactites, stalagmites, and more helictites. The same chromium steel railing surrounded this platform, even though it was only half a foot off the ground. There were lights throughout the caverns, but some spots were cast in pitch blackness. They looked like dark, infinity holes. Brooke looked around and noticed these dark holes were peppered throughout the cavern. There must've been about fifty of them. Brooke imagined them leading into the deepest part of the earth, forking off in several directions, as numerous and twisted as the fingers of the helictites. She imagined getting lost in there forever and dying in the blackness. She repressed a shudder.

"Okay! So that's the end of our 'official' tour," the guide said, using air quotes around 'official'. "You have about 15 minutes of free time here to go to any platform and take photos or videos. But please stay with your party. We'll meet back at the gift shop at 1:30 p.m. Thank you, everybody!" People swarmed around the guide for questions and group photos.

"Hey," Bradley whispered to Brooke.

"What?"

He jerked his head towards the wall of the cavern. He had a devilish grin on his face.

She followed his eyes. She looked back at him like he was crazy. He wanted them to cross over the railing and explore the cavern!

"Are you insane?!" she whispered loudly.

"Shhhh," he hushed. "It'll be fine. Besides, the guide is preoccupied. He'll never notice we're gone."

"That's what I'm afraid of! No!" she said. "It could be dangerous."

"It'll be fine. Just for a minute. We'll be back at the gift shop before the rest of the group. Promise."

Brooke got an uneasy feeling in her stomach. Alarm bells were going off in her head. She felt the whole idea was perilous. She –

"*What are you doing?*" she cried. She noticed Bradley had already hopped over the railing and dropped to the cavern floor below.

"Come on. He did say to stay with your party." He grinned and held out his hand.

Oh, my god. "This is wrong," she said as she raised her leg over the railing. She jerked her head back to the guide. He had his back to them, pointing to a stalagtisomething. She brought the rest of her body over, and Bradley helped her down to the floor. He kissed her on the lips.

"Let's go," he said, and they silently moved, unseen, towards the cave walls, towards the dark infinity holes along the cavern's edge.

"I'm not going in there!" Brooke said, bending over and peering into one of the deep black holes. "It's too dark! I can't see an *inch* into that."

"Just a couple of feet, that's all," Bradley said. "We won't veer off the straight path, no turns. It'll be fine," he said as he stepped into the darkness. In an instant, the obsidian room enveloped him, and he had disappeared from Brooke's sight. She began to panic.

"Bradley!"

He popped out. "What?"

"I...I...nothing." She was already starting to feel a claustrophobic attack coming on. *Oh my god,* she thought. *As long as I hold on to Bradley's hand, I'll feel grounded and safe.* She rolled her eyes and took a deep breath. "Fine. Let's go. But don't you *dare* let go of my hand!"

Bradley smiled, and together, they walked into the inky chamber.

At once, she was blind. There was nothing to see. Like coal-black outer space, she imagined. Pure natural darkness. She attempted to turn and face the opening – or so she believed – but no light was visible from the large room where she had left the guide and the tour. She felt sick. Her heart was beating loudly, and it was the only sound she heard besides the crunching underneath their feet as they walked.

After about twenty steps, Brooke said, "Okay, that's far enough. We should…we should turn back."

"Just a bit further," Bradley said. "I think I see a light up ahead."

Brooke squinted, but it was no use. It was so dark she couldn't tell if her eyes were open or closed. "I don't see anything. Please, let's go back." Fear-induced tears stung her eyes as she gripped his hand tighter.

"I think my shoe is untied," he said, letting go of her hand. "Hold on." He released her hand, and they were separated.

Brooke stood alone. She neither heard nor saw anything, and she had never felt more solitary than she did at this moment. She heard a rustling ahead of her- a sort of light clicking. *What was that?* "Bradley?"

No answer.

She moved a couple of inches forward. At least, she *thought* she moved forward. Could've been backward in this darkness. She was turned around.

"Bradley?" She put her arms out to feel for him. She felt nothing but space. *"Bradley!"* she cried louder this time. "This isn't funny!"

The rustling and clicking became louder. She felt something brush her leg. No. It was moving *on* her leg. Her hand met with something hairy. She yelped. She shook her hand, and whatever it was fell off. But then she felt more. More movement. More hair. Legs. And lots of them. Clicking and hissing.

"Bradley!!!" she cried. *"Help me!"* Something moved in her hair. She screamed, thrashing her hands in her hair to rid herself of whatever was on her. Something moved across her face and down her neck. Something was inching down her skin.

Panic set in full force, and she was turning and spinning, trying to stop whatever it was from crawling on her. Suddenly, she felt someone grab her hand and jerk her down into the darkness. Within a couple of seconds, she was standing in the light, in the big room they had entered the hole from.

She stared at Bradley. His eyes were wide, moving all over her body. She had no idea what he was looking at.

"What is it?" Brooke asked breathlessly.

But she didn't need to wait for his answer. She looked at her left hand, and she saw it. And another. Movement all over her arm. She lifted both of her arms straight out and stared in horror, and she started to shake.

She was covered in gigantic wolf spiders.

She screamed.

Then, she lost consciousness.

"Are you okay?" It was Bradley's voice, only muffled. Brooke heard him but couldn't focus on his whereabouts. Her sight came into focus. Bradley's handsome face was looking down at her. She wasn't sure where she was, but then she remembered. She bolted upright. Brooke started hollering, and her hands flew across her body. She had to get them off!

"Brooke! It's all right. They're all gone. I got all of them off you. You're safe now." He was holding her and trying to calm her down. He pulled her into a tight hug. She was crying.

"It was so dark...and I couldn't find you...and I was scared....and then I heard a noise and...felt...oh my god," she said, burying her face in his chest.

"Shhh. I know. I'm sorry. But I got you to safety, and you're all good now. Right?"

She looked up at him. They were on a bench outside the main gift shop. Some people were standing close by, but turned away when she noticed them. An older lady stepped closer to Brooke.

"You're one lucky young lady. He rescued you, my dear," she said. Brooke recognized her from their tour group. "He was so brave to go back in and get you."

"Come on, Ruth," her husband said. Let's leave them be." The couple walked away.

Brooke looked up at Bradley. "Can we just go home now? I'm over this vacation."

"Of course, hon. Whatever you want," he replied, bending down and kissing her forehead. His eyes showed such kindness. Bradley had saved her from the chasm's darkness.

The woman was right, Brooke thought. *I'm one lucky girl to have Bradley in my life.*

CHAPTER 9

Brooke was relieved to step foot back into her home's familiar comfort. Not like the thick, unknown darkness she encountered in the caverns. She felt itchy at the memory. She went around the house and turned on every light and lamp, then she opened every drape to let every bit of sunlight inside.

"Should I light candles?" she asked.

"Are you trying to ward off something?" Bradley asked

She glared at him.

He raised his hands in acquiescence. "Here, let me help."

She finally sat down to rest after being satisfied with the brightness level in the house.

They ordered Chinese takeout for dinner and had a casual night in on the sofa. It was precisely what the doctor ordered. Bradley decided to stay the night to assuage any recurring fears she might develop in the night. But the way Brooke was now, he had a feeling she'd be sleeping with all the lights on.

"I think I'll just stay home tomorrow," she said, curling her legs under her. "What would you like to do?"

"Unfortunately, I need to head back to Sonoma to start a big new project for our client. Now, she wants us to re-landscape her entire backyard enclosure to make room for a hot tub. I really think it's a pool, it's so big, but she swears it's just a hot tub. It's a pretty large undertaking, so I'll be gone a few days."

"*She?*" Brooke eyed him warily, half-jokingly, digging into her Lo Mein.

He laughed. "Yes. She. But *she* is an 84-year-old great-grandmother of five. I don't think she's too interested in anything else but relaxing in her pool. Er, I mean hot tub."

"Don't be so sure," Brooke said, extending a leg and kicking him in his thigh with her foot. "Hey. Why don't I come with you? I'd stay out of the way, I promise. I'd love to see what you do for a living. What do you say?"

He grinned and gently grabbed her chin. "Nope. I know you. You'd be bored silly." He kissed her then got up to take their plates into the kitchen. She got up to follow him.

"Oh, come on. It'll be exciting." She came up behind him and wrapped her arms around his waist.

He laughed. "No way. I'm not going to subject you to the sun and all the dirt and sweat." He spun around. "Besides, there might be spiders."

She jerked back and slapped his arm. "Ugh! Shut up!"

He chuckled.

"Fine," she pouted. "I'll just stay here and feel bored without you." She paused. "I'm going to miss you," she said.

"Then I better leave you with something to remember me by." He smiled and kissed her deeply. He grabbed her breasts and gently pinched her hard nipples. She moaned, and he pinched harder. Her legs weakened, and he gripped her butt with his large hands, supporting her. He picked her up and carried her to the bed, where they made love on top of the thick comforter. Brooke felt she was in heaven and lying on a fluffy cloud. Only, she was pretty sure the thoughts she was having wouldn't have let her within fifty feet of the Pearly Gates. Together, they rode each other until exhaustion, and then they fell asleep, sweaty and smiling in each other's arms.

The following morning, Brooke awoke to Bongo curled up on Bradley's side of the bed. But no Bradley. *Guess he got an early start to Sonoma*, she thought. She reached over and rubbed Bongo between the ears. He squeaked a little noise and rolled over onto his back.

Brooke got up and went to the bathroom. She began the shower and used the bathroom as the water heated. She stepped into the shower, the hot water cascading down her body. She closed the glass door to the shower and let the steam envelop her, every nook and cranny feeling refreshed and cleansed. The shower wasn't huge, but it wasn't small enough to cause a claustrophobic attack, either. Not like the caverns. Despite the hot water, Brooke shivered at the memory.

She remembered the wolf spiders crawling over her body, their legs clicking as they squirmed across her skin, how they kept getting entangled in her hair. She added more shampoo than normal and lathered up, hoping to exorcise them from her brain.

Then she remembered the blackness and waking up to Bradley looking over her as she lay on the bench. And that older tourist. Ruth, was it? What was it she had said? *"You're one lucky young lady. He rescued you, my dear. He was so brave to go back in and get you."*

Brooke cocked her head. What did she say?

He was so brave to go back in and get you.

Her eyebrows scrunched. *Why would she say that? He went* back in *to get me. Was he* outside?

"That doesn't make any sense," Brooke said. "Why would he be *outside?*" She shook her head. "Why would he leave me?" A heavy weight developed in the pit of her stomach.

Brooke felt horrible for thinking anything remotely bad about Bradley. He had only shown love and affection towards her. And she loved him – more than she had ever loved another person. *Did I misunderstand what the lady had said?*

But she didn't have any answers to her questions about why he would leave her in the dark cavern alone. Even if he didn't know about her phobia, it wasn't something you do to another person. But he had left her. To fend for herself. What if he hadn't come back in for her? The hot water in the shower did nothing to alleviate her worries.

And she found, for the second time that morning, her skin began to crawl. And there wasn't a spider in sight.

Brooke Carson had no idea her world had just started to quake.
Or that in a couple weeks, she'd be dead.

CHAPTER 10

Her phone was ringing. Bradley was still out of town, so Brooke hoped it was him. She hadn't heard from him since he left last week, and she hated where her mind had taken her in his absence. Every time she tried to call him, it went straight to voicemail. Brooke kept telling herself that he was in Sonoma on a large estate, so maybe 1) he had no service, or 2) he couldn't take his phone with him on the job.

Or 3) he was dead somewhere in a ditch.

Brooke rolled her eyes at her own mother's voice in her head. Well, if anything, she hoped Bradley would at least be back next week to celebrate her birthday. She sighed. She grabbed her phone and saw it was Misty calling. Brooke's shoulders sagged for only a second in her disappointment but quickly perked up when she realized she hadn't spoken to Misty in a couple of weeks, what with the traveling and all.

"Misty, hi!" Brooke said cheerfully. "How are you, babe?"

"Don't 'babe' me, heifer!" Misty said. Brooke could hear the smile in her friend's voice. "You don't call, you don't write…"

"Oh, god, there's my mother again!"

"Your mother? What does that mean?" Misty asked.

Brooke laughed. "Nothing. You had to be there."

"Well, you'll have to fill me in later. How about lunch? Wayfare Tavern?"

"I'm on my way!"

The upscale eatery on Sacramento Street was popular with locals and tourists. Brooke always had a crush on Tyler Florence, and his restaurant was no exception. It was spectacular, and the food was perfection. It was crowded when Brooke arrived, but she saw Misty sitting at a table near the back, and she joined her friend.

"I'm sorry," Misty said. "I reserved this seat for my friend. I'm afraid *you're* a stranger. What's your name?"

"Shut the fuck up," Brooke laughed, sitting down. "It hasn't been that long. Only -"

"Three and a half weeks," Misty finished.

"What?" Brooke gasped honestly. "No way!"

"Way."

"Well, you'll have to wait just a little longer. I need to find the bathroom." Brooke was bouncing like a toddler. She set her purse down in her chair and scurried off.

When she returned, a waiter was close behind her. He dropped off two glasses of Beaulieu Vineyard Merlot. The friends clinked their glasses in a cheer.

"Are you ready to order?" he asked.

"I'll have the fried chicken," Misty said.

"And I'll have the Skuna Bay Salmon."

"Excellent," the waiter said before collecting the menus and scurrying off.

"So, have you spoken to Cathy or Dana about your new man?"

Brooke was caught off-guard, and too late, her face couldn't hide her shock.

"Um, no. I haven't," Brooke said slowly. "I haven't...we haven't...."

"Yeah, I figured," Misty said. "Tough time."

Tough time? Brooke thought. That part of her life was the most tragic time of her life. She hadn't spoken to Cathy or Dana since they were bridesmaids together and .... She couldn't even finish her thought.

"Why would you ask me if I've spoken to them?" Brooke asked, her hand resting on her chest. "Have *you?*"

"Well, no. But I've been meaning to. They've been on my mind a lot lately." Misty could see the direction of this conversation bothered Brooke. She knew that time in their lives was devastating to all involved, so she decided to park the conversation for now.

"Look," Misty said, "I know you're...involved...with someone, and your life has taken a very dramatic and interesting turn. And I couldn't be happier. I'm very happy for you, but -"

"But..."

"But you and Bradley have been seeing each other for a couple of months now, and we have yet to be introduced to him. Is he still not wanting to meet us until you guys are more settled into your relationship?"

In a way, Brooke knew where Misty was coming from. She, too, found it a little odd that Bradley didn't want to meet her friends until a particular time in their relationship. What 'time' that was, Brooke did not know. And she dared not ask him. Ever since that time at Bodega Bay, when she asked about his phone call and he snapped at her, she realized he had a short temper, and when he didn't want to divulge any information, there was little Brooke to do to coerce it out of him. She kept her distance from his personal ideals.

"Look," Brooke said, "Bradley is.... different. He has such a big heart, and we are kind of in the newlywed phase of our relationship, and, yes, I agree it's...odd that you guys haven't met yet, but I think he's a private person. He doesn't speak much of his family, or at all, for that matter, so I'm just letting this play out at his speed. Does that make sense?"

Misty cocked her head as if playing with that thought.

"But I promise, you're gonna love him when you finally do meet! You and Tyler will fall in love with him, just like I have."

"You're in *love?*!" Misty gasped. "Isn't that a bit...fast?"

"Maybe, but not really. I mean, I feel it in my bones. He's the one."

"The *one*? Have y'all talked about marriage already?" Misty's eyes were huge and full of uncertainty.

Brooke and Bradley had never mentioned marriage, but Brooke was sure that she wanted to spend the rest of her life with him. He was everything she dreamed of and more.

"No, not yet," Brooke admitted. "But I don't think that conversation is too far off in our future." She smiled, sipping her merlot. She hoped that would satiate Misty for the time being. But there was something else Brooke was reading in Misty's body language. Misty was antsy, and Brooke noticed. She kept fiddling with her silverware and napkin, and her wineglass already needed a refill.

"Okay," Brooke said. "What's going on?"

"What…what do you mean?"

"The silverware. The napkin. Your wine? You seem…nervous. What gives?"

Misty swallowed.

"Out with it."

"Well, I have something to tell you and -"

"Here you go," the waiter said, placing their food in front of them. "Can I get you anything else?"

"More wine, please," Misty said.

"Be right back."

"This looks delicious," Misty said, lifting a piece of the thickly crusted fried chicken off the plate.

"Cut the shit," Brooke said. "What do you want to tell me?"

Misty placed the chicken back down as the waiter magically appeared and filled their glasses with the delicious burgundy liquid.

Misty took a big gulp of her wine. "You know I love you, right?"

"Yes," Brooke said hesitantly.

"And you know my Uncle Mike is a detective, right?"

"Yesssssss," Brooke replied, unsure where this was going.

Misty felt a bead of sweat roll down her back. She twisted her lips and bit the inside of her mouth. There was no turning back now. Her friend would either hate her or hate her more. Misty didn't like those odds. But hopefully, Brooke would understand why she did what she did. Misty did this because she loved Brooke and only wanted the best for her, so that's why she went to Uncle Mike and….

"Misty!"

The blurt came out in full force. "I went to Uncle Mike and had him look into Bradley just to make sure he was on the up and up and -"

"You *what*?" Brooke screeched, not believing she had heard correctly.

"I...I...asked Uncle Mike to look -"

"I heard you! How *could* you?! Misty! This is my private life! Why the hell would you get your detective uncle involved? What were you thinking?" Her voice had risen above the din of the restaurant.

"I...guess I wasn't. I mean, I was thinking about *you*. Bradley just seemed a little possessive and didn't want to meet me and Tyler, and I got a little protective and ...where are you going?"

Brooke had gotten up from her seat. Her hands hit the table, and silverware flew to the floor and clanked loudly. She grabbed her purse and stood up abruptly, knocking her wine glass over in the chaos. Garnet liquid seeped into the white tablecloth.

"I'm leaving!" she snapped.

"Don't go. Brooke, please! Let's talk about this!"

Restaurant patrons started to stare. Brooke leaned in. "How dare you, Misty. How *dare* you!"

Misty looked saddened and felt a hint of regret.

"You know?" Brooke continued, "I was planning a little birthday gathering next week and was going to surprise you and Bradley by having you two meet at the party. But after this little stunt you pulled, you can forget it."

"Brooke! Seriously. I didn't mean any harm by it, but you may want to at least hear me out about what Uncle Mike found."

Brooke stood at her full height. Should she ask what the discovery was? Would it make a difference? She decided it wouldn't.

"Go fuck yourself," Brooke said as she turned and began walking away from the table.

"There was nothing there!" Misty yelled to Brooke's back.

Brooke stopped. She lifted her head, maybe a little triumphant. A satisfied grin stretched across her mouth. She turned to face Misty.

"Oh, really?" Brooke asked. "Well, I could've told you that. Are you convinced now? There's nothing salacious or malevolent about Bradley, so you can just -"

"No. That's not what I meant," Misty said. She stood up and walked towards Brooke. They were face-to-face. "Uncle Mike found nothing on Bradley Harris."

"Correct. As I said, there's nothing there to -"

Misty looked into Brooke's eyes. "He didn't find anything - because there's nothing there. There's nothing to find on Bradley Harris."

"For god's sake, Misty. Spit it out! What do you mean?"

"I mean, your boyfriend, Bradley Harris, doesn't exist."

Misty had information. And she wasn't sure of the best way to proceed.

I did it with the best intentions, Misty told herself. *Brooke is my best friend, and I was only looking out for her best interest.* Misty rolled her eyes. "Who am I kidding?" she said out loud. "Even *I* don't believe that."

Despite how brutal her Uncle Mike's job could be, and Misty knew firsthand just how brutal, the investigation side of his job had always piqued her interest. After telling Brooke what she knew and egged on by what she had learned from her Uncle Mike, Misty took it one step further: she confronted Bradley.

Misty had initially wanted to just talk with Bradley and flesh him out to see if he could answer any of her questions. She figured after cornering Bradley with what she knew, he would have to come clean.

Or not.

Misty thought back to the day she and Brooke had met for lunch at Wayfare Tavern. Brooke had come in, set her handbag down at the table, and immediately used the restroom. Misty took advantage of Brooke being gone, reached into Brooke's bag, and took out her phone. She knew the password was Brooke's birthday, and once in, Misty scrolled through and found Bradley's phone number. She quickly jotted it down and replaced the phone back in the purse before Brooke returned, none the wiser.

When Misty got home, she paced back and forth in her living room, deciding if she really wanted to take this next leap. She listed every pro and con she could think of. But the pros won, and she punched in his number. Her heart pounded with each trill of the ringing phone.

Please don't answer. Please don't answer. Please don't –

"Hello?" his deep voice answered. "Who is this?"

Misty swallowed. This was it. No turning back. "Bradley? Hi, this is Misty Evans. Brooke's friend. How are you?" She tried to sound chipper.

There was a pause.

"Misty, hi. I'm okay."

She waited for something more, but all she got was silence.

"Yeah, well…. we haven't had, uh, a chance to get to know one another….and, umm, I was wondering if maybe, if you're willing, we could meet for a coffee or something and talk." *God, this is awkward.*

She was met with more silence. Longer this time. *He's not giving me anything,* she thought. *Why? Is he suspicious of me calling? I mean, I would be, but he doesn't know me and has no reason to suspect –*

"Sure," he said, controlled. "Compton's? On Fillmore?"

It was a coffeehouse not far from her. "I know it. In an hour?"

"Sure," he repeated before hanging up.

She looked at the now-silent phone in her hand and opened her eyes wide. *Definitely suspicious.*

Upon entering Compton's, she saw Bradley sitting in the far corner. He was wearing a tight black polo shirt, jeans, and zero expression on his face.

You can do this, Misty, she told herself. She placed a broad smile on her face and walked up to his table. "Hi, Bradley!" she chirped, extending her hand. "I'm Misty. Nice to finally meet you." He stood and took her hand in his. They both sat.

"So, what's this all about?" Bradley asked. "What do you want to know?" His demeanor had grown stern.

"Straight to it, I see," Misty said, relieved she didn't have to pussy-foot around playing nice anymore.

He crossed his arms over his big chest and waited for her inquisition.

Misty spoke. "Well, Brooke is my best friend and I'm really just looking out for what's best for her, and I know everything going on in her life. Everything except this." She waved her finger between her and him. "You and I haven't even had a chance to meet, and Brooke said that's because you want to get to know her better before letting anyone else into your lives."

"Yeah, so?" he said, cocking his head to the left.

"I call bullshit," Misty said coolly.

"That so?" he responded, shifting his head to the other side.

"Yes."

"And why's that?" he asked, furrowing his brow.

"Well, I saw you at the grocery store when you told Brooke you were out of town for work. So, there's one lie. Second, you're avoiding meeting any of her friends. Why, I have no idea. But I think it's because there's more to Bradley Harris than meets the eye. I think you're hiding something."

He threw back his head and laughed. "You don't even *know* me! How could you possibly think I was hiding something?"

He uncrossed his arms and squirmed in his seat almost unnoticeably, but Misty picked up on it immediately. She smiled. Any doubt she had about how to handle this situation went out the window, and she found her nerve.

"You're a cool customer, I'll give you that," Misty said. "But there's something that I know about you, even though we haven't really met and become close. And I think Brooke would find it very interesting."

His expression changed. His jaw tightened, and his smile became forced. "And...what's that?" he asked, a little less confidently.

This was Misty's ace, and she was ready to play it. She leaned across the table and looked him in the eyes. "You don't exist, Bradley Harris. Or whoever you are."

He chuckled nervously. "What...what are you talking about?"

She sat back in her seat. "Oh, I have a connection. In the police department." She saw his eyes grow darker. "And, upon my request, he did a little background checking on you and found out that you -" she pointed to him for emphasis, "are not who you say you are."

Misty could see Bradley's body tense and sweat forming at his hairline. *Gotcha.* She wondered what was racing through his mind now: was he worried she would expose him to Brooke or, worse, the police? Although she didn't think this was something the police had anything to do with. Maybe she was wrong about him. A fleeting tick of doubt tickled the back of her mind. *No. Uncle Mike is a good guy. He doesn't lie. If he said Bradley Harris doesn't exist, then Bradley Harris doesn't exist. Simple as that.*

On the other hand, Uncle Mike's report was all the information she had. Maybe there was more to the story, and she had overstepped. She was now worried that Bradley would call her on it and demand more evidence from her, evidence she didn't have. Her heart pounded.

His biceps tightened, and his arm tattoo looked strained. "What do you want?" Bradley asked.

So, it WAS true! His surrender was confirmation. But he asked a valid question: what did she want, exactly? Misty thought about it. And she realized what she wanted would break Brooke's heart. Brooke had never been a fall-in-love-with-one-man show, but suddenly, with this…*stranger* across from Misty now, Brooke had found the one thing she couldn't live without: love. *Finding this out about the man she loved would kill her. Can I really do this to her? She'd never forgive me. But I couldn't live with myself if something ever happened to her, and I hadn't spoken up.* She considered all options. Then, her mind was made up. She took a deep breath.

"I want you to end it with Brooke. Yesterday."

When Misty got home from her meeting with Bradley, she felt better, as if someone had lifted the proverbial weight from her shoulders. She felt like celebrating. She also thought it might be a good time to come clean to Brooke about her coffeehouse meeting with Bradley. But she also knew Brooke needed time to sort out what Misty had told her. Misty decided to wait until Brooke had a chance to cool off and regroup her thoughts.

After all, what difference will a day make?

CHAPTER 11

Brooke was livid.

And very confused.

Ever since Misty told her she had her uncle investigate Bradley, Brooke saw red. "The *audacity*!" Brooke seethed. She paced her home, raising fists in the air as she had a one-on-one conversation with herself about yesterday's conversation. "Ugh!!" But her anger had merged with the revelation of Bradley Harris's non-existence.

"What does that even *mean*?" she stopped in the middle of her den and asked the air. She remembered Misty's comment: *Bradley Harris doesn't exist.* Of course, he exists! Physically, mentally, literally – Bradley Harris most certainly existed.

Then again, Mike Evans was a really good man and an excellent detective. After the difficult task of busting Misty's parents for drugs, he and his wife took in four-year-old Misty and raised her as their own. So why would he fabricate information about Bradley? Maybe there's some truth to what he found. *What do they say? Where there's smoke, there's fire. I should call Mike myself and get this straightened out.*

"This is crazy!" Brooke scoffed. Disbelievingly, she exhaled multiple breaths. She decided to call Bradley and let him in on this hilarious joke. Brooke tried his number, but her call went directly to voicemail. Again.

Maybe he's out on the estate working. Or maybe he's back in town already and just tired from work and asleep. Brooke hadn't been able to reach him for a couple of weeks, so she wasn't even sure of his schedule. She remembered all the other voicemails she had left. *Or maybe he* doesn't *exist.* Her eyes widened. She shook the stupid thought out of her brain. But if he *was* back in town, why hadn't he called to let her know? His disappearing acts were becoming the norm, and Brooke wasn't sure how to process that information.

"*You're* crazy," she said to herself. She heard a beep through her phone and left a sweet, out-of-breath message. She would try calling again later.

Two hours went by, and she tried calling him again. Another voicemail. She looked at her phone. It was 10:47 am. She wasn't positive he was still out of town, but she was really hoping he had already returned and was sound asleep at his apartment. In the kitchen, she discovered the piece of paper with his address and phone number from their first night together. She made a decision: she would drive to his apartment and welcome him home.

Brooke loved the city: the hilly roads, the architecture, and the many lush gardens and parks peppered throughout the concrete jungle. San Francisco was an allegory in opposites: green landscapes offered tranquil escapes from the maddening harshness of the city; tourists came in droves, but a local could pick out a born-and-raised inhabitant a mile away; futuristic modernness coexisted beautifully with the nearly 90-year-old trolley system. Brooke was an original from the city, and she knew every turn and twist on the map. She knew precisely where Bradley lived without using a GPS. This was her town, and it was her first 'boyfriend'. *Its* existence was guaranteed. She smiled as she shifted gears in her BMW.

Once Brooke was on I-280, she kept straight onto Shoreline Parkway until she could exit onto Sloat Boulevard. She passed Lake Merced on her left, then took the fork to John Muir Drive. Bradley's address, Lakewood Apartments, loomed large on the left. She drove into the parking lot and circled around to building A. She parked, got out, and walked up the sidewalk, passing the in-wall mailboxes. Pulling out the sheet of paper, she reviewed the information: Lakewood Apartments, 555 John Muir Drive, Apartment A-205. She went up the stairs, found apartment 205, and knocked. Nothing. She knocked again. Still nothing.

She heard the door behind her open. An older man stepped out onto the landing and wanted to know what all the ruckus was about.

"Oh, I'm sorry," Brooke said. "I was just looking for Bradley. Do you know if he's home?"

"Who?" the old man barked, scrunching his face.

"Bradley. Bradley Harris." Brooke described him. "He's also got a big black dog, Kong. Surely you've heard him bark or something."

But the neighbor said no one by that description lived in this building, and he'd lived here his whole life. "In fact," he groused, "there's no one living there anyway." He pointed to apartment 205. "Hasn't been anyone for five months now. And pets ain't allowed!" The man started to head back into his apartment. Then he turned. "He don't exist!"

Bradley Harris doesn't exist.

"Wait. Please."

"What now?" he asked.

"This is building A, right?" She rechecked her note. *A-205.*

"Yesterday, today, and tomorrow," he smiled, showing gums.

She looked back at the door and then at the note. *Maybe he wrote it down wrong. But why would he write his own address down wrong? None of this was making any sense.*

"So, you're sure no one with the description I gave you lives in this building?" Brooke asked hesitantly. This man acted like he was being bothered, so maybe she should ask a different neighbor.

"I told you, no one lives there. No one in 203 or 204, either. Now go away!" he entered his apartment and slammed the door behind him.

Brooke stood there, shaking. She was embarrassed but also concerned. Why would Bradley give her a bogus address? Brooke was at a loss for words. She hadn't heard from or seen Bradley in over three weeks, and Misty's uncle had turned up nothing on him. Now, this man in this apartment building said no one with Bradley's description lives here.

Bradley Harris doesn't exist.

Oh my god, she thought. Tears burned the back of her eyes. Misty said

Bradley didn't exist, and now his supposed neighbor has never even seen him. What was going on?

She raced down the stairs to her car, her tears stinging in the wind as she ran. She pressed the unlock button on her key fob and jumped in her car. Her hands were shaking like leaves as she placed them on the steering wheel. She sat there for a good ten minutes before finding herself calm enough to drive home.

As she made her way through the hilly streets and buildings of the allegoric city she knew like the back of her hand, she couldn't help but think of the irony that she was in a relationship with a man she knew absolutely nothing about.

Bradley Harris was a total stranger.

CHAPTER 12

Brooke was looking at herself in the bathroom mirror, but she had no idea who was looking back at her. The reflection showed a woman with crow's feet, disheveled hair, puffy, bloodshot eyes, and sallow skin. Gone were the sparkling blue eyes, silky blonde hair, and smooth skin reminiscent of a teenager.

Like Bradley, she was a total stranger to herself.

It had been two days since Brooke had visited his apartment.

Two days since Misty's revelation was confirmed.

Two days since Brooke hadn't stopped crying because her world had fallen apart.

And she still had heard nothing from him. Not a peep. So, Brooke's confusion turned to worry. Was he hurt, or worse, dead somewhere? Was he trying to reach out to her for help but couldn't get to his phone?

Or maybe he was a phony and did this to all the women in his life? Had he been stringing Brooke along this whole time? She stiffened. She thought, in that case, he had better be hurt. *Or dead.*

"Snap out of it, Brooke," she scolded herself. She threw some water on her face from the sink, dried her face off with a thick towel, and went into the kitchen. She felt Bongo rubbing on her legs. He was meowing loudly. She looked, and his food and water bowls were bone dry. She couldn't remember the last time she gave him food and water.

"Oh god, boy. I'm so sorry." She bent down to pet his head, but Bongo looked up and hissed at her, swatting his paw on her hand. "Ouch! I guess I deserved that," she said, filling his bowls. Bongo gobbled up his food and lapped his water until he was content. He walked past her into the den, ignoring her.

Brooke felt sad for failing her boy. She could feel the tears welling up again.

"I'm sorry, fella. I've just been a little out of it and -" she heard her phone ringing. It was an alien ring since she hadn't received a call for weeks. She wasn't even a hundred percent sure her phone *was* ringing. Was it Bradley calling? Did he finally get free and remember he had a girlfriend in his life? He was okay! She was ecstatic. But then the phone stopped ringing.

Brooke panicked. *I waited too long, and* – it began again. She lunged for her phone and pressed the button.

"Bradley?! Is that you? Bradley?!"

"Uh, no. It's me."

Misty.

"Oh, hi. Sorry. I thought you were -"

"Yeah. I heard." There was a brief silence. "So, are you still mad at me? What's going on? I haven't heard from you in a couple of days."

Was she still mad at Misty? If what Misty had found out about Bradley was true, then how could Brooke be angry with her? Or was Brooke just pissed off at the situation? That she had let her guard down and had fallen for a guy who may or may not be real? Who may or may not exist to her, or anybody? Misty wasn't at fault here. If anyone were to blame, it was Brooke for allowing this to happen.

"No, I'm not mad at you," Brooke said quietly. "And I'm fine. Just busy with…things."

"That's good to hear," Misty said optimistically. There was a pause. "Look, I wanted to invite you over for an adult sleepover. I was thinking about asking Dana and Cathy to come over. I've already ordered the pizza, and I have some cheap ass wine here somewhere. Maybe some Tickle Pink."

Brooke laughed. "Oh, you got the good stuff, I see!"

Misty giggled. "Only the best for my friends. So, what do you say? Come over in an hour?"

It was the last thing Brooke wanted to do. And since when did Misty talk to Dana and Cathy? None of the girls had spoken for over a year. *Not since the accident on Alicia's wedding day when….* she let the thought trail off.

Plus, Brooke hadn't heard from Bradley yet, she looked a wreck, and she was sick with worry that her cat hated her. And if Misty *had* been speaking honestly about being in contact with Dana and Cathy, there was *that* situation Brooke wasn't ready to face.

No. She couldn't face them yet. Their past was too intense, and Brooke was not in the right mindset to deal with her past in the present. It was best that Misty didn't know the girls hadn't spoken to each other since what happened to Alicia…

"Hello?" Misty asked into the silence.

"Oh, sorry. No, thanks. I'm just gonna stay in tonight. I'm a little under the weather and don't want to get anyone else sick. Raincheck?"

"Oh, okay. Sure." Misty sounded disappointed. "But I'm pretty sure the boys are gonna crash and do a panty raid."

That made Brooke chuckle. "Which would be all well and good if you wore panties in the first place."

"That's fair," Misty agreed, shrugging. She paused. "Are we okay?"

Brooke let the silence hang for a minute. She had a lot on her mind, but Misty's intentions were sincere, and she would not let that ruin their friendship. "Yes," Brooke said assuredly. "We're fine."

"Whew. I'm glad," Misty replied. She didn't want to say more and push her luck. "Okay, well, we'll talk tomorrow. Have a good night and feel better."

"Thanks. Talk soon." Brooke hung up. She was smiling at the thought of Misty and a panty raid. She shook her head, happy she had her friend back. Her phone beeped. She looked down, and it was a text message. Her hand flew to her mouth.

It was from Bradley.

Meet me at The Lodge.

Five little words. But Brooke knew what the text meant. The Lodge, in Bodega Bay. Where they first made love. After all this time of no communication, Bradley brought up the one place she knew meant a lot to them both. He was letting her know he was ready to move forward with their relationship. It was his way of saying he was sorry he hadn't been in touch for a long time, and he was asking for forgiveness.

Obviously, she was reading a lot into these five little words. *I mean, it was just yesterday he didn't even exist.* She smiled and rolled her eyes at the preposterousness of the idea. Clearly, he existed! The old man at his apartments was delusional and senile, obviously, and probably had no idea who lived where. "Dumbass!" she said to no one.

Is it possible Bradley wrote down the wrong address? Brooke pulled the sheet of paper out of her purse: *A-205.* But now that she looked at his scribbled address closer, the '2' *could* be a '7'. She put the paper back in her bag and headed into the bedroom.

Bodega Bay was only 90 minutes from where she lived, but she did not know how long she'd be gone this time or even what to pack. She jumped up and hurried to the closet, began pulling out clothes that would have to convert from the warm days to the chilly nights of northern California, and tossed them onto the bed. She bent down to grab some comfortable shoes and noticed a black bag on the floor of the closet. It was Bradley's overnight bag.

"Huh. He must've left this when we returned from our trip," she said. She carried it to the bed and decided to bring it with her to Bodega Bay. *He might need this.*

She went into the kitchen and filled four bowls with cat food and water for Bongo, who just stared at her and hissed again. She reached out to scratch his head, and he gave in to the familiarity and nudged the side of her hand. Brooke picked him up, scrunched his furry face in her hands, and kissed him on top of his head. "See you later, boy!"

She headed toward the door but turned back to look back into her house. Bongo had jumped onto the sofa and was circling to find his sweet spot before settling down into a cinnamon roll-like shape. A smile filled her face. She'd never felt everything was as perfect as it was at this very moment. She thought about calling Misty to let her know not to worry. Everything was going to be okay.

She threw her and Bradley's bags into the back seat, jumped in her car, and sped off.

Misty paced her apartment. She was worried Brooke would never *truly* forgive her for what she had done, even though, according to Brooke, they were fine. Misty knew getting Uncle Mike involved was probably going too far, but she only did it out of concern for her best friend. Her uncle was one of the good guys: a decorated detective with a stellar record and a heart of gold. He and his wife, Karen, took Misty in when things in her life went horribly wrong. The family issues she had to deal with were the absolute worst times in her life, and her uncle and aunt stepped up and became her 'parents', the ones who truly raised her into the young lady she was today and – her thoughts were interrupted by a knock on the door.

Pizza, Misty thought.

"C'mon in, door's open," she said as she walked to the table where her purse sat. She heard the door open and, off in the distance, in the back of her mind, she heard the door close, but unfortunately, she thought nothing of it. Misty dug out her wallet and started to pull out some money.

"I hope you have change for a fif -" she started to say but stopped in an instant when she felt two large hands surround her throat and cut off her air supply. She tried to gasp, but as she did, the hands closed tighter, the fingers squeezed tighter on her windpipe. She dropped her wallet and felt herself being lifted off the ground. Her feet dangled only inches from the safety of the hardwood floors, kicking to no avail. She heard something rupture. As the hands crushed more tautly, she felt her windpipe being jammed deeper into the back of her throat. The constriction had stopped all airflow, and she heard something snap inside her neck, her larynx now touching the back of her throat. Her kicking stopped, and the last thing Misty felt was her neck twisting unnaturally before being tossed aside, her body landing against the wall with a loud thud and slumping lifelessly to the floor.

CHAPTER 13

Brooke hit the 101 north, crossed the Golden Gate Bridge, and, within ten minutes, was breezing through Sausalito. The marina town was one of her favorite places on Earth. She loved the on-water experiences and hiking trails from the Marin Headlands to Muir Woods. As she drove, she looked to her right. The views of Richardson Bay from this small town were stunning. It had the perfect mix of artists, boutiques, and dining. Perfect for accommodating a wedding.

Just a couple of months ago, she was as far away from a commitment as anyone, having Oscar, Hank, and so many other men in her life. Brooke never saw herself as the settling-down type, but then Bradley came along, and everything changed.

She knew it was sudden. *Too sudden? I've kissed enough frogs in my life to know when a true Prince comes along.* Maybe marriage wasn't around the corner, but one thing Brooke knew for sure – she'd never been happier.

But then, there were holes in the relationship Brooke needed to be filled in. Like, when Mike Evans found nothing on Bradley Harris and said he didn't exist, was that because there was nothing *bad* to find or nothing to find at all? And there was the stamp thing. Her father once said, "a true philatelist knows everything about stamps. It was their 'stamp' of authenticity". Was Bradley authentic? And how did the neighbor not know who Bradley was? Was it something simple like Bradley gave her the wrong address, or Bradley, with his job out of town a lot, just never crossed paths with the neighbor? And when Bradley goes out of town all the time for weeks at a time, why can't she ever reach him? Surely, there's cell phone service in Sonoma!

Brooke had a lot of questions, and as she drove through Sausalito, she became more determined to get answers as soon as she saw him at The Lodge.

Once she got out of traffic, she stopped in San Rafael for a gas refill and grabbed a large soda. She put the cup in her holder, settled in, and continued her drive. She figured she had another hour to go, and that would put her in Bodega Bay around 9:15 p.m., just in time for a late dinner with Bradley. Maybe they could go back to Drakes for the whole roasted rainbow trout. It was some of the best fish either of them had ever had. Bodega Bay was a special place for Brooke and Bradley.

She smiled to herself. She had never once thought she'd ever have a "special place" with someone. But besides their time there, the Bay was also where they filmed "The Fog", one of their favorite horror movies. Brooke marveled at how much they had in common – even down to their favorite genre of films. She shut her eyes briefly and lifted her shoulders in a satisfied chuff.

Suddenly, a deer jumped out in front of Brooke's car. "Oh, shit!" she yelped. Her hands gripped the steering wheel as she swerved to miss the deer. Brooke slammed on her brakes, and she skidded to a long, gravelly stop on the side of the road. Her seatbelt jammed into her chest, and dust flew up and around her windows. "Oh, my…god!" she hollered. She clutched her chest with both hands and tried to calm her breathing. She was in a quick panic. Her head was bent down, looking at her hands. She lifted her head and looked out her driver's window. The deer just stood there, staring at her silently before walking casually into the dense brush.

"Fucker!" she yelled at the deer, who apparently couldn't care less he nearly gave her a heart attack. "Holy crap!" She ran her hands through her hair. She could feel the sweat on her forehead. Brooke closed her eyes and took several deep breaths until her heart slowed to a somewhat normal rhythm.

When she opened her eyes, she looked around the inside of the car. Her soda had exploded all over the dashboard, and her purse and its contents were in shambles on the floor of the passenger side. She twisted and peered into the backseat. Her and Bradley's bags were now upside down on the floor.

Brooke groaned. She clicked on her hazard lights and got out of her car. She didn't see any traffic, so she got out and walked to the passenger side of the vehicle, which was a few inches away from a grassy hill. She opened the door and put her bag back on the seat. Bradley's bag was on the other side, so she crawled onto the backseat and pulled his bag up. As she did, the contents dropped out onto the floorboard. She was mad at herself for not noticing she should've zipped it shut first.

"Shit!" she exclaimed. "Damn deer!" she said, looking back out the window, hoping to pass more blame its way but seeing nothing. She grunted as she gathered Bradley's belongings, stopping to bring one of his tee shirts up to her nose and taking in a deep breath of his scent. She smiled. "Nice," she whispered.

She grabbed more shirts, jeans, underwear, toiletries, and – *what's this?* It was a small bottle she hadn't seen before. It was a small brown spray bottle. She rolled it over in her hands and read the label: Happy Kitty Catnip Spray.

Brooke scrunched her face. "What does he need this for?" Her mind automatically shifted to Bongo and how much Bongo loved Bradley. "Hmmmm." A loud car horn jarred Brooke from her thoughts as a car zoomed by too close. Brooke jumped. "Gahh!" She made a decision to get the hell out of there quickly.

She looked at her watch: 9:05 p.m. She had wasted over half an hour on the side of the road. Absentmindedly, she put the catnip bottle in her pocket before getting behind the wheel and continuing her drive.

CHAPTER 14

By the time Brooke reached The Lodge, it was well after 10:00 p.m. The ride took longer than expected because once she turned left onto Hwy 1 and her approach reached the bay, a thick fog had rolled in and settled onto the bay and all surrounding areas, turning visibility to nil. The Lodge's grounds swept right up to the cliffs, and the parking lot had a wooden railing that prevented cars from plummeting over to the rocks below. Her heart was pounding as she pulled slowly into the parking lot. She could not make out the parking space lines and had no clue where she was in the lot, so she switched on her high beams. Brooke gripped the steering wheel until her knuckles were white, and she leaned up until her nose was inches from the windshield. As she breathed, the glass fogged up on the inside, and she felt utterly lost.

"Omigod, omigod, omigod!" she repeated, praying she wouldn't smash into another car or, worse, the wooden railings at the lot's edge. Brooke inched the car forward, turning the wheel only centimeters from side to side. Her bright headlights made things more blinding and were unhelpful. She dimmed her lights and suddenly saw what looked like white lines. Brooke carefully parked her car and turned off the engine. She had no idea how far or close she was to the cliff's edge. With a sense of relief, she stepped out of her car. She looked upward but couldn't see the sky, only fog. She thought of the movie that was filmed here and how eerie it was that this night resembled the setting in that film. It was deafening silent, and a thick gray mist surrounded her. She could actually feel it on her skin. Goosebumps quickly rose all over her.

Brooke grabbed both bags from the backseat and began walking through the lot, unsure of her direction. She pulled out her phone and texted Bradley.

I'm here. Where are you?

She saw the three dots signaling him typing a response.

Our room. 411.

Brooke smiled. He got the same room they had before. This was surely a sign.

She saw three more dots blinking.

Come in through the back patio.

Brooke remembered the back patio well. It was the exact spot where they first made love. It was secluded and serene, and you could hear the waves from the nearby bay. Brooke looked up and saw a small sign in the fog: *Main Lobby* with an arrow pointing straight ahead. She sighed a breath of relief and headed in that direction.

After a few minutes, she found the main building, then turned left to walk around to the backside of the resort, eventually coming to the hedges of coffeeberry and the granite pavers that led to room 411. She had made it. Fog be damned!

Brooke took the pavers to the back patio of their room and saw the open French doors leading to their room emerging from the grey-white mist. She saw a pale light on the inside and entered the room. She realized the pale light was coming from a couple of candles Bradley had set aglow. The setting was romantic and perfect for a proposal. She couldn't help but grin.

Brooke set the bags down. "Hello?" she called out but got no answer. She walked deeper into the room and called out again. "Hello? Bradley?" Still nothing. *Maybe he's getting ice,* she guessed.

She stood looking at the bed, a vase of poppies on the bedside table. Red and yellow variegated. Her favorite. Her smile grew. She pulled out her phone to text him again.

> I'm in the room. Where are you?

Nothing. No dots.

She dropped her shoulders. "Hmmpf," she grunted.

"I'm here," she heard a deep voice behind her as arms wrapped tight around her. She let out a short scream.

She spun around and was face to face with Bradley, hair wet and slicked back, body glistening with beads of water. Fresh from the shower, he was naked except for a textured towel wrapped around his waist. Brooke ran her fingers down his abdomen and looked up into his eyes. "Hi," she sighed.

"Hi," he murmured, his breath hot and thick on her neck.

Her fingers released the towel, and his hands were over her, removing her clothes until they were both naked. They fell into bed and made love, both lost in the motion, surrounded by the softness of the flickering candles and the hardness of the crashing waves.

It was a little after midnight before they got out of bed. Bradley poured Brooke some wine. They redressed.

"Come," he said, holding out his hand. "I want to take you somewhere special."

"Oh, really? Where?" She grabbed his hand, and he pulled her close to him.

"Remember that estate I've been working on? I want to show you the finished product."

Her eyes opened wide. "Now? It's so late!"

"Well, yes. The owners come back tomorrow, and, well, I'd like to christen the hot tub before they do." He grinned mischievously and rapidly raised and lowered his eyebrows.

Brooke sipped her wine. She was skeptical. It was after midnight, and
–

"Besides," he said, "the estate is gorgeous, and the moon is just perfect tonight. It'll look amazing." He wrapped his arms around her. "As will you strutting around naked on a forty-million-dollar estate."

"Forty million dollars?" she gasped. "Oh, my god!"

"I said what I said," he replied.

Well, the hot tub did sound nice. She finished her wine, and he poured her some more.

"But isn't that trespassing?"

"Not if I'm still *working and finishing up details*," he said, using air quotes.

She couldn't argue with that. *Couldn't argue with what?* She couldn't remember what they were talking about. Her mind was fuzzy. She remembered she had to ask him some questions. But about what, she couldn't recall.

"This will be a night to remember," he said.

She hugged him. "I love you," she said. Her eyes closed as her head rested on his chest.

"Careful there. I don't want you passing out on me yet."

Yet, she thought. That's an odd thing to say – but everything went blank inside her mind as she lost her train of thought.

He was holding her hand and leading her outside. *Why's it so white out here? It's like walking through clouds. Am I up in the clouds? Will I fall out of the sky?* She tried to widen her eyes but wasn't sure if they did as she wanted. Her feet were thick and heavy, but Bradley was guiding her through the clouds, and she smiled. She loved him, and he would take care of her. He wouldn't let her fall out of the sky. She laid her head against his shoulder. She felt safe.

They reached his truck, and he helped lift her into the passenger side, shutting the door once he got her legs inside. Soon, he was behind the wheel, and they started driving.

"Where are we going?" she asked. "Are we in the clouds? They're so fluffy. Oh, I hope we don't hit any birds. That'd be awful." Her eyes looked worried as she squinted her eyes to look out her window for birds that might be flying too close to the truck. She felt tired and sleepy.

And as the thick fog swirled around the moving vehicle, she laid her head on the cold glass window and drifted off.

CHAPTER 15

The car jolted to a stop, and Brooke's head jerked forward. Her eyes fluttered open, and she grunted. She heard a car door open and close, then silence. She lifted her head with difficulty and stared ahead, but all she could see was a cloudiness. Was that outside? It looked so peaceful and yet menacing at the same time. She remembered a horror movie she had watched about a mist and unimaginable creatures that would emerge from the whiteness and savagely kill anyone they encountered. *I hope there are no giant spider thingies about to leap out at me,* she thought. She felt a sudden impact on her right shoulder as the door to the truck flew open. She started to fall out, but the seatbelt stopped her from plunging to the ground.

She felt numb, tingly, disoriented. Her brain felt as full of the fog as her surroundings. But she was standing, being supported by someone. *Bradley?* They walked through the woods, the trees towering above them. The pine straw and sticks crunched beneath their feet. She looked up, her neck bending back almost cartoonish, and she barely made out branches. The air was thick with a chill, and his arm went behind her back and wrapped around her shoulder, pulling her into him. *This is romantic,* Brooke smiled. She looked at his large hand on her shoulder, then peered down at her left arm, bent in a crook, her hand on her stomach, and noticed a little red dot in her elbow crease. *Whassat?* she thought, suddenly feeling weaker. She had no answer for the red dot.

And still, they walked.

"Are we going to the hot tub?" she murmured. "How big is this property?" She stumbled, and he caught her. "Oopsie," she giggled. She lifted her head and squinted into the foggy darkness but saw nothing. "Where's the house?"

"Just over there," he said. "Not far now."

They walked deeper and deeper into the woods. "Are we in Oregon yet?" she asked. A branch got stuck in her hair, and she shook it loose. "We've walked f'ever. I needa sit." She saw lots of trees. Big, tall ones and her mind went back to their time in the Redwood National Forest. She looked back up at the towers around her now, and the branches started to sway, closing her in. She felt a panic attack start up. She closed her eyes and willed it away.

Without warning, Bradley stopped walking. "Oh!" she said, startled. "Sorry."

"We're here," he said.

She looked around in the dense fog and couldn't make out anything. "Where's here?"

"The hot tub is just over there," he pointed to what she thought was a large boulder. "Go ahead. I'm right behind you. There's a surprise waiting for you." She looked up and saw a smile on his face. He bent down and kissed her on the lips.

Brooke was a little hesitant and was a bit unsure if she was steady enough to stand on her own, let alone walk fifteen feet without support. "Whatever," she mumbled and began to walk. Her legs were a tad wobbly, but she found her footing. She put her arms out for balance and pressed on. After ten feet, she turned to look at Bradley, but he wasn't there.

"Bradley?" she called out. No answer. She swiveled back and kept walking. She began to imagine the warmth of the hot tub and being close to Bradley in the hot, bubbling waters. Making love to the man she was going to – *hoping to* – marry. She felt a smile creep onto her face. She took another step forward, then spun around, looking for something, anything. "Where the hell is -" she began, but then felt herself start to fall. Nothing but air and space, darkness, and earth. She fell for what seemed to be an eternity but was really only three seconds.

She thudded to the ground, landing hard on her back. Hard rocks jagged into her spine, and the wind rushed out of her lungs. "Owww," she moaned when she finally could catch a breath. She tried to push herself up on her hands, but it was no use. She was down and couldn't move. She cast a quick glance in every direction. "What the -" but all she saw was dirt, four walls of it. And then it occurred to her. Her eyes opened in horror.

She was in a deep pit.

Brooke squinted and looked upwards towards the sky, outside the hole she'd fallen into, and she tried to focus on...something. *Or someone.* But for some reason, she couldn't see clearly. Her eyesight was blurred. Tears filled her eyes. She couldn't move her neck, so she blinked rapidly until the tears fell sideways down her cheeks. Her view cleared up. And then she saw him.

Bradley.

And he was looking down at her.

"Help me!" she yelled. "Please, help me!" But to her horror, she could hear no words coming from her throat, only grunts and muffled noises. She couldn't move her lips. She couldn't speak. But then she realized Bradley wasn't speaking either. He was silent, just...staring down at her. She tried to plead with her eyes.

Still, he said nothing. He squatted down and placed his hands on his knees. From this stance, she could see his tee shirt sleeves had slid up on his big arms; his tattoos danced in the foggy moonlight. With one hand, he held up an object and waved it at her. It was her cell phone. Brooke's eyes grew bigger, but she couldn't understand or focus on exactly why he would have her cell phone. And why wasn't he jumping down into the hole to help her out?

Brooke was confused. She felt a sharp pain in her back and suddenly realized the numbness was wearing off. She opened her mouth to speak.

"Help....me..."

Bradley cocked his head. "I see the succinylcholine is wearing off. I wasn't sure how much to give you, so I only filled the syringe halfway."

She remembered the little red dot in her elbow crease. *He drugged me? Why would he do that?*

"I should've never brought you to the hospital that night you hit your head outside your house. I should've just let you stay passed out. But it wasn't my decision. I just do as I'm told."

Suddenly, the memories of Oscar and Hank, the fight outside her house, and ending up in the hospital flooded Brooke's mind. Dr. Kaufman's words reverberated in her head.

It was the young man that brought you in. He witnessed the whole thing. He said his name was Gio, but that's all he gave me. He was a big, strong guy. Carried you in his arms into the E.R.

But that was impossible. *Gio is dead!* But now she knew that the young man who'd brought her into the hospital was Bradley. *But why? Why would he save me only to* – then Brooke realized he didn't intend to *save* her: he wanted to *kill* her. And she had no idea why. She saw Bradley stand up. He looked thirty feet tall outside of the hole. She tried to move but ended up only wiggling a bit.

"Don't worry about trying to move," he said. "I got the succinylcholine from a vet clinic. It paralyzes its victims. Only temporarily, mind you. Not that that matters." He tossed something down into the hole with her. Something flimsy. It fluttered back and forth like a dropped feather, landing on her stomach. He turned and walked away, out of sight.

The panic in her began to rise. She was in a hole in the ground. A large, rectangular hole, probably six feet or more deep. Her claustrophobia started as a spark, then ignited into a full inferno. Her heart raced, and her breathing quickened. She was sure a heart attack loomed nearby. Her eyes darted back and forth and up and down. Then, the realization zapped her like a bolt.

It wasn't just a pit. It was a grave.

My grave!

Her lips moved, but she wasn't sure if she was saying anything. She was screaming but didn't hear any sound. Bradley had left her alone to die. *Why was he doing this? He was always so sweet! He knew my favorite flower and my favorite wine. We liked the same movies. Even Bongo liked him!*

Bongo.

Brooke sighed for her little kitty at home. Would she ever get to see him again? Who will take care of him? Then she remembered the catnip in her pocket. Why did Bradley have this in his overnight case? Then, like a ton of bricks, it hit her: Bradley sprayed his clothes with catnip before coming over. That's why Bongo was so taken with him.

That sonofabitch! It was all fake! But why?

She heard a noise off in the distance. Something started up, a machine. A car? Was he leaving her here? But the sound grew louder until she heard it just outside the opening of the hole. It sounded like.... like a bulldozer. The Bobcat excavator!

As she looked up, she could see the stars through the tall branches of the trees and realized the fog had lifted. She could see movement in the branches from the wind, the large moon just beyond her reach. It was clear. A slight breeze came down into the hole with her. The paper on her stomach lifted, floated silently above her, and landed along the dirt wall. Her eyes focused on the item. It was a photograph.

A photograph from *that* day. The day everything changed.

A picture of her, Cathy, and Dana in matching dresses they'd never wear again. They all had drinks in their hands. They were obviously having a good time celebrating, plying themselves with alcohol. And there was a man in the picture: Gio. He, too, had a drink in his hand. There were vows and music, cake and reverie, smiles and clicks of a camera.

And then there was a crash.

A fire.

And death. *So much death.*

Brooke could hear the Bobcat getting closer, and her mind came out of her memories.

She squinted her lids shut. *This isn't happening.* Slowly, she opened her eyes and saw the poppy necklace lying on her chest. *We all have one.* Ironically, she found herself smiling. The necklace was a reminder of happier times. Of friendships. Of sisterhood. Brooke felt a calmness, surrounded by a love that once was.

The night was clear, and so were her thoughts. For the first time in a long time, her thoughts were as clear as the night sky. And she thought of Misty.

Misty was wrong about Bradley Harris: he *did* exist. He may not live where he said he did, but he was here now. He was somewhere up there, above me. She tried to warn me, and I didn't listen. *Oh, Misty. I hope you'll forgive me.*

She saw a long shadow above her. The elongated arm of the Bobcat. It swung overhead as small pieces of dirt drifted down from its jagged-toothed bucket.

He brought me here to kill me. To bury me alive. And the reason *why* flooded her mind.

"It's...my...time..." she whispered into the darkness. "Payback." Payback for what she did. For what *they* did. The secret she'd been keeping this whole time. A secret that would finally be buried with her. "Oh, Alicia. I am so sorry," she said quietly. Regretfully.

They were the last words she'd utter as a mountain of earth crashed heavily onto her body. She opened her mouth to scream. But earth filled her lungs, and a gritty darkness enveloped her.

When Bradley was done, he placed her cell phone on the ground. He got back into the Bobcat, then drove over the phone, shattering it. He returned the excavator to the nearby estate, its job complete.

He left his truck in the parking lot of The Lodge. Bradley had reserved the room and the vehicle under a different name and picked up the truck after hours. He had worn a disguise just in case there were CCTV cameras around.

Bradley had done everything as he was instructed. Everything had gone off without a hitch, as expected.

He was driving Brooke's car back to San Francisco. He rolled the windows down to let the cool breeze in. The night was clear and crisp as he maneuvered the curves on Shoreline Highway. Bradley saw a sign for an upcoming scenic viewpoint close to the cliffs. That was his signal. He reached into his jacket pocket, pulled out a burner phone, and dialed a number.

After the first ring, the phone clicked as the recipient picked up.

"It's done," was all Bradley said before hanging up. As he saw the highly elevated bridge appear ahead, he switched the phone off. Crossing the overpass, he outstretched his arm and tossed the phone out the passenger window to the crashing rocks below.

PART TWO
CATHY

CHAPTER 16

Cathy Broderick knew her neck was about to break.

Yet she was only halfway to her desired height.

And she hated heights. They were her biggest fear. She was deathly afraid of them. The dizziness swept over her like a wave. She closed her eyes and gripped the wood with all her might. The higher she climbed, the lower her blood pressure fell, and she felt faint.

Perilously, Cathy balanced, holding on for dear life. The ground was so far below her that everything looked as if in miniature scale. And should she fall, she would for sure die with a giant splat.

And with maintenance off for the weekend, who would clean the mess? she thought sardonically. *No one, that's who.* She took a deep breath and took another step, her knees like Jell-O.

Suddenly, the structure she was on shifted and even rolled a bit. Cathy let out a small yelp. She dropped everything she was holding in her arms, and they landed with a bang, and she gripped the rails with such force, her knuckles turned white. Cathy closed her eyes. She shoved her head in between two of the steps, and she held on for dear life as the fixture shook violently, threatening to throw her off. Her glasses jammed into her head and sat cockeyed on her nose.

"Oh, my god!" she cried, her eyes clenched shut.

"Sorry!" a disembodied voice from far below said in a strong whisper.

Cathy opened one eye and peered below. A gentleman was walking away from the ladder she was on. "Watch where you're going next time, Tim!" she called down to him in a hushed tone.

She was still shaking long after he left. She looked around and realized she really wasn't that high up. Not for most people, anyway. But for someone with a phobia of heights, she might as well be scaling the outside of Big Ben. She gripped the wooden ladder rails and started making her way down, one step at a time.

She hated heights, but putting books away, no matter where their shelf-home was, was part of her job at Sarah Tuttle Public Library. She preferred the shelves closer to the floor, of course, but she loved her job. Just not the hazards it came with.

"Cathy, do I need to come up there and help you down?" It was Elaine, Cathy's coworker.

Yes, she thought. "No,' she said. "I've got this." So, rung by rung, Cathy made her way down to the floor. The sweet, solid, un-rolling floor. A breath escaped her mouth.

"Cathy, you know I'd put those high-up books away for you. I know how badly heights scare you." Elaine shook her head in a tsk-tsk manner.

Like this was Cathy's fault. She couldn't help it. She just never did like being up higher than the height of her head. Cathy couldn't explain it. She just had this irrational fear of falling and hurting herself. *Or worse.* She repressed a shudder. But for now, she was on solid ground and felt her heart slowing to a regular beat.

"It's time for you to go home anyway," Elaine said. "I'll finish up. See you tomorrow?" Elaine asked.

"Nope. Off tomorrow. See you Thursday?"

"Yup. Have a good night."

Cathy drove home in her Honda Civic, a dowdy car to go with her dowdy clothes. She sighed. She was well aware of what Elaine – and everyone else, for that matter – thought of her appearance. But she liked how she dressed. It was easy. Comfortable. Non-threatening. It certainly didn't extend an invitation to men to approach her, and she was just fine with that.

Cathy was raised in a strict Catholic family, and she was surrounded by rules. Her father was a manager at the local thrift store, and her mother was a schoolteacher. After school, Cathy had to complete her homework and then could watch Jeopardy and Wheel of Fortune until dinner, which was promptly at 6:00 p.m. every night. During dinnertime, Cathy had to raise her hand to speak, and then, and only then, her conversation was required to be on current topics: politics, religion, world leaders, technology, and books. She especially enjoyed discussing books and the written word. Cathy could read a book a day and discovered there wasn't anything she couldn't learn from reading. She fell in love with books, and her bedroom shelves were filled to capacity with works by her favorites, like Tolstoy, Hemingway, Christie, and Fitzgerald. Cathy preferred older novelists but, on occasion, enjoyed current reads from King, Patterson, Tartt, and even Dr. Seuss. To her, the depth in his simplicity was unmatched.

Cathy had daily chores as well as nightly prayers. Her mom would cook the dinners, and Cathy would clean up. On Mondays, she did the laundry; on Tuesdays, she'd sweep the floors. On Wednesdays, she took out the garbage. Thursdays, she'd mop the entire house, and Fridays were set aside for washing her parents' cars. On the occasional weekend, she'd help her father in the yard with weeding or raking leaves. Every night before bedtime, she would tidy up her bedroom and brush and floss her teeth. She rarely had any downtime, but when she did, she always found a good book to dive into.

Cathy didn't mind the rules her parents handed down. In fact, she enjoyed most of them because they demanded a sort of balance and organization in her life. She was a rule follower, and that was okay with her.

Now, as she was almost home, she was stopped at a 4-way intersection near her home. Out of nowhere, a car zoomed through the stop sign from her left, narrowly avoiding hitting an elderly man walking his dog in the crosswalk. The dog yelped, and the old man flipped his middle finger at the oblivious speedster.

"Holy crap!" Cathy exclaimed, throwing both of her hands to her chest. Her heart was pounding. "It's a 4-way stop, idiot!" she called out. She hated people who didn't follow the rules. The old man looked at her, and she gave a gentle wave and shrugged. She cautiously looked both ways before proceeding through the intersection. Her heart was still throbbing in her chest.

When Cathy got home, she went into the kitchen, plopped a frozen dinner in the microwave, and then turned on the TV. The local news was on. She had the volume level set low, but she could still hear it perfectly. Because of the rule to stay hushed at the library, her ears were acclimated to the quiet, and she could hear just about anything at a low level. The only other noise surrounding her was the mechanical whirring of the microwave.

She headed into the bedroom to get into her soft clothes for the night. She undid her bun and let her thick brown hair fall below her shoulders. As she pulled off her blouse and denim skirt, she stood in her undergarments and saw her reflection in the mirror, and smiled. She liked what she saw. Her body was toned and supple. Cathy knew she wasn't as frumpy as she presented herself. She liked erring on the side of mystery to people around her. *Rule number one: what other people think of me is none of my business,* she thought. She smiled at her reflection. Then something caught her ear, and she cocked her head slightly.

"…missing since last Wednesday…."

It was the newscaster on the television set. Absentmindedly, Cathy listened to the news and began putting on her pajamas.

"…from the Bay area. Once again, Brooke Carson has been missing for the past four days from her home in the Bay area, and if anyone has any news as to her whereabouts, they are to call their local police."

Cathy jerked to a standstill. She pulled her sleep shirt over her head and moved into the den. She found the TV remote and pressed the up arrow to increase the volume. A picture of a beautiful blue-eyed young woman with wavy blonde hair popped up on the screen. The name underneath said 'Brooke Carson'.

The remote slipped from Cathy's hands and slammed to the floor. Her hands flew to her mouth. "Oh, my god. *Brooke!*"

CHAPTER 17

An electronic *ding* echoed in the background, signaling Cathy's microwave dinner was ready. It had been ready for 45 minutes, but despite the incessant dinging, Cathy had lost her appetite and couldn't find the motivation to retrieve her dinner. The Lean Cuisine lasagna would have to wait.

After the news of Brooke's disappearance, Cathy had felt numb, moving slowly and without direction, like a zombie. She had been gut-punched with the announcement of Brooke being missing. Cathy eventually stumbled to her bed, where she propped pillows up against the headboard and leaned back into them. She reached down into the bottom drawer of her nightstand and pulled out a photo album. She marveled that she still kept a photo album because it was so old-fashioned, but Cathy felt she lived a previous life in a different period, one where life was simpler: where kids drank water from a hose, and they stayed outside with friends under the streetlamps until 9:00 p.m. with the June bugs skittering around the light, or households left the doors to their homes unlocked. And where photo albums held tangible memories, smartphones never could. She shrugged and set the album on her lap.

And still, the microwave dinged.

She flipped pages of the photo album, revisiting the many ghosts of her past, pictures from every stage in her life: her first puppy when she turned four, braces when she was eleven, her driver's license on her sixteenth birthday, her first Homecoming Dance with Robbie Cartwright. Seeing a tall, gangly boy in an ill-fitting suit standing next to Cathy, whose hair was teased too big for her head, automatically brought a light smile to her face. "Oh, my god," she said, covering the photo with her hand in embarrassment. She shook her head as she kept flipping pages.

Then she saw them, snapshots of her and the three other girls in various stages of their friendship: graduation, parties, college picnics. A wedding. Cathy was a bridesmaid, along with Brooke and Dana. She saw a picture of the three of them, and there was a man in the shot. They had drinks in their hands, liquid revelry. It was the happiness before the storm.

Tears fell from Cathy's eyes, and her mouth frowned, saddened. "Oh, Brooke. Where are you?" Distracted, she rubbed the orange poppy charm on the necklace around her neck. She remembered when Alicia gave it to all the girls as gifts. It was a bond. A talisman of hope and love.

She closed her eyes and laid her head back on the pillows. Her mind shifted to a celebration of song, light, and love. There was laughing and tears of joy. Drinking and dancing and the click of cameras. Cathy remembered being surrounded by a crowd, but the memory was fuzzy. The details were few and unclear. The sound of a car starting up and then silence. *Until...*

It had been over a year since that day. Over a year since they had spoken to one another. Girls who used to hang out and talk and laugh about anything and everything, never at a loss for words, were now surrounded by a wall of absolute silence.

Cathy squinched her eyes shut and slammed the photo album closed. She set it on the bed beside her, rolled over, and turned off the light. Her pillow was wet with tears as she drifted off into a sleep filled with thoughts of Brooke, her friend once upon a time, and the terrible secret they shared.

A loud noise outside awakened Cathy, and she sat up in bed. It was still dark out, and moonlight pierced through the bedroom window. She climbed out of bed and looked out the window into the backyard but saw only darkness. In the background, she heard the microwave still dinging. She leaned closer to the windowpanes to get a better look, then heard a crash. It was coming from outside the front of the house.

She walked to the front of the house, cutting through the kitchen to shut off the microwave. She noticed the time on the clock was 11:11 p.m., the magical time of having your thoughts turn into reality. Cathy closed her eyes and thought positively about Brooke and her safe return. But what if – *stop it, Cathy! Don't think that!* She could feel the hairs on the back of her neck stand up. She kept walking.

Once in the den, Cathy peered out the front window, and she stood frozen. Across the street, under the streetlight, was a figure- a large figure of a man. Or something. She couldn't see too well, so she ran back to get her glasses. She put them on, hurried back to the front window, and looked out again. But there was nothing there.

The figure had vanished.

She only saw shadows from the trees blowing in the wind. She took and released a deep breath.

"You're seeing things, Cath," she said to herself. Or you're seeing nothing at all, which is more like it." She crossed her arms and hugged herself, still looking out the window. "Probably just a raccoon in the trash again. Stupid varmint."

Her mind flashed to the small pistol she had in her bedside table. Cathy had never used it before, but when Phil and Lauren's house down the street was broken into last month, her mother had cajoled Cathy into purchasing a small gun.

"Better safe than sorry," her mother had warned. With a roll of her eyes, Cathy had broken down and bought the Ruger Max-9 semi-automatic pistol. Its slimness and ability to be easily hidden appealed to her. Gun's made Cathy a bit nervous, but something about the Ruger's alloy steel construction gave it a sleek beauty she could appreciate. And she felt a sort of kinship with the gun: it was hiding its beauty underneath a common casing.

Satisfied there was nothing outside but the wind-whipped trees and a garbage charlatan or two, Cathy went into the kitchen for a glass of water. Even though she was off work tomorrow, she was not a night owl. She needed to get back into bed and –

Her landline rang and jostled her out of her thoughts.

"Why do you still have a landline?" her mother had asked once.

"Well, when the power and cellphone towers go out, I'll still be able to call someone."

"Who?" her mother asked. "All of *their* cellphones will be down!"

Her mother had a point, but Cathy refused to give her the satisfaction. She liked her landline. She even had an old-fashioned answering machine. The old machines were a comfort and a security blanket that anchored her to that throwback period she felt she lived in once upon a time.

Now, the ringing was loud and shrill, and it rattled Cathy to her bones.

"Hello?" she answered.

"What are you doing up so late?" her mother asked. She didn't wait for an answer. "Never mind that," her mother continued, "I guess you heard about Brooke going missing?"

"Yes," Cathy said quietly. "I did."

"Oh, Cathy. It's so scary! Where could she be? Have you spoken to her?"

Cathy hadn't. Oh, she thought about calling her many times, but she could never bring herself to pick up the phone. She wanted to tell her about the new job she got at the library! Or how she was thinking about rescuing a puppy! Or just to invite her to go shopping. But Cathy never told Brooke any of those things. She never found the steel to pick up the phone and call. Once that day so long ago happened, it was as if everyone fell off the face of the earth.

"Cathy?"

"I'm here, mother," Cathy said, bumped out of her thoughts. "No. I haven't spoken to her. Not recently. It's been a…"

"Well, maybe she'll call you then," her mother said. There was hope in her voice.

"Yeah. Maybe," Cathy whispered sorrowfully.

But Cathy knew that would never happen. Not after that day. She had never told her mother why the girls stopped talking to one another. It was too painful to dig up. *No. The past is the past, and this secret is better off staying buried.*

Cathy had no idea just how prescient her words were.

CHAPTER 18

There were a few things Cathy liked to do on her off days from the library, like going to a matinee at the neighborhood theater, making ceramics at "Kiln Me Softly", and selecting the freshest fruits and vegetables from the farmer's market. Sometimes, she'd splurge and get a small bouquet of mixed flowers. They always cheered up her little home.

But more than anything, she adored the outdoors and taking a hike now and then. Once, her family went to Yosemite National Park, and they got to stay in The Ahwahnee. It was a rustic yet breathtaking inn, surrounded by ancient, towering trees and large rock formations, and had the best views of the cliffs and waterfalls. It was here she developed her attachment to rambling alfresco.

She loved the outdoors and hiked the local trails every chance she got. Cathy loved her junk food, too, so the hiking and exercise in the wilderness helped keep her body in check. But even with her affinity for being outside and challenging herself over the different terrains, she never hiked over 1,000 feet elevation, especially near the cliffs, because of her fear of heights.

But today was a special day. Today, her heart was hurting for Brooke, so she needed to rest her mind. She wanted to do one of her favorite activities: take a packed lunch with her and venture off to Little Marina Green Park. The park was located along San Francisco Bay and had unmatched views of the Golden Gate Bridge and Angel Island. From where Cathy would sit on her favorite bench, she could see the Palace of Fine Arts, one of her favorite places to frequent. Tourists always populated the park, snapping selfies with the amazing backgrounds. At the same time, parents with their kids and dogs tramped through the lush grass, and lovers enjoyed picnics under the giant sycamore trees.

Cathy loved sycamore trees. She read once that when they're young, their leaves are covered with tiny "hairs" that, upon magnification, are star-shaped. She always loved seeing star-crossed lovers under leaves that once had stars on them. The irony made her smile.

She found her bench near the lake and sat. A dog barked in the background. She looked around, and as she absorbed the view, she blocked out all ambient noise around her. She just needed to take in the quiet, if only for a moment. A reflection of how lucky she was to be here, to see all this. To be fortunate enough to enjoy the beautiful sun, water, and shade. It was perfect. All of it. She felt nothing was missing.

. Then she thought of Brooke.

Cathy knew it was just a matter of time before Brooke came to the forefront of her mind. Cathy's shoulders sagged, and she took a deep breath. "You'll be found," she whispered. "I just know it."

She reached into her bag and took out her turkey, mayo, and tomato sandwich. The fresh-cut turkey had a delicious aroma, and Cathy put it up to her nose to take a whiff. She smiled before taking a generous bite. She had brought a book from the library, *A Calculated Risk,* by Katherine Neville, one of her favorite authors. In the book, a female financial prodigy is dared to pull off the perfect bank heist within an impossibly short timeframe. The book raced between completing the monumental task and getting caught. The pacing and intelligence of the plot made Cathy's adrenalin course wildly through her blood. Her mind was brought back to reality when she heard the deep barking of a dog.

Cathy set her sandwich down and picked up the book. Off in the distance, she heard playful screams from children on the playground. She smiled and leaned back onto the bench. She turned to her bookmarked page and continued her adventure.

She was so enveloped in the story that she didn't clearly register the warnings. But somewhere in the distance, the muffled cries came.

"…look out!"

"Oh, my god! …. someone stop him!"

"Miss….!!!"

"He's heading…. for her!"

Cathy heard barking, a low growl. She lifted her head. Suddenly, from her left, she heard a ferocious gnarling. She turned and saw a huge black shape racing towards her. It leaped, barreling at her like a bullet, its razor-sharp teeth aimed at her neck.

Cathy screamed.

Instinctively, she threw her book at the beast. It hit him on his dark, wet snout. For a split second, Cathy feared she made him angrier. He yelped and veered off course, landing hard on the ground. Within seconds, he found his footing and turned towards her, his powerful neck muscles stiff and straight, his back low, the hairs bristling. The growling was deep and venomous.

Oh, my god. He's going to kill me! Cathy quickly backed up on the bench, trying to distance herself from the drooling savage. It was inching towards her; its thick lips hitched back in an evil smile, its deadly teeth bared.

Cathy felt she was about to be eaten alive.

"Kong!" a man yelled authoritatively. "Heel! *Heel!*"

In an instant, the massive dog stopped in its tracks. His big tongue licked his lips, and he turned his neck back to look towards the male voice. He whined, looked back at Cathy, then sat his rump down on the ground.

The man approached the dog. His biceps tightened as he gripped the collar tightly. Only then did Cathy release her breath.

"Kong! Bad doggie," the man chastised.

"He…he almost *killed* me!" Cathy exclaimed angrily, her hands resting on her chest to keep her heart from flying out.

"Kong would never…"

"Kong almost *did*! If not by ripping my throat out, then by giving me a heart attack!" She noticed the man held a leash in his hand. She stood up quickly, keeping one eye on Kong.

"Look, he's sorry, aren't you, big guy?" the man rubbed Kong's head, and the dog wagged his tail enthusiastically, then let his tongue flop out and looked up at the man.

It amazed Cathy how quickly the dog's demeanor changed. She didn't buy it for a second.

"Yeah, well...I'm not sorry. Not in the least. He's a beast and should be -"

"Should be what?" the man straightened up. "Put down?"

Cathy looked daggers at the man. "No. The *dog* shouldn't be put down. I don't blame *him*."

"Wow. Okay. Got it," the man said, smiling. "Look, again, I'm really sorry. He was just chasing some birds and got excited and....and probably smelled your sandwich there...and, well...." He rubbed the back of Kong's neck. Kong looked back at Cathy, and she could've sworn she saw regret in his eyes.

"Whatever," Cathy said, flustered. She looked at the man and dog standing there and stormed off.

"Well, now you've gone and done it," the man said to Kong, who just leaned his head back and looked up at him. He licked the man's hand. The man released Kong's collar, and the dog walked over near the bench. He sniffed at a book on the ground. The man reached down and picked it up, looking at the cover: *A Calculated Risk*.

The man opened the book and saw the stamp inside: "Property of Sarah Tuttle Public Library". He looked up and saw Cathy walking over the hill until she was out of sight. He patted the dog on the head.

"Good boy," he affirmed. "Good boy."

CHAPTER 19

When Cathy returned home, she was still shaking.

And pissed.

This was the worst day off. Ever! She couldn't believe how careless some dog owners were to let their dogs run around without a leash. *It's the rule to have your dog on a leash when outside,* she thought to herself. Sure, the man was holding one in his hand, but obviously, he let him loose to run around unsupervised. *Chasing birds! Whatever,* she thought, rolling her eyes. *Hunting for his next meal is more like it.* Instinctively, Cathy raised a hand to her throat.

She slammed the front door behind her and went into the kitchen, tossing her stuff on the table. Her stomach growled, and she realized she'd only had one bite of her sandwich before leaving it on the picnic table. A flicker of a memory hit her, and she glanced around. Then, with a jolt, she smacked her hands on the back of a chair. She closed her eyes and realized she also left her book behind.

"Crap!" she yelled. That book was long gone and, even if found, would be soggy from the dog's snout. She would have to pay for the book out of her paycheck. Cathy didn't think she could reach a new level of anger towards the man and his mutt, but here she was. Her head began to throb.

"Calm down, Cathy," she said as she went to her refrigerator, where she grabbed a cold Pepsi. She placed the cold bottle against her forehead to deter the oncoming headache that was forming. In the den, she plopped down in her oversized leather chair and let the cool material wash over her body, which was tense and still on high alert. She sipped her Pepsi and noticed her answering machine was blinking next to her on the end table. She pressed the PLAY button.

YOU HAVE FIVE NEW MESSAGES, the mechanical voice said. PRESS ONE TO HEAR YOUR MESSAGES.

Five? She scrunched her brow incredulously. No one ever called her, and she never had more than two messages, let alone five. She reached into the end table drawer and pulled out a pen and a pad of paper. She always took notes, a lesson learned from her overly organized father. "Always take notes," he'd say. "The palest ink is better than the best memory." She was pretty sure he had robbed that from Confucius or somebody.

She pressed PLAY.

The first two messages were from her overly cautious mother. If her father was an organized extremist, her mother was identical but in the ways of worrying. The cloudy voice came through the machine's retro speaker.

"Are you okay? I haven't heard from you in a couple hours! Call me!" Cathy rolled her eyes. Even though they had just spoken the evening before, Cathy's mother was taking Brooke being missing very seriously and had automatically jumped to the conclusion that her own daughter was M.I.A.

PRESS SEVEN TO DELETE MESSAGE OR PRESS EIGHT TO KEEP MESSAGE. Cathy pressed seven.

Cathy's mother's second message was from the same ilk, just a little more irritated and heightened. "Cathy, I'm serious! Are you dead? Call me!" Cathy shook her head. Sometimes, dealing with her mother was exhausting. She meant well, as most mothers do, but Cathy felt her mother was in a league by herself. She jotted a note on the pad: Call mom ASAP!! She pressed seven again.

Message three was from West Coast Cleaners informing Cathy that her dry cleaning had been sitting in their facility for 38 days now, and since it had passed the thirty-day mark, if she didn't come pick it up in the next two days, they would happily give it away to Goodwill. Cathy's eyes got big, and she cocked her head in thought. How had she forgotten their thirty-day rule? She pressed eight. Above the note to call her mother, she wrote 'PICK UP DRY-CLEANING NOW'. *Priorities*, she thought.

The fourth message, speaking of the devil, was her mother again. "I'm calling the police!" Cathy sighed. She knew her mother was overreacting, but still. With Brooke missing, her mother might seriously call the police. "And get a cell phone!" her mother said before sending a dial tone through the answering machine's speaker. Cathy drew an arrow, moving the message to call her mother above the dry-cleaning one, resetting the priorities. Haltingly, she pressed seven again.

The last message was from her job, Sarah Tuttle Public Library. It was Elaine, her co-worker.

"Okay, so some *very* hot guy just came in looking for you. Lots of muscles and pretty teeth. Oh, my god, he was so hot! Anyway, he said something about the park and a killer dog and he's sorry and, oh yeah! He returned your book. He saw our stamp inside. He mentioned he didn't want you to pay a fee for a missing book. Wasn't that sweet? Do men like this really exist? Anyway, gotta go. I need some cold water. Or a cold shower. Haha! Hope you're having a great day off. And if you're running into men like this, I know you are!" *click*

Cathy sat there, blinking. So, this man whose dog almost killed her is now stalking her at her place of work? This was unbelievable! The nerve he had! She went from pissed to rolling her eyes to shaking her head to cocking her head and back to pissed again – all in the span of five phone messages. Her breathing became rapid.

Agitated, she repeatedly banged on the number seven on her phone, ensuring the message was deleted forever. Her heart was pounding wildly, and from the memory of a hurtling dog, she rested a hand on her throat. She hurled the notepad across the room.

CHAPTER 20

The next day, Cathy adhered to her priorities and called her mother. They agreed to meet for lunch, and reluctantly, Cathy agreed to let her mother talk, and she would listen. *It's better to appease than displease*, Cathy surmised.

Cathy could walk to the restaurant from her home. As she got closer, she saw her mother already seated outside. Linda Broderick was hard to miss: her makeup was too thick, her clothes were too thin, and her hair and cleavage were both too big—the complete opposite of Cathy in her bunned hair, jeans, and Casual Corner blouse.

They sat outside at Café Deux Oiseaux. Anyone seeing the two women seated across from each other would probably assume Cathy was getting a psychic reading from an over-the-top medium.

"Why haven't you answered any of my calls? Why are you worrying me so? Don't you know I'm a heart patient, and any little thing could cause a rupture with my stent?" Her mother clasped her heart for dramatic effect. "Poor Brooke Carson has gone missing, and it's been almost a week now, and everyone is fearing the worst." She sniffled.

Fake.

"Mother, I -"

"What? Do you think I'm overreacting? You do. You think I'm overreacting," she said, not waiting for an answer. "Well, I'll have you know, I'm not. It's a mother's lot in life to worry about her children. You can be a child or an adult, and the worry will never wane. Never." She paused. "Poor Brooke. Larry and Rebecca must be beside themselves."

Brooke's parents were more than likely in a drunken stupor, but Cathy didn't say that. Instead, she said, "Yeah. Probably."

The waitress brought over their baguette and cheese and filled their glasses with lemon-infused water.

There was a silence. Then Cathy spoke.

"Mother, I'm sorry. For not calling. But I've been busy with work and _"

"And what?" her mother interrupted. "You don't do anything else." She could see the hurt – or was it truth – in Cathy's eyes. "I didn't mean that." She paused. "Not really."

"I know you didn't," Cathy said.

"You know I love you, right?"

"Of course, mother."

Her mother continued, "It's just that you are so smart. You're not only book smart, but you have common sense. Both are usually not found in one person. You either have one or the other."

Here it comes.

"And yet you turned down a scholarship to MIT to go to Pepperdine and then left early to, what? Work in the library? To be lonely and miserable?"

"Mother, I'm not…miserable." She left out the lonely part. "I'm perfectly happy. Can we please not go down this road again?"

"Fine. So, what about…this?" she said, waving her hand up and down in front of Cathy. "Get a makeover. Wear contact lenses. Let your hair down. Maybe that'll help you get a man."

"A man?" Cathy asked incredulously. "A *man*, mother? Oh, my gosh. I *definitely* don't want to go down *this* road with you!" Cathy could feel her face flush scarlet. "And I certainly don't need makeover advice from you." Her mother clasped her heart again. Cathy rolled her eyes.

Cathy shook her head and caught a glimpse of herself in the café's window. Her hair was pulled tight into a bun on top of her head, a blue ribbon tied tightly around the base. She wore glasses and too-comfortable clothes that were too big for her slight frame. But her skin was smooth, and underneath the look, she had a great figure and strong, lean legs. But she kept all of that hidden. *My god. I look like a dowdy school-marm.* She shook her head again.

"Besides, I have friends -"

"Who?" her mother crowed.

"From work!"

"The library? *Borrrring!* All boring."

Cathy looked wounded.

"Oh, Cathy. I didn't mean you. Or maybe I did. I just worry about you. Look at poor Brooke Carson. She's your age, and she's been missing for a week! She's probably -"

"Don't say it, mother," Cathy interrupted.

"– dead."

Cathy slumped in her seat.

"I'm sorry, dear," her mother said quietly now. "Have you spoken with her lately? I'm sure her parents would like to know."

Cathy's eyes widened. She and Brooke hadn't spoken in almost a year. Not since that day. And now it might be too late to speak with her ever again. Cathy felt a tear sting her eyes.

"No," Cathy's voice was a whisper. "We haven't spoken in…in…a while."

"A while?" Linda Broderick asked, surprised. "What does that mean? I thought you two were close."

Cathy had had enough for one day. She needed to go. Between Brooke's disappearance, the dog attack at the park, the shadow outside her home, and now her mother berating her to change everything about herself, she was done. She had lost her appetite for lunch.

"I have to go," Cathy said, getting up from her chair. "I'll call you later."

Her mother's mouth was wide open in mid-sentence, but before she could say anything, Cathy was gone.

Linda was more worried now than before. Her daughter was acting aloof, and even Linda knew something was going on with her. She just wasn't sure what it was. But her motherly instincts were telling her not to let it go. She dug into her purse, pulled out her phone, and dialed a number from her contact list.

She found the name and remembered the sweet man she was about to call. *What a saint. A man among men.* Linda knew of few men who would step up and do what Mike Evans did for his niece, Misty. The circumstances were unimaginable, and yet he became the hero to so many. Mike was always helping everyone however he could and was such an easy person to go to and talk to about anything. She admired him greatly and knew she could count on his confidentiality. A female voice picked up.

"Hello?" the woman on the other end answered.

"Karen, hey. It's Linda Broderick. I need to speak with Michael. Is he home? I have a favor...."

CHAPTER 21

The next day, Cathy was finding it impossible to concentrate at work. There was a stack of books higher than she was tall that needed to be put away, and all she could think about was yesterday with her mother. *How dare she criticize my job! My clothes! My everything! And telling me I need a man?!* Cathy scoffed. The lunch was nothing short of disastrous.

And speaking of lunch, Cathy found it challenging to eat because every time she attempted to take a bite of her turkey sandwich, the memory of Kong almost shredding her throat haunted her.

"Ahem," came a voice next to her.

"Oh, sorry," Cathy said. Elaine was standing next to her with her arms crossed over her chest.

"You're in la-la land," Elaine said.

And she was. Not only with everything with the dog and her mother, but Brooke being missing was taking a toll on Cathy's mental state. More than she cared to admit, truth be told. This morning, the newscaster said they still had no leads to her whereabouts. Her parents were interviewed and, through tears, said, "We just want our baby back." They were slurring their words, but Cathy was sure their sincerity was genuine. At least, she hoped so.

Cathy thought about her and her friends: Brooke was the enthusiastic, carefree one; Cathy, the reliable, intelligent one; Dana, the ambitious, conscientious one; and Alicia.... loving, generous Alicia. Cathy sighed. *It was a horrible way to die.*

"Sorry, yeah. Just a bit preoccupied," Cathy said.

"Well, I, for one, don't want to be here all day," Elaine said. "And this stack of books isn't going to put itself away."

"I'm on it," Cathy replied.

"Then, here. Add this one to the stack." Elaine handed Cathy a copy of *A Calculated Risk*. It was the book she had left at the park, the one the stranger returned for her.

The stranger with the killer dog.

"Thanks," Cathy mumbled.

Elaine sat at the table next to Cathy. "So, tell me *all* about this handsome stranger." Elaine looked up at Cathy like a kid anticipating Santa Claus's arrival.

Cathy huffed. "There's nothing to tell. He's about as boorish as his attack dog."

Elaine's phone rang, and she looked back at Cathy, disappointed in her answer. "Well, poo," she said. She stood up from the table. "It's my dad. I need to take this. There might be some car graveyard emergency," she said, rolling her eyes. She clicked on her phone before stepping away. "Hi, dad. How are things?"

Cathy gave a weak smile.

"You what?" Elaine continued, her voice carrying to Cathy. "Okay. How much do you need this time? No problem. I think I can swing that." She walked away from Cathy.

Cathy felt bad about eavesdropping. Elaine's dad wasn't the most money-conscious person on the planet, but he was a very hard worker. He owned a car graveyard, where cars go to get crushed and are then taken for recycling. That was basically his entire world. And if the crusher wasn't working, neither was her dad. Elaine, bless her, had given her dad money over many years to keep him afloat, and it sounded as if he needed more. She knew Elaine didn't make much money, but her dedication to her father and his junkyard lifestyle was sweet and endearing. She smiled and got back to work. And she knew what she was about to face. Her knees began to quiver.

Cathy turned and faced her nemesis: the ladder.

She inhaled deeply. "You got this. Absolutely no problem." Cathy put three books in the crook of her right arm and squeezed them close to her body. *No problem.* She grabbed the side rails and gripped tightly, placing her left foot on the lowest rung. *Still no problem.* The wheels creaked, and the ladder immediately began to wobble. She closed her eyes and took in a breath. "We've got a problem," she sighed. But she was determined to keep going. As much as she feared heights, she was bound to conquer her fear and not let it stop her from doing the things she loved. *Hiking, yes; climbing a rickety ladder ten feet off the ground to put away books, not so much.* But it was all part of the job.

She looked around. Elaine was still talking to her father about his car graveyard business and would be of no help to Cathy. She was on her own.

Rung by rung, Cathy climbed. Inching her way towards the middle of the ladder where she could safely reach the shelf needed. She placed the first two books in their designated spaces on the shelf. She glanced down at the third book.

A Calculated Risk.

The book.

"What the hell?" Cathy huffed. She didn't mean to get this book this go-round because it didn't belong here. It went three rows over.

Cathy shook her head. She didn't want to have to climb down and start all over, but the only other choice she had was to roll herself over a distance of six feet.

While hanging onto a rattletrap of a ladder.

On wheels.

High up from the ground.

Where falling would mean certain death. *Or at least a good maiming.*

Cathy felt nauseous.

"You can do this," she willed. She closed her eyes, then wrapped her arms tightly around the sides of the ladder and, with her left foot, pushed off from the shelf. The ladder began to roll.

"Aaaaahh," she yelped. The ladder continued its glide, then jerked to a stop, warping back and forth. She froze, and her hold on the ladder was a vice grip. When everything was at a standstill, she felt comfortable moving. Cathy felt those six feet were conquered quite successfully, and she felt her heart swell.

"I did it!" she said triumphantly. "I freaking did it!" She opened her eyes.

She had rolled five inches.

"Well, hell."

She took another deep breath, bent her head with determination, and gave another shove off the shelf. This time, the ladder rolled further, and when it stopped, she was halfway to her goal.

Cathy calculated one more push, and she'd be where she needed to be. But to go that distance, she decided this time she would push with her foot and use her right hand to pull herself along. But that meant taking her hand off the ladder.

"No risk, no reward," she said, trying to talk herself into it. "Let's do this, Cath!"

She let go of the ladder and, with her right hand, got a good grip on the shelf, ready to pull herself along with the ladder. Her left foot came off its rung, and she placed it on the shelf, ready to push as hard as she could. She was balanced recklessly, secured with only one hand and one foot.

She took a huge breath. "On the count of three. One. Two...."

But before she could get to three, the ladder quaked violently and jarred, bending in the middle. The wheels sprung off the ground, and the whole contraption became unhooked from the top gutter.

Cathy immediately lost her balance, and she plunged down. She was falling into space. She screamed, plummeting towards the ground, and she knew her life was about to end. Holding her breath, Cathy braced herself for the hard floor's sudden impact.

Suddenly, her drop ended. But she wasn't on the ground.

She was in someone's arms.

The arms were big but bent from the force of her fall, so the catch wasn't so abrupt. Her head snapped down from the impact, and her eyes flew open, and she tried to catch her breath. She looked around. The right hand of her catcher was touching her boob.

What the…

She looked at her savior.

It was the boorish, handsome stranger—owner of the killer dog.

CHAPTER 22

I t took Cathy all of 5 seconds to gauge the situation and become infuriated.

"Put me down this instant!" she yelled. She kept pushing on his chest to get away, much like a victim would try to escape a kidnapper. "Ugh! Let...me.... *GO!*"

"Fine," he said, tipping her slowly till her feet were on the ground. "I was only trying to help -"

"You were trying to kill me. *Again!*" she huffed. Her eyes flashed at him. "I know you moved the ladder. On purpose, I might add. So, I would fall and break my neck!" Cathy was dusting herself off, straightening her skirt. Elaine ran over.

"No, no. That would be me. I'm so sorry, Cathy! This gentleman," she smiled and nodded in his direction, "needed a book from the bottom shelf beneath the ladder, and I know I should've gotten it for him. I thought he could reach it, but it's my fault. I guess he accidentally bumped the ladder and, oh, I'm so sorry, Cathy! Are you okay?"

Cathy found herself out of breath, panting. Her eyes darted between Elaine and the stranger. She was mad she was going to have to apologize, but she knew she would. "I'm fine, thanks." She turned towards

Elaine. "But please, always help the customer. I could've really been hurt!"

Elaine's eyes hit the floor, while Cathy's went to the stranger. "I'm... I'm sorry. I'm...just still...a bit shaken up." Now, she shifted her eyes to glare at Elaine, who just kept staring at the floor like a scolded puppy.

"It's fine. Apology accepted," he said, his voice husky. He gently touched Cathy's arm. "Are you sure you're okay?"

Cathy couldn't help but notice his arms. They were big, and his tee shirt was not. It was skintight, and his dark, wavy hair looked every bit like a model from the '70s. Deep down, she still wanted to be angry with him, but she was beginning to warm instead.

She found her voice. "Yes, thank you."

Elaine said, "This is the gentleman that brought your book back." Her mouth flew open at a realization. "Is he the one with the attack dog?"

"Attack dog?" he said. "Ha! Kong was just running towards her to be petted."

"What?!" Cathy exclaimed incredulously. "Petted? That dog wanted to be petted about as much as a porcupine does!"

"Well, you don't really know what a porcupine wants..." Elaine muttered.

"Oh, shut up," Cathy said. "What I meant to say was you can't pet a porcupine, or you shouldn't...because of the quills and...well, that would hurt and.... well, it wouldn't hurt the porcupine because...." She saw a big grin spread across the man's face. "Oh, never mind!"

"Look," the man said, "Kong would never -"

"But Kong did," Cathy retorted.

He put his hands up in surrender. "I don't want to revisit this. I am sorry. Truly. For everything. I just came to check out a book and wanted to make sure yours got returned properly. I had no idea you worked here."

Cathy looked at him skeptically but realized there was no way he could know where she worked simply from yesterday's incident. "Okay. I'm sorry," she said. She looked towards the ground and squinted.

"Here," the man said, bending down, "looking for these?" He gave her back her glasses.

"Th...thank you. *Again*." She put on her glasses, and for the first time,

Cathy got a good look at him: tall, great hair, green eyes, broad shoulders- basically, like he literally jumped off the cover of every romance novel in the library.

As if reading her mind, Elaine stared at him wide-eyed, sensing that he really was a cover man come to life.

"What book?" Cathy asked.

"Excuse me?" he replied.

"What book did you need under the ladder?"

"Oh. This one," he said, reaching and grabbing a travel guide to Yosemite National Park. "I've always wanted to go and -"

"I've been," Cathy interrupted. "It's breathtaking. I actually like to do day hikes there sometimes. I stayed at The Ahwahnee Hotel, which has the best views! The trees, the cliffs, the waterfalls, the -" she caught herself before she went any further. She had let her guard down and was gushing and needed to stop. "I mean, I'm sure you'll love it," she said curtly. *This is crazy*, she thought. *There's no way I have something in common with this Neanderthal.*

He was smiling. "Maybe you can be my tour guide there one day," he said.

She gawked at him. "Think again, nature boy!"

He laughed. "That was presumptuous of me. How about dinner first? Or lunch? To apologize further. I promise I'll leave Kong at home."

Elaine's eyes flew open, and she beamed. "Yes!" she exclaimed for Cathy.

Cathy glared at Elaine.

"Sorry," Elaine mouthed. Cathy rolled her eyes.

"I'm busy that day," Cathy said.

"But I didn't give you a specific day -" he started.

"Yes...but..."

"Please? I normally don't beg, but I feel I need to apologize even more," he said.

He looked so cute with his eyebrows raised. Cathy's mind was telling her, "Absolutely not!" but her heart was telling her, "Go for it!". *That's not my heart*, Cathy thought wryly.

Elaine nudged Cathy.

"Fine!" Cathy relented. "But just so you can apologize." She couldn't believe she had given in. She shook her head.

"Awesome!" he exclaimed with a huge grin. "That makes me happy. But right now, I need to run. Can I get your number? I'll call to finalize the plans."

Cathy went to the table, wrote down her number, and handed it to him. "If I don't answer, leave a message on the machine."

"The...*machine?*" he asked quizzically.

"She'll answer," Elaine interrupted.

"Okay, great," he said before turning and walking towards the door. Elaine's eyes followed his walk.

"Wait!" Cathy yelled. "I never got your name."

He turned and smiled big at her. Bright, even teeth.

"Bradley," he said. "Bradley Harris."

CHAPTER 23

The *ding* in the kitchen let Cathy know her chicken pot pie was ready. After the Lean Cuisine lasagna sat in the microwave for fifteen hours last time, she warded off lasagna forever. The pot pie was a safe alternative.

She padded in her slippers across the linoleum flooring. She took out her pot pie and retrieved a small pre-made salad from the fridge. After settling with a TV tray on her sofa, she turned on the television.

That's when she heard a noise outside. A creak was more like it. Just outside the front door. *Was someone on the front porch?* Cathy pushed her tray aside and slowly walked towards the door, clutching the remote control like a wimpy weapon. She inched her way to the door as she heard another creak, then a thud. She stood up straight, startled. *What was that?*

"Hello?" she whispered hoarsely.

Nothing.

A couple of inches further.

"Hello!" a little more assertive this time.

She gritted her teeth and pursed her lips as she put her hand on the knob. She yanked open the door to – nothing. No one. She closed her robe tight to her body and hugged herself as she peered outside. She looked around. The wind had picked up, and a few leaves rustled across the walkway. "This feels like some Halloween horror movie shit," she muttered. "Nope."

She started to head back in but looked down and saw a box. Sealed shut. Just a regular, everyday, brown, unobtrusive, probably-has-a-head-in-it box. *Stop it.*

Cathy saw a piece of paper taped to the top. She read the scribbled note.

HE'S SOWWY, TOO.

Cathy had seen enough creepy movies to know picking up this box, bringing it inside, and opening it was the worst idea among bad ideas. These boxes were always harbingers of doom. She also knew the dumb blonde who did such a thing ended up with her head chopped off by some machete-wielding maniac. But Cathy was not dumb. *Nor am I blonde.*

Confidently, she lifted the box and took it inside. It was lighter than she imagined. *No head.* She looked around outside one final time before closing the door behind her and turning the deadbolt.

The man outside looked at Cathy's house and stood silent, smiling, as if challenged by the sound of her locking the door.

Cathy headed to the kitchen and set the box on the table. With hands on hips, she stared, wondering if she should go through with this.

"Screw it," she said.

Grabbing scissors, she sliced through the tape. Gingerly, she pulled back the four cardboard flaps. There was a lot of tissue in the box, and she carefully took it out piece by piece. "Is there anything in here?" she grumbled. And then she saw it.

At the bottom of the box was a Polaroid turned upside down. She grabbed it and turned it over.

It was a picture of the sweetest little black dog's face she'd ever seen. The eyes were woeful and almost…remorseful. There was writing on the white margin of the photo:

I'M SOWWY. I DIDN'T MEAN TO BE SO RUFF. PWEEZE FORGIVE ME.

Cathy couldn't help but smile. The picture was of Kong. And obviously, Bradley was making sure Cathy knew Kong was apologetic about the park incident.

It was preposterous.

It was idiotic.

It was the sweetest thing she'd ever received.

It never occurred to Cathy how Bradley Harris knew where she lived.

CHAPTER 24

Cathy's phone rang, and it was Bradley calling.

"Thank you for the picture," she said. "It's cute. Odd, but cute."

He laughed. "If you think that's odd, how about going to dinner with me tonight? I know, we just met, and you think my dog tried to kill you, but I promise to leave him at home."

It was her turn to laugh. She had to admit she hadn't been on a date in a while, and besides, he did save her from splatting to the ground in the library. She owed him at least the company of going with him to dinner.

"Sounds good. But only if I pay my own way," she said.

He was tempted to argue with her a little, but after witnessing what a spitfire she was, he thought better of it. "Fine," he said. "But I'm driving. I'll pick you up at 7:00."

Cathy looked at her watch. Thirty minutes. She had to hurry.

No sooner had she replaced the phone in its cradle than it rang again.

"Cancelling already?" she asked, smiling.

"Um, hello?"

"Oh! Elaine, hi! Sorry, I thought you were someone else." At the slip-up, Cathy shifted the left side of her mouth down. *Oops.* Cathy wasn't ready to discuss too much with Elaine about her night with Bradley.

"Obviously."

"So, what's going on?" Cathy asked, hoping to change the subject.

"Oh, well, I was wondering if you'd like to go to the movies tonight?"

"I wish I could," Cathy said truthfully. "But I have plans tonight." She could visualize Elaine's eyes growing in size. She heard a lot of 'ooohs' and 'ahhhs' through the receiver. Cathy rolled her eyes and now knew why she didn't want to discuss tonight's date with Bradley. She checked the time on her watch. She now had 22 minutes to get ready. She had to run. "In fact, I'm running a bit behind. Mind if we catch up tomorrow?"

"Sure! But I want de -"

Cathy had already hung up.

She ran and jumped in the shower. Because of the running water, she never heard the phone ring for the third time, nor did she hear the message left on the machine.

Cathy stepped out of the shower, and before she could wrap a towel around her, she felt a slight breeze on her wet skin. It was coming from the hallway and right into her bedroom. She grabbed a towel and dried herself off as she walked down the hall. She lived alone, so she did not need to worry, but the breeze was a little concerning. Had she left a window open? She stepped into the den and saw the back of a man standing by the fireplace.

She screamed.

She raised her hands to her mouth, dropping the towel in the process. The man turned around.

It was Bradley.

"What the heck?!" she yelled. "What are you doing here?!" Her voice rose in anger. "Oh, my god!!"

"Oh, shit! I am so sorry!" he said, putting up his palms in apology. "The door…it was already cracked open, and I heard your voice say 'hello', so I walked in."

"That's…that's impossible!" she stated. "I've been in the shower and-"

Her landline started ringing. When she didn't answer, the answering machine picked up, and she heard her voice say, "Hello. Leave a message". Bradley must've heard the machine and thought it was her. Cathy closed her eyes and shook her head. "I'm sorry. It must've been my machine you heard."

"Ummm…" he started.

"Someone must've left a message. I'm sorry I got so upset." She noticed Bradley was just standing there. Not saying a word. *A bit rude if you ask me.* "Have you got anything to say?" she asked.

"Ummm, have you got any clothes? Nice necklace, by the way," he said.

Cathy looked down and noticed, except for the orange poppy charm dangling from a necklace, she was totally naked.

She shrieked before running away.

Bradley chuckled and whistled approvingly.

She yelled from her bedroom. "I think you should go."

"Why? We have dinner plans."

"You have to ask?" she said.

"Look, I'm sorry to barge in like I did." He turned around to face the wall, not sure why. "I…I'm really sorry. But if it's any consolation, at least we got the awkward part of our date out of the way already, right?"

Silence.

"And I gotta say, wow! You look amazing!"

"Not helping!" she cried from the bedroom.

"Okay. I'll go." There was a sad lilt to his voice. "Again, I'm sorry. Can I call you later?"

Silence again.

"Okay. Bye…" he said, with one last hopeful note. He headed towards the door.

Cathy was beside herself. She wasn't ashamed of her body. She'd done enough hiking and exercise to get into the shape that she was. But still. A total stranger had just seen everything. And she meant *everything*. She bowed her head and covered her hands with her face. She had to admit Bradley was hot. *Smokin' hot.* And he seemed nice, to boot. When was the last time she had gone out with someone like Bradley? *Never. That's when.* And she felt this chance may never come again.

Cathy took a deep breath and squinted her eyes.

"Wait!" she called out. She poked her head around the doorframe. His back was to her, and he was standing near the open doorway. She smiled sheepishly. "Sit. I'll be right back."

Twenty minutes later, he was opening the passenger side door for her to slide in. He closed the door, then walked towards his side. As he opened his door, she said, "Oh, shoot. I forgot to leave a light on for when I get home. I'm not used to going out this time of night. It'll be dark when I get back." She started to open her car door.

"I'll get it," he said.

"Oh, thanks. Just turn the lamp on that's on the end table." She handed him her house keys.

He bounded up the stairs to the front door and let himself in. When he looked back, Cathy had the visor down, checking her face.

Bradley turned back and shut the door behind him. He remembered the phone ringing earlier. *Always pay attention,* he remembered his mentor telling him. He entered the kitchen and saw a red light flashing on the answering machine. He pressed PLAY.

YOU HAVE TWO NEW MESSAGES, the mechanical voice said. PRESS ONE TO HEAR YOUR MESSAGES.

Bradley pressed one.

"Cathy, hi. It's Dana. [pause] I hope you're doing well. It's been a really long time since we chatted, and, well, I just felt it's time to...I mean, with Brooke missing and...oh, God, did you even know about that? I hope you did because I really didn't want you to find out this way. Shit. I'm sorry. [pause] Anyway, we need to catch up. Work at the clinic is going great, always busy. A lot of pets need my expertise [laughter]. Wow, that wasn't arrogant at all [nervous laughter] [pause] And in less arrogant news, I'm engaged! Yay me! I can't wait for you to meet him. He's a really great guy. Anyway, I'll go before the machine cuts me off. Call me if you want. [long pause] Miss you, babe."

The machine said PRESS SEVEN TO DELETE MESSAGE OR PRESS EIGHT TO KEEP MESSAGE

Bradley's finger hesitated over the buttons. *Dana.* He pressed seven.

MESSAGE DELETED. MESSAGE TWO. PRESS ONE TO HEAR MESSAGE.

Again, Bradley pressed one.

"Cathy, it's mom. Look, there's news about Brooke, and it's not good. She was seeing someone, and now he's a suspect in her disappearance, only – he's disappeared, too. Don't ask me how I know. And since you and Brooke were close, I wanted to tell you myself. There's more, but -" There was a pause. "Geesh, I really wish you'd get a cellphone because-"

Bradley pressed STOP. He had heard enough.

A mechanical voice said PRESS SEVEN TO DELETE MESSAGE OR PRESS EIGHT TO KEEP MESSAGE

Bradley pressed seven.

He quickly turned on the lamp, then walked out of the house.

CHAPTER 25

They ate dinner at Chops, one of the city's best steakhouses. But Cathy was almost too nervous to eat. The waiter brought over an enormous basket of breads and flavored butters. Bradley dug in, carbs be damned. Cathy marveled at how he could eat so much and still maintain his physique.

"What?" he asked, noticing her shocked expression.

"What? Oh, nothing. Just wondering what all that bread would do to my body," she said absently. Too late, she realized she referenced her body, which he had seen every nook and cranny of an hour ago.

Bradley gave a wry smile.

Cathy could feel the red heat bloom up her neck. "Oh, god, I'm stupid! Let's change the subject."

Bradley chuckled.

"Oh, my god, stop it!" she said, her face now completely crimson. She shook her head. Then she joined in on the laughter.

She noticed what a great, hearty laugh Bradley had, how his eyes glistened in the flickering light of the candle on the table, how perfect his hair was, and how his clothes fit him like a second skin.

She also noticed how everyone around them noticed, too. Eyes from women and men alike were ogling the god amongst them. It was kind of creepy if she did say so herself. Cathy needed to stake her claim. She placed her hand on his forearm and slid it back and forth. He raised his eyebrows. Several pairs of eyes got the hint and retreated to the safety of their own dates.

"So, now I know you embarrass easily," he said, "what else comes easy to you?"

Cathy took a sip of wine. She told him about her love for the outdoors and her trips to Yosemite, about her family and how she was twelve when her father left her and her mother, and her favorite band was Fleetwood Mac, and why she felt social media has hindered how families communicate these days, and –

"You're gorgeous," Bradley said, interrupting.

Her butter knife clanged on her plate and echoed throughout the small restaurant. Suddenly, all eyes were back on their table, but this time, she was the subject.

"I...uh..." she had no words.

"I mean it," he said. "I feel like the luckiest guy in the world right now."

At least he sounded sincere, she thought. Admittedly, she had taken a little more time in her appearance tonight than she normally would have. She changed out her glasses for contacts, wore her hair down over her shoulder in a soft wave, and her dress, a slinky black number she wore once to a funeral, fit her perfectly. She knew she looked very unlike the librarian side of her, but to hear Bradley tell her she looked 'gorgeous' was the cherry on top.

"Thank you," she blushed.

He took her hand from across the table, and she felt his eyes boring into hers. She felt a quivering down below. The candlelight suddenly felt like an inferno, and she felt a bead of sweat glide down her back. She reached for her wine to take a sip.

"How do you feel about marriage?" he asked.

Cathy gurgled and nearly choked on her wine. She wheezed but recovered quickly.

"What?" she coughed.

"I mean, do you want a small wedding or a big wedding? Isn't that something women think about?"

Cathy realized he was just asking a question. Not *the* question. Relief washed over her, and a memory swept into her mind, and in seconds, she felt the sting of tears. *Alicia was so happy. She had her whole life ahead of her with Ryan. Had....*

"What's wrong?" Bradley asked, noticing her solemness.

"Nothing," she lied. But Bradley was looking at her hopeful, wanting her to continue. "It's just that.... a friend has gone missing. Brooke Carson. We've been friends for a long time, and well, we've lost touch recently, but now.... I just miss her a little more than ever." Cathy dabbed her eyes with her napkin.

His hand squeezed hers. "I'm sorry for your loss," he said quietly.

"Loss?" she said defensively. "Brooke's not dead. She's just missing. She'll turn up. She has to, right?" Cathy released her hand from his, hurt.

"Of course, of course," he said. "What are the police doing to find her?"

Cathy didn't have an answer to that. She had a contact in the police division she could reach out to, and she made a mental note to call him on Monday.

The waiter brought dinner. Bradley ordered the ham, red beets, and corn; Cathy got a steak, salad, and potatoes.

"I'm not a fan of red meat," he explained.

"I do not like red beets and ham," she said.

"You don't?" he smiled. "Would you eat them in a house? Would you eat them with a mouse?"

"What?" she said, confused.

"Would you eat them in a box? Would you eat them with a fox?"

Then her mind clicked. "No. I would not eat them in a box. I would not eat them with a fox. Not in a house, not with a mouse." *Apparently, he liked Dr. Seuss, too—something else we have in common.*

They laughed.

As they ate, he said, "Tell me about your job. Why the library?"

Cathy noticed Bradley had changed the subject twice now since they talked about Brooke, and she was thankful for the change in topic. She liked him even more for his considerate act.

"Well, I love books and adventures, and even though I don't get to travel abroad or lead an exciting life, books take me away to exotic lands and universes, and I relish the escape. Plus, I learn a lot. Books are full of ideas."

He nodded his agreement.

"What about you?" she asked.

He told her he was in between jobs at the moment but would love to be a gypsy and just travel the world. He liked to work for six months to earn enough money to go somewhere, live and work there for six months, then go somewhere new and repeat the process.

Cathy's heart sank a little. For some reason, she was liking him more and more and the thought of him leaving after six months…! She wondered why this bothered her so much already. He was kind and considerate, and he filled a void in her life she never knew needed filling. She looked over at him, and he was smiling at her with his mega-watt teeth. And his body. She couldn't help but think what those arms would feel like around her, holding her, cuddling her, throwing her down on the bed, and taking control of her. She took a deep breath and came out of her fantasy. Her eyes opened and he was staring at her.

"What?" he asked.

Was it possible for him to read her thoughts? Could he sense her longing? Could he hear her heart pounding? She looked down to make sure her dress wasn't moving with the heart thumps. Cathy was no dating expert, and she'd only had sex a few times in her life. The first time she had sex, well, if that's what you wanted to call it, was after the Homecoming dance. Her date, a drunk Robbie Cartwright, climbed on top of her, and five humps later, he was done and was snoring by her side. So that doesn't really count.

Then there was that one time at the frat party with Ryan. But that turned out to be a huge mistake.

She looked at Bradley across from her and he was still staring at her, his eyes brooding and his biceps twitching, ready to grab her. Suddenly, she felt like the center of attention, like everyone in the restaurant was looking at them and could read the filthy thoughts tumbling through their minds. *You're so hot,* she thought.

"Excuse me?" he asked.

She had spoken aloud.

"Uhh, I'm hot. It's hot in here." *Shit.* She picked up her water glass and swallowed it all in one take. Now she had to pee. "Um, can we just go?" she asked.

"Sure. If you're ready."

And with certainty, she was. She looked at this man across from her and remembered the sweet things about him: the photo of Kong's apology, rescuing her from the ladder, holding the car door open for her, running back in to turn on a lamp for her. And the things they had in common: the outdoors, Yosemite, Dr. Seuss. And Cathy realized she had never met anyone like this man. All doubts flew out the window, and she found herself ready to be with Bradley in every way possible. The tension was palpable.

"I'm definitely ready," she replied suggestively.

Bradley threw some money on the table, and they hastily left the restaurant.

Cathy knew what was coming next, and she couldn't be more excited.

She couldn't be more scared.

It'll be fine. It'll be quick and easy, and I'll probably never see him again. I'll do this just this once, and he'll be gone before I know it.

He left Cathy's bed three days later.

CHAPTER 26

That was a week ago, and Cathy hadn't heard from Bradley since. She and Elaine were talking.

"Three days?" Elaine exclaimed. "My god! Can you give me details? Can you give me any hope for me? Can you give me anything? Can you even walk?"

Cathy laughed. It was wonderful. She had never felt this way before. Bradley was the missing puzzle piece in her life. In three short days, disbelievingly, she found herself falling in love. *Maybe those romance novels know a thing or two.*

Plus, he was a marvel in the bedroom. Although she had little to compare it to, Cathy was pretty sure he was a sexual superhero.

Elaine noticed the grin on Cathy's face. "Well, it has been a week since you've heard from him, so maybe *he's* the one who can't walk," she smirked.

Cathy playfully smacked Elaine's arm. "By the way, how are your dad and the car graveyard? Everything good?"

"Don't change the subject," Elaine said. "But he's good, thanks. Now, back to you."

"Delivery for Cathy Broderick," a UPS delivery man said, entering the library.

"That's me," Cathy said. She signed for the box. There was no return address.

"Nothing suspicious about that," Elaine said warily, eyeballing the box.

Cathy shook the box, and something heavy inside banged around.

"Stop! It could be a bomb."

"It's not a bomb, worrywart," Cathy said. She grabbed a box cutter and sliced through the tape. Slowly, she opened the box. Elaine was next to Cathy but leaning away as if that would save her from an explosion.

Cathy reached in and saw crumpled tissue paper. "Now.... let's.... just.... see.... what's...under.... all.... this.... BOOM!!" Cathy yelled, tossing the tissue paper into the air.

"AYIEEEE!" Elaine shrieked, covering her face with her hands.

Cathy was laughing hysterically, trying to catch her breath.

Elaine was panting, her hands now on her chest. She looked at Cathy. "Have you lost your damn mind?" she cried.

Cathy kept laughing. "That was hysterical!" she said.

"Whatever," Elaine said. "Thanks a lot."

Cathy finally caught her breath and pulled out the contents of the box. She set everything on the table next to the box. There was a compass, a survival kit, a backpack, a map of Yosemite, and a pair of size seven hiking boots.

"What the hell is all that?" Elaine asked.

Cathy shrugged. "There's a note," she said, holding it up to read.

> **YOU'RE OFF TO GREAT PLACES,**
> **TODAY IS YOUR DAY.**
> **YOUR MOUNTAIN IS WAITING,**
> **SO, GET ON YOUR WAY.**

Cathy laughed. *Dr. Seuss.* "Just an inside joke," she told Elaine

"Fine. Have it your way. I hope he turns out to be a serial killer," Elaine said before stomping away, taking her bruised ego with her.

Cathy smiled, but inside, she was a little miffed that she hadn't heard from Bradley in almost a week. She knew living the life of a Luddite and not having a cell phone made things harder for people to reach her. *Still.* She picked up the note again and reread it. Her heart skipped a beat. It really was a sweet gesture.

"Looks like we're going camping," she said out loud to know one. "This should be fun!"

After work, Cathy's drive home was frightening. It was dark, and her pitiful headlights did nothing to shine a path through the downpour. The rain was torrential, and she could barely see where she was going. Her windshield wipers were at their maximum speed, and all they did was smear the deluge of water even more. The inside glass began to fog up, and she started to panic.

The thunderstorm sent lightning bolts so low she felt they would strike the roof of the car at any given moment. She yelped at a couple of close calls. The sound was loud and shocking, and she found herself jumping and shrieking more than once. Her car hydroplaned on Third Avenue and again on Prospect Avenue. Her nerves were completely frazzled by the time she pulled into her driveway.

Before stepping out of the car, Cathy got her umbrella prepped. As she stepped out of the car, she raised her umbrella, and the strong wind turned it inside out. A lightning strike zapped above her, but her scream was drowned out by a clap of thunder. She ran up the steps to her porch and uselessly shook off the rainwater. She stood on the front porch like a drowned rat, her glasses covered in droplets and her chest heaving with big breaths.

"Holy *shit!*" she said. She forced her umbrella back to normal and snapped the straps together. She stepped inside her house and flicked the light switch.

The power was out.

She flicked the switch up and down. Up, down.

Nothing. It was dark outside and in.

A chill swept through her from head to toe. And that's when she heard the noise.

From the kitchen. A *clink.* She froze.

She took a tentative step forward.

Lightning illuminated the room, and shadows briefly danced. The dead room came alive, then died again, and thunder shook the walls.

Gulp.

Another noise.

She stopped in her tracks, wielding the umbrella like a sword in front of her. Her heart was pounding so loudly it practically drowned out the thunder. She was near the entrance to the kitchen. The umbrella entered first.

As she took another step, she saw a shape, a dark, ominous shadow, standing by the refrigerator. Her glasses were still covered with water, so it was still unclear what she was seeing. Then lightning flashed and briefly lit up the room: a person. A boom of thunder.

It was still too dark to make out who it was.

Oh my god, she thought. She held the umbrella high in front of her and spoke.

"Who-" but just then, lightning struck, and the figure turned to look at Cathy.

They both screamed.

CHAPTER 27

"*Mother!* What the hell?!"

"Cathy! You scared the bejeezus out of me!"

"I scared *you*? My heart is *still* pounding. What are you doing here?"

Linda Broderick took a teakettle off the stove. "I was making tea before the power went out. The weather is so dreadful I thought this might warm us up. This should still be hot." She lightly touched the side of the kettle and smiled when she felt the warmth. "Sit. I'll pour you a cup."

Cathy's eyes were still wide, but she sat at the table. "Mother, you haven't answered my question. What are you doing here?"

Linda set two mugs on the table and put a teabag into each one. As she poured the hot water, she spoke.

"I was worried about you, honey. I haven't heard from you in several days. You're not returning any of my calls."

"What calls?"

"I've left messages. And look, I'm sorry about how we ended lunch that day and -"

"I never got any messages," Cathy said. "There were none on my machine. Or else I would've called you back."

Linda waved her hand in the air to dismiss the whole thing. "It doesn't matter. I'm just glad you're safe." Linda sat down to join Cathy.

Cathy noticed that even with all the makeup, big hair, and tight, bright blouse, her mother looked tired. Worried.

"Mom, what is it? What's wrong?" Cathy could see tears brimming in her mother's eyes.

Linda held Cathy's hand. "Oh, honey, I just...I'm just so sorry for everything... and you know I don't mean to judge you or add stress to you." She paused, then spoke haltingly. "I know you're worried about Brooke, we all are, and, well...there's some news that -"

Cathy's landline rang, shrilling through the still-dark room, and they both jumped.

"Now, see?" Cathy said, waving her hand in the dark. "If I didn't have a landline, no one could reach me." She smiled. "Hold that thought." Cathy picked up the phone. "Hello?"

"Hi," a deep voice answered.

It was Bradley! After all this time. Cathy felt a surge course through her body. Was that relief? Anger? Agitation?

She went with relief.

"Hi," she said quietly.

"Hello," he said through the receiver. His voice was husky, and in her ear, it made her tingle.

"I...I've missed you," Cathy said, almost in a whisper. She looked back at her mother. Linda was sitting at the table, sipping her tea, looking down, but her head was cocked at an angle where she was trying to listen in.

"I've missed you, too," he replied. "I've just had a lot going on and have been a bit preoccupied. But can we meet for lunch tomorrow? I'd love to get together so we can discuss our camping trip."

"Yeah, I got your package. That was thoughtful," she said. "Dr. Seuss? Really?"

He laughed. "Thought you might get a kick out of that."

Cathy grinned.

"So, tomorrow?" he asked.

"Sure. Delancey's on the Embarcadero?" It was a favorite restaurant of Cathy's and near her work.

"Perfect. I'll meet you there at noon."

"Noon."

He whispered something in the phone that she could barely hear. Her face rushed red, and she looked back at her mother, who was smiling with widened eyes.

Cathy hung up the phone.

"So, what was that all about?" Linda asked.

Cathy sat back down at the table. "Nothing. Just someone at work wanting to know if I can pick up a shift, that's all."

Linda knew she was lying, but she would let her have this one.

"You started to say something about Brooke earlier," Cathy reminded her mother. "What was it you wanted to say? Have there been any recent developments?"

Linda saw Cathy looking happier than she had in a long while, and after this phone call, it was apparent Cathy might be seeing someone. She didn't want to tarnish Cathy's newfound happiness, so Linda felt a little white lie was appropriate. She found her resolve and lifted her head. "No, nothing new." She patted Cathy's hand. "But I feel they are getting close to finding her safe and sound."

Linda looked at her daughter. Ever since Linda's husband left her to raise Cathy by herself, Linda had been cautious of every man in their lives. Of people in general, to be honest. The abandonment left something broken in Linda. It was just her and Cathy against the world, and she would do anything to protect her little girl. And that's why she had called her friend Michael and asked him for a favor to look after Cathy. She remembered the call.

"Michael. How are you? How's the family?"

"We're good, Linda. And with you?"

"All good, thanks. How's that beautiful niece of yours?"

"Misty? Oh, busy keeping out of trouble. Did you know she moved out? Got her own place now."

When Misty was four, Linda knew she came to live with her uncle and aunt after her parents were busted on drug charges. Michael and Misty's father were siblings, and Michael was actually the detective who busted her parents. It was a big scandal in their little town, but it was a peaceful transition for Misty to *come live with Michael and Karen. Misty adapted wonderfully and became the child Michael and Karen never had. And Misty was friends with all the girls. Misty was never as close as the other four, but she was always her own person.*

"Oh, that's great. But I'm sure you and Karen miss her being around, huh?"

"We miss her like crazy."

Linda could hear his voice thicken with emotion.

He cleared his throat. "Karen said you had a favor to ask of me?"

Linda had to be careful. She didn't want to sound worried, but she wanted to take every precaution. Brooke's disappearance brought things just a little too close to home.

"Yes, I do," she replied. "I understand that Brooke Carson is missing, and, well, she and Cathy were...umm, are friends, and I wanted to ask the detective side of you if you could keep an eye on her for me? You know, just in your travels."

"Sure. I understand where you're coming from. Does she still live in the same house?"

"On Hampton Street. Yes."

"Fine. I'll do what I can, Linda."

"Thank you, Michael. I really appreciate it. If anything changes, I'll call and let you know. Please give Karen my love."

"Will do. Goodnight"

Linda felt better after that call. She would do anything to protect her daughter, but Linda's heart ached for the Carsons. Brooke had been missing for a while now, and her safe return was looking more and more fleeting. She was grateful her daughter was safe and sound, so she decided now was not the right time to discuss Cathy's missing friend.

Michael called Linda a few days later, telling her Cathy just seemed to be doing normal everyday things, nothing to be alarmed about. Relieved, Linda asked if there was anything new where Brooke was concerned. He informed her Brooke's boyfriend, someone named Bradley, was a person of interest in her disappearance, but no one seemed to be able to locate him, and to please keep that to herself. He was only telling her because of their friendship.

Linda debated whether to tell Cathy what she had found out. She had the name of a person of interest! But then again, maybe she shouldn't say anything because that could get Cathy's hopes up. Plus, if the guy was innocent, it could hurt his reputation.

Without knowing whose fate she was about to seal, Linda decided not to tell Cathy a word.

What she doesn't know won't hurt her.

CHAPTER 28

The rain outside was still coming down. It had been raining for two full days, and roads were swollen from the deluge. It wasn't easy getting to the restaurant, but she had made it.

"More water?"

The server asked Cathy if he could refill her glass for the fifth time, and he sounded a bit agitated. " I'm already about to float away, " she thought.

"No, thank you," she said. Cathy felt embarrassed. She had been sitting in the restaurant for over forty-five minutes waiting for Bradley, who was a no-show. She started to gather her handbag and umbrella. "I'm just going to go. I'm sorry I...um, but my party hasn't shown up and-"

"No problem," the waiter said, handing Cathy a black plastic holder with the bill inside.

"But...I just had...water," Cathy said, a little confused.

"Yes, but there's a charge for loitering, and, of course, you had lemons with your water. Soooo...." He cocked his head like, "This isn't my problem, honey."

Cathy's eyes got big, and she conjured up a look of disbelief. *I've never heard of such a thing!* She opened the holder and saw a charge for

$10.50. "But-" she started to say, but the face of the waiter changed her mind. She put $11 in the holder, closed it, and handed it to the server. "Keep the change," Cathy said pleasantly. He opened it up, looked inside, rolled his eyes, and huffed as he walked away.

She was not happy that she'd been stood up and had to pay $11 for a glass of water. Her day was not looking good.

By the time Cathy returned home, she had talked herself into being twice as mad as she was before leaving the restaurant. She called Elaine and told her she'd be coming into work to take her mind off the rotten day she was having. As she hung up the phone, she saw the box containing the camping information sitting on her table.

"Yeah, that's not gonna happen," she said, gathering up the box and walking outside to throw everything away in the trash bin. As she walked back in, movement out the window caught her eye. She heard a crunching noise, like someone – or something – was walking on broken glass. It was coming from outside along the side of her house.

"Damn raccoon," she said. She decided to scare it off. She went to the front door and yanked it open in a flourish, yelling and screaming like a mad woman, hoping to startle the critter into running off. As she turned the corner on her porch, she looked down the side of her house, and there was nothing. No critter. Nothing at all. Her head raises in triumph. "Guess I scared it away," she said. "And *stay* away!" she hollered. She went back inside to get ready to go to work.

"Thanks for coming in," Elaine said. "We've been busy with returns, so there's lots to put away."

"I appreciate you letting me come in. I've just had a weird day and need to take my mind off things."

"Things meaning *him*?" Elaine pushed.

Cathy looked knowingly at Elaine. "I'd rather not talk about it."

"Fine. Then you can start with Travel and Local Interests," Elaine said as she pointed to two large stacks of books on the cart.

Cathy got busy. She was glad none of the books required her to go more than two rungs up the ladder this time. With Bradley M.I.A., there'd be no one to catch her. *Stop it*, she told herself. *Get over it.*

She picked up a travel guide to Yosemite and glared at it as if willing it to burst into flames. She thought of all the plans she and Bradley had made – correction, plans *he* had made - for the two of them. And then he stood her up at the restaurant, and now –

She slammed the book down on the book cart, the loud sound echoing throughout the library. Several heads lifted from their quiet stupor.

"Wow. What did that book ever do to you?" a voice asked from behind her.

She whirled around. It was Bradley. A part of her was relieved to see him, another part not so much. She steeled her posture. "Good to know you're not dead," she growled before turning back to her work. Her knees spasmed. She felt their first fight coming on.

"Yeah," he stammered. "That's really good to know." He noticed her cold shoulder treatment. "Cathy, did I do something wrong?"

She heard a little boy's pleading in his voice. An innocent, unaware of their blunder. But none of that mattered. She spun on her heels and looked at him, confounded.

"Are you serious? You were supposed to meet me at Delancey's for lunch so we could discuss our camping trip, the one *you* planned, I might add, and then you didn't show up. You don't call! You don't do anything! What am I supposed to think?" She could feel a burning in her eyes from tears forming. She hated herself for showing this emotion.

Bradley looked hurt, like a puppy left on the side of the road.

"I'm so sorry, really. But there's a good reason why -"

"What? What could you possibly say that could make up for how you made me feel?"

"There…. there was an accident. With Kong. With all the rain, there were puddles everywhere, and when I took him out for a walk to go to the bathroom, he saw the puddles and, well, Kong loves playing in the water, so I let him off his leash to play a little bit." Bradley's voice started to quiver.

Cathy stood, listening.

"And he saw a puddle and jumped into it, only he missed, and his front legs went into the water, but his hind legs caught on the concrete ledge, and he slipped pretty bad, and -"

Cathy's eyes were wide with concern. "Oh, gosh. And?"

"And he broke his left hind leg. I had to take him to the vet, and we were there all day trying to fix him up. I was too worried to think of anything else. I'm so sorry! He's at Peterinarians right now."

Cathy looked at Bradley, horrified. She felt awful. How could she have jumped to such a despicable conclusion that Bradley had just abandoned her for no reason? She wanted to crawl under the book cart and die.

"Oh, Bradley! I am so sorry!" She went into his arms and hugged him. "How…how is Kong doing now?"

"He's back at my place, healing. Slowly. But he's young and, with physical therapy, should have a decent recovery. It's quite a task to get him from one place to another. He's a large dude."

Cathy knew only too well. But there was something else. Something Bradley had said. *Peterinarians. Why did that name sound so familiar?*

"So, I really am sorry that I didn't call, but the past few days have been pretty trying, as you can imagine. But I want to make it up to you," Bradley said. He grabbed the book about Yosemite she had thrown onto the cart. "I'm going to check this book out and come over to your place to cook dinner. We can discuss our trip tonight."

Cathy put her hand on her chest. "No way! You've got a lot going on. I'll come over to your place, and we can-"

"No!" he said too quickly, then recovered. "Kong is hurt and can't always make it outside in time to go to the bathroom, so sometimes, he accidentally goes inside, and well, my place isn't the cleanest of conditions…." He let the sentence hang, lowering his head as if embarrassed.

Cathy loved him for this. For thinking of her and not wanting to disappoint her.

"I understand," she said. And she did. She couldn't believe she had found the perfect gentleman: one who loves animals, cooks, and looks the way he does. She never saw this happening in her life, and she was overcome with gratitude.

Bradley took her in his arms and hugged her for a long time. Both were smiling.

But for entirely different reasons.

CHAPTER 29

They decided to go on the weekend before schools started back up. Bradley told her most families stayed home this weekend shopping for back-to-school items, and with smaller crowds venturing out of town, it was the best time to visit theme parks, museums, and, of course, Yosemite.

Cathy smiled. She knew Bradley wanted to be alone and not surrounded by a bunch of people. He had already told her he knew of a great remote area where they could set up their tent, far from the masses. The seclusion and privacy would bring an excellent opportunity to deepen their relationship.

He's so thoughtful.

The drive would typically be just under three and a half hours, but Bradley had a lot to show Cathy on the way, so they got an early start at 7:00 a.m. They made stops along Route 120 in quaint little towns with vowel-rich names like Alba, Adela, and Oakdale. They stopped at Arthur Michael Vineyards for a tour of the property and bought a bottle for their trip, then took a right to continue their journey, crossing over the beautiful Woods Creek and finally coming up to Rainbow Pool. Bradley insisted they take a quick dip in the cool, refreshing waters.

Cathy loved it. She could hear a waterfall in the background, and she let the peace envelop her. She couldn't remember a time she was so happy. She decided the sound of the waterfall was a good omen.

Back on the road, Cathy noticed the road had become more twisty and treacherous, with steep inclines and hairpin turns with no railings. One false move, and they'd plummet hundreds of feet to their deaths. Cathy shivered at the sight. She felt Bradley's hand on her thigh, a squeeze. She relaxed a bit. He looked over at her and caught his eyes. There was a kindness there that she hadn't noticed before. Oh, sure, she had noticed his vibrant green eyes and how they seemed to smile whenever they were together, but today, they were different, softer, sweeter. She felt an emotion that she hoped he reciprocated.

And still closer to the edge of the cliffs, they drove. The height was dizzying. She needed a diversion.

"How's Kong doing?"

"He's doing pretty good. I left him kenneled at Peterinarians while I was gone. The vet there is also into pet physical therapy, so she's helping him recuperate."

There's that name again: Peterinarians. Why do I know that place? Then it hit her: that's Dana's clinic. *Bradley probably deals with different doctors there, but I wonder if he's ever met Dana? I'll have to ask him.* But speaking of the vet, Cathy was secretly relieved Kong wasn't along for this trip since the last time they met, he had tried to rip her throat out. Instinctively, she rubbed her neck.

Finally, a little after 2:00 p.m., they pulled into the Yosemite entrance.

Bradley flashed a wilderness permit and drove into the park. He grabbed her hand and held it for the next thirty minutes. He pulled the car ten feet off the road, and Cathy noticed it was completely hidden from anyone who might be driving the path. When Bradley turned off the ignition, the silence was unbelievable. No leaves were rustling or water running. A little crunch in the woods was all she heard, probably from a rabbit inching along the ground. It was unnerving. But Bradley was beaming, and Cathy felt reassured. He leaned over and kissed her.

"Let's go!" he said enthusiastically.

"Go? Go where? Aren't we here?"

He laughed. "No. We have a little hike ahead of us. I'm taking you somewhere secluded. It's a special place. You'll love it. Promise." He opened his car door and hopped out.

Secluded? More secluded than this? Cathy couldn't fathom a more hermetic spot. She got out of the car and went to the back to help Bradley unpack the car.

Once they had their equipment, they hiked about a mile. Cathy was glad she was an outdoorsy type of person because the terrain was a bit challenging, but she found it invigorating, and she loved every minute of the scenery. The flowers and trees and wildlife were amazing. She hadn't seen another soul for the entire hike, and she grinned as she wondered if they had the park to themselves. *Wishful thinking,* she smiled. But she had seen a small black bear off in the distance, wandering through the Douglas firs, minding its own business. *Thank goodness,* she thought.

"Here we are!" Bradley announced, stretching his arms out high as he stood in the tucked-away spot. "Crane Creek."

And Cathy stood, stunned. Her eyes were full and unblinking as she stood in the surrounding mosaic.

Crane Creek wound gently over the landscape, its waters gliding over the large, smooth rocks on the riverbed. Pine violets, primrose, and larkspur grew wild, making the ground look like a glassy kaleidoscope. Cathy and Bradley found a spot near the creek's bank and set up their tent under the Jeffrey pines; their bark smelled of vanilla. Cathy had been to Yosemite before but had never seen it like this.

The air here was cleaner, and it was quiet. *So quiet!* Cathy stood near the large, rushing creek, and on a whim, she released a *whooo hooo* at the top of her lungs and heard the same words echo, running their course through the knolls and rock formations until they found their way back to her. Bradley was right: there were no crowds at all. This spot was as removed as they came. Like it was deserted. Cathy felt it was the most beautiful place on Earth. And that she and Bradley were the only two inhabitants left.

As they sat on the bank of Crane Creek, the sun started to set. The area was quiet except for the trickling of the creek's waters. A light breeze carried a low mooing of a sleepy animal across the tranquil terrain to where they sat. Cathy pulled out a book on Yosemite and started reading aloud about the trees and flowers in the area. She mentioned poppies.

"Like the one on your necklace?" Bradley asked. "Isn't that the flower that makes you sleepy?"

"May I continue?" she asked, smiling.

He gestured for her to carry on.

"And no, it's not the actual flower that makes you sleepy. It's the opiates inside." She read from the book. "The seedpod is first incised with a multi-bladed tool that lets the opium "gum" ooze out. Since ancient times, people have scraped off and air-dried the milky fluid that seeps from cuts in the unripe poppy seedpod." She paused. "And voila! Opium!"

He looked at her quizzically. "Interesting."

"I'm sure there's more to it, but those are the basics. Give or take," she said.

She grabbed another book.

"How many books did you bring?" he asked.

"Enough to get me through this trip," she responded. She started reading up on their hike to the Mist Trail tomorrow. She saw where the trail rested at a 2,900-foot elevation, and for a second, the height caused her breath to catch. But she loved Bradley, and more than that, she trusted him to love her back and keep her safe.

She read out loud.

"The Mist Trail is one of Yosemite's classic and most popular hikes. Many people hike to the top of Vernal Falls using this trail. Vernal Falls stands at 317 feet tall and is among the most powerful waterfalls in Yosemite. You'll find an excellent view of the falls from the footbridge. Or, to proceed directly to the top of Vernal Falls, follow Mist Trail half a mile up a steep granite stairway of over 600 steps. This staircase is protected by a railing, but because of a tremendous amount of waterfall spray, the steps are wet, so place your feet with caution. Prepare for slippery footing-"

"*What?*" Bradley said, his eyes popped open.

"Hush," Cathy said. She continued: "Prepare for slippery footing, and when at the top, under no circumstance should you climb past the railing at the lip of the falls." She looked at Bradley in mock menace. "Or you could die in the frenzied maelstrom below." She smiled broadly and laughed an evil laugh.

"Stop it," he said, suddenly looking solemn. He sniffled.

Allergies?

Bradley said, "I'm going to bed."

Cathy wondered what she had said that made Bradley react the way he had. "Hey," she said as he walked towards the tent.

He turned and looked at her.

She smiled sincerely this time. "I love you," she said. The moon seemed to brighten, and the vanilla-scented air was more fragrant than before. It was the right thing to say at the time.

Bradley looked back at her, his expression unreadable. The corner of his mouth raised a little before he turned and went inside to go to bed.

Cathy felt lost. The change in dynamics was unusual, and she sat there wondering what had just transpired. Ten minutes later, she went into their tent and lay down beside him. They didn't make love that night.

Neither one slept.

CHAPTER 30

When Cathy got up the next morning, Bradley wasn't in the tent. She found him down by the water.

"You okay?" she asked.

He turned slowly and looked at her. "Perfect. Why?"

"Just making sure." But she wasn't sure.

After a couple of protein bars and coffee, they gathered their gear and set off for Mist Trail. They traversed Old Big Oak Flat Road Trail and crossed over large bridges made of fallen Douglas Fir trees. What little light could pierce its way through the thick foliage to the floor of the park spotlighted colorful flowers while dragonflies and lacewings fluttered through the beams. Cathy expected to hear David Attenborough's voice any minute.

Cathy and Bradley had been in Yosemite for a couple of days now, and although spending time and sharing this adventure with Bradley was perfect, Cathy couldn't help but feel a little sad she hadn't shared with her mother yet that she had met someone and was now sharing life with him. The thought of calling her mother crossed her mind, and, for once, she regretted not owning a cell phone. *I'll call her when I get back,* Cathy told herself. Just thinking of getting in touch with her mother and telling her about all the wonderful things going on in her life lately brought a small smile to Cathy's lips. She looked, and Bradley was about twenty feet ahead of her. She jogged to catch up.

Cathy had made sure her research conjured up the safest routes, and they found the trails relatively smooth, but occasionally, because of a steep grade, they would need to stop and rest at viewpoints like Yosemite Valley and Eagle Peak. When they passed Yosemite Falls, they took a minute to refill their canteens with fresh water. Cathy loved the sights. She wished she had brought her phone to snap pictures, but Bradley insisted no technology would accompany them on this trip. He wanted her all to himself, he had said. She found that oddly romantic.

But not as oddly romantic as his next suggestion.

"Let's skinny dip!"

"Excuse me?" Cathy asked, shocked.

"Here, in the falls. Look." He waved his arms out ceremoniously. "There's no one around."

Obviously, his idea of 'no one' didn't include the many families enjoying the falls along the banks of the pool.

"There are *lots* of people around," she said through a gritted smile, hoping to deflect any attention from them in case somebody had heard Bradley.

He walked about fifty steps away from her, finding a spot more secluded behind the plummeting waters. "There's no one over *here*," he yelled. He spun around like he had found Willy Wonka's magical candy room.

"Shhhh!!" she said, putting her index finger to her lips. A smile formed behind that finger. She found Bradley's enthusiasm rather cute. Out of place but cute. But as she looked, she noticed that there wasn't anyone around, and no one could see him from where he stood. *Could we?* she thought. *I mean, anyone would really only see our heads above water and nothing else.* The right side of her mouth twisted up, and she felt devilish. *Do it!* she heard an inner voice say.

She walked towards Bradley, looking left and right quickly with each step, but then realized her twitching might draw attention that she was some weirdo walking alone with some neck spasm. She straightened up, and within ten more steps, she was in Bradley's arms. He had already taken off his shirt, and she realized she was in her happy place.

"You're crazy!" she said. *"We're* crazy!"

"Yup!" he said, pulling his shoes and socks off, a massive smile on his face.

Cathy quickly joined in the disrobing, glancing over her shoulder now and then. They heard a rustling in the tall grass. A critter slinked by, then stopped and looked at Cathy and Bradley. It blinked once, shook its head, then moved on.

"That was a marmot. Harmless," Cathy said, glad she had done her research. "But I think he just judged me."

When the last of their clothes fell to the ground, they stood naked in front of each other.

"My god, Cathy. You are beautiful," Bradley said, giving a small whistle.

"Takes one to know one," she said, sidling up to him, their skin melding together. She leaned up and kissed him, his maleness against her pelvis.

"Mom! What's that?"

Bradley and Cathy froze. Had the kid seen them? Their eyes were wide.

"That's a Western Pond turtle," a female voice said. "It's the only species of turtle here in Yosemite." It was clear the mother had done her research, too. "Don't get too close. It could snap at you." Cathy heard the little boy huff his disappointment, then their voices faded.

"Coast is clear," Bradley said, breaking away from their embrace, running and diving into the cool water.

"Oh, my god," Cathy said as she tip-toed a little more cautiously into the coldness. "Yikes," she shivered.

"Come on, chicken," he goaded.

Bravely, she glided into the water and sank underneath, quickly emerging with wet hair and chattering teeth. Bradley swam over to be with her, collecting her in his arms and holding her tight. They stood facing each other, their feet planted firmly on the hard silt. She could feel his hardness pressed against her. Cathy marveled the cold water had zero effect on shrinkage for Bradley. She blushed.

"What?" he asked.

"Nothing. Nothing at all," she murmured. She looped her arms behind his neck and pulled him into a deep kiss. And there, hidden in the cool, rippling waters of the reservoir, they made love.

Afterward, they climbed out of the water and lay naked, hidden amongst the tall sedges grass and western Azaleas. They dabbed each other with towels to dry off, and suddenly, Bradley rolled on top of her. He looked into her eyes, and once again, she saw the sweetness in his gaze.

"I love you, Cathy," he said.

Cathy had never been happier. "I love you, too."

And as they made love again, she held on tight, their bodies tangled into one ecstatic mound.

And she thought, *if I died today, I'd die a happy woman.*

Rejuvenated, they continued their trek to Mist Trail and Vernal Falls. In a couple of hours, Cathy found the trail a little rockier than she expected, so she placed each foot thoughtfully and gingerly. Thankfully, they both managed to get through the pathway without spraining an ankle on the large stones.

As the low sun disappeared behind clouds and the branches became denser, the temperature dropped a little. The chill bored into their bones and seemingly caused them to rattle inside their skin. The trail continued several hundred yards at an incline, and Cathy was getting a little more winded. Her breathing became thicker. But thankfully, she heard the roar of the falls just ahead.

They had finally reached Mist Trail.

There were no other hikers around. "We're the only stupid ones," she huffed sardonically. She looked back, and Bradley was about fifteen feet behind her, squatting down to tie his shoe. He stood up and leaned on the sign that read, "MIST TRAIL OPEN". He smiled at her and waved before kneeling to tie his other shoe. It was getting late, and Cathy had to admit that even for someone like herself who was used to the outdoors, this hike had been arduous. Bradley stopping to tie his shoes at the sign was a welcome stop. If anything, she was happy for the rest.

"Ready?" Bradley said, bounding up beside her.

Well, that didn't last long.

"Yep. Let's go!" she said with as much enthusiasm as she could muster.

As their approach to the stone staircase and railings lessened, the sound of Vernal Falls became absolutely deafening. Almost violent. Cathy's heart pounded with every thrash of water that went over the edge. She found herself at a complete standstill, her body petrified to the spot where she stood. She was unsure of her next steps. She wasn't sure she even wanted to move forward. Bradley came up and stood next to her and held her hand. They looked up, almost straight up, the back of their heads resting on the napes of their necks. The sight before them looked nothing less than a slippery deathtrap. Cathy's fear of heights began to rise and take over.

They were at the base of the staircase.

"I've got you," Bradley said quietly. "I won't let anything happen to you."

She couldn't hear him over the rush of the water, but she could *feel* him. Cathy looked at him, but he had turned his head away. She furrowed her brow. *Was he scared?* She caught a small glimpse of his face. *No. It was something else.* But she couldn't figure it out.

Holding onto the railing, they began their climb. And the more they climbed, the slipperier it became. The railing was wet and was of no use as a support mechanism. Cathy pulled her nylon hoodie over her head and tightened the cords. Higher and higher, they ascended, over 600 steps straight up; the falls grew more and more deafening until, gratefully, they were near the top. Cathy's nerves were shot, and she felt her legs become frail and unsteady.

Cathy looked around, and the sight was amazing, but she couldn't go any further. The falls were huge and torrential; gushing flumes plummeted over 300 feet straight down over jagged rocks, crashing into a raging churn. She gripped the railing with all her might. Bradley was one step below her. She turned and yelled.

"IT SEEMS TOO DANGEROUS! IT DOESN'T SEEM SUITABLE!"

He leaned in to hear better. "YOU'RE RIGHT! IT'S BEAUTIFUL!" he yelled back.

She shook her head. "NO! I THINK WE SHOULD TURN AROUND!"

His eyes were scrunched to keep the spray out. "I DON'T THINK IT'S OPEN YEAR-ROUND!"

The explosion of the falls drowned out all other sounds, and when she looked around, she saw no other person. Cathy could barely hear her own thoughts. It was almost eerie.

Before she knew it, Bradley had stepped up to join her and lifted his leg over the railing, crossing over to the side only feet from the falls. He seemed to levitate. He gripped the railing with one hand and held out his other for her to grab.

She shook her head vehemently. "I CAN'T DO IT!"

"I GOT YOU," he reassured. "DO YOU TRUST ME?"

That was something she heard clearly. *Did* she trust him? It was a legitimate question. They hadn't known each other that long. And until he came along, she only had women in her life. Like Brooke and Dana. Cathy regretted letting them slide out of her life. But that time was too painful to reflect on. She felt tears fall down her face, mixing with the spray of the falls.

She looked at this man in the eyes and thought of all they'd been through. Maybe Kong really *did* just get loose, and Bradley *did* save her from him. And he did catch her when she fell off the ladder at the library, after all. But then there was that time he was gone for over a week. But then he had brought Dr. Seuss into the mix. Cathy felt a sly grin form on her lips. She felt conflicted. There were several pros and cons to weigh, but, in the end, the pros won. And she realized she did trust him. She loved him. And isn't that what love was all about? *I trust him with my life.*

He was still looking at her, smiling. She answered him by reaching out her own hand to take his. But she also said a little prayer. *Can't be too careful.*

Cathy shut her eyes and stepped over the railing. Her feet slipped and gave way. She released Bradley's hand and fell against the railing, holding on for dear life with both arms. Wobbling, she stood and found her footing. She took several deep breaths before opening her eyes and turning to face Bradley.

He wasn't smiling anymore.

"BRADLEY?" she asked. "ARE YOU OKAY?"

He didn't answer. Or maybe he couldn't hear her.

He reached inside his jacket, took out a folded-up piece of paper, and slapped it onto her chest.

"OW!" she said, instinctively releasing one hand from the railing to press the paper down. Her feet shifted on the moss-covered wetness. She looked quizzically at the paper and then at him, then asked, "WHAT IS THIS?"

He ignored her.

She shook the piece of paper open and looked at it. But it wasn't just a piece of paper: it was a picture. From over a year ago.

There were three girls. All friends. She and Brooke were bookends, with Dana in the middle. And Gio was there, too.

They were smiling. Happy.

Cathy flashed back to that day. *The drinking. The accident.*

The deaths.

Her brows furrowed in question. "WHAT...." she began to ask. "I DON'T UNDERSTAND."

But Bradley was no longer looking at her. He was looking down.

Then, like a lightning bolt, she understood. Something snapped in her, a thought, a recognition of that day. A culmination and a punishment. Brooke wasn't just missing - she'd been *punished.*

And she was never coming back.

And Cathy was next.

Fear leapt into Cathy's heart. She needed to get out of there. *Now!* She grabbed the railing and started to move, but in her haste, she forgot where she was. Her shoe stepped onto some wet lichen, and she lost her footing. Suddenly, she was floundering, trying to grasp onto anything around her to keep her balance. Her legs flailed like a marionette's, trying to find ground, but everything around her was soaked and slippery.

Her clutches were futile, and her feet instantly lifted from the unstable rocks. She became weightless, floating only for a second before getting snatched by the rapid falls and plunging into the violent gush of thick water. The turbulent whirlpool silenced her screams, and then a wet darkness ended all other sounds.

Over an hour later, Bradley stood at the top of the falls. He reached into his jacket pocket and grabbed his cell phone. Then he dialed the number he had been given.

"It's done," he said with finality before tossing the phone into the waterfall and watching it disappear forever from sight.

He made his way down the trail and to the sign where he had stopped to tie his shoes. He walked to the front of the sign. It now read: "MIST TRAIL CLOSED". Earlier, while he was tying his shoes, he had flipped the sign from OPEN to CLOSED so no hikers would come past the sign onto the trail. He needed to be alone with Cathy.

He flipped it back to show the trail was open and then returned to their tent before heading home.

The next day, police and paramedics surrounded the area outside of Cathy's house. The body of a woman had been found brutally murdered near the streetlamp across from Cathy's house. Her throat had been slit from ear to ear.

Two days later, the coroner identified the body as Linda Broderick, Cathy's mother.

PART THREE
DANA

CHAPTER 31

I t was the wailing that made her shiver the most.

The painful sound emanating from the gaping mouth pierced her heart. There was blood everywhere, and it just…kept…coming. Rushing out as if a water balloon had been punctured. In all her life, she'd never seen so much blood. *If death came, it would be better*, she thought. But death was not an option. *Not on my watch.*

Dana was at Peterinarians, the vet clinic she started just out of Veterinary school, and it was a success from the start. The first animal she had worked on was her mother's Cocker Spaniel. Poor little Milo had cataracts in both eyes that covered nearly 40% of his lenses, so Dana decided that surgery was the best thing to restore Milo's sight to normal. She remembered her first surgery clearly.

Her mother had dropped Milo off at the clinic while Dana was in a consultation. Dana had the sneaking suspicion her mother was trying to avoid her. She didn't really blame her mother; she blamed Ray, the man Delores was seeing. He was too possessive for Dana's liking, but he seemed to make her mother happy, so Dana went with it- for the time being.

"Just don't kill him!" her mother cried over the phone, already prejudging

her daughter's abilities. But Dana knew more than just Milo's life lay on the line; so did her already-strained relationship with her mother.

And if Milo didn't pull through......she released the thought from her already crowded mind. She went to work on her mother's pup.

After Milo was gently anesthetized, Dana bent over the tiny dog and proceeded with the phacoemulsification process. She made a tiny incision in the cornea of the right eye, then inserted a needle-thin probe into the lens where the cataract had formed. Dana realized at this point if anything went wrong, poor Milo could hemorrhage or experience retinal detachment. She inhaled deeply. She used the probe's ultrasound waves to emulsify the cataract and then suctioned out the fragments. Dana then implanted an artificial lens to allow light to focus correctly on Milo's retina. With blade-like precision, she stitched the tiny incision. After an hour hunched over the pup, Dana had completed the surgery on the right eye. She stood up straight and cracked her back. Perfect. One down, one to go.

"Everything went fine," Dana told her mother over the phone once both eyes were done and Milo was sleeping off the anesthesia.

"Oh, thank god! My poor little baby," her mother said. "When can I pick him up?"

No "thank you!" or "great job on your first surgery!" or anything else appreciative. Dana sighed.

"We'll keep him overnight, and you can pick him up on your way home from work tomorrow." Dana wondered if she should suggest she take Milo to her mother's so they could have dinner. It would be a nice change for her mother to see her only daughter and for Dana to see her mother. It had been a long time since they'd seen each other. She wondered if Ray would be there. She decided to go for it.

"Mother, how about I bring Milo over, and you and I can have a nice dinner? You know, to catch up. I have some exciting news to tell you!"

Silence.

"Mother?"

"Yeah, I'm here. Look, baby, tomorrow's not a good time. Ray wants me to... to fix him a special dinner – it's our anniversary!"

What? Dana thought. Three months? What gift is that: lint? Dana felt hurt but not surprised. The avoidance continued. Ray was commandeering

Delores's life, and Dana seemed powerless over his persuasion. Not one to give up easily, she decided she'd table the conversation – and reunion – to another time.

That was over six months ago, and Dana still hadn't seen her mother, nor had she told her the exciting news she and Bradley were engaged. *Maybe it's for the best Bradley hasn't met my mother yet,* she thought. Plus, Ray was still in the picture, so maybe it was *all* for the best.

But today, she had other things she needed to focus on, like the 15-pound Maine Coon on her operating table who was wailing from the pain of being on the losing end of a scuffle with a possum. The possum's razor-like teeth had ripped out chunks of the poor kitty, and the blood loss was substantial. Most people would have little hope for the cat, but the cat was in luck: Dana was not most people. She was one of the most dedicated and personable veterinarians in San Francisco. All the reviews said so.

Her technique was renowned. Dana knew pet owners did not understand all the stuffy medical jargon, dire veterinary situations, and complicated diagnoses; they just wanted to know if Muffy, Max, or Mr. Puddles would pull through. So, Dana decided to talk to the clients like they were all concerned little children.

When she was describing terminating a cat's pregnancy, she described the unborn litter "like little furry marbles"; or when a dog had a prolapsed gland of the nictitans, Dana would describe it as 'cherry eye'. The gland had a ligament attached to the orbital bone, and if there were a weakness in that ligament, the gland would pop up so it looked like a cherry. When Dana had to reposition the eye surgically, she would describe it as if putting an edamame pea back into its pod. Dana learned that if the clients could visualize what was happening, they could understand more of what the outcome could be.

People liked how Dana was so personable and brought discussions about their beloved animals down to their level of understanding. After all, when pets were as important as a family member, the last thing someone wanted to hear was something beyond their comprehension. Dana became another part of their family and offered comfort in her conversations. It came easy to her.

But she was afraid this time would be different. How could she calmly describe the visceral tableau on her table to the owners? Dana sighed. She decided she would do what she did best and deliver nothing but good news.

Dana prepared the inhalant anesthesia mask.

Three hours later, Dana was whipping off her surgical mask and safety goggles. The Maine Coon was resting comfortably with several sutures, bruises, and bandages. But he would live to see another day, and that's all that mattered.

"Another great job," her assistant Sheila said.

"Thank you. That was a tough one. He'll definitely be sore for a while." She pulled off her gloves. A *bing* on her phone signaled an incoming text message.

Two interns came and carried the cat to his recovery cage.

"Is that him?" Sheila asked conspiratorially, grinning.

"Yes," Dana said, exasperated. "It's him." She typed in a quick response. "He just got home from being gone a week on some land-scaping job, and he just wanted to know if…." Dana could feel her face heat up.

"Why, Dr. Harris, are you blushing?"

Dana rolled her eyes. "I am *not* blushing. And I'm *not* Dr. Harris." She looked at Sheila. "*Yet.*"

"You might as well be," Sheila responded. "You're both gorgeous, and you two are together enough, and you're already engaged, and the wedding is in a couple of months, and you can't stop sleeping with him and -"

"Sheila!" Dana laughed. "Stop it!" She laughed harder.

"Whatever," Sheila said. "I just wish I had a pre-husband that made me blush like that."

Dana looked at Sheila. Both women, who were young and attractive, had long brunette hair. They would tie it up in a bun on workdays but let it down and be carefree on off days. Both had the same tight bone struc-ture and thoughtful brown eyes. Most people thought they were sisters. *If I can find someone wonderful, Sheila can, too.*

"You will, girl. Soon," Dana said. "I was lucky. The day he walked into this clinic with the poor injured doggie, it was love at first sight- as clichéd as that sounds. The poor creature needed me."

"The dog or the man?" Sheila asked, smirking.

"Both!" Dana said, laughing. "Hey. Do you have plans this weekend?"

"Some girlfriends and I are going to the Wild Oaks Country Music Festival in Thousand Oaks. Why? Wanna come?"

Dana was more of a classic rock kind of girl. "No, but I appreciate it. Since Bradley's been busy with work, we haven't seen each other in a little while, so he's taking me to Catalina Island for the weekend to go scuba diving and -"

"What?!" Sheila said, shocked. "You hate the water! That's, like, your biggest fear!"

Sheila didn't need to remind her. Dana was petrified of the water. There was just something about the inky depths of a sea or lake where you couldn't see the bottom that frightened Dana to no end. When she was a child on a church youth choir tour, she nearly drowned in a massive wave pool at a water park in St. Louis. No one noticed her, and she had emerged from the pool coughing and choking. Since then, she has feared and avoided any body of water.

Until now.

"Look, I know, believe me," she placed her hand on her chest. "I'm nervous as hell, but, believe it or not, I've taken some scuba lessons on the weekends at the 'Y'. They've helped get me prepared."

"So, you're, like, cured?"

"Not by a long shot," Dana said. "But at least I can get in the water over my head and not have to rely on Xanax as a crutch," she laughed nervously. "I just don't want to embarrass him. He's been very patient with me working a lot, and I want to do something for him, and, well, if this is it, then…" She let the sentence hang.

"Yeah, well, sounds to me like you're doing this for your man and not yourself."

Dana knew Sheila wasn't wrong. But Dana was in love, and she wanted to please her fiancé. She wanted to make sure that whatever he did, she would show an interest, too.

"You're a better woman than me," Sheila said. "But I can't wait to hear about it all on Monday!"

"Oh, don't forget, we're closed Monday for the A/C wire maintenance, so I'll see you Tuesday."

"I forgot. Okay, I'll see you Tuesday. And I'll do the inventory first thing. Why don't you head out, and I'll finish up here." It wasn't a question. "Go on, scoot. You've got someone waiting for you."

"Thanks, don't mind if I do," she smiled, then hugged Sheila. "Oh, what about the -"

"I'll enter the notes for the aftercare," Sheila said, referring to the Maine Coon's surgery.

"You're the best," Dana said, grabbing her purse and heading out to her car. She dialed his number, and he answered on the first ring.

"Well, hello there." His voice was sexy and gruff. An upward shiver seemed to touch each vertebrae in Dana's back until the hairs on the back of her neck tingled.

"Well, hello," she whispered.

"Rough night?" he asked.

She thought of the mangled cat on her operating table she saved from termination. "Not really," she lied. "Same ol', same ol'." She switched the phone to her other ear as she got into her car and behind the wheel.

"Aww, well, that's good," he said sweetly. "I can't wait to see you."

Early in her career, Dana had sacrificed her love life for her work life, and there was no balance. She was successful but had no one to share it with. Her mother never wanted to hear about her daughter's success, so Dana had kept quiet. And alone.

Until now.

Everything was coming together in a beautiful kismet explosion. Dana had met the man she was to marry on the day he brought his dog into her clinic. He was beyond worried about the canine's well-being, and Dana's heart hurt for the handsome stranger's pain. She and his owner had bonded over the week that Dana cared for the kenneled dog. One night over the phone, they were discussing the pup's progress, and he had simply asked her out to dinner.

There's no way. It's too soon. He's a stranger. I don't date clients. "I'd love to go," she found herself saying.

"I can't wait to see you," he said.

And so it had begun.

"I feel the same. I'm on my way home now." She hung up and clutched the phone to her chest, smiling. She looked up and saw Sheila walking from the clinic to her car. Sheila was a dear friend and a brilliant assistant at the clinic. Dana was in love and wanted so much for everyone around her to feel what she was feeling. Maybe he had a friend he could fix up with Sheila. She would ask him someday. After all, every woman deserved someone as wonderful as Bradley.

Sheila looked up and caught Dana's eye. She waved goodnight, and Dana waved back. What was it that Sheila had said? *I wish I had a pre-husband who made me blush like that.*

"You will," Dana said to no one. "But for now, stay away from mine," she said playfully. "Bradley Harris is a one-woman man!"

She started up the car and began the drive home.

CHAPTER 32

When Dana got home, it was dark, except for a few faint candle flickers of light snaking up the walls. The scents of vanilla and sandalwood wafted through the house. She set her purse down on the kitchen island.

"Bradley?" she called. She took off her Dansko shoes and left them at the door.

As she walked through the house, her feet stepped on something soft and delicate. She looked down and saw poppy petals strewn around, leading to the back of the house. She smiled lovingly. Poppies were her favorite flower, and they held a very sentimental meaning to her. Automatically, she felt the necklace around her neck.

She was touched Bradley had put so much effort into wooing her, and it did not go unnoticed. She took off her jacket and unbuttoned her blouse. Dana continued following the path of petals into the bedroom, but he was not there. The fragrant trail entered the bathroom. From the doorway, Dana could see more flickers of pale candlelight dancing in the shadows. She walked into the bathroom.

"I see you found me," Bradley said, sitting in the large claw-footed tub. His big arms were resting on the edges. He was surrounded by white marshmallowy bubbles, his large chest just above the fizziness. He looked at her and smiled; white teeth gleamed against his tan, chiseled features.

Dana could feel her pulse quicken. In a flash, her clothes fell off, and she slinked into the tub to join him. Millions of tingly bubbles clung to her body and awakened every nerve ending. She slid towards him, and he brought his arms down to pull her closer. Deftly, he lifted her slightly and then lowered her onto him, filling her. She placed her hands on his broad shoulders, and she moaned in pain, then pleasure; their movements caused the water to slosh and the bubbles to grow. The ride was intense and wet and ecstatic and tumultuous, until they both groaned, reaching simultaneous peaks.

For a moment, they remained in that position until he lifted her again and turned her to face away from him. He entered her, and the fervency began again.

Neither of them had noticed the water had become cold.

Dana was on the soft, cream sofa, her legs curled beneath her, and a thick, fluffy blanket draped around her naked body. Bradley sat beside her and handed her a glass of merlot. As she kissed him, a large black dog with a slight limp in his back leg padded gingerly to the sofa and lay at Bradley's feet. Dana reached down and scratched his head. "Hello, Kong," she said sweetly. She felt guilty for thinking so, but she silently thanked him for getting hurt and coming into Peterinarians with Bradley. That's how they met, after all.

And the rest was history.

"His movement has improved quite a bit," Dana said, noticing Kong's limp was less prominent.

"Thanks to you," Bradley said proudly. "And to the Konginator 2000," he said in a deep announcer voice, gesturing magnanimously towards an arcane-looking homemade device in the corner of the room.

Dana playfully slapped his arm. "Hush," she said. "Kong's doing all the work. I just...I just wanted to help him heal. I guess it's in my nature." She shrugged humbly.

"Oh, come on! This thing is amazing! And you really should patent it. It could help so many other animals out there with broken legs in their rehabilitation."

When Bradley brought Kong into the clinic, Kong had a broken back left tibia. Dana was taken by Bradley's charisma and was determined to help his dog however she could. Dana and Sheila had worked on Kong, but even after their expertise, she knew he needed something more. He was a gigantic dog, and his weight would only hinder the healing process of his weakened bone structure. At the beginning of her career, Dana had contemplated developing a device that could aid in rehabilitating dogs, but she became too busy to ever have it developed. Once she worked on Kong, all that changed. She met up with a friend who was handy with construction, and she provided him with her ideas and a rough sketch. Within two weeks, he had presented her with what Bradley lovingly called the Konginator 2000.

The Konginator 2000 was simple: it comprised of a rectangular plank made of polycarbonate that was attached to a two-foot tower. With a turn of a dial, the plank could be raised in two-inch intervals, depending on what level the animal was on in their recovery. On top of the plank was a button that, when pressed, would 'ding'. The point of the device was to gradually increase Kong's vertical height when raising his back leg, and when his paw landed on the button, Dana would reward him with a treat. It was sort of a Pavlovian instrument to improve the range of motion and to strengthen his biceps femoris and the gastrocnemius muscles in his hind leg. Since starting the process, Dana had raised the plank three notches every other week, so after only a month of work, Kong was up to a six-inch level. Dana smiled at the progress. She couldn't help but feel a little accomplished.

"I'm telling you. If you don't solidify a patent on that thing, someone else will."

"Maybe someday," she said softly. As she scratched Kong's head, he looked up at her and closed his eyes in happiness. His large tongue hung out.

"He's close to being well enough to walk and carry our rings down the aisle for us," Bradley said thoughtfully. "Our wedding is not too far off, you know."

Dana loved this man and was glad she had found someone who was as dedicated to their wedding as she was. But then, Dana's thoughts wandered back to another wedding she was a part of. She was a bridesmaid at Alicia and Ryan's wedding, when they joined in marriage and their families came together, two became one and all that. Their wedding day was a day when so much was gained, but so much was also lost. Loved ones. Best friends. It was an exciting, beautiful day marred by tragedy and death. Dana closed her eyes and willed the memories to disappear.

"Hey. Where'd you go?" Bradley asked, rubbing her shoulder.

Dana lifted her head and opened her eyes. She leaned back into him, into her comfort zone. Quickly, she changed her mind's focus. "Just thinking about our wedding and how happy I am." She carefully maneuvered the next question. It was a touchy subject Dana only broached once, and he coolly shut her down. But with the wonderful mood they were both in now, she decided to go for it. "Have you given any thought to who you'll want to invite from your family?"

Bradley took his hand from her shoulder. "Why do you keep asking me that?"

Uh oh.

She looked at him and took his hand in hers. "I just want them to be happy for us. As happy as we are. Is that too much to ask, darling?"

He let out a small huff. "No…it's not. It's just that I don't speak to my parents or brother," he said, a little agitated. He shifted on the sofa.

"Maybe if I spoke to them. I could tell them -"

"Absolutely not!" he said intensely. "Look, I don't want to discuss this any further, so please, don't bring it up again. Okay?"

This side of Bradley was a rarity, and Dana didn't like it, so she dropped the subject. "Okay," she said.

"Let's get to bed. We have a long day ahead of us tomorrow. Catalina Island awaits!" he said, rising from the sofa. He reached back to take her hand.

"I'll be there in a moment. I'm just gonna finish my wine," she said.

"I could stay up with you…." he suggested.

"Nah, I know how hard it is for you to fall asleep. I'll come to bed in a little bit. Promise." She leaned in and kissed his still-outstretched hand.

Bradley smiled gently at her, then turned and headed to the bedroom.

Dana felt unsettled. Not just at Bradley's reaction to his family but from her flashbacks to Alicia's wedding. *I'm sorry, Alicia. So sorry. Please forgive me.* Dana sniffed. Kong stood up and rested his big head on her lap.

"It's okay, boy. I'm just being nostalgic." Kong cocked his head. She smooched him on top of his nose. "Ready for bed?" Kong's tail wagged, and his tongue danced.

Kong followed Dana as she took the wine glasses into the kitchen to rinse them out in the sink. As she stood there letting the water run, a thought flashed in her mind: *Cupertino.* She remembered Bradley mentioning he was from Cupertino, a city less than an hour south of San Francisco. *What if...*

The thought started to bloom in her head. *What if I did some digging and located his family and invited them to the wedding myself? What if I got a car service to pick them up and bring them here? Bradley may say he doesn't talk to them, but surely his family showing up on the happiest day of his life would be a wonderful surprise! I know him! Deep down, he'll be happy as a kid in a candy store!*

She shut off the water faucet and looked down at Kong standing by her. "Where's my phone, boy?" she asked him excitedly as she went to the den to get her phone. She swiped through her contact list until she found the name she wanted: Mike Evans. He was the father of her friend Misty and, if Dana recalled, was a police detective or something. With her going to Catalina Island, working, and planning the wedding, she hadn't the time to investigate, so she needed Mike Evans' help locating Bradley's parents and brother. She typed out what she needed from him, then read the text before hitting send:

> Hey Mike! This is Dana Emerson, Misty's friend from college. Hope you're doing well. I have a favor to ask of you. I am looking for relatives of my fiancé who I can invite to our wedding as a surprise for him! So, it's all very hush-hush! lol

> Let me know if you have time to look into this and what you need from me. I'm hoping your expert detective skills will be able to give my future husband a wonderful wedding surprise! Thank you so much! I look forward to hearing from you!

Pleased, Dana hit the up-arrow button to send the text message.

"There," she said. "That's taken care of!" She looked at Kong, then cupped his face. "What's the worst that could happen?"

CHAPTER 33

The following day, Dana and Bradley awoke early to pack the car for their trip. While Bradley was loading up, Dana wrote a note for Sheila with instructions for caring for Kong, including his rehabilitation sessions on the Konginator 2000. She hated leaving him behind, but she felt a long car ride could exacerbate his leg. She patted his head and closed the door behind her as she joined Bradley in the car, ready to begin their nearly 7-hour drive to Long Beach.

They hit the 101 and headed south, through cute towns like Shell Beach and Spyglass, passing immense homes and boutique shops in Montecito and Santa Barbara. Once they reached Thousand Oaks and Calabasas, the Santa Monica Mountains loomed to their right, the Pacific Ocean just beyond the smooth peaks, where beachside hamlets like Malibu and Point Dume awaited.

Dana saw a sign that read 'Antelope Valley 86 miles'

"Oh, I wish we were closer," she said.

"Why's that?" he asked.

"The Poppy reserve!" she said, as if he should know.

"The…"

"…Poppy reserve! Millions and millions of California poppies bloom every year. As far as the eyes can see. It's spectacular."

"You and your poppies," Bradley chuckled.

"Yeah, I do love them. They're special to me and…" Her hand went to her shirt, where she could feel the poppy necklace underneath. *Alicia.*

"And?"

"Huh?"

"You sounded like you were going to say something else," he prodded.

"Oh. Nothing." She turned away. She saw another sign. 'Long Beach 60 miles'

"Look. Not much further," she said, closing the subject.

She turned her head and looked at the passing landscape.

In Sherman Oaks, they merged south onto Interstate 405. A little over an hour later, Dana spotted The Queen Mary moored in the Los Angeles River.

Bradley followed the signs to the Catalina Landing in downtown Long Beach. Once he spotted the Aquarium, he went another couple of blocks, then turned into the lot and parked. They carried their duffle bags to the Catalina Express ferry and boarded. The ferry was heading to Avalon on Catalina Island, and the ride was about an hour long. Dana and Bradley found two side-by-side seats at a small table.

"Do you want the seat by the window?" he asked her. "Great views of the water."

"Uh, no thanks," Dana said apprehensively. "You take it."

"Don't mind if I do," Bradley said, taking the chair.

After a small wait, the ferry began its journey to the island.

An announcer's voice came over the speakers.

"Good afternoon, ladies and gentlemen. My name is Dave Mathews – no, not *that* Dave Mathews *(laughter)* - and I'd like to welcome you aboard the Catalina Express ferry. In about one hour, we will reach our destination, so sit back, relax, and enjoy the ride."

Dana snuggled up to Bradley. The announcer continued.

"Catalina Island is the southernmost island of California's Channel Islands. The island consists of two towns: the rustic Two Harbors and the historic, yet more settled, Avalon, which is where our ferry will be docking today. Catalina Island is just 22 miles long and 8 miles across, so small enough to explore but large enough to get lost. *(laughter)*

"The island is best known for its wildlife, scuba diving, charming coastal towns, and Mount Orizaba, its highest peak. Catalina Island is part of Los Angeles County, and Avalon was the 13th city in the county. And for all you sports fans out there, the Chicago Cubs trained on Catalina from 1921 to 1951!" *(oohs and ahhs)*

A lady with a fanny pack yelled from a table near Dana and Bradley.

"Dave, have any movies been filmed on the Island?"

"I'm glad you asked," Dave Mathews said. "As a matter of fact, several very well-known movies were filmed there. *Rosemary's Baby*, *Chinatown*, *Waterworld*, *Apollo 13*, and one of my favorites – *Jaws*! But don't worry, that was just a movie." He paused. "Or was it?" *(laughter)*

"What kinds of wildlife are on the island?" the same lady asked.

"Well, I'm glad you asked again," the announcer said, pinched. "I should pay you to ride every ferry to ask questions." *(laughter)*

"Was that sarcasm?" Dana whispered to Bradley, smiling.

"I think so," Bradley grinned.

"Catalina Island," the announcer continued, "hosts a myriad of animals, ranging from bison, foxes, blue whales, dolphins, eagles and sharks."

Dana's head popped up. "Sharks?"

"Just baby ones," Bradley replied.

"But where there're babies, there're mamas," Dana said.

"Don't worry," he said. "Where we're diving, the sharks don't like to go. Everything's going to be fine." He wrapped his large arm around her and pulled her close.

Dana felt nonplussed, but she eventually gave in to his assuredness and relaxed. She laid her head back down on his shoulder and dozed off.

She was awakened by the jolt of Dave Mathews' voice on the intercom. "Ladies and gentlemen, in about five minutes, we will be pulling into the Cabrillo Mole boat landing. From there, you can take a short walk to Crescent Avenue, which is the main street surrounding Avalon and is packed with restaurants, shops, beaches, and scenic architectural elements like the Serpentine Wall and Wrigley Fountain."

Dana felt the ferry slow and shift right as the motors readjusted for the vessel to dock along the waterfront pier. Once at a complete stop, Dana and Bradley stood and made their way to the gangplank.

"And here we are!" Dave Mathews said. "On behalf of Catalina Express, we thank you for trusting us with your journey to the beautiful Catalina Island. Please enjoy your stay!"

Bradley and Dana held hands as they walked down the busy Crescent Avenue and stopped at Sailor's Delight for an ice cream cone – he had Black Cherry, and Dana chose Banana Cream Pie. They were delicious and perfect on this sunlit day. Dana wasn't sure if she was happiest to be with Bradley on such a beautiful island or because she was on dry land. She grinned.

After a couple more blocks, they arrived at their luxurious hotel, the Zane Grey Pueblo Hotel. Dana eyed her beautiful surroundings. In the lobby, a woman was seated near a man wearing a large-brimmed hat. On the other side, near the Concierge desk, Dana saw the woman with the fanny pack. The Concierge looked overwhelmed with tourists. Dana chuckled.

"Checking in for Harris," Bradley told Megan, the receptionist.

"Of course," Megan said, smiling broadly at Bradley. Dana raised her eyebrow and inched closer to him.

"That's Mr. and *Mrs.* Harris," Dana said quickly.

"Yes, ma'am, of course." More typing. "Ahh, okay. I see you have booked one of our King Ocean Suites for your stay. The bedroom has wonderful views."

The insinuation did not go unnoticed by Dana. *But who could blame Megan,* Dana wondered. *Bradley was probably the most handsome man on the island.* Megan's eyes weren't the only ones eyeing him since they arrived.

"That's great," Bradley said. "My, uh, wife booked the hotel, so I'm sure it's wonderful."

"Perfect. So, all I need is a credit card for incidentals."

When Bradley pulled out his credit card from his wallet, other cards fell out. He handed his AMEX to Megan.

"What's this?" Dana said, picking up one of the cards that had fallen to the floor. "A library card? I had no idea you liked to read enough to belong to a library," she said teasingly. Bradley reached for the card, but Dana continued to read. "Sarah Tuttle Public Library. Cute name. Who's Sarah Tuttle?"

"No idea," he said, taking the card back from Dana and putting it in his wallet. "Some big reader, I suppose." His face was flushed.

"You are just full of surprises, Mr. Harris," Dana said.

Megan said, "It looks like your room is all ready for you. Here are your keycards, and the Wi-Fi password is listed just here." She pointed to the back of the card case. She handed Bradley back his AMEX.

"And we've already confirmed your reservation for dinner tonight at Bluewater Grill at 6:30. Should you need anything, anything at all, please don't hesitate to ask."

Dana caught the wink Megan gave Bradley.

Bold.

Dana watched as Megan inhaled, causing her breasts to rise. The smile on Megan's face grew seductively. Dana's eyes widened, and she shook her head in disbelief. She looked Megan in her eyes and said, "We won't need you any further. I've got it from here." She winked back.

Megan eyed her back as if challenged.

Bradley and Dana left the counter.

"Oh, and by the way," Dana continued, turning back to Megan. "You've got a piece of lettuce in your teeth." She watched Megan's entire demeanor deflate as she quickly produced a mirrored compact. Dana laughed and walked away.

In the lobby, the man wearing the large-brimmed hat swiveled his head as he watched Bradley and Dana head to the elevators.

Later, Dana and Bradley wandered the city, the sun gently beating down on their skin. Cooling breezes blew in up and down the streets, causing awnings and flags over the many boutiques to ripple and waver. Dana went into The Steamer Trunk and bought a wind chime with animal carvings dangling from the top for Sheila for babysitting Kong.

They went to Middle Beach and carried their shoes while stepping through the surf and sand. Kids started screaming excitedly and pointing out into the water. A grey whale breached the surface and hissed out water vapor. The kids squealed louder. Dana snuggled against Bradley.

Dana was in heaven. It had been a perfect day, and she was safe in the arms of the man she loved.

Promptly at 6:30, Bradley and Dana entered Bluewater Grill. Dana wore an arctic blue maxi dress that fell loosely but still hugged her curves. Her sun-kissed skin glowed against the blue fabric, and she looked like a goddess. Bradley had on a crisp white button down, rolled up to his big forearms, and navy chinos with a woven belt. His tan had become more bronze, and his green eyes sparkled. Even with all the beautiful souls on the Island, Dana and Bradley stood out. The hostess greeted them at the dais.

"Hi there. My name is Shaley. Welcome to Bluewater Grill. Dinner for two?

"Yes. We have reservations for Harris."

"Yes, I see it here. Please follow me." As they walked behind the hostess, Dana once again looked around and marveled at her surroundings. The outside deck was large and accompanied several tables. Couples and parties laughed and clinked glasses and ate delicious-looking seafood. Dana realized she hadn't eaten in a few hours, and she was starved.

"Are you enjoying your time here on Catalina?" Shaley asked.

"Oh, yes," Dana responded. "It's a beautiful place. So vibrant and friendly."

"Most definitely," Shaley said. "And here we are," she said, gesturing towards their table. "How's this?"

Dana took it all in. From their table, they had stunning waterfront views of the beach, harbor, and casino. The sun was just starting to set, and the sky was an explosion of tangerines, garnets, and marigolds. Boats with sails folded on their masts bobbled gently on the harbor's surface. It was perfection.

"It's...amazing," Dana said. They sat, and Dana put her handbag on the table.

"Excellent. Can I start you out with some wine or a cocktail?"

"Two merlots," Bradley said.

"I'll get those right up." She handed them each a menu. "Enjoy your meals," she stated before walking away.

"This place is gorgeous," Dana said. "Just breathtaking."

"I'll say it is," a male's voice said next to them.

Dana and Bradley turned to the table beside them. Two dapper men in their forties sat across from each other. One was blonde, and the other brunette. They were wearing matching outfits covered in the Louis Vuitton signature monogram. The brunette had an "S" emblazoned over his left front chest pocket, and the blonde had an "A". They wore wedding rings on their right hands.

"Beg your pardon?" Bradley asked.

"Oh, don't mind him," the blonde one said. "He likes to flirt with everyone."

"Shut up, Aaron," the brunette man scolded playfully. "I mean, am I wrong? They are gorgeous, are they not?" he gestured to Bradley and Dana with his cocktail.

"Hi. I'm Aaron," the blonde one said. "And this is my very subtle husband, Scotty."

Scotty waved with his pinky finger.

"Hi. I'm Dana, and this is...."

"I'm her husband, Bradley." He stood to shake their hands. Aaron shook Bradley's hand firmly while Scotty held his out like a Queen holding court. "Enchanté," he demurred.

"I love your outfits," Dana said. "And your shoes! Those are fabulous."

"Louis Vuitton," Scotty replied. "Cost a fortune, and they're uncomfortable as hell, but they make my ankles look good."

Dana laughed. "I hear ya." She pointed to her Espadrilles.

"At least you have an arch," Scotty said.

"So, what brings you two lovebirds to the Island?" Aaron asked.

"Just a little getaway time from the city," Bradley said.

"L.A.?"

"God, no," Dana said. "San Francisco. What about you two?"

Aaron said, "Real Estate. We're looking to buy a place we can turn into a bed and breakfast."

"Aaron loves to buy things and have me fix them up," Scotty said. "I'm always doing all the work while he just sits back and counts his money."

"That's not true," Aaron replied.

Scotty cocked his head.

"Well, maybe it's a little true," Aaron shrugged. "We own a couple of business properties along the coast and are always looking to expand the portfolio. Anyway, we're looking at a few places tomorrow bright and early, so..." he nudged Scotty.

"Yeah, yeah. We must go. Early night for us." He rose from his seat. "Good night, gorgeous people."

"Good night," Dana said, then turned back to her menu.

Scotty walked ahead, and Aaron turned and looked back at the couple. As he scrunched his face in thought, Scotty grabbed him by his shirt to pull him out of the restaurant.

Their wine came, and they placed their order: a Seafood Louie Salad for her and the Chipotle Blackened Swordfish for him.

"They were fun," Dana said.

"Uh huh," Bradley replied. "Tons."

"Oh, stop it," she slugged his arm playfully. "They were.... eccentric."

"Good word."

A *bing* came from Dana's handbag.

"I'm running to the restroom," Bradley said. "Be right back."

Dana opened her bag as he left the table and pulled out her phone. She saw a text message from Mike Evans. Her heart began to pound. She had asked him to help her find Bradley's family for their wedding. Was he going to help? Was he too busy? Dana was eager to open the message. She clicked on the green text box. Mike Evans' reply popped up.

> Hey Dana. Good to hear from you. I'll be happy to do what I can to locate your fiancé's family. Provide me with his name and place of birth and where you think his family is, and I'll do the rest. I can't promise anything, but I'll do my best. And congratulations on your engagement!

Dana held the phone to her chest and smiled. This was happening. She looked in the restaurant and didn't see Bradley yet. She replied to the message.

> His name is Bradley Harris, and he was born in Cupertino. I believe his family is still there. Thank you! Oh, and please keep this between us! ;-)

189

Dana hit send.

There was a long pause before Dana saw three dots on her phone, signaling Mike Evans was typing her back. She looked up and saw Bradley heading back to the table. She couldn't let him see what she was doing! Her heart pounded. She glanced down at her phone's screen, willing it to pop up with a message. Bradley was now only a few tables away. *Oh my god, hurry!* She didn't realize she was squeezing her phone tightly. Now, Bradley was three tables away and....

Bing!
Dana looked at her screen and read the message quickly.

> No problem. No problem at all.

She threw her phone into her bag and moved it to the chair beside her. Dana's heart fluttered. She felt more excited than she had in a long time. She looked up and Bradley was sitting down.

This was coming true! She was going to surprise Bradley at their wedding. She had a feeling it would be a day neither one would ever forget.

CHAPTER 34

Today was the day Dana was going to die.

A heart attack, drowning, seizure, aneurysm, underwater panic attack – something! I just know it, she thought. *Today was the day.* They were going scuba diving.

She felt sick to her stomach, queasy. But for some reason, when Bradley suggested they eat a light breakfast at Toyon Grill, she found herself saying 'yes', and she had no idea why.

As they were walking to their table, they heard a familiar voice. "Well, hello there, gorgeous people!"

It was Scotty, and he was with his husband, Aaron. Both were drinking coffee and had an assortment of danishes on their table. And both, once again, were wearing matching outfits. Today, the outfits were a gaudy head-to-toe, black and red tartan plaid, and the "S" and "A" initials were again on display.

"Alexander McQueen," Scotty said in response to Dana's stare.

"They're beautiful," she said, hoping she sounded sincere.

"So, what are you two loveys up to this bright morning?" Scotty's eyes bore more into Bradley than they did Dana when he asked the question. Aaron was reading the paper but looked over the top of his glasses and smiled. His brows furrowed, and his smile stayed in place as his eyes focused on Bradley.

"Scuba diving!" Bradley said excitedly.

Dana slumped a bit but put on a brave face. "Yeah, not my favorite thing, but I'm going with the man I love, so I should be okay." She saw Scotty leering at Bradley and then registered Aaron's pensive look.

"And you two are going bed and breakfast shopping, right?"

"Yes," Aaron said, "and we should be going. Our first appointment is in fifteen minutes. Come, Scotty."

"Well, I must go," Scotty said, standing. "Aaron said so."

"Good luck today on your hunt," Dana said.

"Good luck to you, too, gorgeous people," Scotty said as he and Aaron left the restaurant.

Dana saw the two men talking out of earshot.

"Odd couple," Bradley said.

"I think they're fun," Dana said. "In small doses." They laughed.

While they were seated eating their breakfast, a waiter brought them a picnic basket filled with sliced meats, breads, cheeses, dried fruits, and small pastries.

"What's this?" Dana asked.

"Lunch," Bradley said.

"But I'm not even finished breakfast yet," Dana said.

Bradley laughed. "This will be for after we dive. Diving uses a lot of energy. You'll need to regain your strength somehow, so I called ahead and had them make this for us."

Dana loved his thoughtfulness. She had no idea Bradley was such a planner. He surprised her with the library card, dinner reservations, and now the picnic basket.

I thought I knew him, she thought, smiling. *But I don't really know him at all.*

Dana and Bradley took a taxi to Pleasure Pier, where Bradley rented scuba gear and a 24ft Bayliner Trophy boat called *Titanic 2* to take them out into the Gulf of Santa Catalina. He tossed the scuba gear onto the boat.

Dana stared at the vessel's name. "Seriously?"

"Oh, come on. It's funny!" Bradley chided playfully. Dana huffed her skepticism. He was carrying a white five-gallon lidded bucket.

"What's that for?" Dana asked.

"It's ice for our drinks," he smiled, jumping onto the boat. "Come on."

Surrendering, she handed him the picnic basket and started to climb slowly onto the boat. As soon as she had one leg on, another craft zoomed by, and its wave caused *Titanic 2* to rock violently. Dana yelped and fell into Bradley's arms.

"Got you!" Bradley said.

"Yeah, whatever," Dana said, already regretting her decision to do this. But she knew she needed to do this. She felt safe with Bradley and fear or no fear, this was important to him, and she was determined to conquer this phobia. She sat in the passenger seat near the helm.

Bradley unmoored the boat from the dock and started her up. In five minutes, they had left the safety of the pier and were on their way out to the deep blue sea.

Thirty minutes later, Bradley shut off the engine and threw out the anchor. Dana couldn't see anything around them except Catalina Island, which looked mighty tiny in the distance. They donned their scuba outfits, pulling the hoods onto their heads. Next, they helped each other with their weight belts and scuba units. Once they put their masks and fins on, they sat on the edge of the boat with their backs to the water.

Except for the pounding of her heart in her ears, the silence inside the suit was unnerving. Dana willed her training to kick in pronto. She didn't want to chicken out; she had come too far. Dana controlled her breathing through her mouthpiece, the heavy sigh sound emanating from deep in her throat. Bradley looked at her and gave her a thumbs-up before falling back and landing in the water with a big splash.

It was now or never. *Do I stay within the safety of the boat, or do I fall back into the blue abyss?* Dana was not a religious person, but she needed every bit of help she could get. She made the sign of the cross and threw herself backward over the edge.

At first, darkness surrounded her. But once the millions of minute bubbles dissipated, Dana felt herself floating, suspended with zero gravity. She could see her world had gone from a confined, stodgy boat to an endless, crystal-blue ocean. It was the most peaceful experience she'd ever had.

She flipped her fins gently and glided closer to Bradley. He pointed behind her, and she rotated and saw what he was pointing to: a kelp forest. Hundreds of strands of the algae rose 65 feet from the ocean floor and were thick and lush, swaying drunkenly in the under-surface current. The waving leaves were a murky brown, but because of how the sun penetrated the surface, they glowed in colors like chartreuse, forsythia, and red currant. It was a living mosaic.

Dana and Bradley propelled closer and could see large kelp bass and sea fans near the bottom. A startled octopus shot across below them along the ocean floor. Dana felt her heart swell at the sight. She loved all animals, and witnessing them in their natural habitat was awesome.

Together, they left the kelp strands and swam further down. A school of bright orange garibaldi fish swam ahead of them. Dana noticed they were unbothered and seemed comfortable with strangers in their wet world. She smiled behind her mask.

Bradley was further ahead and seemed to hover in the water, moving his arms to the front and back of him to stay in his position. Dana moved her fins, and she was soon by his side. When she saw what he was looking at, her eyes widened.

A large bank of purple hydrocoral, sharp and beautiful, like underwater alliums, spread across small hills on the ocean floor like wildflowers. Shadows above them moved, and she looked and saw six reef manta rays gliding close to the surface, their wingspans over 15 feet wide. They were majestic and silent, and Dana felt she was visiting another world, like *Avatar*. She thought of how she healed animals on land, but for the ones underwater, what took care of them if they were injured?

She took a breath through her mouthpiece and got a lungful of fresh air. She exhaled, and bubbles came out of her regulator, ascending upwards towards the surface. Her eyes followed the bubbles, and she saw something above her: a vast, shadowy blob. It wasn't another manta ray. This blob was reddish in color. *A school of rosefish*, she guessed. She had heard about the rosies that lived off the coast of California, and now there seemed to be a school of them above her, nearly blocking out the sun. It was a spectacular sight.

Dana could hear herself breathe, but other than that, she was enveloped in silence. She was in a beautiful place with her fiancé and hadn't even thought about her fear of deep water once. She smiled behind her mask. Speaking of her fiancé, she could no longer see Bradley. She looked around, spinning slowly in a suspended circle, but there was nothing except an endless blue universe.

Bradley was nowhere to be found.

She was all alone in the sea, and suddenly, her fear resurged back to her. Dana started to panic and spun wildly in the water. Her breathing quickened, and bubbles escaped her regulator at an alarming pace. Feeling lost and confused, Dana suddenly became aware she had absolutely no clue of her whereabouts. She wanted to scream but knew she couldn't open her mouth. She looked up. The school of rosies had moved, and she could see sunlight. Flapping her fins, she began her ascent to the surface...closer.... closer...her arms pulling through the water to help thrust her body to the water's crest.

After what seemed like an eternity, Dana could feel her arms breaking through the surface. She pushed her mask up on her suit's hood and took in a deep breath, bobbing in the water and staying afloat by using her fins.

She spiraled around but couldn't see anything around her. The salty seawater stung her eyes and sloshed into her mouth.

"Bradley!" she yelled. But she was alone in the ocean. "Bradley!" *Oh, my god. I'm going to die!*

She spat out water. *There.* A glint. Something sparkled in the sunlight. *A boat.* It was about a hundred yards away and coming closer. As it slowly closed the gap, Dana could see someone on the deck, and they were waving their arms in a crisscross motion above their head. *Is that Bradley? Yes! Thank God!*

He was yelling something, something she couldn't make out. She couldn't hear him; the hood on her head blocked her ears.

"What?" she yelled. He said something, but it was muffled. She yanked the hood off her head. "I can't hear you!" she yelled back. The surrounding water sloshed intensely.

"You...not.... true!" Bradley hollered.

You not true? What does that mean? You not true?

The boat was slowing down, inching towards her cautiously. Dana motioned with her hand to hurry. She decided she would swim towards the boat.

"No!" he waved to her. "You.... not.... move...."

Wait. What? It's not "you not true"; it's "do not move"? He's telling her not to move. Her eyes grew wide, and she froze in place. *Why can't I move?*

"W-w-w-why can't I move?" she asked feebly. The boat was now only ten feet away.

He looked worried, but she had no idea why. Her legs were cramping from trying to keep afloat.

The boat was now two feet away. Bradley shut off the engine, went to the stern, and leaned over the edge. "Dana, I don't want you to panic..."

"Too late!"

"Stay perfectly still," he urged.

She nodded a feeble approval. "But w-w-why? Bradley! Why?"

"Just don't move, sweetheart, okay? Everything is going to be fine."

"W-what is it? Oh, my god. What is it?"

She looked him in the eyes, and she saw terror. Something nudged her fin.

Bradley took a deep breath. "You're surrounded by sharks."

CHAPTER 35

Dana wanted to scream but feared the sound might attract more sharks. She knew movement would make her a magnet to the beasts, and at that moment, she could feel the waves from the boat causing her to bob up and down in the water like bait. She tried to stay perfectly rigid, moving her swim fins imperceptibly to stay afloat. Dana imagined her leg or side being sliced open by gnashing, razor-sharp teeth.

"I've seen three," Bradley said as he leaned over the boat's edge. "Something must have attracted them." He looked worried. His head lifted, and his eyes shifted to her left.

"What?" she asked, trembling.

He said nothing.

She looked slowly to her left and saw a large fin forty feet away slice through the water and head directly towards her. Dana wasn't sure what scared her the most: the one she could see barreling towards her or the two she could *not* see, probably circling her dangling legs. Suddenly, something brushed up against her back.

"Help me!" she cried hoarsely, looking up at Bradley. She turned her head, and the fin on her left slowly sank below the surface. Now, all three sharks were invisible to her. Her mind imagined the poster for

Jaws, and she pictured them all coming straight up from below to swallow her in one vicious gulp.

"I've got you," he said. "Just stay still." The boat quietly glided closer next to her. "Raise up your arms.... slowwwwly...." he said.

She did, just as a shark bumped against her thigh. Instinctively, she flinched, worried now she just kicked a shark and pissed it off.

Bradley reached down and grasped her hands. "On the count of three."

"How about on the count of one?" she begged.

Suddenly, the water around her churned violently, and he whipped his head up and looked behind her to the right and left. They both knew the sharks were coming for her like savage killing machines.

"THREE!" he shouted without waiting, yanking her out of the water, her legs still hanging over the edge of the boat. At that instant, a shark breached the water in a fury and sideswiped the boat, snapping a swim fin into its jaws and yanking it off her foot before disappearing back into the blue depths.

Dana screamed as she felt the tug on her leg, and she fell on top of Bradley onto the floor of the boat.

She burst into tears and shook uncontrollably. He held her until the sobs subsided.

"Let's get out of here," he breathed.

Bradley got behind the wheel at the helm and started the engine. He pushed the lever forward and began their journey back. Dana got up and sat in the chair next to him. She was wrapped in a fluffy towel but still shivered as if she had just plunged into icy waters. It would be a while before her heart returned to a normal rhythm. She kept her eyes forward, silently wishing the shores of Catalina Island would come into view.

She never once looked back to where the sharks had been to where she had come *thisclose* to dying.

For if she had, she would've seen the chunky red chum being stirred up in the wake of the *Titanic 2* and realized it wasn't a school of rosefish that had been floating above her head after all.

CHAPTER 36

"Can we just go home now?" Dana asked that night back at the hotel. They were sitting on the sofa in their suite.

"The ferry's not operating until tomorrow. We'll leave first thing," he promised. "Let's just enjoy our last night here. On land," he iterated. He smiled.

Despite how she was feeling, Dana weakly smiled back.

"You saved my life today," she said. I'll never forget it." She leaned over, wrapped her arms around his neck, and kissed him softly.

"Nah, you would've done the same. I'm no hero," he said.

"I would've tried, but I couldn't lift you out of the water like that!"

"What? You'd leave me as shark food?" he teased.

"They'd probably break a tooth on you," she said, poking his hard chest.

He chuckled.

"I'm going to take a shower," she said.

"Okay, and then we'll get dressed and have a nice leisurely dinner out. Some wine, fresh seafood-"

"Seafood?! I'm never eating seafood again!" she exclaimed. "Just turf from now on. I was almost a seafood meal today, and as of this moment, I'm a carnitarian!"

He laughed. "Fine, fine. No seafood. Just go and get cleaned up."

"I'm serious," she said as she left the room. "Ugh!"

Dana went into the bedroom and plugged in her phone. She pulled up Mike Evans' last text to her:

> No problem. No problem at all.

Dana had heard nothing further from Mike, and she hoped he was having better luck in his investigation than she was in her scuba diving. She sighed and set her phone down on the bedside table.

Dana stuck her hand in the shower and turned on the hot water as far as it would go. She removed her clothes and stood in front of the mirror. Her hair was matted, she had dark circles under her eyes, and her lips were dry. "Hello, gorgeous person," she said sarcastically. *Scotty would be proud*, she thought.

She put toothpaste on her toothbrush and cleaned her teeth. It felt good to get all the salt water out of her mouth. The taste lingered, along with the memories. She closed her eyes as she brushed. She bent over, spit out the paste, and rinsed her mouth. When she stood up, the mirror was steamed over.

She reached into the shower and turned the knob a little so she wouldn't scald. Gingerly, Dana stepped into the shower with her back to the spray. The thin jets of water felt like wonderful little hot needles on her back, and she let out a sigh. She leaned her head back to wet her hair, then reached for the shampoo. Something hit her foot. Dana looked down. The water in the bottom of the shower was a pale red color, and a small chunk of something was trying to get down the drain.

"What is *that*?" she said. "Ick!" She stepped on the squishy chunk with her foot, forcing it down the holes in the drain. It went down, albeit reluctantly, then disappeared from sight. "Was that part of the kelp? Still in my *hair*? Oh, my god, I hate today so much!"

She filled her hand with shampoo and washed her hair, the chum residue washing away while her eyes were closed.

Bradley took Dana to Descanso Beach Club for dinner. She was wearing jeans, an oversized fisherman's sweater, and espadrilles. Her hair was pulled back into a simple ponytail. Outwardly, she looked confident, pulled together; inwardly, she was a shivering mess. But it was their last night on the island, and she couldn't be happier.

As they walked to their table, Dana looked around at all the patrons. A gentleman was wearing a large-brimmed hat with his back to them, two couples were dining together and laughing over drinks, and another couple was gazing into each other's eyes, oblivious to the food stacking up on their table. *Honeymooners*, Dana decided. If these people only knew, they would be shocked to find out that she might not have been here at this very place, this very minute. Life is short; life goes on. She was amazed at the irony: today, she almost lost her life, and these people are living their best ones.

The hostess led them out onto the terrace and to their table near the railing overlooking the beach.

"Two glasses of merlot, please," Bradley said. The hostess nodded and scurried away. Dana and Bradley sat in silence at their table, staring out at the waves gently crashing onto the sand. Distant gulls squawked. Their wine arrived, and Dana took a large gulp.

"Small world, gorgeous people," a voice announced.

"Hey, you guys," Bradley said as Scotty and Aaron approached their table. Today's matching designer outfits were by Gucci, including identical sunglasses resting on top of their heads. Their initials "S" and "A" were monogrammed on the shirt pockets in Gucci's signature red and green colors. Bradley smiled at them and showed bright, even teeth against his tan skin.

"Hard to imagine you could get more handsome, but here you are," Scotty said. Aaron slapped his arm.

"But what happened to *you*?" Scotty asked, glaring at Dana, his hand on his chest. "You look like a white bike reflector. Why so pale?"

Dana glared back. "Don't start." She emptied her wineglass, and the waitress instantly appeared for a refill. Dana mustered up enough energy to change the subject. "Did y'all have a productive day? Find any interesting properties?" She began to drink again.

"Three," Aaron said. "One was perfect but too expensive. One was a fixer-upper that Scotty loved, and the third was not on the beach but was the right price and fully furnished."

"It's like we're on fucking *House Hunters*," Scotty exclaimed, exasperated.

"What about you two," Aaron asked. "Anything exciting happen today?" His eyes went to Bradley, and he cocked his head.

Dana spewed her wine across the table.

Bradley started wiping the table.

"That bad, huh?" Scotty said. "Do tell."

"Just an exciting day scuba diving," Bradley started. He saw Dana shoot him a look that told him she did not want to relive their afternoon. "But, uh, other than that, nothing too exciting."

"You know," Aaron said, pointing at Bradley, "This has been bugging me for a couple of days, but you look so familiar. Have we met before?"

"Um, yesterday?" Bradley said, shrugging.

"No, no. Before. I never forget a face -"

"He doesn't," Scotty interrupted. "He could recognize one of my ex-boyfriends on an overcrowded cruise ship. Hypothetically."

"Where do you think you've seen him?" Dana asked.

"I'm thinking," Aaron said. Then he looked at Bradley. "Have you ever been to Bodega Bay?"

Bradley showed no reaction. "Can't say that I have. Why?"

"Well, we own a property there, The Lodge at Bodega Bay. It was the first one we bought and fixed up together -"

"Beautiful views!" Scotty added.

Aaron continued. "And I want to say I've seen you there before. Not too long ago...."

Bradley shrugged and raised his eyebrows. "Nope. Wasn't me. Maybe it was my twin brother, Wesley," he teased.

"A twin of *you*?" Scotty said, flustered. "I wish!" He fanned himself with the menu.

Bradley laughed. "Sorry to disappoint. No twin here."

Scotty lifted a corner of his mouth. "My loss."

"Well, I do have landscaping work up in Sonoma sometimes, so maybe you've seen me around town or something. Wouldn't that be a neat coincidence?" He slowly raised his eyes and met Aaron's. The look was unmistakable.

Aaron decided to abandon the thought. "Well, my mistake. You two have a good evening." He grabbed hold of Scotty's shirt to leave. "Let's go."

"What about dinner?" Scotty asked, stumbling.

"I'm not feeling well all of a sudden," Aaron said, his eyes quickly meeting Bradley's before darting away.

"Oh, okay then…. bye, gorgeous people," Scotty barely got out of his mouth before they turned to leave. In his haste, Aaron backed up too quickly and bumped into the chair of the man wearing the large-brimmed hat.

"Oh, so sorry," Aaron said before quickly exiting.

The man barely lifted his head. "No problem. No problem at all."

CHAPTER 37

The drive back home seemed longer to Dana than the ride to get to Catalina Island. But maybe that's because of what she had been through, and her mind felt like it was stuffed with cotton balls.

On the way, she decided she'd try to take a nap, but she was restless, and sleep was fleeting. Every time she closed her eyes, she kept having visions of being torn apart by vicious sharks. One grey behemoth would clamp down on her air tank and shake her like a rag doll, while the other two would take turns ripping off her limbs one by one in their grinning, toothy jaws. She would wake up gasping for air. And the cotton balls were replaced with questions.

Once they arrived home, they carried their belongings into the house and set them down in the den. They plopped down on the sofa, moaning.

Dana looked over at Bradley. His hands were behind his head, and his eyes were closed. He looked peaceful, calm, and collected, like he was living without a care in the world. Not at all acting like his fiancé had been mere seconds away from being a shark's chew toy.

She turned to face him.

"Bradley?"

"Hmm?" he responded.

"Why did you leave me?"

He brought his hands down and placed his right hand on her knee. "Sorry, what?"

Dana removed his hand. She needed him to be serious about this and for her mind to be clear. "Why did you leave me? Out in the ocean? When I came to the surface, you were nowhere to be found. *You left me*," she said with emphasis.

"I didn't leave you."

"Well, you weren't *with* me, that's for damn sure." She could feel the heat on the back of her neck intensify.

"I was on the boat. I came back for you."

"But *why?!*"

"Oh."

"*Oh?*" she asked, stunned.

"Well, my air tank was running low. I was afraid if I didn't get it replaced or fixed, then I would run out of oxygen. I had to get back on the boat to get a new tank." He looked at her. "Is that what this is all about?"

"No, that's not *all* what this is about. Fine. You got on the boat. First off, you didn't signal to me you were leaving while we were in the water, and you *know* how I hate the water. Second, you were over a hundred yards away when I surfaced. What the hell?"

"I guess the boat floated away while I was on it and -"

"I thought you anchored the boat," she challenged. "So, how did it just float away?"

"I don't know," he said, agitated. "Maybe the anchor didn't reach the bottom. It's pretty deep out there."

"Trust me, I know it's deep," she spat.

"When you came up and were so far away, I was just as surprised as you. Are you sure you didn't swim away from our spot? It's easy to get disoriented down there-"

"No, I didn't swim away from our spot! I stayed with the kelp forest the entire time- unless it got up and walked a hundred yards away." She rolled her eyes.

"No need for sarcasm," he said.

"Well, what do you expect? I could've *died* out there, Bradley." She stood up. Out of anger, tears filled her eyes.

His voice lowered to a whisper. "Look, I'm sorry, okay? I guess I wasn't paying attention to everything, and I should've done a better job of protecting you out there." He reached out and took her hands.

Dana tried to pull her hands from his, but his grip was too tight. "Stop," she said through tears.

"I won't stop. I won't stop loving you. I won't stop protecting you. I love you so much, and I'm so sorry this happened to you. I'm just glad I was there to, I don't know, rescue you from everything, but it shouldn't have happened in the first place."

"No," she said. "It shouldn't have." Dana wrested her hands from his. She was still angry and felt fatigued. She hadn't had a good rest since all of this. Lassitude overtook Dana. "I'm going to bed." She paused. "You can sleep in the guest room." She turned and walked away from him.

As she laid her head on her fluffy pillow, she remembered the clinic was closed tomorrow for the A/C wire maintenance, and she didn't need to go in until Tuesday morning.

She slept for 18 hours.

When she awoke, it was 3:00 Monday afternoon. She was alone in bed, and she was groggy. She went into the kitchen and saw a note from Bradley saying he had to go to Sonoma for the day to continue a project. She was relieved she didn't have to face him after their fight.

Kong padded up next to her and licked her hand. She scratched between his ears, and he let out a content chuff. She noticed his walking had less of a limp. "I'm so proud of you, boy," she said. "Show me what you can do." She walked with him to the Konginator 2000. Dana noticed the lever with the button was now up to at least eight inches off the ground, two more inches since they went away. *I see Sheila worked on Kong's rehabilitation while I was gone,* she thought happily.

Kong stood next to the contraption and looked up at Dana. She nodded. "Go on," she urged. Kong lifted his left hind leg until his paw was above the button. He lowered his paw onto the button, and Dana heard a *ding*. He lowered his leg and repeated the process three more times.

"Oh, that's wonderful, boy," she said excitedly, rubbing his plump face in her hands. Dana went to the cupboard and pulled out a treat for him. He snarfed it down without even chewing it. "Now it's time for *my* treat," she said.

She fixed a cup of coffee from her Nespresso then headed to the bedroom. Kong followed and plopped down in his doggie bed. Dana got into the shower. The water was invigorating, and by the time she emerged, she was relaxed, awake, and feeling like herself.

Later that day, without Bradley there, she decided to get some reading done. She grabbed the latest DeMille book and curled up on the sofa. She held the thick book in her hands and, for some reason, thought of Cathy. Cathy loved books. Dana realized she hadn't heard back from her since she called and left her a message. *Had she gotten my message and just decided not to call back? Was it too soon to talk? Maybe it's for the best. I'll send her a wedding invitation, just in case. If there is still going to be a wedding.*

Dana laid her head back on the sofa and closed her eyes. She dozed off and dreamt of a swaying kelp forest and a school of rosefish gliding quietly by. The fish suddenly darted left and right, panicky. The school became separated, and their swimming was frenzied as if startled. Without warning, a huge shark torpedoed into the school, bobbing its head and gnashing its jaws, impaling the fish on its sharp teeth. Faster and faster, the shark flew through the water. The poor rosefish never had a chance, and soon they were all devoured. Bits and pieces of red scales floated in the water. The shark spun and was face-to-face with Dana. It seemed to grin an evil, monstrous expression. The dorsal fin lowered in the ready, then the beast reared back and shot like a bullet straight toward Dana, its mouth wide and aimed directly at her.

Dana woke up screaming.

She looked at her watch. It was 6:00 a.m. Tuesday morning. Time to get ready for work. It was going to be a long day.

"Good morning," Dana said to Sheila.

Sheila was sitting in a chair, hunched over in front of a medicine chest. She had a notepad and pen. "...twenty-one, twenty-two, twenty-four. *Shit.*"

"Oops," Dana said. "Sorry. Forgot about inventory."

Sheila craned her neck back and let out a sigh. "It's fine. I need to stretch anyway." She stood up, walked over, and hugged Dana. "Welcome back! I can't wait to hear all about your trip."

"Thank you," Dana responded. She didn't reply to the second half of Sheila's statement. She wasn't ready to talk about her scuba diving incident quite yet.

"By the way, did you know we are all out of succinylcholine?" Sheila asked.

"What? The bottle's empty?"

"No. I mean, we're out. There's no bottle. But there's an empty space where it used to be -"

Dana's phone let out a *bing*. It was a text from Mike Evans. Distracted, she walked away from Sheila, ignoring the last statement.

> I'm still looking into the matter we discussed.
> But I feel like I'm getting closer. I'll keep you
> apprised of any information I find.

Despite recent events, Dana felt a surge of hope. She pulled up her phone and checked her work calendar to see what patients were coming in today: PawPaw, an older mutt that needed to be dewormed; Hello Kitty, a polydactyl Siamese cat that was getting her nails trimmed; and Thunder, an elderly German Shepherd who was going to be euthanized because of liver failure. Dana sighed. Those were never easy, no matter how good a veterinarian you were. Dana loved all animals – even sharks – and putting one down, no matter the reason, was heartbreaking. She hated seeing families going through the pain -

Sheila was saying something. *Was she still talking about the missing succinylcholine?*

"What?" Dana asked.

"I said, did you hear about what happened on Catalina Island yesterday?"

Dana swallowed. So much happened on the island while she was there. What could Sheila have possibly heard about?

"No, what happened?" Dana asked cautiously.

"I mean, it's so weird! You were just there, and now there's this big thing going on there? So wild -"

"Sheila -"

"- I mean, when I travel, nothing ever happens. It's always so boring. Except for that one time when I thought someone stole my purse, but it turned out to be in my suitcase the entire time -"

"Sheila-"

"- or that one time when my taxi had a flat tire and -"

"Sheila!"

"What?"

Dana took a deep breath. "What happened on Catalina Island yesterday?"

"Oh yeah! They found two dead bodies. Both men, they're pretty sure."

Dana's breath caught. "Pretty sure? What does that mean?"

"Well, their bodies were pretty mangled. Their heads were smashed in, and they had no teeth, and their hands had been sliced off, so there were no dental records or fingerprints."

Dana started feeling nauseous.

"The police can't identify them, but as stated in the autopsy reports, it looks like they've been dead for at least 48 hours, according to decomp and liver temp."

Dana looked at Sheila quizzically.

"What?" Sheila said. "I watch C.S.I.!"

"Are you kidding?" Dana asked.

"No! I love that show."

"I meant about the bodies."

"Oh. No. Not kidding."

Dana really wished Sheila would stop talking about Catalina Island. She just wanted to put everything about that place out of her mind.

"Here, look," Sheila said, placing her phone in Dana's hands. "Spoiler alert: It's not pretty."

Dana was suddenly looking at photos on DRT, the online news organization that never held back when exposing affairs of the rich and famous, indiscreet crimes, and deadly accurate gossip. They didn't care who got destroyed by the news they broke; they only cared that they got the scoop before anyone else. DRT changed the face of how the public got the news and was one of the most sought-after sources of information in the world. And so, it was today that Dana was viewing such news. Her knees buckled, and she fell into a chair.

"You okay?" Sheila asked.

"Wha-what am I looking at –?"

Sheila sat down in a chair beside Dana. Her voice was soft. "The bodies. Of the two men."

Dana stared at the phone. There, before her eyes, were the bodies of two men lying on a cold, marble floor. The pixelated picture showed the gore and crushed faces, but the clothes remained intact and in clear focus. She gasped, and her hand flew to her mouth.

The torsos were both wearing matching Gucci outfits with unmistakable "S" and "A" initials on the pockets.

CHAPTER 38

How she made it home, Dana had no idea. Absentmindedly, she plopped her purse on the kitchen counter. Kong limped his way over to her and expected a pat on the head. He got none. Refusing to be ignored, he nudged her hip. Dana shuffled into the den in a daze and sat on the sofa. She heard a *ding* from the Konginator 2000, but she gave no response.

Scotty and Aaron! What had happened to them? Who could've done this?

"I should call someone, but who?" she said, not sure who she was asking. She wasn't sure of anything. She looked at her phone and tried to Google Catalina Island Authorities, but her hands were shaking too much. Dana couldn't complete her thoughts. *I could be wrong. But I'm not wrong. Those were the outfits they were wearing the last night we saw them. I'm sure of that.*

She racked her brain to remember the property in northern California Aaron said they owned. *Bay Park? Berryessa? Bodega Bay? Oh, God. Think, Dana, think!*

She thought back to Saturday night, dinner at the beach club restaurant. That was the same day she had gone scuba diving and the sharks.... her memories caused her to get a chill. *I wasn't thinking straight that day.*

There's no way I'll remember. She walked around the house, hoping a sliver of remembrance would come to her. But it was futile. What kept popping back in her mind was how kind Scotty and Aaron had been. And yet someone had done the most heinous, malicious thing to them: smashed their faces in so all their teeth fell out and then chopped off their hands. She felt sick to her stomach.

"Hello, gorgeous people."

"You look like a white bike reflector."

"You look so familiar to me. Have we met before?"

Suddenly, arms wrapped around her from behind. She yelped.

"Sorry!" Bradley said. "Are you okay? You're awfully jumpy."

"I'm...I'm fine...but..."

"But?"

Dana hadn't forgotten her and Bradley's recent argument, but this information hit too close to home not to tell him about. Dana took a deep breath. "Do you remember Scotty and Aaron?"

Bradley furrowed his eyebrows. "The couple from Catalina Island?"

Dana nodded.

"Yeah, sure. Why?"

She told him that the bodies of two men were found murdered on Catalina Island and how she believed the bodies belonged to Scotty and Aaron because the clothes were an exact match to what they were wearing. "It has to be them, right?"

"I'm sure you're just overthinking this," he told her.

Dana looked scolded. She pulled up the images on the DRT website. For a lightning strike of a second, Dana thought she saw something in Bradley's eyes, a recognition. But then it was gone as quickly as it had flashed.

"They could be anyone," he said.

Dana was indignant. "But the timing! And their clothes! That's what they were wearing. Not everyone is going to be wearing matching Gucci outfits on the island at the exact same time we were there. This is not a coincidence!" Her breathing started to become uneven.

"Darling, hush," he soothed. He took her phone and put it in the back pocket of her jeans. "It'll be alright. Please don't worry about this. Even if it *was* them, which I'm not a hundred percent on board with, we didn't really know them, and there's nothing we could do for them at this point."

Dana knew Bradley was right. She had to let it go. She had enough on her mind with her clinic and the new interns coming in this week and –

"So, what do you think?" he was asking.

Her head turned. "Sorry, hon. About what?"

"About going away for a couple of days to take your mind off all this. I know we just got back, but I feel like I need to make up for a crappy Catalina trip." He looked at her, hopeful. "And an even crappier first day back from the trip." He lowered his head. "By the way, I'm sorry about all that. Truly. But a trip like this will be so relaxing – I promise!"

"I can't possibly!" she said. Work is backing up after this weekend, Sheila is going bonkers, and we have four new interns starting who need to be trained."

"How long till they're trained?" Bradley asked.

"Two weeks." She eyed him suspiciously. "Why?"

"Then we'll go in two weeks," he said. "You'll have Sheila and four assistants to run the place. Besides, it's only for a couple of days."

"Hmmm," she thought. "I really don't think -"

"Oh, c'mon! I need to do this for you." He pulled her into a tight hug, his big arms enveloping her.

She was weakening. "Where is it exactly you want to go?"

"Lake Oroville."

She snapped back as if she'd been struck. "Are you insane?"

"What?" he asked innocently.

"You know I hate water I can't touch the bottom in. Especially now after what just happened in Cata -"

"I know, I know, but you learned how to scuba and overcame a big fear. Well, until-" He smiled at her menacingly. "Duh dum. Duh dum. Duh dum duh dum duh dum -"

"The theme to *Jaws*? Seriously?" She smacked him on his arm.

Bradley laughed. "Oh, come on. You'll be fine. There are no deadly animals in the lake. It'll be fine."

"No!" she said emphatically.

Bradley pushed his bottom lip out and pouted.

Dana couldn't resist that look. He looked so cute – and hot at the same time. *How does he do that?* He pulled her back into his arms and hugged her tight. She could feel his hardness, and her legs turned to jelly. *Damn him,* she thought.

He looked down in her eyes. "Please? I promise you'll be safe. Besides, you know what they say about falling off a horse."

"Horses don't eat people."

He smiled. "Look, didn't I keep you safe in Catalina? I promise no harm will come to you."

Dana had to admit that he did save her from the sharks, and she's never felt safer than when she was with Bradley.

"So, how about tonight we just have some fun? We can go to Escape-Goats. I know you love a good escape room."

She did! It was one of her favorite things to do, and the more challenging, the better. "Yes! I'd love to go!" she said.

"To the lake?" he asked, turning his head.

She smirked. "We'll talk about that later. But right now, I'm ready to break out of jail!" She wrapped her arms around him and kissed him. "I love you," she said softly.

"Love you, too," he said back. He paused. "Oh, next week, I'll be away for three nights. Another project." He shrugged.

Dana was happy Bradley was so busy with work, but it sure cut into their intimate time together. Maybe a lake getaway was just what the doctor ordered.

"Okay," she said, "but until then, your ass is mine!" She squeezed his butt and pulled him tighter towards her. She heard her phone in her back pocket *bing* a text message.

"Let me get my keys from the bedroom, and we're all set to go," Bradley said, leaving her.

She pulled her phone out of her back pocket and clicked on the message. It was from Mike Evans.

Call me.

"All set?" Bradley asked, returning to her side.

Dana put the phone back into her pocket. "Yep. Let's go." *I'll call Mike back later.*

As they drove away, Dana had forgotten all about the two slaughtered men on Catalina Island.

CHAPTER 39

The following week was a whirlwind for Dana. Bradley was away, and it was her mother's birthday. She made a mental note to call her mother and invite her to lunch one day. Hopefully, her mother wouldn't expect Ray to accompany her. *I'll let her know it's a mother-daughter lunch. No men allowed. See how well that goes over.* Dana heaved a breath. *Like a lead balloon, probably.*

With Bradley out of town, Dana threw herself into her work. And it turned out to be the week from hell.

This week alone, she drained two skin abscesses from a Maltese, performed a prophylactic gastropexy on a young Great Dane, fixed a ruptured cranial cruciate ligament in a Himalayan, removed 22 rubber bands from the stomach of a domestic shorthair, spayed and neutered thirteen cats and dogs, removed a ten-pound intestinal tumor from a potbellied pig, and treated a bearded dragon for pinworms.

She was exhausted.

On top of that, one new intern got two files mixed up, nearly resulting in a surgical procedure on the wrong dog who just needed a distemper shot.

Another intern decided to rearrange all the files under a new system that failed miserably. As a result, no files could be found on time, and the waiting room became a zoo. Literally.

One day, near her breaking point, Dana said, "What is going on here?" Shelia looked overworked and defeated. She had no words. "And what are all these files doing here?" Dana pointed to an enormous stack on top of the filing cabinet.

"Oh, sorry," an intern said. "I was just trying to -" She saw Dana's face and decided to stop talking. "I'll move those now." But as she went to grab the stack, and in her nervous haste, they all fell to the floor, scattering everywhere and out of order.

"I'll handle it!" Dana said impatiently. The intern skittered away.

"Good lord, what a mess," Sheila said, helping Dana pick up the files. "I'm starting to think training four interns at one time was a bad idea."

"Ya think?" Dana asked incredulously.

They looked at each other and burst out laughing.

"Look, I shouldn't have expected you to handle all four of them," Dana said. "Why don't we each take two. You work with Jalynn and Emily, and I'll take Camryn and Shirey. Deal?"

"Heck yeah!" Sheila said happily.

Dana laughed.

"Aww, look," Sheila said. "Kong's file." She held up the manila folder like it was a plaque or something. "I remember when that sweet doggie came in with his broken leg. And that hot man he was with." She put her finger to her chin. "I wonder whatever happened to him?"

Dana's eyes grew wide. "Last I heard, he was being held captive by some crazy veterinarian who was having her way with him. Shocking."

Sheila laughed. "Well, I know your little rehab machine works well. We got to go up two more inches while you were away."

"Yes, and thank you for working with him," Dana said. "Actually, I'm pretty impressed with myself. His leg has gotten so much stronger, and his range of motion has greatly improved. The limping is almost unnoticeable. But he's gained, like, seven pounds from all the treats," she laughed.

Sheila opened the file. "I felt sorry for Kong. He had slipped in a puddle and broken his back left tibia clean in two. That was some slip."

"Let me see that," Dana said. She flipped through the charts and X-rays. Her brows creased. "Well, that's strange."

Sheila picked up more files. "What's strange?"

'Well," Dana hesitated, "it might be nothing, but take a look at the X-ray. See there? Where the tibia is broken?"

Sheila's eyes traveled the X-ray. "Yes. What about it?"

Dana spoke as her mind traveled. "If he slipped, then he must've slipped and fallen off a 20-foot cliff. That tibia is a clean break. Right in two." She shook her head. "Why didn't I notice this before?"

"Because you were distracted by *him*," Sheila stated matter-of-factly.

Dana blushed. "Yeah, maybe. But still….it is a bit odd."

"I don't know," Sheila said. "Isn't that a normal break for a fall?"

"Yes, and no. If a dog of Kong's size slips, sure, he'll sprain something, or in a worst-case scenario, get a hairline fracture that could result in the bone breaking all the way through if it's not treated."

"But…." Sheila egged.

"But Kong is a big dog. It would take a lot to endure a clean break of this magnitude."

Sheila looked puzzled. "So, what exactly are you saying? That Kong *didn't* break his leg?"

"Oh, he broke his leg alright. But I don't think a slip in a puddle would do quite this type of damage." She looked at Sheila. "I don't know if I completely understand it myself. It's like someone just grabbed his leg with both hands and -"

"And what?" Sheila asked.

Dana spoke incredulously. "…. just snapped it in two."

CHAPTER 40

Bradley was due back tonight from his long work week and Dana knew he'd be tired, so she just ordered dinner in. DoorDash was a wonderful thing. When she was ordering the food, she remembered she had failed to call her mother for a mother-daughter lunch. She winced. *She probably had plans with Ray*, Dana hoped. It had been an arduous week, and her mind was anywhere but on her mother. Dana let the guilt pass.

She poured herself some wine and sat on the sofa, curling her legs up under her. Kong padded over and rested his head on her thigh.

Dana thought of the X-ray. "What happened to you, boy?" she whispered, scratching behind his big black ears. He smiled contentedly, and his tongue flopped out. His tail began wagging.

The situation with Kong was bothering her, and she wasn't even sure *what* she had discovered, or *if* she had even discovered anything. She felt a headache coming on. Her mind was reeling, and she took a sip of wine.

She didn't want to bring it up to Bradley because it was a sore subject to him. He already felt guilty enough that he let Kong run in the rain and that he slipped in the puddle. But if someone did this to him deliberately, Bradley had a right to know. Maybe Kong was out of sight for longer than Bradley thought, and an aggressive neighbor who didn't like the big mutt did something on purpose to get back at Bradley. But who? Whoever it was, they needed serious help. Dana made a mental note to ask Bradley if he had any neighbors that fit the bill.

She raised her head and gazed at her bookshelves. There was a photo there, one of her and her three friends: Alicia, Brooke, and Cathy. People who knew them called them the 'AlphaBabes' because their names started with the first four letters of the alphabet. All four girls wore a matching necklace with an orange poppy charm. Alicia had given it to them as a bridesmaid's gift.

Dana remembered a time....

They were seated in the dark-paneled bar in el PRADO Hotel. After several glasses of champagne, Brooke was toasting the group.

"To the AlphaBabes! Because we are the hottest babes, and men are lucky to have us!"

Cathy quietly sipped her champagne and blushed at the mention of being called a 'babe'.

The other girls laughed at her naiveté.

Dana said, "Oh, please, Cath! We know you! You could be the hottest girl in college. All you have to do is take out that blue ribbon and let your hair down. Literally!"

Cathy raised a hand to the bun of hair on top of her head.

Dana continued. "Need I remind you of Ryan's party when you got a little drunk, whipped out that bobby pin, let your bun down, and you had him hooked -" but she stopped herself when she saw Brooke shooting daggers at her to shut up.

Cathy's glass fell to the table with a smash.

"Wait," Alicia said, sitting straighter with a jolt. "Ryan? My Ryan?"

There was an awkward silence.

Alicia looked at each girl for an answer.

Dana spoke first and quickly. "I must've been mistaken. It was Brian. Brian Hoover." She looked to the other two girls for help. "Wasn't it?"

Brooke picked up on the cue. "Yes. It was Brian Hoover. Or Steven Andrews. Or Lee Strickland. Or Thomas Graham. Or..." she was ticking off boy names on her fingers.

Cathy laughed nervously.

"Probably all of them," Brooke said. "Our Cathy here isn't as innocent as she'd like us to think." Brooke glanced at Dana. The look on Brooke's face asked, "Was that convincing?"

Dana nodded her agreement. She needed to change the subject. She grabbed Alicia by the arm and said, "You're going to make a kick-ass bride, and nothing is going to spoil it!"

"Here, here!" Brooke and Cathy said in unison.

Alicia had grown silent. Her eyes squinted as if in thought.

"Cathy, you need another glass," Dana said, grabbing one from the empty table next to them and quickly filling it with the golden, effervescent liquid. She handed Cathy the glass and mouthed, "I'm sorry."

Cathy's lips thinned, and her eyes rolled to the side.

"So, let's toast to many years of friendship! To the AlphaBabes!" Dana whooped, raising her glass. Brooke and Cathy followed suit, but Alicia did not move.

"Come on, sis!" Brooke goaded.

Alicia smiled, but it was brief. She knew her friends had said something they shouldn't have, and now they were trying to sway her to forget. You can't unring the bell, girls, she thought.

"To me," Alicia said, adding her glass to the toast. As they drank, her eyes darted over the rim of her glass to the three girls.

Dana looked hopeful.

Brooke looked satisfied.

Cathy looked nervous.

But Alicia, however, looked fucking pissed.

Dana held the photo in her hands. The four of them used to be each other's ride-or-die. *Used to be.* Until the wedding. That day, everything changed. It was their fault she was dead. And it was a secret they all swore they would take to their graves.

Now Brooke was missing, and Cathy wasn't answering her calls. But Dana and the girls hadn't really spoken since it all changed. They agreed silence was the best way to keep their secret buried.

The doorbell shrilled through the house, causing Kong to bark loudly and Dana to jump. *DoorDash.* She put the photo back on the shelf and headed towards the door. "One minute," she called as she grabbed her purse to get a tip. She opened the door and gasped.

"Mike!" she cried as she stared into the eyes of Mike Evans. "I thought you were…that you were…. what…what are you *doing* here?" She looked behind him quickly to see if anyone was around him. She grabbed him by the hand and yanked him inside. "Bradley is due back any minute. He can't see you here! The surprise would be spoiled!"

"I've left a couple of messages for you," he said, unbothered.

She was sure he was right and vaguely remembered a message to call him. But with everything going on, she had forgotten about their arrangement. She glanced nervously at her watch.

"May I sit?" Mike asked. "I have news."

"Sure," she said nervously. They made their way to the sofa. *I have to make this quick. If Bradley comes home and learns I was looking to find his family* – she couldn't finish the thought.

"I found them," Mike said. "All of them. His parents and his brother."

"Really?" she asked excitedly, forgetting she needed to hurry this along. "Bradley said he doesn't speak to them anymore. But maybe they'll speak to me." She was babbling. "Do you have a way for me to contact them? I'll even fly there if I must speak to them in person. Surely, they'd want to come to Bradley's wedding. He's their only son and brother. Do you think that's possible? That I could see them?"

"It's a bit complicated," he said.

"Oh? Well, then, what do you suggest? I really would like to see them."

Mike Evans pulled out some photos. "Okay, sure. But as I said, it's a bit complicated." He handed her the pictures.

As Dana flipped through them, her face drained of color, and her mouth opened wide. Her hand raised and covered her mouth in shock. "Oh, my god!" she cried out in horror. "What…what are these?"

"They're the crime scene photos. That's his family. Or what's left of them. They were butchered."

Dana shot him a look. She kept flipping through the pictures, each one worse than the last. "When…?"

"About three years ago," Mike filled in the blank.

These poor people! Who could've done this? And poor Bradley! No wonder he didn't want to talk about his family. No one in their right mind would want to rehash this tragedy.

But then her eye caught something. Her brain danced, and it registered something familiar. But what? *There was something….* And then either her heart stopped, or it raced so quickly she couldn't feel it. She flipped through the photos faster and re-examined all of them again.

And there it was- the thing she missed the first time, but the thing that could not be mistaken.

"Sweet Mary," she said, staring at the photos.

"What is it?" Mike asked.

Dana spoke haltingly. "They have no faces. No mouths. Their faces have been crushed."

"Oh yeah," Mike said. "That's pretty gnarly."

"And…and their hands have been chopped off." She paused. "No teeth and no hands." Flashes of matching Gucci outfits streaked across her mind. *Surely this is just a coincidence, she told herself. I mean, what are the odds? And Bradley seemed to be the connection.* She shook her head of the invading thoughts. *Why did I just think that? Oh, God, this is not making any sense!*

She was holding the pictures of Bradley's murdered family in her hands when she heard a noise off in the house, but it seemed further in the distance, in another part of her mind. She felt lightheaded and her hand rested on Mike's leg for support. Her thoughts were a whirlwind, and she didn't know what to do next. When Dana looked up, her eyes widened.

Bradley was standing over them.

CHAPTER 41

H is deep voice cut through the night. "What's going on here? Dana's racing heart stopped.

Mike Evans paused for only a second. He stood up and went to shake Bradley's hand. "I gotta tell you, this young lady is a helluva vet. She took care of my Dexter and had him almost as good as new in just one day. What did you say was wrong with him? Gastric dilation and volvo -"

"Uh, *volvulus*," she corrected him. "Gastric dilation and volvulus. Commonly called bloat." As she stood, she inconspicuously hid the photos in the sofa cushions. Kong jumped on the sofa and sprawled out. "It's really just when the stomach fills with gas. It was nothing. I was happy to help."

"Nothing? Oh, it was everything to me and the missus. Little Dex has been with us for fifteen years. From what I understand, he could've died. You saved him."

She waved off his appreciation. Her eyes flickered to Bradley. What had he seen?

"I just came by to thank her in person, is all," Mike said.

Bradley's eyes narrowed.

Mike Evans looked at Dana and nodded imperceptibly as if to say, "It's all good.".

"I appreciate you stopping by," Dana said, walking towards the door.

"Yeah, I'll get out of your hair. Thanks again, doc," he said as he closed the front door behind him.

Dana counted to five before turning to face Bradley.

"Really? A client that makes house calls. At night?"

She opened her mouth to speak just as the doorbell rang again. Startled, Kong jumped up and down on the sofa before hopping to the floor and barking savagely.

"Let me guess: another client. Kong hush!" Bradley headed towards the door. He turned the knob and swung open the door. Kong's bark was a roar. Bradley's huge frame swelled to fill the door like a giant ogre defending his castle. "What the hell do you want now?!" Bradley bellowed.

The DoorDash girl yelped and dropped the bag of food. Kong rushed to the bags.

"Oh, shit," Bradley said, helping her get the food up. "Kong, get back!"

"I'm...I'm so sorry," the girl stammered. She was near tears.

"No, no. I'm sorry," Bradley said.

Dana stepped up, grabbed Kong by the scruff, and pulled him back in. She gave the girl a crisp twenty-dollar bill for her troubles and thanked her as she left.

"I figured you'd be tired when you got home, so I ordered dinner. Hope you like scrambled whatever this is," she laughed.

He grinned sheepishly. "I'm sorry. I don't know what came over me. I come home and see a strange man in my house with you on the sofa and _"

"Shhh," she said. "There's nothing to worry about. He was just a client. A very nice one. I guess I need to tell my clients not to visit me outside the clinic. Or else I'll start charging them," she smiled. "We good?"

"We're good." He kissed her on the lips.

"Welcome back, by the way," she said. "How was your weekend away from me? How'd your project go?"

Bradley looked her in the eyes. "Went great. Killed it."

Dana's smile was slow to form. "Well, I'm glad you're back."

"Thanks. Long week."

"I bet I have you beat," she said

"I'll take that bet," he said. "I'll take this, too." He took Kong from her and handed her the food.

Dana headed into the kitchen to unload the dinner. "You can pour us some more wine. Grab a fresh bottle from the cabinet." Bradley headed into the den.

"So, just wait until I tell you about my week," Dana said from the kitchen. "I had so many patients, which I loved, but it was so busy. And poor Sheila. She was overwhelmed with the interns. Oh! And the interns! Let me tell you, they are going to need a lot of work, but I think a couple of them have promise so I'm excited about that and – Bradley, do you want to eat out of the container or on a real plate?"

Silence.

"Bradley? Container or plate?"

No response.

"Hon?"

Bradley walked back into the kitchen.

"There you are," Dana said. "Didn't you hear me talking to you?"

Bradley just stood there, his face ashen.

"Honey, are you okay?" Dana asked, setting down the dinner and siding up to Bradley. She placed the back of her hand on Bradley's forehead. "My god, you're burning up!" She led him to a chair at the table. "You sit. I'm going to get you some Tylenol."

"I'm fine," he said.

"Well, I'm still getting you some Tylenol. It'll help reduce the fever."

"Okay," he said.

She left the kitchen and entered the den on her way to the bathroom. As she passed the sofa, she noticed Kong had made a mess of the cushions when the doorbell rang.

Dana froze.

"No!" she whispered. "*No!*"

She stood in front of the sofa and stared down in panic. There, amongst the disheveled sofa cushions, now completely unhidden, were all the grisly photos of his butchered family.

And Bradley had just seen them.

CHAPTER 42

"Oh, my god!" Dana exclaimed. Her hands flew to her mouth. Her heart pounded in her ears.

"Do you need help finding the Tylenol?" Bradley called from the kitchen.

Bradley! She couldn't tell if he sounded different or not. He can't come in here. But if he's already seen the pictures – *which way did he walk into the kitchen?* If he came from the foyer, then he missed the sofa, but if he walked into the den to get the wine – *did he come into the kitchen with the wine?* Dana couldn't remember anything. Her panic had risen to an explosive level. Sweat dripped down her back.

"Dana?"

"Yes!" she called out. "Be right there!" Grabbing all the photos, she hurriedly made her way into the bedroom. She was sweating and her hands were shaking. The photos slipped from her grasp and scattered across the floor by the bed. She fell to her knees to collect them all, gathering them up in a bunch. Dana lifted the bed skirt to make sure none had slid under the bed. Confident she got them all, she ran to her dresser, yanked open a drawer, and hid the pictures under her tee shirts.

Flying into the bathroom, she grabbed a bottle of Tylenol from the medicine chest. She was hot and nervous, so she popped two of the blue and red pills herself. "Coming!" she called, hoping he didn't notice the shaking in her voice. She raced to the kitchen and stopped just outside the entry, composed herself, then stepped inside.

Bradley was there holding their wine glasses.

She forced a smile and handed him the bottle of Tylenol. *Were my hands shaking?* Dana was looking at him, trying to gauge how he was looking at her. Is that the look of someone who just saw pictures of his butchered family and now he knows she knows? Or of someone who just has a fever?

Or maybe it's the face of a man she knows nothing about.

Either way, Dana felt she was screwed.

He handed her a glass of wine. He swallowed three pills and chased them with the merlot.

She drank slowly, eyeing him over her glass.

"Thanks," he said. "Appreciate it."

Dana squinted her eyes. *Well, he doesn't act like he's about to go off the deep end at me for nosing into his business.* Despite her assured smile, she harbored worry. She shouldn't have done this! She should've listened to him and dropped the subject. But she couldn't leave well enough alone. She had to know. Justifying it by saying she was trying to surprise him at the wedding. Her intentions were good, but everything could've gone to shit quickly. *I need to fix this.* She tipped her wineglass to her lips and finished the burgundy liquid.

"So, uh, hon. I was thinking, why don't you go ahead and plan that trip to Lake Oroville? The sooner, the better." *Like, tomorrow.*

"Really?" he asked, his eyes popped open.

"Yes, really. It'll be fun." She couldn't think of anything *less* fun. But she had to get his mind off tonight's matters. But her doubt lingered. *This trip might afford me some alone time to take a gander at some of the information Mike gave me.* Dana made a mental sidenote to bring her laptop. She hated having these nagging feelings, but -

"What changed your mind?" he asked, interrupting her thoughts.

"Well, you were right: I conquered a big fear in Catalina. And I shouldn't be afraid of a little ol' lake when I survived a big ol' ocean." She wrapped her arms around his neck. "I mean, barely, but still."

He laughed. "I promise. You'll have a good time. It's a holiday, so there might be fireworks. I'll make all the arrangements." He kissed her lips, then moved to her neck, sucking gently on the side. He cupped her ass with his large hands and pulled her up and into him, his muscles taut and strong. She went limp in his arms. He scooped her up, carried her to the bedroom, and laid her on the bed.

His hands went under her shirt, and he grasped her breasts, pinching her gently and making her writhe. She tossed her head back and moaned.

And there, in the middle of her ecstasy, and for a brief moment, Dana's worries melted away.

CHAPTER 43

"What's the gun for? You know I don't like guns. Hate them, in fact."

Bradley was packing for their trip to Lake Oroville.

"Just in case."

She eyed him suspiciously. "Just in case of….?"

"Well, there could be…. bears," he whispered, almost inaudibly.

"Excuse me? What did you say?"

He turned to face her. "Bears. There might be bears."

"*Bears?*" she shrieked. "There are *bears* there?"

"Honey, it's California. In the woods. By a lake. Of course, there are bears." He walked over to her and held her. "But remember, I've got you. Promise." He headed back to his suitcase to pack.

Dana remembered how unprotected she was when she was floating bait for the sharks in the ocean. She felt helpless, and she hated that feeling. She stood there with her hands on her hips, looking at Bradley, and she made a decision.

"Don't forget the bullets."

The drive took less than three hours northeast to the lake. The roads were twisty and curvy, and the scenery was breathtaking. Dana enjoyed every minute. They stopped in the town of Oroville at a mom-and-pop store for a few groceries and wine.

"The wine has a screw top? No cork?" she whispered to Bradley.

"It's a mom-and-pop. Guess we should just be thankful they have wine at all," he shrugged.

"If you say so," she said.

A few minutes later, Bradley pulled the car up to their cabin, and a doe crossed their path on the driveway. A good omen, Dana thought.

Entering the large A-frame building, Dana immediately noticed the floor-to-ceiling windows that let in a ton of light and a fantastic view of the entire lake. They set the groceries on the kitchen counter, and Dana headed outside onto the expansive covered deck. From where she stood, she could see the beautiful Bidwell Marina and Eastern foothills. The only sounds she heard were the quiet creakings of the tall trees as they barely stirred in the breeze. She felt Bradley's arms wrap around her from behind. He placed his chin on her shoulder.

"See? It's beautiful, isn't it?"

She raised her eyebrows and shook her head. "I'm speechless."

"Oh. I should've brought you here sooner."

She scoffed and gently jabbed him with her elbow.

The water rippled in the wind, and now and then, a fish or turtle would cause a streamline across the surface. Dana's fear of the water lingered, but she needed this trip. She needed Bradley to enjoy this time away so he wouldn't think anything more about why Mike Evans was at the house or the pictures on the sofa of his murdered family. If he indeed saw them. She didn't want to take any chances.

Bradley had said he wanted this trip to be perfect because he felt he needed to make up for the Catalina calamity. And Dana was determined to make his wish come true—anything to divert his attention.

There were a lot of undertones to this trip and so much riding on its success. Dana looked at the water. It was dark and calm, but what lay beneath – she shivered. It certainly *seemed* idyllic. But there was something a bit unnerving she couldn't put her finger on.

She spun around. "So, what's first on the agenda? Hiking? Horseshoes? Tennis?" Anything that kept her on land.

"I was thinking about doing a paddleboat."

232

"In the lake?" she said a little too loudly. Her voice echoed through the woods.

He pulled his head back. "Yes. In the lake. Where else?"

"Don't they have a kiddie pool or something? Something where I can touch the bottom? I need to touch the bottom."

He laughed. "You're going to be just fine, trust me. Don't you trust me?"

For the first time, she felt a hesitation in finding her voice. *Did* she trust him? He wasn't honest, really, about his parents. He kept the truth about their murder from her. He just said he didn't talk to them anymore. Was she splitting hairs? And then there was the issue with Kong and his leg. Why didn't Bradley tell her how he really broke his leg? Or does he even know? She was baffled, but ultimately, she loved him. And with that love came trust. So, yes, she trusted him. She loved him with everything she had, and they were going to be husband and wife.

She smiled. "Of course, I trust you, darling. I love you. And to prove it...." she slowly got to her knees in front of him and unzipped his shorts. Bradley's breathing quickened, and he leaned back on the deck's railing, his head lolling back. She was gentle at first, the way he liked it. But in a short while, she brought him to an uncontrollable fever pitch. He moaned loudly, and then it was over. He raised his head back up and opened his eyes.

"Uh, we have company," he said.

Dana looked over her shoulder, and there, at the edge of the deck, was the doe they had seen earlier in the driveway.

"I hope you were taking notes," Dana said to the deer, who nodded and walked away.

They both burst out laughing.

After a quick lunch, they took the hiking trail down to the lake. Dana took in the wonder of nature all around her: bright pink Red Maids, yellow mariposa lilies, and delicate maiden-hair ferns.

"Look!" she cried, pointing to the left, where a never-ending field of bright orange California poppies bloomed. It was as if the entire landscape was ablaze. "I missed seeing them in Antelope

Valley, and now they're up here with us! Oh, they are magnificent," she said.

"They certainly are," Bradley agreed.

Once they arrived at the recreation center, they found the paddle-boats lined up along the pier.

"I don't see any attendant," Dana said.

"Maybe they're at lunch," Bradley shrugged. "But since we're renting a cabin here on the property, we get full use of the facilities and equipment."

He helped her with her lifejacket, and they hopped in one of the paddleboats and left the comfort of the dock. Dana started breathing heavier, just knowing the only thing separating her paddling feet from the water's murky depths was a couple of inches of fiberglass. Bradley noticed and grabbed her hand, reassuring her. Her fears began to dissipate.

They paddled around the corner of the lake and found a slew to pull into. Bradley suggested they park the paddleboat on the shore and take a quick dip.

"I didn't wear my bathing suit because I wasn't planning on swimming," she said, hoping that would be the end of that.

It wasn't.

She caught the mischievous little boy's look on Bradley's face and knew what he was thinking: *who needs a bathing suit?* She rolled her eyes and kept paddling, giving in. Once on shore, they parked the boat. She quickly looked all over the shore and saw no one. They quickly disrobed and waded into the water, the liquid cool to their bodies.

Dana walked about fifteen feet into the water, so her feet were still planted firmly on the slanted floor of the lake. She felt comfortable at this stage and decided she would stay put. She would not move for anything. Bradley swam up in front of her. Suddenly, her eyes widened, and she screamed. *"Snake!!"* She frantically pointed to below the surface.

Bradley jumped and thrashed in the water, trying to escape the snake. He whooped and hollered, not knowing which way to run. When he stopped moving, he saw Dana double over in laughter.

Giggling, one of her hands covered her mouth, and the other pointed to him below the surface. "It *does* kinda look like a big ol' snake," she purred. He grabbed her arms and wrapped them around his neck.

"Well, I oughta-"

She giggled some more, then wrapped her legs around his waist.

His face became serious, and he looked down in the water. His head swooped back and forth, scanning the dark water.

"What?" she said, her eyes big. "*Are* there snakes in here?" She jumped off his waist and started running back to shore.

He laughed. "No. Well, maybe."

"I'm out," she said.

"Oh, come on. I was kidding. I think." He bellowed in laughter.

"No way!" she announced. She reached the shore and pulled her shorts back on. "I survived sharks in the ocean," she said as she snapped her shirt over her head and shoved her arms through the sleeves. "And I'll be damned if I'm about to die in this lake!"

CHAPTER 44

The following morning, Dana fixed herself a power smoothie and a heartier breakfast of eggs, sausage, pancakes, and juice for Bradley. She brought it to him out on the deck. Dana looked at the water: it was calm and dark, undisturbed, awaiting the many revelers.

Dana's head cocked to the side. *Come to think of it, I haven't seen any revelers. Not one.* Her brows furrowed. "Hmmm," she murmured. She shrugged, chalking it up to being too early in the morning for vacationers to be awake. She gave it no further thought.

They spent most of the day hiking around the cabin. He took her back to the poppy field. Dana pulled out her necklace with the orange poppy charm.

"Where'd you get that?" Bradley asked.

"From a friend," Dana said quietly. "It was a long time ago." *But not really.* It just seemed like forever ago when she was a bridesmaid for Alicia. Brooke and Cathy, the other AlphaBabes, were there. "Ironic, huh?" she smiled. "Like me being here is meant to be."

Bradley took Dana's hand, and they laid down amongst the flame-colored flowers.

"I feel like Dorothy in *The Wizard of Oz*," she said, yawning.

"Just keep the flying monkeys away," he said, going in for a tickle. She shrieked and jumped up, running through the field. Bradley laughed and followed her. He caught up to her, gently wrapped his arms around her, and placed her on the grass. She was still laughing when he kissed her, his hands holding her arms above her head. She relented, and there, amongst the flowers she loved, she made love to the man who owned her heart.

"I love you," he said, looking down into her eyes.

It was a perfect day.

Once back at the cabin, exhausted from the afternoon, Bradley napped. While he slept, Dana snuck into the kitchen, sat at the table, and pulled out her laptop. What she was about to do caused Dana's heart to volley around in her chest. She heard a creaking noise behind her and jerked her head over her shoulder. There was nothing there. Turning back to the computer, she entered her credentials and hit ENTER. Her screen flickered.

INVALID LOGIN OR PASSWORD ENTERED.

She re-entered the information slower this time. She hit ENTER. There was another flicker, and then her screen went blank.

"What the…?" she asked. "Stupid computer." She hit the touchpad with her index finger and moved the cursor to the systems section at the bottom of her screen. She looked back over her shoulder to make sure the coast was clear. Once in the menu, she moved the cursor and clicked the NETWORK icon.

Wi-Fi NOT AVAILABLE

"Well, hell." She looked for unsecured Wi-Fi connections, but there were none. In fact, there weren't any Wi-Fi connections or personal hotspots at all for her to choose from. *No revelers at the lake,* she remembered thinking earlier.

Dana got up and opened drawers in the kitchen until she found what she was looking for: CABIN INFORMATION. She looked over the information and found the Wi-Fi name and password, then went back to her computer. She entered the login and password information and hit ENTER.

Wi-Fi NOT AVAILABLE

"Crap," she said. "Now what?" She closed her computer, went to the bedroom door, and peeked in. Bradley was on his side and exhaled a light snore. *It'll have to wait,* she thought. She padded barefoot to the bed and spooned him from behind. *If you can't beat 'em, join 'em.*

When Dana awoke, Bradley was on the deck grilling out steaks for dinner, her wine already poured. She wrapped herself in a fluffy blanket and joined him outside. He smiled at her and sipped his wine while she wiped some of the burgundy liquid off the corner of his mouth.

She decided everyone came with baggage, and if Bradley wanted to share his with her, he would when he was ready. *I need to stop being so paranoid,* she thought. *I am so in love with this man. My life is perfect. And nothing will ever spoil it for me.*

After dinner, they were sitting inside on the sofa. Her head rested on his shoulder.

"So, I have a surprise for you," Bradley said.

"A surprise? For me?" she asked, sitting up.

"Yup. But you'll need to put on something warmer. It's chilly out."

She sat up further. "Out? We're going out*side*?" She got up, walked to the deck's sliding doors, cupped her hands on the glass, and peered out. She saw nothing but pitch blackness. Nothingness. She walked back to Bradley on the sofa. "You can't see anything out there," she said incredulously, pointing toward the black hole outside the glass doors. "And you want to go out there?"

Bradley chuckled. "Yes. Now scoot," he said, smacking her playfully on her butt. She yelped, then walked into the bedroom, shaking her head.

"Where are we going?" she called from the bedroom.

"You'll see," he said.

"In this darkness, I can't see anything," she muttered under her breath.

"So, what's this surprise all about?" she asked, emerging from the bedroom.

"Fine. I'll tell you," he huffed in mock surrender. "It's a holiday, and they're having fireworks over the lake. I thought it would be nice if we went out to see them. Have a little wine, celebrate our upcoming wedding…" He held up two bottles of wine. "One for me and one for you, m'lady."

It was the first time Bradley had mentioned their wedding in a while, and it made her heart swell. Of course, she would go with him. It would be a perfect night.

They both held flashlights as they hiked towards the marina. The stars were dazzling, like millions of diamonds in the sky; the sight was mesmerizing. It was something Dana had never seen before. The moon shone on the surface of the lake, making the ripples shimmer in the pale light. Dana felt the night was very romantic.

Once at the marina, they turned right and walked along the lake's edge. There was a five-foot drop, nothing too dangerous, but it was dark, and Dana was in unfamiliar territory. A chill swept across the lake and through her bones. She shivered, and her teeth chattered. Within five minutes, the trail became rocky, and she stumbled more than once. She began to doubt the stability of her foothold. The last thing she wanted was to trip and fall off the trail's edge into the inky water.

She stopped and lifted her head from the trail. Her flashlight wavered in the dark, and she noticed Bradley was a good twenty feet ahead of her.

"Wait up!" she called to him.

She no longer felt the night was romantic.

"Where are we going?" she demanded.

"Almost there," he hollered back over his shoulder. "Promise."

Dana huffed her annoyance. She tripped on a large rock and felt her ankle turn a little. "Ow," she muttered. She began to crave her bottle of wine, but it was twenty feet ahead of her. *I'm not even going to bother with a glass,* she thought.

Fifteen minutes later, Dana had had enough. She was done. Her ankle hurt, she was tired, and she was no longer interested in seeing the fireworks. She was ready to go back.

"Bradley-" she whined.

"We're here!" he announced.

"Thank you, Jesus!" she exclaimed. *But where was 'here'?* She looked around; on her left was the shimmering, dark water of the lake, and to her right was a pitch-black forest filled with God knows what. *That's not creepy at all,* she thought.

But once she took a closer look, she had to admit it was beautiful. The full moon reflected off the obsidian water and illuminated nearly every edge of the lake. Dana felt she was on another planet. It was spellbinding. A Great-horned owl hooted, escaped from the forest, and flew across the lake, disappearing into the dark. *It's like something out of the movie 'Twilight',* she marveled. Her eyes shifted, half-expecting a pale vampire to leap out from behind a tree. She shook her head back to reality.

"Here," Bradley said, interrupting her thoughts. "Let's sit."

Dana took his hand as he helped her to the ground. The cold from the grass permeated through her jeans, and an icy chill ran up her spine. She heard him unscrew the top from the wine they had gotten from the mom-and-pop store. At this point, she didn't care it wasn't a quality vino. "Give me that," she said. He handed her the bottle. She took a generous swig. "Yum," she grimaced. "This is swill." She took another long sip.

Bradley stood up and walked towards the water. He put his hands on his hips and looked out over the lake. As he turned back towards Dana, he froze and pointed.

"Look!"

Dana jumped up, certain a bear was reared up behind her, ready to slice through her body. *"What?"*

"A boat!" Bradley was walking fast towards the water's edge. He pointed.

"A – what?" Dana's heart was pounding. She rolled her eyes. Safe from a non-existent bear, she took another gulp of wine. Her shivers were gone as she started to feel warm inside. She joined him on the shore. And sure enough, there was a long wooden Adirondack guide boat just resting on the bank. "That's nice," she said noncommittally.

Bradley said nothing but kept smiling at her and pointing to the boat.

And like a shock to her body, she understood what he was thinking, and her eyes flew open. "Are you *crazy*? Absolutely not! You are *not* getting me in that…that…death trap!"

"Aww, c'mon," he coaxed. "We'll see the fireworks better from out there. They'll be right over our heads."

"I don't want nothin' over my head," she said, drinking her wine.

Bradley got in the boat and sat down. "Look! It's very sturdy. We'll be fine."

Dana wasn't sure if the wine was making her feel braver or more stupid. *More stupid*, she decided. *Stupider.* She was feeling lightheaded.

Bradley reached out his hand to take hers.

Feeling outplayed, Dana found herself stepping inside the guide boat. She tripped over a large block and plopped down on the bench. She took another sip of wine. *For courage*, she reasoned.

Bradley stepped out of the boat and started pushing it into the water. The boat wobbled as it became situated on top of the water. Dana yelped and gripped the sides of the craft. Bradley hopped in and sat next to her on the same bench. He picked up an oar and started a slow paddle. The boat glided gracefully further from shore.

"Jusss, like, ten feet out, m'kay?" she slurred.

He laughed. "The trees will block our view. We need to go out further than that, hon."

"Wha 'ever," she mumbled. *This could be fun.* Her eyelids felt heavy. She forced her eyes open. *Don' wanna miss the fireworks.* They were moving faster now. She looked back and couldn't see the shore. "Bye-bye, shore," she waved.

"How's the wine?" Bradley asked.

"Issss good." She held up her near-empty bottle. She noticed Bradley was paddling like an expert. *He's so talented*, she thought. *Sure was lucky this boat was there.*

Bradley stopped rowing, and he let the boat coast a little. They were now in the middle of the lake. A breeze whipped around her, and she scooted closer to him, causing the boat to rock. She shrieked.

"You really should sit still," he advised.

Dana leaned into him and rested her head on his shoulder. She was in her happy place. She yawned and closed her eyes.

"Finish your wine," she heard him say. She tipped the bottle until there was nothing left.

"Done," she said triumphantly.

"Then you should sleep."

She liked that idea. "M'kay," she said. "G'night."

It was the last thing she remembered before passing out.

She dreamt of running through fields of poppies and getting increasingly tired, the smoky, earthy fragrance from the flowers invading her senses. Her feet felt heavy, and she couldn't run anymore. She wanted to sit and rest. She was standing in the middle of the field; her feet felt cemented to the ground. She looked around, but she was all alone. She called out for Bradley but got no answer. She could not move and, in a panic, awakened with a jolt.

Her face was being tickled by her hair blowing gently around her. Dana tried to raise her hands to wipe the hair out of her eyes, but she could not lift her arms. She was still groggy, and nothing was clear in her mind. She felt a gentle rocking back and forth and remembered that she was in a boat with Bradley. But where was he?

Dana looked at the end of the boat and saw two of him sitting, staring. She blinked hard and shook her head. When she reopened her eyes, he had come into focus, merging into one. He was still staring at her. She didn't recognize this look.

He was looking at her.

No. *Through* her.

"Bradley? What...what is going on? Why...can't I move...?" Her arms felt pinned down, and when she looked, she saw her wrists were bound together by a rope that was tied around her waist. She struggled to move her arms to no avail. "Bradley! What is going on? Answer me!" Her head pounded.

But still, he said nothing.

Dana went to stand but couldn't. "What is...?" She looked and followed the rope with her eyes. It went to the floor of the boat. She looked down at her feet, and her eyes widened in terror: her feet were tied to cement blocks. *What? What is happening?*

Suddenly, she was wide awake, and her fear was at a fever pitch. She whipped her head at Bradley. He was like a zombie, dead, sitting there without emotion. But with a smirk on his face.

"Bradley, I demand to know what's going on! Get me out of here, now!"

He didn't budge.

"Please!" she begged. "Honey, I love you! Why are you doing this?"

He lifted his head. He looked sad. "I saw the pictures. Of my family. Why did you have those?"

Dana looked at him in disbelief. It took her a moment to register, but then the clarity knocked her. *So, he* had *seen them.* "I...um, I wanted to... to invite your family to the wedding as a surprise....and Mike -"

"Mike? That's his name?" he growled.

"He's just a friend. Not even," she said. "I had him locate your family because I was going to surprise you with them as a gift. For you. At the wedding."

Bradley glared at her. "Well, he found them, didn't he?"

Dana looked down at the floor of the boat. She felt ashamed. But then, she thought maybe she could spin this to her advantage. "Bradley, I love you. You have done so much for me, and I just wanted to do something nice for you in return, that's all. Is it really that bad?"

He paused. "So, I guess he told you I killed them, too?"

"Wha-" Dana froze. She looked at him. "Bradley, what? Why would you...no! He didn't tell me anything of the sort. He would never make up something so ridicu -" Then she stopped talking. She took her scene in once again: her tied-up hands and cement blocks on her feet. *He* DID *do it! He actually killed his family! And now he wants me dead, too. But why? Does he think I'm going to tell someone? Oh, God, this cannot be happening! Things like this only happened in the movies.*

"Bradley! You have this all wrong, darling. I would never tell anyone about...about your family. Never! You must believe me." Then she remembered something in the back of her mind, a tickle. But what? And then – Catalina Island. Scotty and Aaron. Their deaths were identical to Bradley's family's. *Oh, my god. He killed Scotty and Aaron, too!*

Bradley stood up in the boat. "I don't care about my family," he said. "We didn't want to be associated with them, so I took away their identities." He looked her in the eyes. "But you really don't know the half of it."

We? He said 'we'. Who's 'we'?

243

He stepped over a planked bench and stared down at her. He looked at the water. "But what you *do* know, and what you *did*, you will take to your grave."

Dana fully opened her lungs and screamed, but it echoed back like a boomerang.

"Scream all you want. No one can hear you. Have you seen another person since we got here?"

She thought back to this morning and how she had thought she had seen no one else. Not a soul. *Only a stupid deer.*

"That's because the lake is closed. Its level is being raised for the season, and the dam is being recalibrated, so the lake is not open to the public." Bradley moved closer to her. He raised his hand. He was holding something.

Dana squinted in the moonlight. It was a little black box, some mechanical walkie-talkie-looking thing.

"What's...?" she started to ask.

"It's a Wi-Fi jammer. Just to be safe," he said, tossing it overboard. They watched it sink out of sight.

That's why I couldn't log onto my computer today, she thought, her eyes widening. Uselessly, she squirmed, but she was tied up too tight. *When did he do this to me? How did I sleep through this?*

"Because I put a shit ton of the tincture from the poppies in your wine. It made you sleep rather soundly."

She had spoken aloud.

Dana knew what was coming but didn't know why. Tears flowed down her cheeks.

"Please, Bradley! You don't have to do this," she pleaded.

He ignored her. Moving up behind her, he lifted her and moved her closer to the edge of the boat.

She flung her head back and forth, her hair whipping around her head. Her body tensed, and she willed herself to be too heavy to lift, but she knew Bradley would have no trouble raising her out of the boat. She screamed with all her might.

He reached in front of her and shoved something in between her arms. A photo. She looked down, and the first face she saw in the picture belonged to Gio. Her eyes focused, and she saw the rest: her, Brooke, and

Cathy. Drinking at the wedding. Her friends, once upon a time. But now Brooke was missing, and she hadn't heard from Cathy. Did Bradley have something to do with them being missing? The realization hit her like a truck, and immense sadness overcame her.

She was sad about her past, for she had no future.

Dana saw Bradley pull out a cell phone and dial a number. She saw her chance and took it.

"Help me! Please, help me! I'm at Lake Oroville, and I'm about to die!" She hoped whoever was on the other end of the call heard her and would help her, but her hopes were dashed when she heard the two words Bradley spoke into the phone.

"It's done."

He snapped off the phone and shoved it into her jeans pocket. "Normally, I call after the fact, but I thought this would be more dramatic."

Normally, I call after the fact.

And Dana knew.

"And just so you know," Bradley continued, "We are at the deepest part of the lake – 722 feet deep." He saw her eyes grow in horror. "Now, you did say you wanted to be somewhere where you could touch the bottom."

With the ease of someone lifting a ream of paper, he lifted her entire body, cement blocks and all.

"And now you will," he said as he tossed her over the side of the boat.

She opened her mouth to scream but gulped in water. Her lungs filled instantly with the cold lake water, and after that, she gurgled twice, then her breathing ceased.

The poppy charm floated around her neck for a millisecond as the rope stretched to complete tautness, and she suddenly felt her body rapidly plunge deep into the sinister, liquid darkness.

PART FOUR
BRADLEY & ALICIA

CHAPTER 45

"You're a pussy!" the voice yelled. "Pussy! Pussy! Pussy!"
Bradley cowered behind the slide on the school's playground. He hated recess. It was always the time he got bullied at school. He was a skinny, gangly boy. The runt of the 4th grade class. And all the students, especially Al, never let him forget it.

Al was the most brutal of all. Forceful. The leader of the school and feared by all students – and most of the teachers. A year older than Bradley but even smaller in stature. Al didn't care how harsh the attacks were – the more abrasive, the better. And every punishment served the purpose of setting ranks in the school. Al always ranked first, the top of the heap, ruling with an iron fist.

And Bradley always ranked dead last.

But today was especially vicious.

Earlier in the day, Bradley witnessed Al place a thumbtack on the teacher's chair, but before Mrs. Gibson sat down, Bradley told her, and the jig was up. Al's trickery was exposed. When Mrs. Gibson asked Bradley who the culprit was, he began to sweat and swore he wouldn't divulge who the miscreant was.

But his eyes deceived him, and in his nervousness, he looked straight at Al. Mrs. Gibson knew Al was trouble and even though the child made her heart flutter in fear, she figured she would set an example of the problem student. As a chastisement, Mrs. Gibson gave Al detention for the rest of the week. Unfortunately, she knew Al was not one to back down lightly and that this punishment would most certainly result in trouble for Bradley. But Mrs. Gibson had no choice. She had to do something. Silence was permission, and she would not let Al get off so easily.

Because of being singled out, Al's anger thickened. Al decided to get even with Bradley by punishing him on the playground for the entire school to see.

What else was there to lose?

"You're a pussy!" Al was yelling at Bradley. Groups from all around encircled Bradley and joined in the verbal accost.

Bradley tried to run, to hide. He covered his ears, closed his eyes, and tried to hold on to his sanity for dear life.

Then, to his horror, he wet his pants. A yellow puddle formed around him, and his thighs warmed. His face colored in embarrassment.

Al pointed and jeered at him.

With all eyes on Bradley, he lowered his head, his bottom lip trembled, and he began to weep.

Al walked up to him. "Look at me!"

Bradley raised his head slowly.

"You're pathetic," Al said. "I can't believe I got detention all week because of you!"

"I'm…I'm sor-sorry," Bradley wailed. "I'm sorry!"

"Oh, you will be," Al sneered. "You pissing yourself was just the beginning. Trust me."

This scared Bradley even further. He looked up into the guileful face of his tormentor, his eyes pleading.

Al's eyes swooped around the scene, eyeing Bradley sitting in his own urine. A yellow river beginning to snake down the sidewalk. An evil idea formed, and the corner of Al's mouth raised. "Lick it up."

Bradley's eyes filled with terror. "Wha-what?"

"Lick. It. Up."

"I…no, please." Bradley's eyes shifted around the playground. Every eye was on him. Some looked sinister; others looked mortified. But every one of them knew Bradley better do as he was told.

Bradley cried harder. He had no choice; he knew that. He got on his knees and looked down at the yellow liquid pooling around him.

Chants of "Drink! Drink! Drink!" filled the playground.

Cornered, Bradley knew he must do this or suffer an even harsher punishment. He shuddered at what that may be. Bending over the puddle of urine, he squinted his eyes closed and stuck out his tongue. He lowered his head until his tongue came in contact with the wetness. He licked once, cringing at the taste. He forced himself to swallow the tiny drop of urine.

Suddenly, he felt a foot on the back of his head, shoving his face down onto the sidewalk, crunching his face around in the liquid. Bradley could feel his lips scraping on the rough concrete, blood mixed with the yellow pee.

"I said lick it up!" Al bellowed.

Bradley surrendered all and started inhaling and sucking up the warm liquid until there was none left. He sat up and scrambled backward until his back was against a trashcan. Tears were still flowing down his cheeks.

"Good, boy," Al smiled, walking up to him. "How does it feel to get beat up by a girl? Your own sister?"

"Alicia...I-I'm sorry!" He buried his head in his lap.

Alicia kicked him in his thigh. "I think I'll make you my personal slave this whole week. It'll make up for the week I have to stay behind in this shit hole." She grinned at him. "Yeah. My personal slave. I'm gonna like making you do things for me." She laughed as she walked away from him.

The rest of the kids followed Alicia's lead and left the playground, leaving Bradley alone.

Alicia had won.

And so, the days of Alicia making Bradley do things for her began that very day. Right there on the playground, piss and all.

CHAPTER 46

Growing up, Alicia did not live in a home filled with laughter and love unless that's what was playing on the television set from some generic sitcom. Instead, her life was a snapshot of tension and humiliation, anger and anxiety, brutality and blood. Her parents, Lucinda and Stanley, were not fans of each other, and, more than once, Alicia wondered how they paused even for a minute to love each other to have children.

She would soon find out love was never in the picture.

The fights would start almost tenderly, playfully. But eventually, someone would end up with a bloody body part, a sizeable purple-black bruise, ripped-out hair on the floor, an errant tooth in another room, or an injury unseen by the human eye. And ten times out of ten, that someone would be her father, Stanley.

Alicia liked her father, but she wasn't sure if she loved him or not. She wasn't even sure if she knew what 'love' was. But one birthday, he gave her an antique locket to wear around her neck.

"Look, Alicia," he said, opening the locket. "There's a picture of you on one side and a picture of Bradley on the other. My two precious children." His voice tightened. "Wear this always and know your father loves you."

"It's beautiful, father," Alicia said, letting her father hook the necklace behind her neck. "Thank you. I'll never take it off."

"Be careful with the clasp. The necklace is antique and very fragile. Keep it beneath your shirt, and don't flaunt it in front of your mother. She wasn't happy when I bought this for you. She got mad that I spent my allowance on something besides groceries."

Alicia should've been shocked her father received a monthly stipend from his wife, but she recognized from the get-go her father was a mouse of a man: weak and timid, a spineless coward who allowed his wife to control him. He was her puppet. An allowance was just another way her mother held authority over him.

Alicia's mother was a monster.

And where Bradley was terrified of their mother, Alicia worshipped her.

Lucinda Harris, for all who knew her, led a charmed life: she had two charming children and a husband who doted on her every need. Lucinda rarely cooked, but on special occasions, Stanley would grill outside, and the family would enjoy a feast. And if things were really good, there would be some decadent dessert for everyone to enjoy. They lived in a beautiful home with the proverbial white picket fence. Lucinda regularly attended P.T.A. meetings and brought her delicious lemon squares; she never let the recipe pass over her lips. "If I told you my secret, I'd have to kill you," she would say, then toss back her red hair and laugh.

Yes, on the surface, all the neighbors envied the Harris's.

Behind closed doors, however, was another story.

Her children were lovely mostly because their mother threatened them.

"If you don't fucking behave in public, like normal, non-retarded children," she said casually one day to Alicia and Bradley, "then don't be surprised if your sweet pets over there," she pointed to the glass terrarium where their two guinea pigs stared back wide-eyed, "end up in the front yard one day, and run away from you, forever."

Young Bradley started crying. Next to his sister, he loved those guinea pigs more than life itself. He vowed never to act up.

"I...promise..." he gasped through his tears.

"Yes, mama," Alicia said.

Lucinda Harris sighed heavily. "Good. Now go to bed."

"But...but we haven't had dinner yet. And it's only 5:30," Alicia mumbled.

"Fine," Lucinda Harris smiled. "No dinner for *two* nights. And you will do as you are told." She glared at them. "Do you understand?" their mother barked.

Bradley couldn't catch his breath from crying so hard. Alicia just said, "Yes, mama."

Their mother arched her left brow, spun, and walked away. "Stanley!" she bellowed to her husband as she headed towards the den.

Alicia heard something crash and shatter in the distance.

"I'm...hungry," Bradley stuttered.

"Shhh, don't let her hear you." Alicia reached over and wiped away her brother's tears. She took him in her arms and hugged him. "I have an idea of how to get us something, okay? Just hold on."

Bradley loved his sister. Whenever she said something to him, it seemed to comfort and assure him. He would do anything for her.

"Okay," he said, feeling better.

Later that night, Alicia opened her locket from around her neck and looked at the pictures of her and Bradley. He was cherub-faced with bright green eyes, and he had a smile that would beguile all who met him. To meet him would be to fall in love instantly with him. And yet, he was helpless. Bradley took after their father: insecure and timorous. But he was her brother, and Alicia decided she would do whatever it took for them to stick together, even if she had to be the one to call the shots.

Tonight, they were hungry, so Alicia decided she would sneak into the kitchen and make a peanut butter sandwich they could split. It wasn't much, but it would have to do.

She crept from her room and down the hall, the soft carpet squished between her toes. As she came upon her parents' closed bedroom door, she heard a horrible noise, as if someone was being hurt. It wouldn't be the first time. Alicia pressed her ear against the cold, wooden door, careful not to make a sound. Just beyond the door, she could hear the bedsprings protesting beneath movement. She moved her head lower, closer to the keyhole. Muffled voices became clearer.

"Now, Stanley! Do it harder! Deeper! My god, I am cursed with a husband who has a tiny dick!"

Alicia heard her father moaning. Or was he whimpering?

"Small or not, you *will* get me pregnant! Now hurry and come! I haven't got all night."

Stanley grunted, then gave a slight whine, and it was over. Alicia heard him sobbing.

"Stop your crying. My god, you are pathetic!"

"Lucinda...I...."

"What?!" she bellowed. "Get from underneath me. I'm through with you."

Alicia heard the bed creak, and then there was a pause.

Her mother spoke. "Well, I think that was rather successful. I can almost feel your little swimmers doing their thing."

"How can you.... I mean, we don't know..."

"Don't question me!" she said sternly. "I can just tell."

"Oh, god," Stanley said.

Alicia knew for certain that if her mother willed herself to get pregnant, then there would be no doubt in the world she would be. She heard her mother's voice change to a low tone.

"Congratulations," Lucinda said. "You're going to be a father."

"I'm already a father," Stanley said. Alicia thought she heard the tiniest bit of a quiver in his voice.

Lucinda laughed. "Oh, please. That little thing has never given me children. Until now."

"What are you talking about?"

Alicia pressed her ear harder on the door. If she leaned any closer, she would be inside the room.

"Oh, what's the point anymore?" Lucinda sighed. "Alicia and Bradley belong to somebody else. But this one, this one inside me now, is yours."

"No! I...I don't believe you!" he stammered.

"Believe what you want, I don't care. Their father – their *real* father –

is no longer in the picture, and, well, I was in the mood for another one. You fit the bill, little dick," she laughed.

The news made Alicia gasp. She covered her mouth with her hands. Too late, she realized she might have been heard.

Inside, the room had suddenly fallen silent.

Panicking, Alicia turned quickly to bolt but slammed into the door-frame. She stifled a yelp of pain but kept running to her room. She closed the door quickly and quietly behind her. Out of breath and panting, she cracked open the door and peered down the hallway.

Alicia could see her mother standing outside their bedroom door, looking up and down the hall. It was dark, and her mother couldn't see her bedroom door cracked open. She was safe. Alicia felt her heart rate slow to normal. *I got away with it,* she thought.

Lucinda was scrutinizing every nook and cranny and floorboard of the corridor. And then, in an instant, she stopped all motion. Her eyes looked down towards the floor, and she cocked her head. Bending over, she grabbed something off the top of the carpet and held it up for closer inspection.

Alicia's eyes grew wide at her mother.

She was holding the locket.

Two nights later, without having eaten for 48 hours, Alicia and Bradley were beyond starving, but blessedly, the time had finally come for them to join their parents for dinner. Alicia never made it to the kitchen to make the peanut butter and jelly sandwich after the complete debacle with her losing her locket, so when they finally sat down to eat, the grumbles in their stomachs were loud and low.

Stanley was outside grilling, and Alicia saw a two-tier chocolate cake on the kitchen counter. A special occasion was brewing, but what it was about, exactly, was anyone's guess. Her father walked in carrying a tray of mouthwatering grilled chicken. The steam rose from the tray and wafted to Alicia's nostrils. Her stomach growled even more at the wonderful smell.

"Tonight is a momentous night," Lucinda said, standing at her end of the table. "I have an announcement to make. And, despite the recent, insolent behavior of you two," she snapped her head to look at Alicia and Bradley, "I'm happy you are here to join in our happiness. Isn't that right, Stanley?"

Alicia and Bradley both turned to look at their father. He had a smile plastered on his face.

"Yes, dear," he said.

"What is it, mama?" Alicia asked. She wanted the news to hurry and get here so she could eat.

Lucinda clasped her hands together. "It's still early, but I'm having a baby. A boy."

Bradley's mouth dropped open.

Alicia wasn't sure how her mother already knew she would have a boy, but she was confident if Lucinda wanted a son, then a son she would have. Alicia recalled what she had overheard her mother yelling at her father the other night. *You will get me pregnant!* It was at this moment Alicia realized her mother, as domineering and controlling as she was, held all the power. Lucinda bent Stanley to her will, and he still loved her. It was a fascinating dynamic to witness.

Alicia took note. *Our mother likes to win.*

"So, this feast honors our wonderful news," Lucinda continued. She sat and spread her hands over the meal. "Eat. You two must be starving." She eyed the children. "You really must take better care of yourselves."

Over the next thirty minutes, not another word was said. Alicia and Bradley devoured their grilled chicken and even asked for seconds of their vegetables. Large pats of butter melted on the fluffy, sweet rolls. The only thing left on their plates were the bones. Bradley ate so fast, he developed hiccups. Alicia giggled each time his throat spasmed.

After dinner, they all enjoyed a thick slice of chocolate cake; the icing was rich and velvety. Alicia let out a little burp.

Bradley chortled.

"That was a delicious meal, Lucinda," Stanley complimented.

"Yes, it was. The meat was just perfect. Tender and seasoned just right. Don't you agree, children?"

"Oh, yes, mama," they said in unison.

"I'm glad you enjoyed it. You may be excused now." She stood and began clearing the table of the dinnerware.

"Thank you, mama," Alicia said. She and Bradley headed towards the den, but as they walked, something across the room glinted in the light and caught Alicia's attention. She squinted her eyes and stepped closer. She stopped dead in her tracks.

There it was.

Hanging from the guinea pigs' glass terrarium.

Her locket.

Alicia's heart pounded. She lifted the locket from the enclosure and quickly opened it. The photos of her and Bradley were still there, intact. Alicia held the locket to her chest and sighed in relief. *She's just returning it to me,* Alicia thought to herself. *Nothing to worry about.* She closed her eyes, thankful there was no more punishment.

"Alicia?" Bradley asked.

She turned to him and smiled. "Yes, brother?"

"Where are they?"

"Where are who?"

"Them," he said meekly.

Alicia followed his eyes. He was pointing at the terrarium.

She didn't fully understand at first. *What exactly am I looking at?* But then it hit her: the glass aquarium was empty.

The guinea pigs were gone.

Alicia crinkled her brow. "I...I don't know." She heard a scraping noise from behind her. *Had they gotten out?* She spun and looked down but saw nothing. Raising her head, she looked in the kitchen. Her mother was smiling, standing over the garbage can with a plate in her hand.

And she was scraping the bones into the trash.

Although Alicia had her suspicions, she never got confirmation what exactly had happened to the guinea pigs that day: *had their mother set them in the front yard like she had threatened, and they had simply run away? Or had they been grilled and -* Alicia couldn't finish the thought. But either way, the message sent was clear as day: don't fuck with mama.

Alicia never mentioned any other possibility to Bradley other than they must have gotten out of their cage and wandered off. He cried for three days at their loss, worried they were out in the world with no one to care for them. *It was better than the alternative for him to think this,* Alicia thought. *He was weak. Reality was not for him.*

He would need guidance, a mentor. Someone who could guide him through life. Someone to pull *this* string to go one way, or tug on *that* string to go another way. Bradley was just like their father. *A puppet.* And although he may be helpless, he could be useful. He just needed the right controller.

And so, after observing and noting her mother's actions for so long, Alicia thought of a second message she had received loud and clear that day: manipulation was all about control, and the controller always won in the end.

And like her mother, Alicia loved to win.

CHAPTER 47

When Bradley was thirteen, he was nearly sent to juvie. When he was fourteen, he had sex for the first time. When he was fifteen, he killed his first human being.

The near-stint in juvie was for petty robbery. Once, Alicia wanted a training bra. And just to humiliate Bradley, she, of course, made him try it on first. Then she made him steal it. Alicia cried in front of the officers and her parents when he was caught by store security, saying she had tried to dissuade him from stealing it, but he had insisted on getting the bra for her as a gift. His parents bargained with enforcement that instead of sending Bradley to juvenile detention, their own punishment would be harsh and swift. After getting hit with a thin weeping willow branch, Bradley was withheld dinner for two weeks. Alicia could barely contain her glee.

Upstairs in his room, he told his sister he wanted to confess to their parents that she made him steal the undergarment. Alicia picked up a hardback book and sat next to Bradley on the bed. His heart began to pound. Her smile was not a cheerful smile, but a blistering one. She placed the book under his left hand, his fingers splayed out.

"Don't fucking move," she said.

She grabbed his ring finger and started to bend it back.

"You will not confess anything to our parents. Do you understand?"

The pain was excruciating. He grunted. And that made her pull back his finger more, the rest of his hands supported by the hardback book. He winced.

His finger was almost at a 45° angle, and it was really starting to hurt. Bradley was afraid but still adamant his parents not punish him for something Alicia made him do. "It...it was…you…"

Alicia bent the finger back further, the skin stretched to the hilt, the bones now in an unnatural position. "Listen to me, dear brother. This was all you, right? You don't want me to hurt you now, do you? Just keep your mouth shut and -"

"Stop it, Alicia! That hurts! Stop kidding around. Please! You -"

She leaned into his ear and whispered. "If you make one sound, I'll break them all." And with that, she forced his finger back until it snapped. The bones made a short crunching noise so loud it was more of a pop.

Bradley's eyes nearly shot out of their sockets. As he inspected his finger, it simply collapsed like a noodle, lacking any ligaments to keep it attached to his hand. He bit his lips until he drew blood, but he didn't make a sound. He had learned his lesson.

"Good boy," she said. "Now, who stole the bra?"

He spat through gritted teeth and fire-red cheeks, "I...did. It...was me." Spittle escaped his clenched mouth. She kissed him on the cheek, licking up a lone tear.

"You better get to a doctor about that finger. It looks pretty warped," she said, pulling a face as she left his room.

It was Jenna, Bradley's next-door neighbor, who took his virginity.

Jenna was twenty-six, buxom and blonde, with legs that seemed to go on forever. Her boyfriend looked like he had just escaped from jail and had a score to settle.

To a fourteen-year-old boy in the middle of puberty, he lived next door to both his dream and his nightmare.

It was summer, and Jenna invited Bradley over to do some land-scaping for her one day. It started with him mowing her yard and turned into him digging holes and planting flowers and fruit trees. Afterward, he was hot and sweaty, and she invited him to use her pool if he'd like to cool off.

"I don't have any swim trunks," Bradley said.

"I don't see a problem with that," Jenna replied softly. "You don't need to wear any."

Bradley had read about situations like these and thought they only existed in cheap books and tawdry movies. "No...no, thank you," he said nervously.

"Chicken," she smiled at him. "I'll turn around even," she cooed.

He had to admit he was hot, and the pool looked pretty amazing. And maybe he'd get a kiss from her and have something to tell his buddies in school.

"Fine," he said, pulling his shirt off and dropping his shorts. He whooped and jumped into the cool water, and his entire body and every crevice were instantly relieved. When he came up for air, he was standing, tossed the water out of his eyes, and saw Jenna standing on the side of the pool. She had also disrobed and stood before him, completely naked. Bradley could feel himself getting hard and was glad it was underwater.

Jenna dove gracefully into the water, and when she came up, she was right in front of him. She put her hands on his shoulders and, in one quick move, lowered herself onto him. She began a slow motion up and down, and Bradley's eyes grew large. His hips found a rhythm to match hers. The water sloshed around them, and their moans coursed across the water's surface. In a few minutes, it was over, and she slid off him and got out of the pool to lie down in a lounge chair to dry off. Bradley stood there for another minute before getting out of the water to join her. As he walked towards her, she looked at him and saw he had not lost his hardness and was ready to go again.

Thank God for teenagers, she thought.

Over the course of the summer, Bradley often did odd jobs for Jenna, but landscaping was the principal work. Jenna taught him many things that summer, and for the first time, he found himself enjoying being told what to do by a woman. He didn't dare tell Alicia of his times with Jenna because she'd use it against him.

But things were about to take a turn for the worse.

On one particularly hot day, Jenna and Bradley were in the pool having sex when her boyfriend came home. The large man was venomous, and the veins in his neck pulsed his anger. Outraged, he threatened to kill the young lad. Bradley jumped out of the pool, and the large man lumbered towards him, his large, calloused hands ready to choke the life out of Bradley.

Bradley ran to the backside of the pool by the newly planted fruit trees and picked up a shovel for protection. The man roared out a laugh at the young boy as the shovel quivered in his shaking hands.

"You're dead!" the man said before taking three huge strides towards Bradley. Closing his eyes, Bradley swung the shovel into the man's stomach, causing him to double over. While bent over, Bradley brought the shovel down heavily onto the man's head, and he heard a crack. Suddenly, blood poured out of the cracked skull like a geyser. The man slumped down and flopped lifelessly onto the concrete.

"You killed him!" Jenna cried.

Bradley saw how scared she was and looked around at his surroundings. He had to act quickly. He knew what needed to be done and used the tool to shovel a deep hole near the new garden. Once it was big enough, he rolled the heavy body into the hole and filled it in.

Jenna was in near hysterics, but Bradley, oddly, was calm. He threw the shovel on the ground. He knew this would be the last time he'd ever see Jenna, so he walked up to her and kissed her deeply. "Thanks for everything," he said before heading home, smiling.

Two weeks later, Jenna suddenly moved away, leaving Bradley – and a dead man's body – behind.

One day in October, Alicia and Bradley adjourned upstairs to his bedroom for one of their talks.

Alicia got up and paced the room. She stopped at his window and stared out. "You know, you really do have a better view than I do."

"We can switch rooms if you want to," Bradley said.

"If I wanted a better room, I'd take our brother's. His is bigger than both of ours." Alicia remembered the night she overheard her mother forcing their father to impregnate her. She made a face. "I can't stand that child. Always stealing the spotlight. You do know he's mother's favorite, don't you?"

Bradley nodded.

"But I like your room, too. You can see so much from up here." She stepped closer to the window and looked down. "Where do you think Jenna moved to, huh?"

Bradley's heart skipped a beat.

"J...Jenna?"

"Yes." Alicia spun around to face Bradley. "Your lover."

"I...I..."

"Oh, stop your yammering," she scolded. "I know everything."

Each word was like a blow. "You...what?" Bradley stood up.

"Come here, Bradley, darling, and see for yourself." She held out her hand for him to take.

Once he held her hand, she yanked him to the window.

"There. See? That's her backyard. And you can see everything," she flourished her hands.

Bradley felt sweat beading on his forehead.

"I know you fucked her." She grinned. She leaned into his ear. "And I know you killed *him.*"

Bradley jolted back as if he had gotten shocked. He looked her in the eyes. She was calm, and it terrified him.

"I know what – *fertilizer* – is making the daylilies bloom in the garden," she said.

"Alicia -"

"You really are a sloppy one," she chided. "And it's a good thing you have me around to clean up your messes."

"What are you talking about?" Bradley asked.

"I saved you," she breathed. "From a lifetime in jail."

Bradley furrowed his brows and stared at Alicia.

She was getting annoyed with his naiveté, and she huffed. "Jenna was going to turn you in. She was going to tell the police everything. But I, dear brother, saw everything from here." She pointed to his window. "Soooo, I talked to sweet Jenna, and I simply made it clear that should she have the urge to talk to the authorities, then I, in good conscience, would have to do the same and inform them she had slept with a fourteen-year-old. A minor. Thus having committed a Class B Felony. And in California, she could face imprisonment for up to twenty-five years."

Bradley's eyes grew wide. "But...what about the -"

"I mentioned I would tell the police I saw her struggle with her boyfriend and eventually killed him. And you tried to stop her." Alicia smiled. "Poor Jenna. Never stood a chance. I owned her."

Bradley's heart swelled. "And she believed you?"

"She left town, didn't she?"

Bradley couldn't believe it. He was safe. For now. But he knew his safety came with consequences. Alicia would have this in her arsenal, ready to be used against him whenever it suited her. He didn't know to be grateful or frightened. Inwardly, he shivered.

"How much do you love me?" she asked him.

"A lot. I do," he said.

"Good. Because now, like Jenna," she grinned sweetly, "I own you."

Defeated, knowing he had no choice but also certain he would do anything for his sister, he smiled back. "I'll do anything you ask," he said.

Her head cocked, and she looked at him. "I'm glad you said that." She walked towards the bedroom door. "We're going to have a wonderful life, brother dear," she said sinisterly. "Just the two of us."

CHAPTER 48

Over the years, Alicia never claimed Bradley as her brother to others, nor did either of them claim their baby brother as a blood relation. Later in life, before college, Alicia would use her middle name, Madison, as her last name to further separate herself from her family. Their parents loved the youngest more and seemed to choose to focus more on him than them. It would turn out to be a terrible choice.

Ironically, it was the one thing Alicia and Bradley bonded over. Because of their new brother, they felt the youngest child stole all their parent's attention away from them, so it was three against two, and two separate families were born.

But Alicia's indifference towards Bradley was always hovering. She couldn't care less he was her brother, but making him her puppet meant everything. She would ignore him for weeks, sometimes months, and would only talk to him if she needed something. And as much as Bradley despised his sister, he loved her. Besides Jenna, Alicia gave him more attention than anyone else in his life, and he thrived on it. She was his drug, and when she wasn't using him, he went through withdrawals. He was caught between a rock and a hard place with Alicia: he hated doing the things she asked him to do, but he loved she trusted

266

him and him alone to ask. And that love outranked the hate every single time.

And so, it was a gleeful day in Bradley's life when Alicia came to him and said she needed something from him. Like a puppy receiving affirmation, he sat and listened with breathless anticipation.

"It's Mr. Stillman." *Her eleventh-grade Chemistry professor.* Alicia was hiccoughing, upset. "I'm failing his class...and...and...he said the only.... the only way I would pass...is...is..." She put her face in her hands.

"Is what?" Bradley asked, concerned.

"Oh, it's horrible! I can't believe he said it!"

"Alicia. What did he say?" Bradley didn't like seeing his sister upset; her crying made him laser-focused on her feelings.

Alicia looked painfully at Bradley as if the following words out of her mouth would spell the end of her existence. "He said the only way I would pass his class is if...is if I slept with him!" Alicia was mortified at the outpouring of words.

Bradley's shoulders pulled back. He saw the hurt in his sister's eyes, and Mr. Stillman's request infuriated him, but he still wasn't sure why she was telling him this. What did she need from him? He saw the pleading in her eyes; the distraught look bore through him, and he suddenly understood.

"What do I need to do?" he asked.

After listening to Alicia explain everything, Bradley was only too happy to obey because her plan was meticulously detailed and foolproof. He could prove his dedication to his sister and eliminate Alicia's problem at the same time. *Two birds with one stone,* he thought. It would all go down on Friday, but first, he needed to make a couple of stops.

On Wednesday, Bradley went to Walmart and bought a cheap black duffle bag, a long neck funnel, and thick gloves. On Thursday, while Alicia's class was in the cafeteria eating lunch, he snuck into her classroom window Alicia had unlocked. He went to Mr. Stillman's desk, took out the key, unlocked the cabinet, and took what he needed. He replaced the key and snuck out the window unnoticed. The whole thing took less than two minutes.

Last, Bradley confiscated two bottles of whiskey from his dad's liquor cabinet. His father would never miss the two bottles.

And now, Friday had arrived. It was time.

Bradley was all set.

The day was foggy, and Bradley dressed for the occasion. He wore gloves and a grey hoodie that blended into the background, and he went unseen as he squatted behind the professor's car in the school's parking lot, the duffle bag rested by his feet. The students had gone for the weekend, and as Alicia had informed Bradley, Mr. Stillman liked to remain behind two hours on Fridays to finish grading papers – or spending "special" time with a student. Bradley was disgusted.

The fog made the parking lot chilly, and Bradley was glad he had worn the hoodie. He checked his watch: 4:27 p.m. Mr. Stillman should be coming out soon and –

Out of the corner of his eye, Bradley saw the teacher heading towards his car. Stillman was a small man, and Bradley knew he wouldn't be any trouble. He could feel his heart pick up speed, and he closed his eyes to put his breathing under control. The teacher was closer, only steps away. Bradley raised up on his legs a little but remained out of sight. The cloth and bottle he had stolen from Alicia's chemistry lab were ready in his hand. Mr. Stillman rounded the front of his car and opened his door.

Like a large cat on the Serengeti, Bradley sprung behind the professor and covered his nose and mouth with a chloroformed rag. Despite his size, Stillman put up quite a struggle but, ultimately, was no match for Bradley. After holding the rag tightly to the teacher's mouth for three minutes, Bradley heard the man drop his keys to the ground. Then Stillman went limp, unconscious. Bradley scooped up the keys and dragged the professor to the back of the car, where he shoved him into the trunk. Bradley picked up the duffle bag, jumped into the driver's seat, started the car, and drove away.

Bradley knew he had less than twenty minutes before the chloroform wore off, but where he was going, he would have time to spare. *Remember, you only have until 5:02 p.m. After that, it'll be too late.* Alicia's plan insisted Bradley drive the same route to the professor's home as the teacher would take: from the school, go down Hanover Street for four miles, then take a left onto Fayetteville Highway. The house was seven miles down on the right, but he first had to pass the quarry and train station. *Look for the stop sign.*

He felt he was close. Then, through the fog, he barely saw the stop sign coming up and began to slow down. He hadn't seen another car the entire drive, which made him happy. *No one else lives out in that remote area, so you shouldn't see too many other people out and about,* Alicia had said. Once again, she was right.

Bradley drove the car slowly over several rough bumps. He could hear the alcohol in the duffle bag sloshing in the bottles. Satisfied he was situated correctly, he stopped and parked the car. He grabbed the duffle bag, got out, and inspected his parking job. *Perfect.* He walked to the back of the car and opened the trunk. The professor was still unconscious. Bradley lifted him up, dragged him along the ground, placed him behind the steering wheel, and then buckled him in. *Safety first,* Bradley thought sarcastically.

He forced the professor's mouth open with his gloved fingers and held it open while he grabbed the funnel from the bag. Without hesitation, Bradley shoved the longneck end of the funnel down the professor's gullet. When he felt resistance, he pushed harder until it stayed in place. He opened one of the bottles of whiskey, put the bottle up to the funnel, and began to pour, and like putting oil in a car, the liquor flowed into the professor's throat easily.

Bradley heard a moan, and Stillman's eyes fluttered open. Bradley just smiled down at the man and emptied the bottle of alcohol, tapping the glass neck against the funnel's opening just to make sure every drop was down. He tossed the empty bottle into the back seat.

Stillman was still too groggy from the chloroform to realize what was happening, and he moved his body and struggled a bit, but the seatbelt held him firmly in place. Bradley opened the second bottle and poured. Once half of the bottle was ingested, he pulled out the bottle and the funnel, poured the rest of the alcohol around the car's interior, then threw the second empty bottle into the passenger floorboard. The professor tried to scream from the pain of the alcohol burning his scraped esophagus.

Bradley shut the car door and picked up his funnel and duffle bag. As he walked away, he heard the distinct horn of the oncoming train. He looked at his watch—5:01 p.m. *Perfect timing.*

He had driven the car over the bumpy tracks and parked the car to await the train. From a safe distance, Bradley heard the warning horn from the colossal engine barreling down on the car. In the fog, the train saw the parked car too late. Bradley turned and watched as the train helplessly smashed into the car, disintegrating it. A tremendous explosion mushroomed into the sky. Smiling, Bradley walked away unscathed. They would rule the death an accident from drinking and driving.

Alicia would be proud.

And she was. But not of Bradley; she was proud of *herself* that her plan worked and that she had manipulated him. She found no need to tell Bradley it was Mr. Stillman who had rejected *her* advances. She had wanted him, and he wanted nothing to do with her. And for turning her down, he paid with his life.

No one ever *told me no.*

CHAPTER 49

After high school, Alicia Madison went to the costly Santa Clara University and insisted Bradley attend the more affordable, further away Sonoma State University. Alicia always got what she wanted, including her idea that Bradley would attend a cheaper college ninety miles away from her. *Far enough away that we won't be connected, but close enough that should I need him, he'll be ready when I want.*

While in college, Alicia met her three best friends: Brooke, Cathy, and Dana. They instantly connected as the AlphaBabes because their names all started with the first four letters of the alphabet. Since Alicia's name came first, she naturally became the group's unofficial leader.

When the conversation about their families came up, Alicia casually mentioned she was an only child, which, to her, was the truth. One brother didn't exist to her, and the other didn't exist to others. Bradley was a well-kept secret, and she didn't feel the need to tell the girls about him. There were some things that even best friends never divulged.

The girls were close from the beginning. On their first day of meeting in Econ 101, Brooke snapped a selfie with her phone of the four girls.

A fifth girl, Misty Evans, also became part of the group.

"Unofficially," Alicia once made clear.

In reverse fashion, Misty was more like a lone backup singer for the four leads. Misty was prettier than the others, a dead ringer for Halle Berry – her father was black and her mother white - and Brooke, Cathy, and Dana secretly wondered if Alicia was a tad jealous, and that's why she never formally allowed Misty to be an AlphaBabe.

"Her name's too far down the alphabet," Alicia would chuckle. "But her uncle is kinda cute. And he looks hot in his police uniform."

Police Detective Mike Evans was Misty's uncle, and he and his wife, Karen, took Misty in after her parents decided drugs were a better child to nurse than a real one. In a twisted irony, it was Mike who actually busted his own brother and sister-in-law for dealing drugs. It was a natural transition that Misty would live with her aunt and uncle.

The three girls felt sorry for Misty and accepted her into their clique. She giddily accepted and never looked back. She was closer to Brooke, Cathy, and Dana, as Alicia was more standoffish. Alicia wouldn't really pay too much attention to Misty, but she was nice enough. She was, what Misty called, "half-nice": Misty would be invited to study groups because she was smart, but not to sleepovers; she would be asked to go with them to the clubs, but she would be expected to be the designated driver; she would be expected to give Alicia compliments on her outfits but was never invited to go shopping with them. And they never, ever discussed guys with her. Because, as Alicia would point out, "She's weird! Her parents are drug dealers! I don't want her to get me arrested!" The other girls would just roll their eyes.

Misty remembered the day her world changed: it was the day Alicia decided to be "whole-nice". That night, they went to Alcatraz Bar, and Alicia was the designated driver. She even told Misty she looked "bangin' in that outfit!". The weekend continued with a sleepover at Alicia's house, which she personally invited Misty to. The following week, Alicia let Misty use her personal tutor to help her write her Econ paper for her final, bought her a new dress for Homecoming, and even baked her cookies.

Misty wasn't the only one shocked.

The three other girls cornered Alicia on campus one day.

"What the hell are you doing?" Brooke asked Alicia.

"What are you talking about?"

Brooke's eyes bugged out. "With Misty. Why the sudden Fairy Godmother act?"

"What? Can't I be nice?" Alicia asked, fluttering her eyelashes.

"I don't know, can you?" Dana chimed in.

"Yeah. This is off, even for you," Cathy added. Her eyes squinted suspiciously at Alicia.

Alicia just smiled, shrugged, and walked off.

"Hmmm," Brooke humphed, plopping her hands on her hips. "This doesn't bode well. What is our girl up to?"

"Whatever it is," Cathy said, "it's gonna be fun to watch!"

They all burst out laughing.

Turned out, they didn't have to wait long to find out.

The following week, all five girls sat on the grass, enjoying a picnic on the green in front of Kenna Hall. Dana passed around some marshmallow-topped brownies.

"Holy shit, these are amazeballs!" Brooke announced.

"Mmm hmmm!" Cathy muttered her agreement with a stuffed mouth.

"My grandmother's secret recipe, never to be shared," Dana said.

"Well, thank her for us," Cathy said.

"She's dead," Dana said matter-of-factly.

Cathy's mouth was agape.

"I bet the boys love that," Alicia said, pointing to Cathy's open mouth.

"Speaking of boys," Brooke said, "I've got this hot-as-hell one in my Liberal Arts class. I think he's from the South because that accent just gets me all wet."

"Good lord!" Cathy said, her face reddening. "How do you have time for boys? I swear my professors are out to kill me."

"Tell me about it," Alicia spoke up, shifting on her legs. "I am struggling with my Criminology elective so bad!" She leaned in and aimed her conversation toward Misty's direction. "And if I fail this class, my parents will yank my ass out of this university, no doubt." Her voice quavered.

Brooke, Cathy, and Dana looked at Alicia, then at each other, eyebrows raised.

Alicia continued, "And I really don't want to leave. I mean, I've gotten so close to each of you." She placed her hand on Misty's leg at that exact moment.

Misty's shoulders sank. Inside, she couldn't bear to have Alicia leave just when they were becoming close. If there was something she could do – and then she got an idea!

"I could get my Uncle Mike to help you," Misty interjected.

"Umm, your uncle?" Alicia asked. Her eyes were as big as a doe's.

"Yes! He's a detective. He knows all about criminal things, or whatever. I could ask him for you. Maybe you could come over to the house, and you could ask him whatever you needed."

Alicia had no intention of ever setting foot in Misty's house.

"That's sweet, but I don't want to impose. I'm afraid I'm just going to fail and have to move back to-"

"Or he could come see you!" Misty added quickly. "I'll give him your phone number and address, and you guys could plan from there. Would that work?" Misty sounded eager to keep Alicia close by.

"Well, I guess so. Think he'll call?"

"I guarantee it!" And in her mind, Misty was thinking she'd do anything to get her Uncle Mike to help Alicia. If he did, then Alicia and her friendship would be unbreakable. She'd be nice to her and invite her to things all the time. "I'll go call him now." She got up and left the group, her phone already to her ear.

As Misty walked away, Alicia smiled and looked down at the picnic food. She plopped a grape in her mouth. She looked back up, and three sets of eyes were glaring at her suspiciously.

"What?" she asked innocently.

They all leaned in.

Brooke spoke up. "Seriously? What was that about?"

"What do you mean?" Alicia asked. "I need help with my Criminology elective."

"Criminology, my ass," Dana said. "Your elective is Basic Anatomy, like me. We're in the same damn class."

"Well, yes," Alicia responded. "You're studying to be a vet and I'm just learning anatomy of a different kind." She grinned. "The *man* kind. And her hot Uncle Mike is going to be my specimen. And you know what they say about black men...."

Brooke and Dana giggled. "My god," Brooke said. "Everything has to fit your agenda perfectly. Poor little Misty never saw you coming. You are such a rogue."

"She's not a rogue," Dana said. "She's anal."

"Well, anal's what we need right now, don't you think?" Alicia said, sucking on a carrot stick.

Brooke and Dana burst out laughing.

Cathy gasped, and her hand flew to her mouth.

Alicia looked at Cathy. She was a beautiful girl with an intelligent face and long brown hair, usually pulled into a bun on top of her head and tied with a blue ribbon – that blue ribbon she wore everywhere and would never part with! - and a great figure always hidden behind some dowdy, shapeless outfit.

"Oh, please. Jealous?" Alicia asked Cathy. "Don't act all innocent. I'm sure you've read worse than that in one of your *Fifty Shades* books before. Or are you really as innocent as a nun?"

Cathy blushed.

Brooke laughed, "Well, I, for one, *am* jealous. He's definitely a hottie. I say go for it. And if you don't, I will. Wife or not." She started fanning herself dramatically with a paper plate.

"Back off, Blanche," Alicia said.

"Aww, she was always my favorite Golden Girl."

Dana pointed her finger at Alicia. "Is this why you've been so nice to Misty all of a sudden? To get closer to her uncle?"

"Who, moi?"

"Yes, *toi*! What are your plans?"

"Why do you think I have a plan?" Alicia balked.

Dana shook her head. "Because you always have a plan. You're always one step ahead of everyone. You plan every detail. So, spill."

The other girls nodded in agreement.

Alicia smiled. "Take the risk or lose the chance," she said.

"Can I make a suggestion?" Brooke asked. "I love you girls so much."

A chorus of "I love you, too!" overlapped through the friends.

Brooke continued. "So, can we agree that we all stick together no matter what happens in life? Through thick and thin?"

Dana smiled and grabbed Brooke's hand. "Agreed."

Cathy took another bite of her thick brownie. "I agwee, tuh."

Alicia looked at Cathy. "Keep eating like that, and it's going to be through more 'thick' than 'thin.'"

An awkward silence settled on the group.

"Oh, fuff off," Cathy mumbled with a full mouth, then burst into laughter and threw her brownie at Alicia.

All the girls collapsed in a fit of giggles until they couldn't breathe.

"Is everyone okay?" a voice said.

The girls looked up and saw Misty headed their way.

Misty walked back to the group and sat down on the grass. The girls all sat up straighter and acted like nothing had just transpired.

"My uncle said he'd be more than happy to talk with you! He'll call you this evening so you two can plan your get-together." Misty grinned ear to ear.

"Oh, that's so sweet. Thank you, Misty!" Alicia said sincerely. She looked at her girlfriends and then placed her hand on Misty's knee again. "I just love a good plan!"

CHAPTER 50

Alicia was living a double life, and she was loving every minute. The first life revolved around Ryan.

For the four years she was in college, she dated Ryan Rosling, a tall, thin, bespectacled man whose fop of blonde hair belied him being ten years older than Alicia. They met freshman year when Ryan came to speak at a law symposium for Santa Clara University. Alicia and the rest of the AlphaBabes had volunteered to be the welcoming committee for the visiting speakers from various local law firms. As soon as Alicia saw Ryan Rosling in his three-piece suit, wearing expensive shoes and carrying a briefcase, she fell in love. She had never seen anyone so beautiful in her life. His aqua eyes were bright and piercing, and Alicia was a goner whenever she gazed into them. But it was his deep, baritone voice that made her insides mushy, the butterflies fluttering chaotically in her chest.

She remembered the day he walked into Mayer Theater for the meeting. He stood a full head above everyone else, and as he entered the theater, his clear eyes swept the room as if he were a lion searching amongst the gazelles of which one to attack first. His eyes met Alicia's, and then his mouth slowly opened into a smile of intense wattage. Everyone else in the room seemed to vanish. Alicia could feel the heat in the room increase, and not one to shy away, she made her way over to him.

"I'm Alicia," she said, extending her hand.

"Ryan." He held her hand in his longer than necessary. There was a shock of electricity in the air around them. "This is nuts," he said. "I know we've only met, but, God, this is going to sound like a cheesy Lifetime movie, but I feel like we've met before."

"Maybe in a previous life," she purred.

"Do you believe in that sort of thing?" he responded, still holding her hand.

She looked him in the eyes and said confidently, "I do." There was no mistaking the message.

"Um, Alicia, I have to speak today, and to be honest, I can't, for the life of me, remember what I'm supposed to be saying. I've lost all train of thought."

She released his hand and took his briefcase from him. Opening it, she took out a folder from the top. She looked inside and flipped through a couple of pages.

"Here. These are your notes."

He couldn't take his eyes off her. He was mesmerized. "Oh, yeah. Thank you," he said.

Alicia lifted her head to look him in his eyes. Her smile was pure and sweet.

"I have to say, I never do this. But I must ask," Ryan said, "are you free tonight?"

Her grin grew. She had forgotten all about Brooke, Cathy, and Dana on the other side of the room. She had forgotten her duties to welcome others into the theater as many arrivals passed her by. She had forgotten even where she was for a brief moment.

But she was certain of one thing. She took a breath.

"Mr. Rosling, I happen to be free forever."

And so, their love story began. She loved Ryan Rosling with every single fiber of her being. No matter how busy he was at his law firm, Wagoner, Walker & Lee, he never failed to make time to be with Alicia. He would leave love notes in her shoes, in the refrigerator, or on her car seat. He surprised her with flowers just because – and where he found tulips year-round was always a mystery to Alicia.

Cooking was never Ryan's specialty – he could barely make a peanut butter and jelly sandwich - but occasionally, he would make her favorite meal – Ossobuco alla Milanese - and it would be perfect. She later learned he took cooking lessons from a professional chef just to make the difficult Italian dish for her.

It was during one of these dinners Ryan proposed marriage, and it was the happiest night of Alicia's life.

The next day, while Ryan was at work, Alicia looked at the ring on her finger. She couldn't wait to show off her enormous ring to the girls! They would be so happy for her! *And maybe a little jealous, I hope,* Alicia laughed to herself.

But before she could tell the girls about her engagement, there was something she had to do. She slipped the ring off her finger and tucked it into her jewelry drawer. She got in her car and drove to see Mike Evans.

Her lover for the past four years.

Life number two.

Alicia loved Ryan, but she lusted after Mike. Mike did things to her that Ryan, bless his heart, never would or could. Where Ryan was a gentle, thoughtful lover who could barely fulfill her needs, Mike was powerful and ferocious and would swell inside her until she could take no more. It was also the secrecy of their meetings that added to the illicit-ness, knowing both Mike's wife, Karen, and Alicia's friend, Misty, were blissfully unaware. The excitement level was breathtaking.

Ryan was tall and thin, whereas Mike was muscular and more like a fireplug, stocky and forceful. Mike started as just a fun thing for Alicia to play with in college, but he eventually grew on her. Ryan was the real thing, and Mike was a plaything.

It started with their initial meeting that Misty had arranged so Alicia could get help from Mike Evans with her Criminology class. Alicia had always thought Mike was hot, and of course, her plan was to meet him and seduce him and let things take their course.

Alicia's nonexistent Criminology course came as a shock to Mike, but it also piqued his curiosity.

"Why lie about it?" he asked.

"Why not?" was her sharp reply. She moved closer to him, and he could feel her breath on his face. She grabbed his crotch and squeezed.

Mike raised his left eyebrow in suspicion. "I don't...I don't understand...I mean, I'm married and -"

"Sit!" she ordered, and without thinking, he did. Alicia could see sweat forming on his forehead.

This is going to be easier than I imagined, she thought. "This is going to be fun," she told him. She smiled as he sat there and nodded.

Mike Evans had proven to be an excellent student, one who asked few questions, could be controlled easily, and never failed her. Alicia was pleased.

But that was four years ago, and now her fiancé, Ryan, was only 12 months away from making Equity Partner at his firm, and Alicia couldn't be happier. She felt now was the time to rid Mike from her life because she was to be married, and she didn't want to risk it all just when she was about to have everything she wanted. The tug of war in her mind was exhausting.

But the sordidness of the affair tickled Alicia. She was with another woman's husband, and that was the ultimate control. *No. I will keep Mike a secret to only me.*

Bradley had heard about Alicia's engagement through the newspapers and became incensed. He reread the headline: **Ryan Rosling of Wagoner, Walker & Lee Law Firm to wed Alicia Madison.**

Rage boiled inside him like a molten eruption. He wanted to destroy everything around him. He felt he was losing her to another man, and that turned his anger into jealousy. And he felt scared. Someone besides him was going to be in her life, and he felt threatened.

"Who is he?" Bradley asked Alicia one day at her home.

"Only the most successful up-and-coming lawyer of the most prestigious law firm in all of California!" she squealed. "Did I mention he's in law?"

If she said "law" one more time, he just might punch her. "Never heard of him."

Alicia's lips closed around her teeth, but she kept her grin. She looked at him exasperatingly and turned up a corner of her mouth. "You wouldn't, now, would you? You're just a dumbass that probably can't even spell 'lawyer'."

Bradley slouched. As brutal as Alicia was to him, he loved her with his whole heart, and so he took her abuse. He had no one personal in his life that really stayed, except for Alicia. She threw all her feelings at him until they stuck, and he was left with the hate and vengeance and mock empathy, but at least he *felt*. 'Hurt' was a feeling. And he let that fester until he learned to live with it. Getting hurt by his sister was the only feeling he related to, and he lived for it. He was obsessed with pleasing her. He made no friends in college because his sole responsibility was to his sister. Sure, he had a couple of girls he would hook up with now and then, but no one truly understood his loneliness and longing for a happier life.

"Oh, don't look so pathetic," Alicia spat.

Bradley snapped out of his thoughts.

"Besides, you'll never get to meet him, so don't worry your pretty little head about it." She turned to him and poked him in the chest. "And don't you *dare* fuck this up for me! You keep your distance, or I'll make your life miserable, you got that?"

He got it. He'd keep his distance until she needed him. And she would need him. Of that, he was certain.

One week later, she, indeed, needed him. And he came running.

Ryan Rosling's parents were high society, Country Club patrons who had wings in hospitals and libraries named after them because of generous donations. The parties at their home in Russian Hill were legendary, and everyone from heads of state to billionaire celebrities would attend. They were known drinkers who never had an empty glass in their hands. They only served and drank the best. At one party for six visiting members of Parliament, the Roslings gifted each guest a bottle of Macallan 64-year-old Whiskey in Lalique glass bottles worth $625,000 each.

They were members of the St. Francis Yacht Club and were dear friends with famed author Danielle Steele. The Roslings' name was connected to several non-profits near and dear to their hearts that improved the betterment of living in San Francisco. Secretly, it made them feel better about themselves. They were the definition of the crème de la crème. And this was the world Alicia was about to live in. As confidence was her number one ally, panic became her number one nemesis.

Desperate, Alicia needed Ryan's parents to approve of her. They loved their only son and were skeptical of any girl he introduced them to.

"She's only after your money. Now, sweet Ruthie McAlister has her own money."

"She's attracted to the prestige of being a successful lawyer's wife. Shelby Gleeson would make a much better lawyer's wife."

"She's not from the right side of the tracks. But Mary-Beth Hollings would make an excellent wife."

Every time, it was the same indifference, just a different girl.

Alicia couldn't prove she wasn't after his money, explain she didn't care about the prestige, or convince them she lived a quiet life in a wonderful neighborhood. So, she needed a different tactic.

And, like always, she came up with a plan.

One that would change the course of her and Bradley's lives forever. She would be welcomed into the Rosling family, and Bradley would be under her control forever. For Alicia, it was a win-win. But Alicia knew this would be one of the most significant tasks she could ever endow to Bradley. She would have to use every bit of charm and coercion in her arsenal for him to agree to this one. As confident as Alicia was, she felt nervous going forward with this plan.

She took a deep breath and picked up the phone.

She called Bradley at his home ninety miles away and told him she needed him. In less than two hours, he was seated by her side.

Alicia told Bradley she needed him to do something for her, something big. She conjured tears and a shaky resonance in her voice. She stood and paced the floor, wringing her hands as if wrestling with the toughest decision she ever had to make. At one point, she feigned lightheadedness and had to sit. Bradley rushed to her side, on his knees. She caressed his strong face with both of her hands and looked him in the eyes, tears flowing down her cheeks. "Oh, but I can't ask this of you. It's simply…too much." *I should get an Oscar for this performance.*

"No, please. Ask me," he said eagerly. "I…need you to ask me."

"If you insist. And just know that it would mean the absolute world to me. And I promise I'll be less controlling in the future if you would just do this one itty, bitty favor for me."

Less controlling? Oddly, that worried him. He was a little concerned she might not need him as much anymore if he carried out this request. Bradley didn't like being between a rock and a hard place, but once again, he had no choice. Of course, he would say yes.

"Of course!" he said breathlessly, his heart in his throat. Ultimately, he was thrilled at the opportunity to do his sister a favor. He *lived* for her. To him, she was the only family he really had. "What is it? What can I do?" He could feel his eyes moisten with happiness.

She placed her hands on his knees, leaned in, and whispered.

"I need you to kill our family."

Two weeks later, a local newspaper reported on a family – father, mother, and young son – who had been found gruesomely murdered in their home. Their faces had been smashed in, all their teeth removed, and all their hands had been sliced off. Neighbors confirmed the bodies more than likely belonged to the family that lived in the house, but it baffled the police why the identifying markers were removed.

But Bradley and Alicia knew why.

Mike Evans called to offer his condolences. Alicia thought that was sweet. He wanted to see her. The adrenalin coursed through her body after what had happened to her family, and with Ryan out of town, she agreed to meet Mike. She would make him fuck her brains out in celebration.

Ryan's family was distraught over Alicia's tragedy and welcomed her into their family with open arms. She was the perfect project for them to help and feel good about themselves.

And in losing one family, she gained another. They had accepted her. Alicia could finally breathe a sigh of relief.

CHAPTER 51

Two weeks before the wedding, Alicia, Brooke, Cathy, and Dana got together for lunch at Waterbar on The Embarcadero. Alicia set a gift bag on the floor by her feet.

"Can you believe it?" Alicia said excitedly, showing the girls her ring. "Alicia Rosling. Mrs. Ryan Rosling."

"And his name is Ryan," Brooke said. "Like Reynolds and Gosling all rolled into one. He's the perfect Ryan!" All the girls laughed.

Alicia's phone rang, and she picked it up. Her lips pursed. She pressed the side button and sent the call to voicemail.

"So, where is the honeymoon going to -" Cathy started to say, but Alicia's phone rang again, interrupting her thought. She saw Alicia click the side button again, sending the call to voicemail.

"Uh, should you get that?" Cathy asked.

"Nah, just some caterer who wants my business. Too late!" she smiled. "Now," she continued, her eyes lit up with excitement. "I have something for each of you." She reached into the gift bag and pulled out three small boxes wrapped in embossed ivory paper and tied with a beautiful black velvet ribbon. She handed each girl their own box. "For you, my sisters."

She clasped her hands together on her chest as each girl excitedly tore through their gift.

Brooke was the first to hold up the piece of jewelry: a gorgeous 18k gold necklace with an orange poppy charm attached.

Alicia spoke. "I know being California girls, we love our poppies, and, well, I just thought this was the perfect way to solidify our love for each other." She reached under her shirt and pulled her matching necklace out. "We all have one. Our connection."

Cathy wiped a tear away. "I love it," she said.

"We all do," Brooke agreed. "Here, help me put mine on," she told Cathy. Each girl helped another put theirs on. They were admiring their charms when Alicia's phone rang again.

But Dana was quick to the draw, and she grabbed Alicia's phone before Alicia could. "You really should answer your phone," she said. Alicia tried to grab the phone back from Dana. Fail.

"Hello?" Dana asked into the phone. "This is Dana, Alicia's answering service. How may I be of service?" Brooke covered her mouth and giggled.

Alicia got up from her seat and started heading toward Dana like a bull to a red cape, but Dana stood up and walked away.

"I can hear you breathing," Dana said. "Who is this? Ryan, is that you? You're breathing hard." Dana's face contorted in amazement.

"Give me that!" Alicia seethed, stretching out her arm to get her phone back.

"Wow, I gotta hand it to you, Ryan. Your breathing is getting me hot and heavy," Dana teased.

Alicia reached Dana and pushed her into a chair. The stiff wooden back of the chair jabbed into Dana's side.

"Hey!" Dana shouted, rubbing her hip. "That hurt!"

"Give me…. the fucking phone!" Alicia spat through gritted teeth.

Dana grunted. "Fine. Take it," she said, shoving the phone into Alicia's hand.

Alicia looked at the number and recognized it as the previous caller. *They can't know,* she thought, still pissed.

"They hung up," Alicia mumbled. "I have to go."

"Don't go," Brooke said. "She didn't mean anything by it, did you, Dana?"

Still rubbing her side, Dana was confused. "No, I didn't mean anything by it. I'm sorry. But next time you want to rumble, let me know so I can bring my padding."

"Yeah, don't be this way," Cathy added. "Sit. Let's talk more about the wedding, okay?"

But Alicia was not relenting. "I told you to give me my phone back, and it was none of your business anyway! Why do you have to be so nosy all the time?"

"What?" Dana asked, bewildered.

"And you!" Alicia said, pointing her finger at Cathy. "You slept with my fiancé. That's low!"

Cathy sank into her chair. "But…he wasn't -"

"He wasn't your fiancé at the time, Alicia," Dana interjected. "It was a random one-night hook-up at a party." But her words fell on deaf ears. Alicia had gathered up her purse, spilling drinks in the process, and started to storm off.

Cathy had tears flowing from her eyes. "I didn't know…."

"Alicia," Brooke said. "C'mon. Stop it. What is really going on? I mean, everything was cool until that phone call. Is something else going on? Something we should be concerned about?"

"You shouldn't concern yourselves about shit with me anymore," Alicia fumed. "You've all had your fun. When you first brought this up at the bar in the el PRADO Hotel, you tried to make it not a big deal, but I knew. Deep down, I knew those two slept together," she hissed, waving her finger at Cathy and a non-existent Ryan. "And all of you held this from me this whole time. You're all fake and phony, and as far as I'm concerned, we're through!"

As she walked away, Brooke, Cathy, and Dana could feel a seismic shift in their friendship.

Then Alicia stopped walking.

The three girls sucked in a collective breath, hopeful Alicia saw the mistake she had just made.

Alicia spun around and looked each girl in the eyes before speaking.

"You can all go to hell."

CHAPTER 52

Alicia had two problems.

For one, she had just told her best friends to go to hell. She sighed. *For fuck's sake,* she thought. She didn't know if she should be mad at them or herself. Mike had been blowing up her phone, and Alicia didn't want to speak to him while she was with her friends. Their affair was still a secret Alicia needed to fiercely protect. And Dana – *nosy broad!* – wouldn't leave well enough alone and had grabbed her phone off the table. *And answered it!* It was a very close call that sent Alicia over the edge.

But even Alicia knew most people wouldn't have reacted so dramatically simply from a close call. Something else more sinister was at play.

Which brought Alicia to her second problem.

It wasn't a huge problem at the moment. But in nine months, it would be.

In less time than that, actually, she thought, looking at the pregnancy stick.

She had read that she should start showing at fifteen weeks. Fifteen weeks until the world knew she was pregnant.

Fifteen weeks until my secret would be blown.

She began to panic. Alicia checked her calendar. She hadn't had her period for five weeks, so that would mean she only had nine weeks left, at the least, before she had to explain why her belly looked like a volleyball.

She placed her hand on her stomach. The baby was probably just the size of a pea, but still.

I'm pregnant! A most joyous time for women. A time for women to celebrate the miraculous growth of life.

"This is a fucking disaster," she said to no one. "I can't have a baby now." And she meant it. Once it was born, the brown skin would give away the baby wasn't Ryan's. And anyone good at math would figure out Ryan was out of town when she got pregnant. Alicia knew if the baby were born, she'd have to lie about the date of conception. She silently cursed her misfortune. Her parents and brother had just been killed, and Mike came over, and she celebrated. The reason, unbeknownst to Mike. She couldn't talk to Mike about this.

And for a split second, she wished she and the girls were still talking. This was a special time when she needed someone to talk to. But they were out of the picture now. *It's probably for the best. This wasn't anything I would share with them even if I could,* she thought. Alicia decided she didn't have the time or stamina to deal with their judgment right now.

She heard her phone ringing and glanced once again at the ClearBlue pregnancy stick. A big blue plus sign filled the testing spot.

Shit.

Alicia tossed the stick into the garbage, then looked at her phone. It was her fiancé, Ryan.

Shit shit.

"Hey honey," she answered, hoping she sounded sincere.

"Hey babe. You almost ready for dinner with the folks? I'm leaving work in a few to come pick you up."

Dinner with Ryan's parents was the last thing Alicia needed right now. The pregnancy was already making her feel dowdy and sad, but she had no idea why. *Maybe I should tell him I don't feel well, which wouldn't be a complete lie.* She loved Ryan but now felt the relationship, unbeknownst to him, was a bit tarnished because of what had happened with him and Cathy all those years ago. Everything seemed a little topsy-turvy now, and sitting down with a couple of stuffy, judgmental golden oldies drinking bottomless glasses of expensive champagnes and cognacs was not exactly what Alicia had in mind.

But then, something clicked in her mind, and a plan began to form. *Maybe I can use this dinner to my advantage.* Her eyes darted back and forth, and she licked her lips. *Yes! This could work.*

"Babe?" Ryan was saying. "You going to be ready?"

She grinned and touched her belly.

"Oh, yes. I'm totally ready."

Dinner consisted of a full seven-course meal. Alicia had never seen so much food. For starters, they had cheese-stuffed mushrooms and pancetta crisps with goat cheese and pears, followed by a warm chestnut fennel soup. At this point, the server continuously filled and refilled Alicia's wine glass. As more wine was being poured, a wilted spinach salad with warm apple cider and bacon dressing was placed in front of her. She sipped her wine and wondered if she could even eat another bite.

The conversation was aimed more towards Ryan and his becoming Equity Partner soon and where they might live after they get married. Ryan wanted the more enchanting Nob Hill, but his parents leaned more toward the ritzy Pacific Heights. In the end, Ryan won when he said it was a better place to raise a family and closer to his parents in Russian Hill should they want to come visit.

Alicia had just finished half of her salad when a butternut squash gnocchi with sage brown butter landed in front of her. She felt a small burp rise in her throat and she tried to cover it with a cough. No one seemed to notice. Or else they were too drunk to care.

Afterward came pasta, then the entrée, followed by the main course. She gulped down her wine.

Alicia was about to explode. *If I pop,* she thought, gulping her wine, *my baby might come out.* She giggled. She placed her hand on her stomach and felt a churning. *Oh my god, I can't eat 'nother bite,* she thought. *I'm gonna puke.*

"Sorry, dear?" Ryan's mother asked.

"N-nothing," Alicia said. "The food was wunnerful." Her words slurred.

"Thank you, dear," Mrs. Rosling said curtly.

They've drank – drunk? – dranken? – drinked? – Alicia couldn't think of the word. But she knew what she was trying to think. *So much alcohol, and they were still functioning.* She shook her head in disbelief. Alicia was grateful for the drinks. It would help her with what she needed to do, but she needed to remain focused: she still had a plan to carry out.

"Alicia, dear, won't you help me in the kitchen with the dessert?"

"Of courth," Alicia garbled. She looked at Ryan. There were two of him. She blinked to focus. Her eyes widened, and she pushed herself up from the table, and, in a rush, the alcohol coursed through her veins and to her head. She found the room spinning around her as she grasped the side of the table. "Whooo," she said under her breath, the lightheaded-ness taking over.

"You okay, hon?" Ryan asked, placing his hand on hers.

"Yup. Hunky dory." She headed into the kitchen. Everything was swaying. "Whooo," she repeated. She leaned on the edge of the long marble island and saw Mrs. Rosling on the other end slicing up a cheese-cake. The more Alicia stared at her, the further she seemed to move away. Alicia placed her hands on the island to steady her balance. She needed to get to Mrs. Rosling. To the right of the island were the double sinks, and to the left were high-back barstools.

Alicia squinted her eyes in thought, then chose the path to the right. As she started walking towards Mrs. Rosling, the room continued to rotate, and Alicia swayed to the left. Her foot got caught in the legs of a barstool. As she lost her balance and began to fall, the metal back of the barstool slammed into her stomach. She screamed as she fell face-first onto the floor with a loud crack, and then it all turned dark.

When Alicia opened her eyes, she was in a white room- a hospital. Her eyes adjusted to the bright light, and her mind came into focus.

Had the plan worked? I mean, if the alcohol didn't kill the baby, then the fall surely did. Ryan's parents would feel even more sorry for her, and they would permanently solidify her acceptance into the family. Even with the death of her own family, Ryan's love was simply not enough of a guarantee; Alicia needed a backup plan. And this was it.

She looked around the room and saw Ryan and his family. A doctor entered the room. Mrs. Rosling rushed to Alicia's side. Tears filled her eyes. The father looked ashen and aged, and Ryan's red eyes showed he'd been crying.

Oh, my God, it worked, Alicia thought. *It actually fucking worked.* She felt the sting of tears in the back of her eyes, not for the loss of her baby but for the realization that she was successful in what she had set out to accomplish, and now she would be a part of this family forever.

Mrs. Rosling was shaking, inconsolable. Her husband went to the other side of the bed and sat in the chair. He could not look at Alicia. Ryan sat on the bed next to Alicia and held her hand.

"Honey. Are you okay? How are you feeling?"

"I-I guess I'm okay," she said weakly. "What happened?" She forced herself to hide her smile.

"You had a nasty fall, but the doctor assured us you'll be fine." He looked at her and saw her lips were parched. "Here," he said, handing her a cup with a straw. "Take a drink."

Mrs. Rosling whimpered.

"Oh, this is all our fault," Mr. Rosling said. "We shouldn't have given you so much to drink at the house." His eyes were moist. "We are so sorry."

Alicia decided she needed to play this to the hilt, to feel guilty for losing their grandchild. "I... I'm fine," she said. "I mean, I will be…. oh my gosh, I'm so sorry!" She lifted her hands to her face and cried. When she raised her head, she saw Mrs. Rosling staring at her, smiling.

What the –

"We thought we almost lost you there," Mrs. Rosling said, placing her hand on Alicia's stomach.

"Oh, don't be so dramatic, Carolyn," the father scoffed.

"What?" Alicia said.

"Not you, dear," Carolyn Rosling said. "The baby."

Alicia lowered her eyes and looked at her stomach. "The…*what?*" she blurted out, shocked, sitting up in the bed. "I…I was pregnant?" She couldn't let on she knew she was pregnant and then drank alcohol at their house. *They'd think I was a horrible person.*

"But thank god you're both alright!" Ryan said, jolting her from her performance.

Alicia's eyebrows creased. *Both? What is he talking about?*

She looked around the room and saw his parents were smiling at her. It creeped her out.

Oh no!

"But I lost the baby, didn't I?" Alicia asked, hoping she didn't sound disappointed.

"Oh, honey, no. The baby is fine! *Our* baby is fine!" Ryan leaned in and gave her an awkward side hug. "Isn't that wonderful news?"

Alicia had no words. Her plan had failed, and her plans never failed. She was surrounded by people who were giddy with happiness, looking at her to reciprocate the same happiness. But it would never come.

Ryan was ecstatic, a goofy look plastered on his face.

But Alicia would never feel the same joy for this child, and once this baby was born, no one would.

CHAPTER 53

The sickness hit Alicia like a Mack truck. Her panic set in, and she raced to the bathroom and threw up.

"Hon, are you okay?" Ryan called from the kitchen.

Damn, he's still here. He should be on his way to work.

"Fine. Just…. dandy," she stammered. "Just some pre-wedding nerves, is all." She bent over the toilet and vomited again.

Ryan popped his head into the bathroom, all grins. "That's morning sickness, my love," he said cheerfully.

At that moment, on the cold tile floor, her hair mussed and sticking to her forehead from sweating, her mouth caked with bile, she would love nothing more than to shove that cheer down his throat.

"Can I get you anything before I leave?" he asked.

"Nah, I'm fine," she said, grunting as she stood. She went to the sink and washed her mouth out. She dabbed a cold, wet towel on her forehead.

"Well, I love you," he said, going in for a kiss. She leaned her neck up and pursed her lips, but he bypassed her mouth and kissed her sweaty forehead.

"Hmmpf," she grunted.

His phone rang in his pocket. "It's the boss, gotta go." He punched a button. "Lou, hey. I was just heading in. Yeah, I have the Eckley deposition with me, and I'll..."

Alicia heard the front door close. She loved Ryan, and she worked too hard to put it all in jeopardy. She knew she was walking a tightrope with her affair with Mike Evans. She had finally gained acceptance into the Rosling family, and being no one's fool, she was fully aware everything she had worked hard for could blow up in her face at any given moment. Alicia had a lot of fun over the years, and this would be news to him, but it was time for their relationship to end. Alicia placed her hand on her stomach. As much as it displeased her, she was carrying his baby—more news to him.

She dreaded the call. Mike wasn't like Alicia: he couldn't turn his feelings off for her as easily as she could for him. She liked Mike. He had served her well. But she had bigger plans, plans that did not include him just yet. Alicia would have to play this next move carefully. *Rip off the band-aid.* She picked up her phone and dialed his number.

He answered on the first ring.

"Alicia. How are you?"

"I'm good, Mike." She paused. "Look, I have something to say and -"

"How are the wedding plans coming along?" Mike's voice sounded rushed.

"Mike -"

"I know being married might make us getting together a little more difficult, but we'll sort all that out. If you need to take some time to figure out -"

"Mike!"

"Sorry. I just care for you so much, and I will do anything for us to -"

"Mike. We're done. Over. There is no more *us*." Alicia took a breath. "Not anymore."

There was a silence.

"What?" he finally asked.

"Mike, I care for you, I really do. But I'm getting married, and I can't be -"

"I'm *already* married! Or did you forget that piece of information? And that didn't stop you from jumping into my bed!"

Alicia could hear the fury in his voice. *Or was that fear? Band-aid.*

"I'm sorry, Mike. I really am. I've had a wonderful time, and I thank you for everything you've done for me. I won't forget it."

"Alicia! Don't -" he yelled, but it was too late. She had hung up.

Alicia looked at the phone in her hand. She took a deep breath and crooked up the left side of her mouth.

"Pity."

She looked in the mirror and saw a mess: her hair was sticky and matted, her cheeks were blotchy, her eyes were puffy, and the inside of her mouth tasted like last night's spaghetti and garlic bread. She smacked her lips and pulled a face.

Ever since that night she spent in the hospital two months ago, Alicia was in a tizzy, trying to figure out a way not to have this baby. She turned sideways and looked in the mirror. She cupped her nightshirt under her belly and saw the bump.

"This isn't going to work," she told herself. She knew that once the baby was born, one look at the skin tone, and everyone would know it wasn't Ryan's. Married or not, she would be ousted from the Rosling family without ceremony, and everything she did to gain their acceptance, including the death of her own family, would go down the drain.

No. I need to fix this now.

A plan started to develop, but it would require research.

And some help.

Alicia went into the bedroom, sat on the edge of the bed, and looked at her phone. She went to Google, typed a few things in, and began reading. Silently, she looked up to the ceiling, unsure. Then her eyebrows furrowed, and she squinted. She was thinking. She had little choice – or no choice, for that matter. Letting the phone rest in her lap, she closed her eyes. After a minute, her eyes slowly opened.

Twenty seconds later, her mind was made up.

Alicia headed into the bathroom, showered, then put on some makeup. She found herself humming "Papa Don't Preach." She loved Madonna.

She headed to her closet and saw a lot of pretty dresses and blouses hanging on the rod. She flipped through the hangers slowly, methodically. The clothes passed by in an array of colors. Alicia was determined to find exactly what she needed. The hangers slid down the rod, one at a time. She stopped when she found what she was looking for. *Perfect.* She lifted the hanger and the dress off the rod. The dress was a beautiful maxi dress by Pucci, something Ryan had given her when they first started dating. Removing the dress from the hanger, she tossed it onto the bed.

She picked up her phone and dialed. Bradley answered on the second ring.

"What can I do for you?" her brother asked dutifully.

This is for Mike.

"Come over this instant." Her voice was steel. "I need an abortion." She looked at the empty wire hanger in her hand. "And you're going to give it to me."

CHAPTER 54

Alicia had no one with her to celebrate.

It was her and Ryan's wedding day, and she should have been surrounded by those she loved. The guests were friends of the Rosling's. Alicia had no one. But there was Ryan. The man of her dreams stood by her when she hemorrhaged and lost their baby. At least that's what she told him happened.

"We'll keep trying, love," he had said through a smile, although his tone was one of a distant sadness.

Alicia should have felt guilty, but she didn't. It was a necessary act for everyone. Even Mike.

She stood in a room at the chapel with no one to help with her final preparations. Ryan was in a separate room with his three groomsmen, waiting to go to the altar, where he'd wait for his bride to meet him.

Bradley was not invited to the nuptials because Alicia did not want him in her life, until she did.

And the girls. Well, the girls had been gone ever since that day at the restaurant, when Alicia had said some terrible things to them – especially to Cathy – and she knew they were out of her life forever. *It was for the best*, she thought solemnly.

Alicia placed the pearl and gold clip in her upswept hair and looked in the mirror. A beautiful bride was looking back. She wore a Claire Petti-bone laced, long-sleeved Victorian dress with pearl accents and lavishly embroidered tulle. A French lace sash tied around her waist and flowed to a graceful, scalloped edge train.

I would've never fit into this if I were still pregnant, she thought. *Beauty is pain, or whatever they say.*

There was a knock at the door. *Who could that be?*

"Come in," she announced.

The door remained closed.

Another knock.

"I said, come in!" she called more loudly.

Nothing.

She spun in her dress and huffed towards the door. She yanked it open. "Are you deaf? I said come -"

And there, wearing their bridesmaids' dresses, stood Brooke, Cathy, and Dana.

Alicia's mouth was agape.

"Is that any way to greet your babes?" Dana asked.

"Yeah, we could just, you know, leave," Brooke said, hiking her thumb behind her.

"I...I..." Alicia stammered.

"Never saw *her* speechless before," Cathy said as they all walked past Alicia and into the room.

"Now hurry up and come here," Dana said. "We don't have much time."

"What...what are you doing here?" Alicia stood stunned, her eyes brimming with tears.

"Aren't you getting married today?" Brooke asked. "Or did you tell Ryan to go to hell, too?" She raised a sarcastic eyebrow and placed her hands on her hips.

"No...I mean, yes...I-"

"We'll take that as a 'yes'," Cathy interrupted. "Now, we have some things for you." She walked towards Alicia, grabbed her hand, and dragged her towards the girls.

"Okay. Now, you need something 'old'," Brooke said. "Here." She handed Alicia a framed photo. It was the selfie Brooke took of the four girls on the first day they met.

Alicia's hand flew to her chest. "Oh, my god. I remember this day like it was yesterday."

"And you already have the something 'new'," Brooke continued, pointing to Alicia's engagement ring.

Alicia smiled.

Dana stepped up. "For the 'borrowed', I'm breaking all the rules. I'm lending you this – the keyword is *lending* – because my grandmother would pop out of her grave and haunt me forever." She gave Alicia a recipe card. It was a handwritten recipe for Dana's grandmother's marshmallow-topped brownies.

"Oh my gosh!" Alicia exclaimed. "These were delicious! We had these on the green in front of Kenna Hall. I remember!"

"They're amazeballs!" Brooke chimed in.

"That was the day Misty got you hooked up with her Uncle Mike, remember that?" Cathy said. "That was a good day."

Alicia's face reddened at the mention of Mike's name, but she quickly recovered. "I can't wait to make these to impress Ryan," Alicia said, waving the recipe card.

"And last," Cathy said gently, "something 'blue'."

Alicia looked at Cathy, and flashes of that day at the bar in el PRADO Hotel, where she found out about her, and Ryan whizzed through her brain. It devasted Alicia, and she almost let it ruin their friendship. That seemed like a lifetime ago. Cathy had made the effort to be here today, but it was still a sore subject to Alicia. It was hard to let bygones be bygones. The memory was an ember inside her and ready to blaze again. *If only –*

"Here," Cathy said.

Alicia looked into her hands. There, laid across her palms, was a blue ribbon- the very blue ribbon Cathy always wore in her hair- the one Alicia thought she'd never part with. And now, she had given it to Alicia.

Alicia was touched. A tear flowed down her cheek.

"I thought it would be a nice touch for this," Cathy said, taking the ribbon and tying it around the stems of Alicia's bouquet. It looked beautiful.

There was another knock on the door.

"Yes?" Alicia said, her voice soft.

A man's voice spoke in Italian: "Siamo pronti per te, Alicia." *We're ready for you, Alicia.*

"Thank you, Gio. We'll be right out."

"Sexy voice," Dana gestured towards the closed door. "Who's Gio?" Dana asked.

"The limo driver, but also a good friend of Ryan's. He's helping out today."

"They're ready for *you*," Brooke said. "But are *you* ready?"

Alicia looked around at the girls surrounding her. Her AlphaBabes had returned. She smiled. "More than ready."

Tears welled up in the eyes of all the girls. After a brief pause, Alicia extended her arms, and they all embraced one another. Hurtful words and angry thoughts flew out the window, and for a brief moment, all was right in the world.

Bygones were, in fact, bygones.

The wedding and reception were gorgeous and lasted six hours.

The man sat alone in the back of the church, unnoticed. He was nervous and used his pants to wipe off his hands. He was gone before the couple kissed.

Ryan's parents were more than generous with the event, from the massive flower arrangements to the stringed quartet. A ten-piece band played while revelers danced after hitting one of five open bars around the venue. Knowing Ryan's parents' penchant for liquor, it was no surprise to Alicia there were five bars scattered around the reception hall. Except for one celebratory toast, Ryan and Alicia had no other drinks. They didn't have time to eat, and by the end of the night, they were exhausted and with cramps in their cheeks from smiling.

The limo driver, Gio, socialized with Brooke, Cathy, and Dana and spent most of his time at the bar or on the dance floor. He was a tall, well-built Italian with dark, swarthy looks, and the girls loved hanging with him, flirting with him, and bringing him drinks. They were all together when the wedding photographer came around and gathered them for a group shot. Gio and the girls whooped and hollered and held up their drinks in conviviality and camaraderie. Gio stumbled into the girls, and some of their alcohol splashed out. This only made them laugh more.

Alicia was across the room and looked over. Seeing her three besties together again, celebrating her, caused her heart to bloom with euphoria.

Alicia turned back to Ryan. The smile she wore on her face was bright and beautiful. She was with the man she loved more than life, and her secret second life with Mike was still unrevealed. And for once in her life, she felt she no longer needed Bradley. Life now was too sweet and wondrous to include anything negative.

She had seen him in the back of the church, sitting in the last pew, alone, probably hoping to go unnoticed. As she said her wedding vows to the man she loved, knowing the man she controlled was in the church watching it all unfold sent a thrill up and down her spine. Alicia couldn't hold back a smile. *I do still need him*, she thought. *I can have my cake and eat it, too.* She made a mental note to text him while she was in the limo.

It was a perfect day, full of peace and gratefulness. And it was a day she would never, ever forget.

Finally, the time had come for the newlyweds to leave the reception and begin their lives together. Gio pulled the limousine around to the front of the church and screeched it to a sudden halt. He got out and walked around to the side to open the door for the couple but had trouble raising the door handle. The door was locked.

"È chiuso. Un momento per favore." *It's locked. One moment, please.* He started laughing.

He staggered back to the driver's side and fiddled with the key fob, clicking every button until he heard the vehicle unlock. He lifted the door handle and opened the door.

"Are you okay?" Ryan asked.

"Yes, yes, my friend. Just happy with love," Gio responded. "Si."

Ryan and Alicia climbed inside the long black car and settled in.

Quickly, Alicia pulled out her phone and sent a text. *He'll be surprised,* she thought, smiling. As Gio went back to the front of the car, Alicia packed away her phone, then lowered the window so they could wave goodbye to their guests. She saw Brooke, Cathy, and Dana in the front of the crowd and blew them kisses. They raised their glasses and blew kisses back.

Behind the wheel, Gio blinked to adjust his eyesight, then started the car and put it in drive.

"Bye! Love you all!" Alicia yelled from the departing car.

"Goodbye! We love you!" the crowd yelled in return.

The limo picked up speed and sped away from the church.

Sometime over the next fourteen minutes, the limousine carrying Gio, Ryan, and Alicia, going 75mph around serpentine back roads, would crash head-on into a massive tree and turn into an inferno of jagged metal, shattered glass, and a blaze of immeasurable heat. Death came quickly.

Her life had just begun.

Her life was over.

CHAPTER 55

The funeral service for Ryan and Alicia Rosling was held the following Thursday.

Ryan's family held a huge memorial for their only son and Alicia. A bank of two hundred white roses cascaded over each closed casket, and the same stringed quartet that played at their wedding accompanied their deaths. Hundreds of people attended the service in memory of the couple, but mostly in honor of his influential parents. It was a magnificent display of wealth and sorrow.

After the ceremony, the girls gathered at Waterbar.

"I can't believe she's gone," Brooke said quietly. "I mean, it just doesn't seem real." She paused. "And why was Alicia cremated?"

Dana spoke. "She didn't have any relatives. Bodies of decedents without family are turned over to the state, and they usually cremate them. It's the same when animals die without owners."

"His poor parents," Cathy said. "They looked so weak. Their only son, dying so young, lying there. Thank God the casket was closed."

Cathy sniffled and placed her hand over Brooke's. "It's so surreal."

Brooke and Cathy squeezed each other's hands.

Dana's eyes shifted between the two. "Snap out of it, you two. You know this is our fault, don't you?"

They raised their heads and stared at Dana.

"What are you talking about?" Brooke asked.

Dana lowered her voice. "The police report said Gio was driving drunk. Three times the legal limit. *We* did that. *We* kept giving him drink after drink."

Cathy's eyes flew open.

"But we didn't force the alcohol down him," Brooke stated.

"Oh, come on. You think he would drink alone? No way. We were flirting with him and handing him drinks left and right. We were all drunk."

'Oh, my god," Cathy said. "We – we killed her!" Her voice carried.

"Shhh!" Brooke quieted her down. "I need to think!" She didn't want to believe Dana, but it was true: they fed Gio a ton of alcohol for hours. And he was stumbling to get the car unlocked. He really shouldn't have been driving.

Cathy turned her attention to Dana. "But we didn't make him get behind the wheel," she said rationally.

Dana raised and lowered her shoulders. "No, we didn't. But he had a job to do, and he was Ryan's friend. I doubt he was going to cop being too drunk to drive."

Brooke sighed. She knew what they had done. And even though it was an accident, the result was the same. An umbrella of guilt covered the trio.

Cathy was crying, already convinced she was responsible for the death of her friend. "So…so…what do we do? We have to tell someone."

"Absolutely not!" Dana said. "We can't tell anybody. What's done is done, and as sad as it is, we have to move on with our lives. Do we really need to make matters worse? For everyone? For once in your life, Cathy, you don't need to follow the rules." She sounded exasperated.

"Dana's right," Brooke chimed in. "Alicia is dead, and, well, it breaks my heart, it really does. But I'm afraid the authorities might see us as accomplices, and I can't go to jail. I just can't!"

"Jail?" Cathy gasped. "Why would they send us to jail? It was an accident."

"It was an accident for *Gio*," Dana countered. "And he's dead. But they could hold us responsible for three deaths. It could be considered manslaughter."

Cathy's eyes were huge.

"But I'm a vet, not an attorney," Dana continued. "I have no idea, quite honestly!"

"Oh, my god!" Cathy wailed. "No! No! I…I can't. We…can't go to… *jail*," she whispered.

Something had shifted, a tectonic movement in the atmosphere. The din of the crowded restaurant had vanished, and it seemed the three girls were alone in the world. No one said a word. No one could. Finally, Brooke broke the silence.

"Then we all agree? We take this secret to our graves?"

Dana nodded her head, her eyes filling with tears.

Brooke laid her hand in the middle of the table. Dana placed hers on top. Both girls turned to look at Cathy.

Cathy was shaking her head. *I can't do this. I can't! We killed Alicia and Ryan and robbed them of their new life together! Someone had to be told. They would understand it was an accident. Wouldn't they? No. I won't be a part of this coverup. Absolutely not! Oh, Alicia. I'm so sorry!*

Dana and Brooke stared at her, and by the look in Cathy's eyes, they knew they had lost. They could sense Cathy would not acquiesce, and they would soon be against a judge and jury. Their hearts sank.

Cathy swallowed. Conceding, she placed her hand on top of Brooke's and Dana's.

"Agreed."

The pain was excruciating. A million needles were stabbing her, piercing her tender flesh.

Or what remained of it.

She was awake in the hospital, but she was having trouble focusing her eyes through the gauze. She had been there for weeks, getting grafts and fresh bandages daily. Her sores oozed, and with each new dressing application, she would scream from the horrific pain, tears flowing from her lidless eyes.

An unidentified stranger brought her into the Bothin Burn Center, and he did not divulge any information about the patient. Her skin had melted, and a dark crust covered her from head to toe. Round nubs had formed at the end of her wrists as her fingers had fused together. Her face was a macabre plaid of burn tissue, and her lips were stationary in a horrible rictus of a smile. The doctors gave her less than 24 hours to live.

While lying nearly comatose in pain for weeks, she remembered the accident: she had no more husband, no more life ahead of her. And she wanted to die.

But someone wouldn't let her. The girls had stolen her life from her, and someone had pulled her from the wreckage, stealing her *death* from her. But she was *not* grateful; she was enraged. Without her husband, without her identity, she felt life was not worth living. But someone took that away from her.

And there in that hospital bed, Alicia swore someone would pay for robbing her of that opportunity.

That was over two months ago, and now they were sending her home.

Where she had time to reflect.

And, like always, Alicia started developing a plan.

Bradley was by her side 24/7. When she was released to go home, he personally transported her to her home. He stayed with her and took care of her. He bathed her and fed her and loved her and would do anything for her. Alicia didn't want a caregiver; she wanted Bradley. She needn't even ask – he was all too happy to help her with whatever she needed.

While Bradley cared for her, her plan formed. She knew who had really caused all this. They had killed Ryan, her life. She had died that day in the limo the moment Ryan died in her arms.

Brooke.

Cathy.

Dana.

Alicia knew they were responsible for getting Gio drunk at the reception. She let her mind sharpen at the memory of that day, when she saw the girls and Gio across the room, laughing, dancing, drinking.

Hatred surged through Alicia, and venom coursed through her veins. She would look at the fused protuberances at the end of her wrists and curse. She couldn't do anything physical to the girls. Not by herself, anyway. She needed muscle.

So, for five days, she sat across from Bradley, going over her plans and the machinations of how it would play out. She told him to pay attention.

Then, she educated him on their phobias (heights, enclosed spaces, and water); on their likes (slasher movies and picnics at Little Marina Green Park); and odd connections (Brooke's father was a stamp collector, Cathy liked Dr. Seuss, and Dana liked escape rooms).

Alicia told Bradley that Brooke had a big, mean cat and gave him a small spray bottle of Happy Kitty Catnip to spray on his clothes before going to her house. *"Bongo won't be able to resist you, and Brooke will swoon over your bonding with her cat."*

She told him about the importance of the poppies and how to use them to his advantage. She told him to use the bobcat to dig the hole, how to train Kong to attack, and where to buy the chum at Pleasure Pier for the scuba outing. She gave him addresses and phone numbers.

She made sure he knew he had to save each girl from *something* that would build their trust in him. With Brooke, it would be the caverns. He would save Cathy when she fell off the ladder, and he would rescue Dana from the sharks. After each rescue, the girls would not be able to live without him. Bradley trusted her assessments.

Alicia told him about each girl's romantic ideals. With Brooke, she loves to sleep around, so Bradley would need to abstain from sleeping with her. *"For a while,"* Alicia informed him. *"Absence will definitely make her horny heart grow fonder."* Cathy is a prude and, as far as Alicia knew, had only slept with one other person. Alicia bristled at the memory of Cathy and Ryan's tryst. *"You'll have to really make her believe you're in love with her in order for her to open her legs to you."* And Dana believes in love at first sight. *"She's been so caught up in her work all of her life that she'll jump at the chance to get married. She'll be the easiest of the three to cajole."*

She instructed him how important it was to do things in advance, like get a library card to Sarah Tuttle Public Library, obtain a wilderness permit to Yosemite, destroy the wires to Peterinarians' A/C unit, and cut a hole in the fence around Lake Oroville and place the Adirondack boat just off the shore. She told him what the bottle of succinylcholine looked like (*"It's a clear bottle with black lettering and a red cap."*) so it would be easier to find when he broke into the clinic that Monday when it would be closed for A/C repairs.

"Brooke will need to be killed during the off-season of The Lodge at Bodega Bay—fewer eyes to witness you there. Plus, the owners of the property where you'll bury her will be out of town during this small window. No interruptions."

"With Dana, you'll need to go to Lake Oroville on the 4th of July. You'll trespass onto the property, and she'll be none the wiser. Normally, people would crowd the lake, but this year, the lake will close for the dam's recalibration. She won't need to know this until the end."

"And Cathy. Dear sweet Cathy. School starts back up at the end of August, so that last weekend, families will be ultra-busy buying school supplies without a single thought of traveling and visiting a National Park. Practically, no one should be at Yosemite."

She had told him he would need a big dog. *"You will not like this part,"* Alicia had said tonelessly. *"But it's necessary."* She watched as Bradley knitted his brow in anticipation. *"In order to get to Dana, you will need a legitimate reason to visit her clinic. You will need to break the dog's leg by hand."* She watched Bradley flinch, his head going rigid. *"I'm not asking you to do this. I'm telling you."* He gave an imperceptible nod.

She slid three identical photographs across the table. *"Give one to each girl at the very end of their lives. I want them to know."*

Alicia sat up straighter in her chair. The pain meds were wearing off, and her body was stinging. She didn't have further to go with Bradley, so she plugged on. She took a deep breath.

But Alicia saved the most important item for last. Alicia gave him three burner phones with one number already added: hers. He was to call her only once from each telephone after he had killed each girl. It was to be the only contact between the siblings. *"Do not forget the phone call."* It wasn't a suggestion.

She was unsure he was disciplined enough, so she refused to allow him to leave the table even to eat, drink, or go to the bathroom. If he could do that, if he could prove his loyalty to her during these five days, then she would be satisfied. He had already shown his dedication by murdering her professor and slaughtering their family.

And by killing her unborn child.

What would be a few more?

When she asked if he was ready, he spoke for the first time.

"Consider it done."

And Bradley had succeeded. He had done everything Alicia had instructed him to do.

"Do not forget the phone call," she had said.

He hadn't forgotten. He hadn't forgotten *anything* with the girls.

He had called Alicia each time.

They had all suffered, one way or another, at his hands. It truly was done. And now he and Alicia could live their lives in happiness. He was counting on that. He was counting on Alicia to be content and for her to be proud of him. She knew everything there was to know about him.

Well, almost everything.

Bradley was nervous, more nervous than he had ever been before. His palms began to sweat. He wiped his hands on his pants. He hated being defiant, especially against Alicia. He knew her and was not looking forward to being at the end of her wrath.

He had done everything Alicia told him to do over those excruciating five days at the table. He loved Alicia, but he realized that what she was doing to him, he was doing to the girls. *Do unto others,* he thought wryly.

But he still had a job to do. He had killed all the girls she had instructed him to kill.

Except for one. One, he kept alive.

And when Alicia found out, she was going to be surprised.
Or mad as hell.

CHAPTER 56

"It's done."

Alicia always got a thrill from those two words. She hung up the phone from Bradley.

"Three down, zero to go," Alicia said icily after Bradley's last phone call. She put the phone to her side and smiled. It was an awkward smile because of the new shape of her burned lips, but inside, she was happy. She was satisfied.

Almost.

She still had something to do.

It was her backup plan. One she never told Bradley about.

But that would be later. For now, she reveled in the fact the girls had gotten their punishment. They had destroyed her new life with her husband, Ryan. The future she worked so hard to get, including the death of her unborn child, had gone up in smoke. Literally. She lifted a side of her mouth at the irony.

The girls had gotten Gio drunk, and because of that, he drove the limo into a tree and crashed. The crunching noise of the grinding car was eerie and one she'd never forget. Then the fire...oh, the fire! It had burned through the car's cabin with a ferocity and took with it every bit of Alicia's happiness and future in a flash.

A tear fell from Alicia's lidless eye. *The girls brought this revenge upon themselves. They lit the fuse to this whole thing.*

She stood and walked through her apartment and stopped at a mirror. The hideousness of her unfamiliar face glared back. She knew she had once been beautiful, but she didn't feel sorry for herself, even though the world could be cruel. The way children stared and screamed as if she were a monster; people purposefully moving away from the sight of her; the pitiful looks and wrinkled faces and shaking heads, not knowing to feel sorry for her or to feel horror. Her suffering knew no end.

They don't know me, she thought. *They're the true monsters.*

But Alicia knew the girls inside and out and used that to her advantage to make them suffer. *I made sure Bradley gave them the picture from my wedding showing Gio and them all drinking so they would know why this was happening to them. It was the perfect revenge.*

And Cathy! She had slept with Ryan at his party, blaming it on being inebriated. She knew what she was doing. And for the girls to have kept this from her all that time? *No! They all got what they deserved.*

But there was still that one matter needing to be cleaned up. She was glad she had a second plan in motion because she wasn't sure Bradley would be careful enough not to get caught. He had, without a doubt, proven his loyalty, and for that, she was proud of him. She had disciplined him well. But he was still weak. They had been through a lot together, but she was right all those years ago: Bradley was a pussy. A weak boy who turned into an even weaker man. And she could leave nothing to chance.

Alicia sighed. She felt melancholy. Her work with Bradley was done. In fact, her work with everyone involved was done. She had no need for assistance anymore, and she had accomplished what she had set out to do. Alicia was ready to end this once and for all. She raised her head in assuredness, picked up her phone, and scrolled through her contacts. *It's time to tie up the loose ends.* Finding the contact she needed, she pressed the number. A voice on the other end greeted her.

"Come over now," Alicia said. "The door will be unlocked." She ended the call. She knew he wouldn't be long. He couldn't help himself.

Alicia waited two minutes before sending a text to someone else.

The time had come for the two men in her life to meet face to face.

She marveled at the fact that she had not one but two men willing to do her bidding. It proved to her that men were the weaker of the two sexes. She smiled.

She walked into the bedroom to select her clothes; she needed something light and colorful. Her mood was picking up, and she needed the right outfit to accommodate that. Alicia opened the closet door and saw her beautiful clothes in front of her, designer outfits she had acquired when she was with Ryan. And there, among the expensive name brands, was the starkness of a shovel, wrapped in plastic to preserve Bradley's fingerprints. Ever since Alicia witnessed Bradley kill and bury their next-door neighbor, Jenna's boyfriend, with this shovel, she knew she wanted it for insurance. *Just in case.* She had kept it all this time and hadn't found a reason to use it against Bradley: he was a willing participant, after all, but after tonight's meeting…. *well, we'll have to wait and see how things unfold.*

And then there was Mike Evans.

Ever since their first meeting when she was in college, he had become infatuated with Alicia. She gave him things his wife, Karen, never could. It wasn't all about the looks; it was about the control. Alicia dominated Mike's life and curbed a side of him Karen had never seen.

But Alicia did not need Mike to be a permanent fixture in her life; he needed to be with Karen but just within reach of Alicia's talons. And Alicia had used Mike and his detective skills to her benefit. Unfortunately, Mike's obsession with Alicia backfired, and he had disappointed her more than anyone. He was a liability she needed to quash. And so, her eventual plan was about to come to fruition. She needed Mike Evans out of her life, but that would require a few strings to be pulled.

Mike Evans had done the unthinkable, the unimaginable.

The unforgivable.

And now, he must pay.

Alicia didn't have feelings anymore; she couldn't care less she was eliminating all of those around her. No one understood what she was going through. Without Ryan, she had nothing. And if she was to live the rest of her life forever alone, then so be it.

She checked the drawer in the end table. The Glock was still there. She grasped it in her hand as best she could. Cold, hard, steel. Powerful. Since she had no fingers to pull the trigger, she had rigged an eight-inch-long, thin wooden stick in front of the trigger. She would brace the gun in a pillow on her lap, pull back on the stick with both hands and fire the weapon.

Alicia knew the meeting would be an explosive one, and she steeled her nerves.

She was ready.

Alicia sat down on the sofa and placed a pillow in her lap. Underneath, she held the gun and stick.

And she waited.

CHAPTER 57

"Come over now," Alicia had said. "The door will be unlocked."

After he got the phone call from Alicia, he felt the hairs on the back of his neck begin to rise. He was excited; he had done so much for her, and his love for her was eternal. And he was confident she felt the same; otherwise, she never would've asked him to do the things he did.

He wasn't just captivated by Alicia; he was obsessed. She was the lifeblood that ran through his veins. It was why he had to be at the wedding. After she had forbidden him to be there, he showed up anyway, sitting in the back unobserved.

When Alicia and Ryan got married, the minister asked the age-old question about whether there was anyone who objected to the union should better speak now or forever hold their peace. He sat in the back of the church on the last pew, willing himself not to burst up and yell, "Stop! Don't marry him! I love you!", but he had seen the happiness on her face, and he loved her enough not to destroy her fantasy. Even after the way she had treated him. He could live with it. For now.

He looked at his hands. They were dirty from a task he had just finished. He wiped his hands on his pants to clean off the residue. The wedding was coming to an end, but he left before the kiss; it was too much for him to watch.

But then he got her text and bolted in a feverish terror.

He followed the limousine. He had to stop it. But the limo was going faster than it should along the winding roads, more than 40 miles per hour over the 30mph limit, and he couldn't catch up. As it made its way through Berkeley Hills and wound its way around the wet, curvy Grizzly Peak Boulevard, he noticed the black car wasn't slowing down – it was speeding up! His heart pounded out of his chest.

"NO!" he yelled.

As if in slow motion, the tires suddenly hydroplaned, and the large vehicle swerved, its backend fishtailed back and forth as the back tires desperately tried to grip the asphalt. In a horrifying instant, he watched the car fly out of control and careen off the embankment, into the heavily wooded area and out of sight. He heard a loud crash and then the boom of an explosion.

Oh, my God!

He slammed his car into park and ran down the slippery hill. The sight of the mangled limousine engulfed in flames took his breath away. From 100 feet away, the heat from the fire singed the hairs on his arms.

He half-ran, half-stumbled down into the ravine, closer to the car. Thick black smoke shrouded the entire vehicle, and he had no idea where he stood. But she was in there, and no matter the heat, no matter the smoke, he would rescue her.

He raced around the long car, trying every door, feeling the scalding handles sting his hand. All the doors were locked. He yanked off his jacket and used that to protect his hands and kept trying doors.

"Alicia!" he yelled. *Oh, God! Please!*

Finally, he saw smoke billowing out of an open window, the one Alicia had opened to wave goodbye. He reached in and unlocked the door, yanking it open in seconds. He stuck his head into the car, now a fiery pyre, and saw her. A body laid on top of her lap. Her eyes were wide open, only…

She was engulfed in flames, and he did the only thing his heart told him to do: he grabbed her by the legs and tugged her out of the car onto the ground. He threw his coat over her to extinguish the flames, but most of the effort was futile. She wasn't moving. He feared she was dead, but he kept pounding the coat on her fire-drenched body.

Mercifully, the flames licking her body went out, and her head fell to the side, and she was staring at him.

His face is so kind and caring, yet he looks worried. He's looking at me, but I can't tell how he's looking at me. He looks pained. Horrified. Why?

She started coughing. Black smoke emitted from her charred lungs. He bent down and attempted to breathe clean oxygen into her, but he, too, was overcome with smoke. She kept coughing, but eventually, it subsided.

"My God, Alicia." He was on his knees beside her, out of breath. "I… I…" he had no words. "I'm so sorry!"

Don't be sorry, darling. She waivered in and out of consciousness. *I remember the wedding. So beautiful. Ryan looked so handsome. There were friends and family. Drinking and dancing and….* She heard the squealing of tires, and then the sound of the crash suddenly filled her mind. She tried to close her eyes but couldn't…

He saw her looking at him. "Oh, Alicia," he cried.

His skin is glistening with sweat, and he's still so handsome. And once upon a time, there were feelings reciprocated. I did love you. But I was engaged to the son of a prominent family that I needed to be a part of. It's why I had to get rid of your baby. I'm sorry for keeping it a secret that you were a father….

She was overcome with a sense of sadness for this man. Her lips were dry. She licked her lips but could not feel them. Nor could she feel the tears rolling down her scorched skin. For the first time since he'd pulled her from the inferno, she spoke in a coarse whisper.

"Mike…."

CHAPTER 58

Mike Evans remembered how it all began…

Since the first day he saw Alicia Madison, when they met to work on her Criminology elective, he was inexplicably drawn to her. His niece, Misty, had called and asked him to help her friend.

"Well, she's a new friend, and I really like her, so do you mind?" Misty had sounded so enthusiastic and happy to have a female friend in her life. She was a bit of an odd duck, but a lot of that had to do with the fact both of her parents were drug addicts and dealers and had emotionally and physically replaced Misty with meth. Things got more awkward for Misty when Mike was the one who actually busted his own brother and sister-in-law. And that's how Misty, at age four, came to live with the Evans.

As Misty grew older, she was the shy one at school, and she didn't have any friends. Although she desperately wanted to fit in, she just never knew how. Square peg, round hole sort of thing. Misty's mixed racial makeup made her classmates guarded and uncertain about which side she identified with: was she black? White? They couldn't make up their minds, so instead, they decided not to deal with her at all. As a result, they didn't trust her, and she didn't trust them. Finding friends in life never came easy for her.

So, when she came calling about her friend Alicia, Mike Evans was only too happy to help his niece. Even though he didn't have the time or energy to help a college girl with her classes, he was committed to helping Misty.

He had decided he would meet with Alicia, go over a few basics to get her through a few tests, and then let her be on her way. He counted on her getting bored with the subject matter quickly, making his tutoring session very short-lived. Then he could hurry home to his wife, Karen.

Mike was a good enough detective to realize off the bat Alicia Madison was not taking a Criminology course. Still, curiosity got the better of him, and he went along with her ruse. He would have fun teasing this one, knocking her down a peg, and maybe, just maybe, he would get something out of it. She was attractive and had an impressive figure. Mike was a little out of shape and had a little belly, but he had the build of a strong linebacker who had let himself go. But he prided himself as a ladies' man. Alicia would be no different.

He had thought wrong.

Alicia Madison was unlike any woman he had ever met. She was confident (cocky?), smart (brilliant?), funny (hilarious?), and savvy (calculating?). And upon first meeting her, Mike Evans became utterly enamored with Alicia Madison. Everything about her enveloped him and had taken over. She had complete control over him, revealing a hidden part he never knew existed, and he had never been so impacted by a woman. Two things happened: 1) he started working out, eating better, and getting into the best shape of his life, and 2) he let everything else in his life disintegrate.

His job no longer mattered.

His social scene and friends no longer fit into his schedule.

His marriage to Karen crumbled, and she had no idea why.

Mike was a man possessed and on a daily mission to make Alicia happy. He never wanted to fail her.

His one mistake was in thinking he was the only man in her life to feel this way.

Mike and Alicia had carried on illicitly for years, through her college days, bleeding into the years afterward. He was married, and Karen was a wonderful wife: dutiful, agreeable, and not opinionated at all. His equal. But where Karen was the calm in Mike's life, Alicia was the storm. Alicia provided the danger and forbidden life of an affair, and he was addicted to it all. She was courageous, confident, sensual. His superior.

Mike was a man usually in control, but Alicia would shake his confidence to the core, and he would gladly (helplessly?) turn all control over to her. He was bewitched.

As her wedding to Ryan approached, Mike could feel Alicia pulling away, cooling things down with him. And then, with one phone call, she had ended things. From then until the wedding, things were a blur. Then, the accident happened, and Alicia became nearly invisible in his life. He had saved her, bringing her into the Bothin Burn Center, and she seemed all but grateful...

Shortly after he had brought her into the burn center, he sat at her bedside. The bandages on her body were tight and stained with blood and salve.

"I...I need to be...dead. I should....be.... dead," she hissed through burned lips. "You...owe me."

He lowered his head.

"I have...nothing," she spat. She tried to turn her head away from him, but the slightest movement caused her sharp pain.

"I don't understand," Mike said. "I saved you!"

"You saved me? You...saved me?" she said incredulously, her voice raspy and harsh. "You robbed me...of dying. I have nothing...nothing....to live for. This is unforgivable. I should've...died." She started to cough. He stood and put the water straw to her lips. She drank.

"Alicia. I'm sorry. I love you and..." He wasn't sure what to say. What could he say? He needed this to be rectified. "What can I do?"

She winced and forced her head to turn so she could look at him. She groaned in agony as she spoke.

And he understood.

Mike let Bradley take Alicia back to her apartment, where she would be cared for. Without any relatives to approve of her passing, it was easy to get his coroner pal to sign the death certificate. Mike told his friend of Alicia's accident and subsequent death.

"Terrible situation, Mike," Ed Silverman said. "I hope it was quick."

"Unfortunately, she hung on for a few days. I'm sure she was in terrible pain."

"No doubt," the coroner said. "So, how can I help?"

Mike remembered Alicia's instructions and chose his words carefully.

"Well, the deceased had no immediate relatives, so there was no one to pay for the funeral. The state requires a death certificate in order for the funeral to be funded by the county."

"Damn government," Ed Silverman said. "They cut my budget in half, and I lost both of my assistants. I've got procedures and bodies backed up for two weeks."

"That's terrible," Mike agreed. "So, maybe you can just fill out her death certificate and a cremation authorization form, too, while you're at it, so we won't have to add her body to your backlog." He chuckled and gently slapped Ed on the arm.

"My pleasure!" Ed said, relieved his workload didn't get any heavier.

And just like that, Mike Evans had proof that Alicia Madison was 'dead and cremated'. He could now ensure the casket would be closed at the funeral with no meddlesome questions.

Alicia could now carry out her agenda.

He smiled, knowing Alicia would have to forgive him.

But sadly, for Mike, things only went from bad to worse.

Alicia cut off all contact with him, and his calls to her went unanswered. He couldn't fathom what he had done wrong. She had disappeared entirely, and Mike felt a huge chunk of his soul was missing.

That seemed a lifetime ago. He got nervous; the end was approaching, and his life became a complete shambles. Karen threatened to leave him, and his lieutenant had put him on final notice. Mike became listless, and living became a burden to him. *It all needed to go away.*

Without Alicia, life equaled death. He put his gun in his hand and walked somberly out to his car. He trembled as he sat behind the wheel but was confident there was no other way. There were no tears, for there was no sadness. Only regret. He placed his finger on the trigger. As he raised the gun to his temple, he could feel the cold, hard steel of the gun's barrel. Mike closed his eyes. As he began to squeeze the trigger, the shrill of his phone startled him. He looked at the screen.

Alicia!

Within two hours, he was seated across from her.

She was still self-conscious about her looks, but Mike saw through the burns and loved her completely. Despite her disfigurement, he never stopped loving her. He had rescued her, and she was completely oblivious that she had just rescued him.

She spoke.

Alicia told Mike about her plans for Brooke, Cathy, and Dana and how she was using Bradley to carry out her agenda. She asked him to listen, and he moved closer to the edge of the sofa and listened intently. He was happy to be back in her good graces.

"But Bradley can be, well, unpredictable," she said with a wave of her arms. "I trust him, but he gets so focused sometimes that he forgets his surroundings. It's just about observations. I need you to watch him and…"

"…follow him?" Mike asked.

"In a way. But only as insurance."

"Insurance?"

Alicia cocked her head as if she were thinking this through for the first time. "Yes. While he's doing what I need him to do, I'm sure people will not be so oblivious to him and might become a bit…suspicious. Dangerous to the plan." She looked him in his eyes. "You understand, this is just for backup, right?"

He nodded. "I understand."

"Mike," she said, gently placing her hand on his knee, "you don't have to do anything you don't want to do. This is just me asking a favor." There was a pause. "I want nothing you do to affect Karen."

At the mention of his wife's name, he sat up straighter. Defiant. "This has nothing to do with Karen," he assured her. "This is about you. I love *you*. Karen will never…"

Alicia knew she had him. "Then, if you're okay with this…" she let the sentence hang in the air.

He nodded his approval.

"Good." She removed her hand from his leg. "Then here's what I need you to do…"

She began to spell out his duties, and when she was done, Mike knew he was in. He knew his *observations* would probably become *participations*, and he was okay with that.

Nothing about her surprised him.

Everything about her surprised him.

He wouldn't let anything – or anyone – stand in his way of seeing things through.

And that's why Mike had to kill Cathy's mother, Linda. And the two gay men on Catalina Island. And his niece, Misty. *I'm so sorry, Misty.* His throat thickened. *I know I lied about Bradley Harris not existing when you asked me to investigate for Brooke's sake. I had to. I followed him to the coffeehouse that day you confronted him. Oh, how I wish you hadn't done that. You got too close.* They all had. They were all *thisclose* to exposing Bradley, and Alicia couldn't have Bradley outed, so Mike had to step in. *Participation.*

Misty's boyfriend, Tyler, had to have a reason not to contact Misty, so Mike had dug a little into his past and found he had been charged with a misdemeanor two years ago for theft. Mike puffed his chest and intimidated Tyler, telling him he wasn't good enough for Misty, and if he didn't cut off all contact with her, he would expose him as the criminal he was. Tyler complied and never called Misty again. *Not that he could have reached her.* Misty's selfless gesture of looking after her friend Brooke ended up being fatal for her. Mike sighed. That was a tough one. As it turned out, Misty wasn't nearly as important as his alliance with Alicia.

He had hidden behind trees staring at Cathy's house and had received the call from Linda Broderick asking for a favor.

"*I understand that Brooke Carson is missing and, well, she and Cathy were...umm, are friends, and I wanted to ask the detective side of you if you could keep an eye on her for me? You know, just in your travels."*

"Sure. I understand where you're coming from. Does she still live in the same house?"

"On Hampton Street. Yes."

"Fine. I'll do what I can, Linda."

"Thank you, Michael. I really appreciate it. If anything changes, I'll call and let you know. Please give Karen my love."

"Will do. Goodnight"

Linda Broderick was onto something, and Mike Evans knew it. He was afraid she would talk, so he slit her throat, cutting through her vocal cords. *No more talking.*

The gay couple on Catalina Island got closer than they should have. Mike wore a hat with a large brim to disguise himself while seated at restaurants close to Dana and Bradley, and he could overhear everything. It was a coincidence the men recognized Bradley from his time at The Lodge at Bodega Bay when he was there with Brooke. Mike had lured the couple into a home under the guise of being a seller of a potential Bed and Breakfast property. When they had their backs turned to him, he smashed them over their heads with a hammer. They fell hard to the marble floor. He decided to be creative and killed them the same way Bradley had murdered his family: no teeth, no fingerprints. He was having a bit of fun with Bradley and knew that if Bradley ever saw the photos, he would be thrown off his game and would have to focus more.

And it had worked. Bradley straightened up and took care of Dana with no apparent problems.

But throughout it all, Bradley had been sloppy. Alicia was right: he was unpredictable. He had no idea just how close he had gotten to being discovered. But Alicia's plan to have Mike follow him and help keep Bradley on track was executed brilliantly. He was happy to do it. For Alicia.

For them both.

But mercifully, it was all over. The three girls had been taken care of, and he could once again focus on his love for Alicia. He had come very close to ending it all, but with his mission successfully carried out, he was sure she could change her mind and have her closer to him than ever before.

And now she had called him and told him to come over. He smiled.

This was it.

Mike grabbed his trusty bag with his belongings and headed over to see Alicia.

CHAPTER 59

Over those five days when Alicia was giving Bradley the sequence of steps to carry out her plan, she had casually slipped in that he would be dating all three girls simultaneously, a challenge Bradley wasn't sure he could triumph over. But the more invested he became in the process, added with a compulsion to honor his sister's wishes, he found it easier than expected.

When he was with Brooke, he left her to spend time in Sonoma to dig the makeshift grave; after he and Cathy spent three days in her bed, he left her and took Kong to Peterinarians to meet Dana; and on the weekend before California schools started back, he left Dana to take Cathy to Yosemite. The timing and coordination of events had to be immaculate. For anyone else, the organization and implementation of the plans would've been overwhelming. But Bradley was smart. He had executed everything beautifully.

But now, quizzically, he wasn't so sure.

Bradley stared at the text on his phone.

> Come over, dear brother. We need to talk.

This was never a good sign.

He racked his brain over and over, trying to figure out what he had done wrong, where he had slipped up. *No. I did nothing wrong. I followed every instruction according to her plan. Except…*

"Shit!" he said aloud, coming to a possible realization. Had Alicia found out about *her*? *I was so careful.* He was confident that nobody had found out, even though it was tricky to keep her hidden. Yes, he knew about the man who kept following him. He wasn't an idiot! When Bradley encountered the man in his living room, posing as a veterinarian client of Dana's, he knew he had recognized him from the restaurant on Catalina Island. Bradley was pretty sure this man was the one who provided Dana with the photos of his family. *But why?*

Bradley couldn't worry about all that now; his life was turning for the better. He was in love. For the first time in his life, he felt a different type of love. It's why he had saved her at the last minute from death. It was a tough conversation to confess everything, but, in the end, she had recip-rocated his love and promised to help him with his plans. And now Bradley was ready to tell Alicia everything.

He knew it wouldn't be easy to tell Alicia – she counted on him as much as he counted on her. But he needed to tell her he was leaving her to better his life. His eyes had been opened, and he realized Alicia was poison to him. And yet, at the same time, she would no longer be a part of his life. He felt a sadness unlike any he'd experienced.

Bradley got in his car to drive to Alicia's. He took a deep breath before starting the engine. Then, he got out his phone and sent a text.

> Heading over to her house now. SUS.

He found his hands were shaking. Can I do this? He shut his eyes hard and took several deep breaths. *Better.* His nervousness about Alicia was waning. He now had a confidence that usually came from loving someone. Yes. Bradley found himself in love with a wonderful woman. And he couldn't wait to re-introduce her to Alicia, to surprise her. It'd been over a year since the two women had last seen each other, and they were practically strangers. But not really. They used to be friends: *AlphaBabes.*

He was supposed to have killed them all, but as Alicia was soon to find out, one of her friends was very much alive.

CHAPTER 60

S he read the text:

> Heading over to her house now. SUS.

SUS. See you soon.

She smiled. *Yes, my darling,* she thought. *You most certainly will.* She kissed two fingers and then gently placed them on the phone screen.

She grabbed her car keys and heavy handbag and felt something nudge her hip. She looked down at the large black Russian Terrier.

"Well, hello there, Kong. Mommy's leaving for just a little bit, but I'll be back soon."

Kong licked her palm and then walked over to his device, the Konginator 2000.

She chuckled and tossed back her long hair. "Fine. Show me how you've recovered."

The dog stood beside the machine, its bar now a full 12 inches off the ground. He lifted his long back leg and then dropped his paw on the button. *Ding.*

She rushed over to him and cradled his furry face in her hands. "What a good boy!" she said.

Ding. Ding. Ding.

She laughed and got him a treat from the jar.

Perfect, she thought, smooching him on top of his head. She ruffled his floppy ears.

She opened the door and left.

CHAPTER 61

Alicia heard the front door open and then shut. She felt her heart beating faster than usual. She hid the gun under the pillow on her lap. *Not yet.*

She looked up and saw Mike, the first to arrive. He walked into the den and saw her sitting on the sofa.

"Hello, my darling," he said, heading over to her. He bent down to kiss her on the forehead, his bag still over his shoulder.

Alicia knew the time had arrived. She needed this to succeed, but she was still waiting for one other person. *He will be my alibi.*

"Hello," she replied coolly.

"So," he said, grinning ear to ear. "What's going on? Why did you need to see me? Another project? Because I'm ready to -" But a knock on the door interrupted him.

"Would you get that for me, please?" she asked, shifting in her seat.

"Sure," he responded, heading out of the den.

Alicia heard the door open. Male voices. They were getting louder.

"You!" *Bradley.* "What are you doing here?"

"I could ask you the same thing, asshole." *Mike.*

"I was invited." *Bradley.*

"You should leave." *Mike.*

"Not until I speak to my sister!" *Bradley*

She saw them enter the den, both looking a bit confused and angry. The energy in the room crackled with electricity.

"Alicia -" Mike started, but he stopped talking when he saw what was resting on a pillow in her lap. She had a gun aimed at his head.

"Whoa.... honey, wait. What's going on here?" Instinctively, he dropped his bag to the floor and raised both hands in surrender.

"*Honey?*" Bradley asked. He was confused. He had come here by request but was going to tell Alicia about the woman he loved and how he would no longer be his sister's puppet. But this! She had a gun pointed at the man who had been following him for months. And he had just called her 'honey'. What the hell was happening?

"Ahh, look at you two. Both of my men in the same room. Face to face. This thrills me to no end." She tried, but her misshapen lips refused to form a smile. She wasn't able to show her pride by using her facial expressions, but the tone of her voice conveyed the message perfectly.

The two men stood, staring. Alicia broke the silence.

"It's really quite simple, Mike. I needed you to make sure Bradley didn't fuck up." She saw both men bristle at her words. "And you succeeded, and now, well, to put it bluntly, I don't need you anymore. Capeesh?" She shifted the gun a little and gripped the wooden stick in front of the trigger.

Mike's eyes enlarged in horror. He couldn't believe it! The woman he loved was going to kill him! Kill *him*? His world was crashing down, and he felt he only had seconds to change the situation in his favor. His mind's wheel spun, and he pointed his finger at Alicia and shouted to Bradley. "She's got the shovel!"

Alicia turned rigid.

Bradley cocked his head. "Shovel? What...shovel?"

"The shovel! The one you killed your neighbor with! It has your fingerprints on it, and she was going to use it to set you up if you didn't do what she asked you to do!"

Alicia's face turned red with anger. If she were a dragon, she'd be breathing flames.

Bradley looked at his sister in disbelief. Her hands were shaking, the gun wavering.

"Bradley! I would never use that against you…. I promise! You believe me, don't you?"

He had always believed his sister. No matter what she had asked of him, he had believed her. But suddenly, he found he didn't. He looked at Mike, who had a smug expression on his face. Bradley was devastated. The room began to spin. The sister he loved with all his heart. He knew she was controlling and ferociously mean, but she was blood! How could she do this to him? He found he was crying, the tears falling from his eyes onto his beet-red cheeks. His anger was a bomb waiting to explode. This was the final straw!

Bradley reached behind him, pulled out a gun from his jeans' waist, and pointed it at Alicia.

"I should kill you right now!" he spat.

Horror overcame Alicia. None of this was making sense. All she wanted to do was to kill Mike and have Bradley be her alibi - that she had killed Mike in self-defense. Hell, she might even coerce Bradley into taking the blame for the murder, like he took the blame for stealing her bra when they were kids. *When it had all started.*

But now, Alicia found herself backed into a corner as the tables turned. She stared at Bradley, dumbfounded. Her eyes darted to Mike.

He had grabbed a gun from his bag and was aiming it at Alicia.

This is insane! Alicia thought. A triangle of people was in her den. Everyone had a gun, and blame was being tossed around like confetti. *The world has gone batshit crazy!* Everything was spinning out of her control. Her breathing became harsh and rapid. She decided to take a page out of Mike's book. She turned her venom towards him.

"Bradley forced me to abort your baby!"

Mike stiffened. *"What?* What are you…what are you *talking* about? My *baby*?" He stammered his words.

"I got pregnant, but Bradley didn't want a mixed-race baby to be brought up in my life, so he forced me to abort the fetus. He tied me down and used…. he used…a hanger and….it hurt so bad…I…I'm so sorry, Mike…." Her sadness became palpable.

Something in Mike shifted. *After all I've done….* He knew he had lost - both Karen and now Alicia. Mike had nothing more to lose.

And then the universe was hushed; all sound was muted as if

plugged into noise cancellation. An awkward lull of quiet that seemed to stretch on and on.

Then, it started as a stifled titter and became a hearty chuckle, growing louder and louder until a sonic boom of laughter filled the room. The maniacal roar stuffed the den, corner to corner.

Alicia's tears suddenly stopped as she looked towards the source. Bradley scrunched his brows as he looked, too. Their eyes rested on Mike. He was nearly doubled over in hysterical fits, covering his stomach with his free hand. Finally, he let the laughter subside, and he wiped his face with his shirt's sleeve.

"What's so funny?" Alicia demanded. "Didn't you hear what I just said? Bradley made me -"

"Oh, shut up, Alicia," Mike bellowed, suddenly stern. "You think you have it all figured out, don't you? You are delusional, you know that?"

Alicia shivered. She was taken aback by the sudden attitude swap and now wasn't sure where to take this conversation. Mike was clearly upset, and he still had his gun pointed at her. She noticed his hand was shaking. His finger could easily squeeze the trigger without warning and –

"I have a confession," Mike said, interrupting her thoughts. "One that you might find rather funny." He shook his gun at Alicia. "Well, it's not so much funny as ironic."

Alicia didn't want to lose control of the situation, but she knew she needed to find her resolve and remind him of her position. "Do tell," Alicia said, lifting her chin.

"When you called me and ended...*us*," he spat, "I was angry. You knew I loved you. You *knew* how I felt." His voice grew more robust with each sentence. "You came into my life and turned everything I knew upside down. I hated you for it." He took a deep breath. "I loved you for it."

Alicia sat listening. Stoic. Her face was void of all expression.

"You were getting married and....and I had to see it for myself. So, I went to the church and sat in the back to watch."

"Yes. I saw you there."

He looked to the floor. "But that was after what I did."

Alicia felt the first sting of worry. She shifted in her seat, the gun still resting on the pillow. *What did he do?*

"What…. what did you do, Mike?" she asked, not sure she wanted to hear the answer.

Mike looked at Alicia. His eyes began to water. "I tried to stop it! I swear, I tried to stop it! But it was too late," he cried. He wiped his face again. "It was too…. late."

"Too late for what?" Bradley asked.

"Mike. Tell me what you did," Alicia coaxed.

Mike took a deep breath. "I…I was out of my mind with anger. You were getting married to…*Ryan!*" He said the name as if it was poison on his tongue. "The wedding was going to happen, and I wasn't a part of it. I would never be a part of anything with you again!" Mike's voice ping-ponged between sadness and ferocity. He waved his gun erratically.

"Go on," Alicia urged, never taking her eyes off the loose cannon in his hand.

"I couldn't think! I…I was so angry with you. And so…*disappointed* in you." He looked at her; anguish filled his eyes. "I stormed around the church, not knowing where to go or what to do! I went to my truck to sit and think and saw my tool bag in the back." He paused. "And then I knew what I had to do. I grabbed the bag and went to the limousine. The car that would take you to your happy ever after." Defeat consumed his voice. "I opened the bag and took out the tools I would need, got under the car, and…."

"And…?" Alicia asked apprehensively.

Silence hung in the air.

"….and I drained the brake fluid. From the limousine." *His hands were dirty from a task he had just finished. He wiped his hands on his pants to clean off the residue.*

"I…I don't understand," she said.

"I wanted revenge. I wanted you to crash. I wanted you to suffer." Mike was speaking fast, his words coming out in a torrent. "But then you texted me. You said you saw me in the church and were sorry you had ended things and still needed me. I…I was ecstatic. I couldn't believe it. I *knew* you had come to your senses and realized your mistake." His eyebrows raised, and his mouth turned into a hopeful smile. He looked sad and remorseful.

"Oh, my God -" she started. Her spine started to tingle.

"Holy shit," Bradley muttered.

"But then...then I saw you leave in the limo and...and I realized...the brakes...what I had done to the brakes.... I followed you as fast as I could, but...the roads were wet, and the limousine was going too fast and...and...then...." he couldn't finish the sentence.

Alicia's eyes were wide and searing. The realization of what had happened to her smacked her hard against the head. She wasn't sure if she comprehended the entirety of the situation.

"*You?* You did this?"

Mike turned his head and looked at Alicia. His face had changed. His demeanor was no longer soft and apologetic. He no longer looked sad and hopeful. He looked vengeful.

His acting job was over.

His voice deepened. "Yes, I did. I caused the accident." He stood up straighter and cracked his neck side to side. "At first, I felt horrified that I had let this happen. I had tried to stop the limo from crashing and tried to rectify what I had set in motion. But it happened. I was frantic trying to get you out, not being able to get to you, but I finally did. I *rescued* you from the fire!"

Alicia didn't move. *Mike had done the unthinkable, the unimaginable. The unforgivable.*

"And you were...*ungrateful!* Angry that I had done so. I couldn't believe it!"

Alicia found her voice. "I wanted to *die!*" she hissed. "I didn't want to live like this! You stole my death from me! You killed my *husband,* and I had nothing else to live for -" She saw the trap too late.

"Ahh. So, I wasn't worth living for. Is that it?" Mike asked. "And here I thought you loved me like I loved you." He laughed. "I was just a sap, wasn't I?"

"No, Mike, that's not true. I just -"

"Oh, it doesn't matter anymore," he said. "My revenge is still in the works."

"What does that mean?" Alicia asked nervously.

"You still don't get it, do you?" Mike asked.

"No. I -"

"Here's that ironic part I was talking about earlier, remember?" He glared his eyes at Alicia. "The girls? The AlphaBabes?"

Alicia's head cocked slightly.

"Turns out, drunk driving was not the cause of the wreck. It was the faulty brakes." Mike could almost hear the wheels spinning in her mind.

"What?" Bradley asked. "That's impossible!"

"It's actually not, Bradley, my boy," Mike said, turning to face him. "The brakes gave out long before the alcohol gave in."

Alicia's breathing intensified. Mike turned back to her.

"So, now, do you understand, my sweet?" Mike asked her.

And finally, she did. All her carefully thought-out plans, everything she worked for up until this moment, every skillfully planned out death.

It was all for nothing.

"The...girls...they...they didn't..." she stammered.

Brooke.

Cathy.

Dana.

"That's right," Mike said, confirming her suspicions. "The girls died needlessly. They had nothing to do with your accident." He leaned in closer to deliver the final blow. "You killed all your friends for no reason." He stood up straight. "Just like you killed my baby for no reason," he growled.

"*Noooo!*" Alicia wailed. "*Nooooo!!*"

"But I will say, my anger is no longer with you," Mike continued. He slowly swung his arm to the right, his gun now pointed directly at Bradley. "Is it true?" he asked him. "Did *you* kill my baby?"

"She told me to. I...I had no choice," Bradley said. He sucked in a breath as he stared deep into the barrel of Mike's gun.

The game had suddenly changed.

All three people had a gun pointed at someone different. Everyone had a motive. And everyone had a short fuse.

It was anyone's game to lose.

Then there was a noise.

The front door opened, then closed. The clack of high heels echoed through the apartment as stilettos hit the hardwood.

No one moved.

From the corner of her eye, Alicia saw someone walk into the room. At first, she didn't recognize her. She was beautiful, and her long hair cascaded over her soft shoulders. She wore a body-hugging, emerald green Hervé Léger bandage dress, tall heels, and a killer smile. Recognition finally came to Alicia's brain like a bolt, and her mouth gaped open slowly.

Alicia was looking at a ghost.

Then Alicia saw the gun in the woman's hand, down by her side.

Alicia shifted her eyes towards Bradley and saw a smile of content spread across his face; a knowing, secretive smile.

And Alicia knew. She knew Bradley had lied when he said, "It's done". He had saved her – a second time. But worse than that, he had fallen in love with her.

"But…how? *Why?*" Alicia asked. She looked at Bradley and then at the woman.

"Imagine my shock when Bradley told me you weren't dead. We all thought you had died. That we were responsible for your death." The woman stood there and looked at Alicia with disgust; regret filled her eyes. "As for the 'why', well, you tried to kill me." She shrugged. "You're not the only one that can play dead, you know." She took a step closer. "Now, I'm going to do what you *tried* to do to me. It's the Golden Rule, you know. And I love to follow the rules," she smiled sweetly.

The look on her face sharpened. "Plus, this is for my fallen friends. You took them from me." She lifted the gun and pointed her weapon at Alicia.

Alicia was overjoyed to see her friend again. She hadn't died! Everything had been a mistake, and now they could be friends again and start over.

"I'm sorry," Alicia whispered. But the look in the woman's eyes told her it was too late to feel for apologies.

The tension in the room suddenly magnified, and everyone could feel the next step coming. Intuitively, everyone steeled the aim of their guns.

The guns were raised. Aimed. Triggers poised.

Almost unnoticeably, the woman tapped her foot on the floor.

Alicia's eyes grew wide. "Oh, my God – *don't!*"

Two shots rang out.

A pause.

Then another shot.

Silence.

Then, a thud as a body hit the floor.

EPILOGUE

S he couldn't believe she was living with the man she loved- or thought she loved. Because it wasn't long ago, she didn't trust him as far as she could throw him.

After all, he tried to kill her.

But he *had* saved her at the last minute, rescued her, and told her the whole sordid tale, claiming his love for her surpassed all loyalties to his sister, Alicia. *Who knew she had a brother?* she scoffed. He had told her Alicia wanted revenge for something they had done.

Well, revenge was a two-way street, my dear.

When Bradley told her the story, she initially didn't believe him. She was soaking wet, like a rat that had gone down over the side of a ship. He didn't *have* to save her, and he didn't *have* to tell her everything. But he had. And then, to her surprise, she found her disbelief had over-turned. It took a couple of months, but eventually, she came around. And she, too, fell in love.

In love with a plan, Cathy thought smugly.

"Cath?" Bradley called from the kitchen.

Kong came padding up to him but kept his distance. Kong had lived with Bradley and Cathy ever since he killed Dana. He felt sad about what he did to Kong, but it was necessary. Kong growled at Bradley, then lumbered over to his little leg therapy mechanism. Bradley was happy Cathy insisted they bring the homemade machine from Dana's so Kong could continue his therapy and keep a sense of familiarity. Kong lifted his left hind leg and pressed the button with his paw. His range of motion was near-perfect. *Ding.*

Cathy walked into the kitchen and witnessed the exercise. "Good boy, Kong!" she said, patting him aggressively on his massive head. She gave him a treat, which he scarfed down in three chomps. Kong gnarled at her playfully and bumped his large head into her, almost knocking her over. She laughed.

We've come a long way from the days of you trying to rip my throat out, haven't we? She thought of that day in the park.

Cathy was humming and began making breakfast: half a grapefruit for her and cinnamon oatmeal with raspberries for Bradley. She placed the food in front of him and joined him at the table.

He dug in and smiled. "My favorite. What's the occasion?"

"What? Oh, no occasion. I just know how much you love it. It's not rocket science to make it, you know. Easy peasy," she smirked.

He laughed and continued eating his oatmeal.

"Bradley, can you believe how our life has become so-"

"So normal?" he asked.

"Yeah, I guess. I mean, just a month ago, we -" her voice broke.

"Hush, hon. I know. I didn't think we were going to talk about that again."

She sighed. "But it's hard not to at least *think* about it, right?"

He looked at her. "It is, I know," he agreed. "And I can't apologize enough for my part in all of it. I mean, if it weren't for me, you'd still have your friends and-"

"Now *you* need to hush!" she interrupted, gently slapping his arm. "I've forgiven you, and we're stronger for it. Don't you agree?" She placed her hand over his.

He nodded silently.

She paused for a beat. "Do you miss her?"

He looked up at Cathy. "No. I mean, yes. Sometimes." He lifted a shoulder. "It's complicated."

"Tell me."

He looked pensive. "I miss my sister, but not the monster she was."

"I get it. She was my friend. My sister, too, I suppose." Cathy shrugged both shoulders. "But then she wanted me dead. All because of an *accident!* We couldn't stop Gio from getting behind the wheel, and then Brooke mentioned jail..." Her voice became agitated. "Alicia went from being my sister to my -" she paused to think of a word. "My nemesister!"

Bradley threw back his head and laughed.

"What?"

"Nemesister? That's just a clever word." He laughed harder.

She glared at him, then broke her stare and joined in the laughter. Then she got serious. "But that night -" she began, "- what if it hadn't gone according to our plan?"

He sighed. It almost hadn't. It had nearly gone entirely awry. "But it did. It went down perfectly. Once she texted me, it had begun, and from then on, it was up to our sharp brains to finish it." He tapped his temple with his finger.

Even though it was over, Cathy was still unsure. She remembered the beginning of it all...

They had concocted a plan to double-cross Mike and Alicia, and then Alicia had texted Bradley to come over. Bradley, ecstatic Cathy had finally joined the 21st century and bought a cell phone, texted her:

Heading over to her house now. SUS.

The plan had begun.

When Bradley arrived at Alicia's, he was angered and caught off guard by Mike's admission that Alicia had the shovel to use against Bradley whenever she felt the need. He was disappointed in Alicia. After all he had done for her! And then she blamed him for her abortion! How could she? Technically, yes, Bradley did the deed, but he did not tie her down and force this upon her. It was Alicia's idea, not his. Oh, how he hated his sister at that moment. Bradley wanted to kill

Alicia then and there. Cathy had warned him that Alicia might try throwing him off his balance, but he needed to stick with the plan. So, he had pointed his gun at Alicia to scare her, but he kept his nerves intact. This was all for Cathy. He couldn't afford to mess up.

Once Cathy had gotten to Alicia's – and she had made sure to dispose of the dowdy looks Alicia loved to poke fun at and, in Alicia's honor, had made herself look amazing – almost all hell had broken loose, but Cathy assessed the situation quickly. People pointed their guns in all directions, and then she silently tapped her foot. It was the signal. The signal she and Bradley had rehearsed over and over, heard only by them. And it inferred to pull the trigger.

Three shots. And it was over.

Cathy's bullet entered Alicia's leg as planned. Maimed, Alicia dropped her gun. She moaned, the pain searing.

Bradley swung his arm and shot Mike straight on, a bullet to the carotid artery. His body slammed hard into the wall, cracking the sheetrock. Mike's mouth opened, but he said nothing. He was dead against the wall, suspended in a standing position.

In a flash, Bradley moved to Alicia's side and placed his own gun under her chin. He leaned into her ear and whispered, "Goodbye, sis," then pulled the trigger. Alicia's head exploded in a red mist across the room. It was messy but would prove beneficial.

Bradley turned and watched Mike's body slide down the wall and then fall forward onto the hardwood floor with a thud.

Cathy and Bradley then worked quickly and methodically. First, they collected Alicia's and Mike's guns from the crime scene and packed them away in Cathy's purse to take with them. Next, they wiped the fingerprints off the other two guns. For the bullets to match, they placed Cathy's gun in Mike's hand and Bradley's gun in Alicia's. The coroner would report that Alicia shot Mike, his gun went off and injured Alicia, and then she turned the gun on herself. The deaths would be ruled a murder-suicide.

And finally, before leaving Alicia's apartment, they swiped the shovel and took it with them.

"How did you think of all this?" Bradley had asked, astounded.

Cathy thought about the question. "From reading. It's like I told you: there's nothing you can't learn from reading. Books are full of ideas." She paused. "Some better than others," she smiled.

But that was a month ago. Today was a new day, and it promised to be a big one!

Cathy was getting ready for the day. They had finished their breakfast, and she told Bradley she'd like to go for a picnic lunch on this beautiful Saturday. She wanted to go to Little Marina Green Park, her favorite place and where she had met him and Kong. She had been cooped up for so long while hiding at her friend Elaine's, and now she just wanted to live life to the fullest! They could take Kong with them and see how well he would run on his healed leg.

Bradley loved the idea. He decided he would pack Kong's things while she prepped the food and wine.

She went to her closet, pulled down a shoebox from the back of the upper shelf, and removed its contents: a small, zippered pouch and a black-and-white doctor's photograph. Cathy glanced at the small image. She smiled while holding back tears of happiness, gingerly running her fingers over the small form captured by the ultrasound. "Soon, my darling," she whispered. "Soon."

When she showed Bradley the picture, she hoped he would be as surprised as she had been when she first saw it. She clutched it to her chest and smiled. She was so happy today was finally here that her smile was hurting her cheeks.

She had planned for this day ever since she almost died in Yosemite at Mist Trail's Vernal Falls....

She and Bradley were alone on the stairs leading to the falls. She thought it odd there were no other hikers around. He had crossed over the railing and was holding out his hand. Nervous, she was shaking as she closed her eyes, said a silent prayer, and then took his hand, gripping it tightly. Cathy was soaking wet and felt as slippery as a seal. One false move and... She brushed the thought from her mind.

Once on the other side of the railing, he slapped the wedding photograph of her, Brooke, Dana, and Gio onto her chest. Cathy was confused and wanted to ask him why he gave that to her. She looked at him, trying to meet his eyes, but he turned away from her. He looked almost...sorrowful.

"Bradley!" she cried, raising her voice to be heard over the roar of the falls.

She reached out to him. Cathy took a step forward, forgetting where she was, and her foot landed on some slippery moss. She began to fall.

Cathy found herself surrounded by the water, and her mouth and ears became clogged. She panicked, and her arms flailed, trying to find something – anything – to grab hold of. But there was nothing! She knew she was going to die.

But then something happened: she felt a tug, a pull from her back. She felt one angry yank and found herself on solid ground, choking up water and trying to catch her breath.

She looked up and saw Bradley. He was holding onto a rope, which was attached to a carabiner he had latched onto her backpack.

He had saved her.

He had tried to kill her.

He dropped the rope, then fell to his knees. She heard a faint noise and realized Bradley was crying. Then, for the next hour, he told her everything. He freed himself. And he knew he was no longer Alicia's puppet.

After Bradley spilled Alicia's plans, Cathy was impressed. Her mouth hung open, but she had to hand it to Alicia: the plan was meticulous and left little to no margin for error.

"But what if we had talked to each other and shared we were dating a guy named Bradley? It would've been too much of a coincidence, and everything would've been exposed," Cathy said.

"She knew you three hadn't spoken since the accident, and she didn't worry that you would all suddenly pick up the phone after this length of time just to talk about your love lives. She was confident about that point," Bradley stated.

"Wow," Cathy exclaimed, shaking her head. "She certainly has a set of balls on her."

But Bradley had more to say. He told Cathy that Alicia wanted them to feel death slowly. She wanted them to be aware they were going to die, like she had been aware in the fire. He hung his head. Saying all this out loud was a relief to Bradley but also a confession he knew could be the end of everything for his and Cathy's future. He looked up with woeful eyes wet with tears.

Cathy's thoughts were distant. She was conflicted. She wanted to kill Bradley – and Alicia! – for everything they had done. Brooke. Dana. Kong. But ironically, he had saved her, and that's when she got a plan in her head. She sat him down on a wooden bench and told him what they should do. If he truly loved her, he would do this for her. He kept nodding his head in agreement. And reverence.

"It's just the seeds of a plan," she told him. We'll expand on the details later." But Cathy was already forming the details in her head.

"Yes," he said. "I love you and will do whatever you want."

The control had shifted, and the strings moved from one hand to another. And for Bradley, one thing became crystal clear: he belonged to a new puppet master.

There on the Mist Trail, Cathy made Bradley make the call to Alicia.

"It's done," he said into the phone before tossing it into the waterfall.

On their way down the mountain, Bradley flipped the sign from "MIST TRAIL CLOSED" to "MIST TRAIL OPEN".

Watching this, Cathy realized just how calculated Alicia was. If Cathy were going to make Alicia pay for what she had done, she would have to do precisely what she had done unto her. After all, rules were rules.

During the drive home from Yosemite, Cathy had a thought, a question that nagged at the back of her brain. She turned to Bradley.

"Why me?" she asked him.

"What?"

"Why me?"

"What do you mean? Alicia wanted-"

"No. Not Alicia. You. Why did you save me? And not Brooke or Dana? Why me?"

Bradley kept his eyes on the road. Slowly, he pulled the car over onto the road's shoulder. He shut off the engine, then turned to face her.

"Mrs. Gibson."

Cathy blinked. "Who?"

Bradley laughed. "Mrs. Gibson. She was our teacher growing up and the first person – and the only person I know of – who ever stood up to Alicia. She punished her and sent her to detention for something she did. And even though I paid the price," Bradley rubbed his ring finger, remembering when Alicia broke it on top of the hardback book, "it was still satisfying to see her get some type of punishment. I have respected Mrs. Gibson since that day."

"So, what does that have to do with me?" Cathy asked, curious.

"You weren't afraid of me. You stood up to me."

He saw her eyes squinch in thought.

He reminded her. "In the park? The library?"

Cathy's brain ricocheted back to the day she was at Little Marina Green Park when Kong leaped at her throat, teeth gnashing. Cathy had indeed scolded Bradley for his inept ability to keep Kong restrained. And then that day when he showed up at the library, and she fell off the ladder into his arms. She had viciously accused him of knocking her off the ladder when it was really Elaine's fault.

"Oh. Yes. I remember," she said sheepishly.

"You reminded me of how Mrs. Gibson stood up to Alicia. You weren't afraid. And I respected you."

"Okay...."

"Brooke and Dana are — were — sweet girls..." He saw Cathy's eyes fall when he corrected his word. "Sorry," he said remorsefully. "And, well, Brooke was a little too needy, and Dana was a little too fast. I knew I had a responsibility to Alicia, but you just broke through all that and made me rethink my assignment. For lack of a better analogy, it was the Goldilocks Principle: you were just right."

Cathy's smile was small.

"You were — are — different," he said.

Her smile grew at his word correction this time.

"I fell in love with you. You're nothing like Alicia. You're everything she's not: kind, caring, honest. You don't have an evil bone in your body. You're everything that is right in the world."

Bradley saw her face redden.

He grinned. "Plus, you love Dr. Seuss. I mean, how could I not have fallen in love with someone who can recite the entirety of Green Eggs and Ham?"

Cathy smiled. She had her answer. Finally, Cathy could understand why Bradley and many others, including her, Dana, and Brooke, had been bewitched by Alicia: she possessed confidence and a hunger for power. She was angry, manipulative, compelling, and had an undeniable allure — everything the others lacked. Alicia was a born leader, and everyone else was a follower. It was an easy spell to fall under.

And as for Bradley, knowing what she put him through - the schoolyard bullying, making him feel worthless, the constant demeaning, shaping his mind to believe she was the only person that mattered to him, basically planning his entire existence – it's no wonder he did her bidding. If he wanted his only remaining family member to show him the slightest bit of compassion or concern, then he had no other option.

Oh, she's good, *Cathy thought.* But I can be better. I have the upper hand with Bradley on my side. Together, we can take her down. And after that –

"Cathy?" Bradley had asked her a question.

"Sorry. What?"

"I asked if you were ready to go home and start working on our plan."

Cathy looked him dead in the eyes and smiled sweetly. "More than you know."

Bradley started the car again and eased back onto the highway. He reached over and grasped Cathy's hand as they went home.

Since that day, Cathy had remained hidden. Bradley had told her he thought Alicia had someone following him, so it would be best that she kept hidden until this was all over. She stayed with her friend Elaine from the library. She couldn't go out in public for fear of being spotted, and any word back to Alicia would've meant the jig was up. So, she stayed hidden. It wasn't easy.

Cathy wanted so badly to reach out – to someone- anyone! - but that would mean exposing the plan. She didn't even go to her mother's funeral. Just some-thing else Alicia robbed me of, she thought bitterly. First her friends, and now her mother. But she and Bradley would talk regularly on another burner phone he had purchased, and Alicia was the principal topic of conversation. And the more they talked, the more the plan began to form.

Elaine felt differently.

"My father knows people," Elaine offered. "I mean, he owns a car graveyard and crushes cars for a living," she laughed. "He's not exactly from the upper echelon." She placed her hands on Cathy's knee. "Maybe he can help."

"No," Cathy said. "But thank you. This is something I need to do on my own. Your friendship means the world to me." And she meant it. She could feel a tear forming in her eye. "Helping me hide is plenty."

As they drove to their picnic, Bradley was in the passenger seat, and Cathy was behind the wheel. Bradley said he was a little tired and wanted to rest a bit. He leaned his head against the window and almost instantly started a soft snore. Cathy looked in the rearview mirror and saw Kong sprawled across the entire back seat, also sound asleep.

"Men!" she said, smiling. She looked over at Bradley. He was so handsome. Really a stunning man. *I'm very lucky to have ended up with him.* Moving her eyes back to the road, she caught a glimpse of her own face in the rearview mirror. She was no slouch herself: her eyes were a deep brown and perfectly almond-shaped, lashes long and full; her hair was a silky, deep chestnut brown. Whenever she was working at the library, she wore plain clothes, put her hair up in a bun, and hid her eyes behind thick glasses. She was always uncomfortable with putting the beautiful side of her on display, even back in school. But as of late, ever since Bradley entered her life, she had felt freer and more exuberant.

Cathy heard a gruff from the backseat. Her eyes flicked to Kong, and a grin formed across her lips. *Patience,* she told herself.

Her eyes shifted back to the mirror. Yes, this was the real her, and she loved the freedom. Bradley loved the real her, too. But truthfully, he didn't really know the real Cathy Broderick.

Well, not yet.

As she saw the signs for Little Marina Green Park, she smiled. *Nope. Not today.* She pressed the gas pedal down and continued to drive.

His head was hurting, and he moaned. He tried to lift his arm to touch his scalp but couldn't. *What the hell,* he thought. He tried to move his other arm. Nothing. His eyes were squinted shut, and when he opened them, he saw a windshield. And then a steering wheel. He felt a breeze. The windows must be down.

He was in a car. *But who's car?* At first glance, this one seemed older, and he didn't recognize it as his. The seatbelt stretched across his chest and lap, buckled in. Bradley started to feel the first bubble of fear. He tried to turn his head to look for Cathy, but his head wouldn't move. He darted his eyes back and forth but couldn't see her anywhere. Nor Kong. *Where were they?*

He tried calling out to her, but the only sound he could make sounded like "Cuthee". His lips were not moving. Terrified, he realized he couldn't feel anything except his heart, which thumped hard and fast like an elephant stomping on the ground. Full panic set in.

"It's succinylcholine, baby," he heard someone say, but he couldn't turn his head to see who said it. "It's what you used to paralyze Brooke. I found it in your bag of tricks, along with some other things which I confiscated." She was waving the small, zippered pouch she had gotten from the shoebox in her closet earlier. "I put just the teensiest bit in your oatmeal this morning. Just enough to make you sleepy. But then once we got here…." She waved a syringe in the air.

Bradley's eyes darted down, and he saw a small trickle of blood in the crook of his elbow. *She had given him a shot!* Then someone came into view: Cathy.

She was standing in front of the car, holding a megaphone. A big black figure lumbered up beside her and stood resolute: Kong. She set the megaphone on the ground, left Kong's side, and walked over to the driver's side. She leaned her arms on the open windowsill.

"Oh, Bradley," she said. "Poor, poor Bradley. Did you really think we were each other's happy ever afters?" She made a face of pity. "After everything you did? What is wrong with your brain? You should really get that checked out." She slapped the back of his head. His eyes slammed shut. "Aww, did that hurt? Oh, wait. You couldn't feel that!"

His head began to turn slowly towards her. He was coming out of the medication stupor.

"Or could you?" she said, surprised. "I better hurry." She rose up.

He grunted.

"What you did to me, my friends-" she looked and pointed to the front of the car – "and to *Kong!*" She shook her head back and forth, adding a 'tsk tsk' for good measure. "What you did to all of us is reprehensible, but our revenge on Alicia was our retribution. But *Kong?* How could you just…snap his leg in two?" She winced. "Now *that* is just unforgivable! You're a *monster!*" she spat. She took a step back.

"Cuthee…don't…" he said, his lips now able to move a bit.

"Oh, don't worry. I won't." She walked back up to the car, reached inside the open window, grabbed a chunk of his shoulder with her fingers, and pinched. He grimaced. "Good," she said. "You're starting to feel things again."

Cathy raised her head and looked to the sky, placing her hands on her hips.

"Do you know where you are?" she asked quietly.

"N…n….no," he said, spittle sliding out of the corner of his mouth.

"You, my friend, are in a car graveyard. My friend Elaine from the library – you remember Elaine, right, babe? Anyway, her dad owns this place. But it's Saturday, and it's closed today, so we're all *alone*." She emphasized 'alone', and her smile told him screaming would be useless. She continued. "I found this book at the library on how to work this, oh, what do you call it-" she waved her hand in the air – "car crusher thingie. And to be honest, it's really not that difficult."

Bradley's eyes grew to saucer size. "No!" he managed. "Please! I…I love…"

"Oh, hush," Cathy snapped. "We're running out of time, and I need this to happen quickly."

From her pocket, she took the black and white ultrasound photograph she had gotten from her closet and tossed it into the car. It landed on Bradley's lap. As she walked to the front of the car, she grabbed a rectangular box that was attached to a long, thick cable. Cathy stood next to Kong. She pointed to a sign that said to wear protective goggles. She put hers on her face to cover her eyes, then bent down, pulled the hair out of Kong's eyes, and placed a pair of goggles on him.

"Cute!" she squealed.

She picked up the megaphone from the ground and spoke through it.

"Bradley. Can you hear me? Blink once for yes." She looked down at Kong. "I've always wanted to say that." He chuffed.

Bradley didn't answer her. He struggled to break free from the numbness that coursed through his body. He screamed and writhed behind the steering wheel. His level of alarm was unimaginable.

"So, this is what's going to happen," she said, ignoring his pleas. "You're about to be crushed to death. I have here in my hands a two-button pendant station. One button, the green one, will start the machine, and the other one, this red one here, will stop it." She paused and bent towards the car. "We won't be using the red one today." She grinned.

"Anywho, when the big crusher thing comes down onto the car, it will not stop until the car is eighteen inches thick. Everything in the car will be a foot and a half thick – including you." She set the rectangular button station on the ground between her and Kong.

Bradley's head popped up, and he stared at Cathy. "You bitch!" He grunted and yelled a drawn-out cry, but his arms and hands were not fully usable, and the seatbelt remained buckled.

Cathy continued to speak through the megaphone, her tone becoming more serious.

"And by sitting up in the driver's seat, your bones will first crunch into abnormal positions until they snap into shards inside your skin. Some may protrude, but most will be turned to dust inside your body. Your head will be the first to be impacted. The crusher will force your head down onto your spinal cord and will not stop until your head is inside your stomach. Your eyes will pop out of their sockets, and your organs will explode. And by the looks of things," she pointed and acknowledged he could now move a bit, "you will feel all of this."

As if zapped by a cattle prod, Bradley jerked his body harder, trying to do anything to break through the thickly woven polyester seat belt. His legs were feeling more agile, and his arms and hands were regaining sensation. He fumbled with the buckle. He was so close to freeing himself and escaping this death trap.

In his struggles, what Cathy threw onto his lap caught his eye. He grabbed it clumsily and held it up to get a better look. It was a black and white photograph. An X-ray, to be exact. Of an animal's leg. He read the words at the top of the X-ray: *broken back left tibia*. And next to that, the patient's name: *Kong*.

"You broke his leg on purpose!" Cathy yelled through the microphone, her voice shaking with fury. *"Who does that to an innocent animal?"* She reached into her pocket and pulled out a dog treat. She looked down at Kong and smiled.

Ever faithful, Kong looked up at Cathy, and as he had done many times in the past with his Konginator 2000, he raised his left hind leg vertically. Cathy gave him a gentle nod. And with that, Kong lowered his leg onto the green START button.

A booming chug and a thick start-up noise rumbled through the graveyard. A long mechanical buzz followed a whir as the crusher lowered onto the car with a screeching, metallic clang. It resisted at first connection to the roof but then continued pressing down without so much of another pause.

The stentorian noise of the crusher drowned out Bradley's screams. The car's roof had just begun to press downward onto Bradley's head. Cathy heard a loud pop but was unsure if it was metal or bone.

Cathy yelled through the megaphone one last time.

"The Golden Rule doesn't just apply to humans, Bradley! Kong is just doing to you as you have done to him." She looked down at the dog proudly.

"Isn't that right, boy?" she said as she gave him his treat.

THE END

ACKNOWLEDGMENTS

I once read a version of The Golden Rule that said, "Do Unto Others Before They Do Unto You." So basically, get 'em first! I don't know if that's a good thing or a bad thing, but in the case of these acknowledgments, I'm using it as a good thing. I'm going to thank people before they get a chance to thank me.

As always, I want to thank my family for always being there as my biggest supporters and fans. My mom (Betty), my sisters (Becky and Bonnie), and my nieces (Shirey, Shaley, and Jalynn – yes, their names are in this book. I owe them!) – I love you all, and thank you! I appreciate how you all encourage me to keep writing, no matter how much I cringe when you read certain parts.

My Aunt Anna Lee, who lives five states away and still champions me to her friends and family no matter how far apart we are geographically. I love you for that and for so many other reasons!

Thank you to Dr. Susan Carastro, Dr. Jacey Morrow, and Dr. John Augsburg for your invaluable veterinary input. You are my family, and I'm beyond thankful you are in my life! Y'all made things so much clearer! Any inconsistencies or incorrect statements are purely my own. And everyone: please be kind to animals! Don't be like Bradley.

Freida McFadden, Rob Kaufman, Natalie Barelli, Alessandra Torre – your books are incredible, and I thank you for inspiring me daily to do my best not to disappoint the readers. Whenever I read one of your books, I am taken to places I never knew existed. The talent you guys have in your pinkies could rule the book world! I appreciate your support so much more than you can imagine. Thank you a million times over.

Jake, Anna, and Paige: you held my first-ever book signing at Tower

Taproom (my fave!), and it was a perfect way to begin this amazing journey. And to all my friends from work and classmates from Jeff Davis's class of 1984 who showed up, thank you from the bottom of my heart. I'll never forget it!

And to you, the reader, I thank you the most. Without you, books would just be doorstops and things to dust. And I hate to dust. Your support by reading my books means the world to me. I'm grateful beyond measure.

I hope you loved *Do Unto Others,* and if you did, I would be very grateful if you could write a review. I'd love to hear what you think! You can also email me at markjenkinsauthor@gmail.com

So, there. I thanked everyone before they could thank me. Not that anyone would ever thank me for writing this book- well, except for maybe the people who really like to dust things.

Mark

Made in the USA
Columbia, SC
14 September 2024

42250930R00217